THE RIDER EMPIRE
The Lost Riders
Book 6

JASPER ALDEN
D.K. HOLMBERG

ASH
PUBLISHING

Chapter One

THERE WEREN'T MANY SOUNDS THAT COULD BE HEARD above the roar of a Northern Circle blizzard in the Wastes. Among the many scattered warring tribal kingdoms of the circle, it was said that the scream of the blizzard was the last sound most people heard before their death if they went out into the cold unprepared. Some even said it was the last lullaby for the many babies and young children abandoned in the Wastes by their parents.

But there was one sound that rose above the roaring winds, the constant swirl of snowflakes and ice, and the stomping of desperate feet in the drifts seeking shelter from the storm: The loud, painful cry of a baby.

Boca heard it before her sisters. Clutching her thick fur coat tightly around her body, the eldest Snow Witch gazed slightly to the north, listening to the baby's cry as it grew louder and louder.

"What's the problem, sister?" Ericha's sneering voice called out. "We need to return to the compound *now*, unless you fancy getting eaten by an ice worm or worse!"

Snapping out of her thoughts, Boca glanced toward her sisters. Kiko, the second oldest, as well as the shortest, stood next to Ericha, the tallest and youngest, not too far away from her. Both of her sisters, just like Boca herself, were dressed to the nines in thick fur coats and hoods, every inch of their bodies protected from the freezing wind that cut through skin like a knife.

"Don't you hear that?" Boca asked, raising her voice to be heard above the roaring wind, crying baby, and the scarf wrapped around her head. "I think it's a baby!"

Ericha looked at Boca incredulously. "A baby? Out here? Are you sure? Because I don't hear—"

The baby's screams suddenly intensified, along with the whipping of the winds, nearly knocking the three sisters over. Even Boca, despite her clothing, was starting to feel the cold now.

"It's screaming," Boca said, turning her gaze north. "It must be somewhere nearby if we can hear it."

Kiko grunted, tightening her scarf around her face. "Poor child. Probably abandoned by its parents."

"Or maybe they were eaten alive by an ice worm," Ericha suggested. "The ice worms have been unusually aggressive this time of year. Just yesterday, in fact, I found evidence of those awful beasts eating my petunias—"

The baby screamed again, making Boca hold up a hand. "You two stay here. I am going to check on it."

Boca made her way through the deep drifts, casting a heat spell to carve a path through them. Even with her heat magic, however, it was slow-going, mostly thanks to the intense winds that seemed to be deliberately telling her to go back.

But it wasn't long before Boca found what she was

looking for: A cradle in the snow, covered by a blue blanket which did nothing to muffle the baby's screams. Kneeling before the cradle, Boca pulled the blanket aside just enough to see the baby.

A tiny blue-skinned Glacian baby—likely no older than a few weeks, if that—lay bundled inside the cradle. Wet tears ran freely down the boy's face, only to freeze and make him cry even more. A whiff told Boca that the baby had likely soiled himself, too.

"Sister, what are you doing?" Ericha said suddenly.

Boca looked up to see Ericha and Kiko standing around the cradle looking down at her, Ericha frowning in clear disapproval, Kiko keeping a stony face as usual.

"I told you two to stay put," Boca said.

Ericha chuckled. "And let you disappear into the drifts, never to be seen again? You know what happens to those who travel the Wastes by themselves, big sister."

"We were worried about you," Kiko said calmly.

"You should be more concerned about the baby," Boca said, lowering the blanket slightly to prevent snow from entering the cradle. "Look at him. I doubt he's eaten in hours."

Ericha wrinkled her nose. "Or had a change of diapers, for that matter."

Kiko glanced around. "I do not see the boy's parents. Definitely abandoned."

"Or victims of ice worms," Ericha said.

Boca shook her head. "Regardless of what happened to the boy's parents, we can't leave him out here. We should take him back to the compound with us."

Ericha gave Boca a look of sheer disbelief. "Are you serious? We're not running an orphanage, sister. We are the

Snow Witches of the Wastes. We are the stories that parents tell their kids to keep them in line. We don't raise children ourselves."

"I'm not saying we should *raise* the boy," Boca said defensively. "I'm just saying that this is the first time we have stumbled upon a living abandoned child in the Wastes. We can take care of him long enough to find a village that will take him in. I'm sure there are couples out there who would love to have a child of their own."

Ericha snorted. "If his parents indeed abandoned him, then they probably did so for a reason. He was probably the runt of the litter or maybe was born with some horrible disfigurement or disease that would have crippled him for life. Abandoning him out here would undoubtedly be a mercy for him, given the kind of life he would probably live if spared."

Kiko nodded. "And the storm is getting worse."

Boca could not disagree with Kiko's last comment. The sky had grown darker, despite it being midday, and the winds roared even more loudly than ever.

But the baby's cries were louder still.

Boca bit her lower lip. "We don't know any of that for sure. I still say we take the baby until we find it a home. And if I have to do it myself, I will. I will not ask for either of your help."

Ericha tilted her head skeptically. "I don't know if I would be able to sleep through such racket, though. Babies are very loud and I need my beauty sleep if I am to keep these good looks of mine."

"I will make sure he never cries," Boca said, reaching in and stroking the baby's face. "I will make sure he never wants for anything, in fact. He will be my responsibility. I promise."

Kiko looked at the cradle curiously. "The baby ... he's not crying anymore."

It was true. Even Boca hadn't noticed. She had only noticed how soft the baby's skin was, how fragile he felt. He felt every bit as soft and warm as Boca, a childless woman herself, imagined babies would feel.

And that just made her feel more protective of him than ever.

Ericha folded her arms in front of her chest. "I see. You've always wanted a child, but since none of us can have children, you've decided to take whatever baby you happen to stumble upon in the Wastes. Kiko and I see through your plan. You can't fool—"

"You can have the baby," Kiko said.

Ericha, stunned, glared at Kiko. "Are you joking? I hope you are joking, even though I know your sense of humor is poorer than whoever this baby's parents probably are."

"Boca has already shown that she can calm down the baby when he is upset," Kiko said, calmly meeting her sister's gaze. She gestured at the cradle. "And since the baby will only be with us until Boca can find suitable parents for him among the surrounding villages, I see no reason not to let Boca take care of the baby if she wants."

Boca smirked at Ericha. "Two to one. I believe you have been outvoted."

Ericha scowled and muttered under her breath, "I hate being the youngest."

Boca peeked under the blanket again. The baby had not only stopped crying but even seemed to have fallen asleep, his eyes closed and his tiny chest rising and falling with each breath.

He was perfect … and he was Boca's.

But then the wind practically screamed in Boca's ears and she dropped the blanket over the cradle. Grabbing the cradle's handle, Boca stood up and walked back in the direction of the compound, Ericha on her left, Kiko on her right.

The sky was getting darker.

"I know we aren't keeping the baby forever, but surely we should give him a name," Kiko said, glancing at the cradle in Boca's hands.

Ericha sniffled. "No way. We aren't giving that *kralot* a name. If you name something, you become attached to it, and then you will never get rid of it."

Boca, however, considered Ericha's words carefully. *Kralot* was an old Glacian word for 'orphan,' said to have predated the Cataclysm that made the Wastes into what they were today.

And she found herself liking it.

My little Kralot, Boca thought, her smile hidden behind her scarf, feeling the weight of the cradle and the baby within it in her hand. *Whether I have you for one month or one thousand years, you will always be my little Kralot.*

Chapter Two

ONE THOUSAND YEARS LATER ...

Hal didn't know if Boca was *deliberately* trying to kill him and Keershan or if the Snow Witch simply overestimated their strength.

Standing on a plateau that jutted out over the void below them, Hal gazed upward and shouted, "Boca! Can we rest for a bit? We've been climbing the cliffs for hours."

Boca, standing on an outcropping above them with one hand reaching toward the next handhold, shook her head. "No. We aren't far now. The gates should be showing up soon."

Hal heard a rumble below and gazed down to see Keershan, his dragon Steed, clutching the face of the cliffs just below him, claws dug deeply into the rock. Although dragons were much better climbers than humans, even Keershan was running out of stamina.

"Why can't we just fly again?" Keershan said, raising his voice to be heard over the howling winds. "It would have been faster and easier than climbing."

Boca rolled her eyes. "As I said before, the Endless Cliffs are only considered endless if you fly. The only way to scale them—and thus see the gods—is by actually scaling them. There is a reason few have ever successfully climbed them, much less survived."

Do you think she's lying to us or telling the truth? Keershan asked Hal mentally.

Hal shrugged. *The Snow Witches have been honest with us so far. On the other hand, they also clearly have a sadistic streak to them, so who knows?*

Keershan sighed. *I just hope she is at least telling the truth about being close to the top. If we have to climb for another several hours, then I'm done.*

Hal understood Keershan's feelings.

A week ago, Hal and Keershan had arrived with Boca, the eldest of the Snow Witches, at the foot of a cliff face she referred to as the Endless Cliffs. Located far to the north of even the Northern Circle, the Endless Cliffs were said to be the entrance to the Gates of the Gods. And if one could access the Gates of the Gods, then one could also enter the Abode of the Gods, said to be the dwelling place of all gods.

Unfortunately, the Endless Cliffs did not earn that name for no reason. Standing at the foot of the cliffs, Hal recalled how endlessly huge they had looked. They even went up above the clouds, making it impossible to see their peak from the bottom.

Not that they had a much better view from their current vantage point, however. When Hal gazed up after Boca, he could just barely see her clutching the handholds and footholds through the cloud cover that seemed to permanently cover the place.

But we won't get to the abode standing around whining, Hal thought, rolling his shoulders. *Have to keep going.*

Hal resumed climbing the cliffs, being careful to get a good grip on the slightly slick rocks before moving on. Hal had almost lost his grip about an hour ago and would have plunged to his death if not for Boca casting a floating spell on him at the last minute.

Boca's stamina was what amazed Hal the most. Despite being over a thousand years old and looking like it, Boca had stayed ahead of both Hal and Keershan the whole way. Hal assumed that she must be using her magic to give her such strength and speed because, otherwise, he couldn't explain it.

Then Hal heard Boca's voice above the clouds say, "We made it."

Curious, Hal increased his speed until he climbed above the clouds and reached for the next handhold …

Only to feel empty air, at least until he brought his hand down on the solid earth and hefted himself up onto it. Rising to his feet and brushing the sweat and moisture in the air off his forehead, Hal took in his new surroundings.

They had indeed reached the top of what appeared to be a massive mountain peak rising out of the clouds. In every direction Hal looked, he saw a sea of clouds spreading out for as far as the eye could see. The rays of the sun shone down on them overhead, the sun itself looking bigger than it did from the ground. The warmth from the sun's rays felt warmer, too, restoring some of Hal's strength.

But his attention was captured by the massive gates that stood before them.

They were unlike any gates he had seen before. They stood as tall as the tallest buildings in the Northern Circle, seemingly made of solid shining gold that somehow was not painful to look at. The faces of dozens of various gods were carved into the surface, along with text at the top that appeared to be written in a language Hal could not read or identify.

And standing in front of the gates was easily the biggest statue Hal had ever seen. Standing directly in the middle of the gates, the statue seemed to have been based on a warrior. Broad shoulders ended in muscular arms with biceps bigger than Hal's head, their hands resting on the hilt of a sword that was easily twice his size in length. A stern face with closed eyes made Hal feel as if he was being judged already.

Boca spread her arms. "Welcome to the Gates of the Gods, our first—though by no means final—destination."

Keershan suddenly crawled up beside Hal, panting hard, flicking his tongue in and out of his mouth like a snake. "I am never doing that again."

"Amazing, isn't it?" Hal said, gesturing at the gates. "I've never seen anything so beautiful or ornate in my life."

Keershan rose to his feet, the exhaustion in his body leaving him as quickly as it left Hal. "In my studies, I've only ever found scattered references to the Gates, to the point where I wasn't sure how much was myth and how much was fact. But they are *beautiful*, more beautiful than even the most flowery descriptions of them in the ancient texts made them out to be. I want to touch them."

Keershan took a step forward, but Boca held out a

hand, saying, "Wait, Keershan, do not approach the gates without—"

Boca was interrupted by the sound of stone grinding against stone, breaking the otherwise peaceful silence that had descended upon the area. It took Hal a moment to realize that the sound came from the statue in the center of the gates.

The statue was stirring. Bits of pieces of rock broke off its shoulders and neck as the statue raised its head, eyes blinking. Its gaze swept across the peak until it landed on Hal and Keershan, a disapproving frown on its carved features.

"Who dares approach the Gates of the Gods?" the statue demanded in a booming voice that echoed across the sea of clouds around them.

Hal, hesitating, said, "Er, I am Captain Halar Norath, a Dragon Rider, and this is my Steed, Keershan. We have come to—"

"State your business," the statue boomed.

Hal bit his lower lip, not appreciating the interruption. "We have come to ask the gods to help us."

The statue went silent again, making Hal wonder for a moment if that answer satisfied it and it would let them inside.

But then the statue said, "Have you brought a proper sacrifice?"

Hal and Keershan exchanged puzzled looks, prompting Keershan to say, "Proper sacrifice—?"

"No proper sacrifice detected," the statue said. Its eyes began to glow red. "Perish."

Red energy beams lanced out of its eyes toward Hal

and Keershan. The energy beams came too fast for them to dodge or block.

But Boca stepped in front of them and, holding up her hands, said, "Wait!"

The energy beams, shockingly enough, stopped inches from Boca's face, and the statue said, "Who dares approach the Gates of the Gods?"

"I do," Boca said, her voice firm despite the energy beams directly in front of her face. "Boca Secha, daughter of the wizard Framo de Secha."

"State your business," the statue said.

Clearing her throat, Boca said, "I seek an audience with Gotcham Nubor to discuss a matter of grand importance to both the gods and the mortals."

"Do you have a proper sacrifice?" the statue demanded.

Boca glared at the statue. "Do not play dumb with me, Protector. You know what my standing with Gotcham Nubor means."

Hal raised an eyebrow. Standing with Gotcham Nubor? Did that mean that Boca had not only been here once before, but had even been granted an audience with one of the gods during her last visit?

Before the implications of that could fully set in, the statue's energy beams suddenly shot back into its eyes. Blinking, the statue lowered its head. "You may enter, Boca Secha, as well as your two companions."

The statue then sank into the ground, disappearing like it had never existed at all.

In the next moment, however, the Gates of the Gods slowly swung open inwards. A beautiful golden light poured out from beyond the gates, forcing Hal to hold up a hand to protect his vision while Keershan folded one of his wings in front of his eyes to do the same.

Boca, however, strode forward, the brim of her witch's hat protecting her eyes. She stopped and looked over her shoulder at Hal and Keershan, a slight frown on her face. "Are you coming?"

Hal nodded. He and Keershan followed Boca through the Gates. Having heard legends of the Abode of the Gods for much of his life, Hal wasn't entirely sure what to expect. He supposed he expected to see a golden city laid out before him in splendid glory, but the truth was that Hal spent little time thinking about the matters of the gods.

So when he stepped through the Gates and found himself on a hill, Hal was in awe of what he saw.

Chapter Three

A SPRAWLING CITY COVERED THE SIDE OF A MASSIVE mountain that made the Endless Cliffs look small. Spiraling towers made of crystal and gold rose up to the skies, a few even ascending beyond the clouds. Streets were paved with solid gold, and odd winged figures and flying horses wheeled in the sky overhead.

The entire city was dominated in the center by the largest building Hal had ever seen in his life. It was bigger than Kryo Kardia's citadel in the Northern Circle, dwarfing it by several sizes, although Hal thought the structure looked vaguely familiar somehow. Four spires rose up from its corners, but it had no walls or gates separating it from the rest of the city. A huge bell stood on the rooftop of the building, though it was currently not being used.

A beautiful river, itself seemingly liquid silver, flowed through the city, the city itself seeming to have been designed around it.

What Hal did not see, however, was people, aside from the winged figures in the skies.

"Is this the Abode of the Gods?" Keershan said, glancing around excitedly. "It's so *big*. Even I feel small here."

"Yes," Boca said with a nod. She gestured at the city below. "This is the Abode of the Gods spoken of in legend. I've been here only once before, but it hasn't changed a bit since then."

Hal shook his head. "It's truly awe-inspiring. I actually feel a little dirty just being here."

"That is because we are mortals," Boca said. "The Abode of the Gods is home only to the gods and similar divine beings. We are not deities ourselves. If we linger here too long, the consequences could be … difficult for us."

"Difficult?" Hal said. "What do you mean?"

A neighing sound in the sky overhead interrupted Boca before she could elaborate. Gazing up into the sky, Hal saw an armored figure riding on the back of a winged horse swooping down toward them. The armored figure carried a lance, making Hal reach for his sword.

But Hal was too late. The winged horse landed in their path roughly and rose to its full height. It had to be at least twelve feet tall, maybe taller, and the armored figure sitting on its back was probably half that height, gazing down at them through the eyeholes of his helmet.

"Welcome to the Abode of the Gods, mortals," said the armored figure. "What are your reasons for coming here?"

Hal frowned. "We already told the Protector. We want an audience with the gods. Although I'd like to know who *you* are, exactly."

The armored figure chuckled. "My name is Captain Raniel. I am the captain of the Divine Guard. It is my job to ensure that those who seek an audience with the gods have proper—"

Raniel stopped speaking when he looked at Boca, seemingly noticing her for the first time.

"Raniel," Boca said with a nod. "Long time, no see."

Raniel nodded curtly in return. "Same to you. Although I am surprised you have chosen to show your face around here again, given how your last visit went."

Hal looked from Raniel to Boca and back again, raising an eyebrow. Boca had obviously not been upfront with them about what she had done the last time she had come here, but whatever it was, Hal didn't think it was any good.

As if to break the tension, Keershan said, "Are you riding a *pegasus*, Raniel?"

Raniel glanced at Keershan, clearly puzzled. "Yes. This is my steed, Yano. Together, we faithfully patrol and protect the gods from those who would wish to do them harm."

"What's a pegasus?" Hal said.

Keershan cleared his throat. "Pegasus are creatures in myth said to be winged horses. Legend has it that pegasuses can only be found in the Abode of the Gods. Seems like the legends are accurate." He sniffed the air. "They even smell like honeysuckle, just like the stories say they do."

That explained where that nice smell came from, although Hal was a bit more interested in the history between Boca and Raniel than in that.

"Thank you, dragon, but I am afraid I must be going," Raniel said, glancing at the skies. "Now that I know who you are, there's nothing else for me to ask from you. But I do have one parting bit of advice to give: Do not anger the gods."

With that, Yano flapped her wings, and both

guardsman and pegasus shot back into the sky. They were fast, even faster than dragons in Hal's estimation. In seconds, both Raniel and Yano were little more than tiny figures in the sky, going over to the west side of the city, joining a small group of other guardsmen and their pegasuses.

"Raniel seemed nice," Keershan said. "Nicer than I would expect from a guy with a lance that big, anyway."

"He was polite," Hal said. He looked at Boca. "What happened the last time you visited?"

Boca grunted. "That is the past. Although the gods have long memories, I am sure they will listen to us once they find out what we are here to ask of them."

Hal nodded. Prior to leaving the Northern Circle, Boca had told Hal and Keershan that they were going to ask the gods for a weapon they could use to claim Kryo Kardia's soul. The logic was that undead magic, similar to what Kryo Kardia was using, was against the 'divine laws,' as Boca called them, and that the gods would grant them that request, as the gods did not like it when any humans broke or violated the laws they set in place after creation.

But after seeing Boca's interaction with Raniel, Hal wasn't so sure about that anymore. If Boca had angered the gods during her last visit, whenever that had been, then Hal hoped that the gods were forgiving.

Because they were going to need them to be if they were going to stop Kryo Kardia.

The streets of the Abode of the Gods were strangely quiet and empty of people. And as beautiful as the architecture was, Hal could not help but find it a bit creepy.

"Where are all of the people?" Hal asked Boca as they walked. "The streets seem … empty, to put it nicely."

Boca gestured at the buildings around them. "Probably asleep. The Abode of the Gods operates on a different time schedule than the world of mortals. While it is day outside, here, it is night."

Hal glanced up at the shining sun overhead, squinting his eyes. "This is night? But the sun is out."

"The sun is *always* out here," Boca said. "But the angels do not need darkness to sleep."

Keershan gasped. "There are even *angels* here? Gosh, you make it sound like all of the legends are true."

"Of course there are angels," Boca said, gesturing at the sky. "Raniel is one of them. They are stronger and longer-lived than mortals, but not as strong as the gods themselves."

Hal suddenly looked around the streets hopefully. "If this is the Abode of the Gods, then does that mean—?"

"Don't get your hopes up," Boca said. "The spirits of the departed do not go here. In fact, technically speaking, this isn't even the gods' natural realm, either. This is simply a physical manifestation of the spiritual realm in which they normally reside."

Hal furrowed his brow. "So this place isn't real?"

Boca rapped her knuckles against a signpost they walked past. "It's real. So are the angels' and gods' bodies. But should, say, an angel's physical form be slain here, they would simply return to the spiritual realm to be reborn as the gods see fit."

Hal grimaced. "Like the demons, whose spirits simply return to the well after their physical forms are killed."

"Very similar," Boca agreed. "But do not worry. Angels are far less petty, vindictive, and outright evil than demons. However, demons are corrupted angels, so it makes sense that they have similar natures."

"Corrupted?" Keershan said. "Corrupted by who?"

Boca smiled wryly. "Guess."

Hal, of course, already knew who had done so, and could sense that Keershan had already guessed as well.

The Nameless One.

The Nameless One was an evil god who had died twice. First to the original Dragon Riders, where his dying words unleashed a terrible curse on the world, known as the Fall, that the world was still dealing with even today. Then to Hal and Keershan a little over a year ago, shortly after his followers resurrected him.

I don't see the Nameless One here, Hal said to Keershan mentally.

Makes sense, Keershan said. *The Nameless One, after all, was cast out of the abode according to legend. Given how everything else we have seen so far matches up with the old legends, it's safe to say that the other gods probably don't care for him very much, either.*

I hope you are right, Hal replied, *because if we have to deal with both the Nameless One and Kryo Kardia—*

Hal was interrupted by shouting and screaming up ahead. Snapping out of his mental focus, Hal looked down the street to see a growing assembly of angelic beings gathering. There had to be dozens and dozens of angels clad in white robes, all scrambling together to see something. Overhead, Hal saw a lot of guardsmen on their pegasuses flying toward the group, wings flapping faster than ever in the wind.

"What in the world is going on over there?" Keershan said. He looked at Boca. "Didn't you say that the angels should be sleeping?"

"They should be," Boca said, frowning. "If they aren't, then something is *very* wrong. Let's go see."

Boca took off at a brisk pace toward the crowd, forcing Hal and Keershan to increase their speed just to keep up with the old witch.

The closer they got to the group, the more Hal could make out individual voices and what they were saying.

"… impossible. How could this happen …"

"… a trick, I tell you, a trick …"

"… do you think we're still safe …"

Hal did not like any of those comments, but he had to admit they piqued his curiosity.

Boca didn't even slow down. She pushed her way through the crowd of angels, not even apologizing, though to be fair, none of them even seemed to take note of several mortals making their way through the group. They were so focused on whatever horrible thing they had witnessed that none of them seemed to care about Hal, Boca, or Keershan.

And once Hal and the others reached the front of the crowd and got a clear look at whatever it was that had drawn the attention of the angels, Hal understood, at least in part.

A beautiful young woman with flowing golden hair and robes whiter than snow lay in a pool of sparkling golden blood. Her eyes were glassy, blood leaking out of her neck. She did not have wings like the angels, but Hal sensed that she was important, perhaps more important than the angels, and certainly no mere mortal like himself or Keershan.

"Poor woman," Keershan said. "Looks like she got murdered."

A female angel standing near them glared at Keershan. "Show some *respect*, mortal. This is no 'poor woman.' This is—"

"Shirataka, Goddess of Light," Boca finished for her in disbelief. "And she is dead."

Chapter Four

"DEAD?" HAL REPEATED. "I MEAN, THAT MUCH IS OBVIOUS. But, no disrespect intended, I don't see what the problem is. The gods' physical bodies aren't their *actual* bodies. Even if Shirataka was murdered, that just means that her spirit is back in the spiritual realm, doesn't it?"

The female angel gave Hal an indignant look. "I forgot how ignorant mortals are. *Painfully* ignorant."

Before Hal could ask what she meant, Raniel suddenly landed in the open area where Shirataka's corpse lay. Dismounting from Yano, Raniel carefully approached Shirataka's body, kneeling before it. He held his hand over her body and squeezed his fist tight.

A golden liquid—different from the blood that Shirataka bled—dripped out of Raniel's fist and onto Shirataka's face. The liquid rapidly spread over her body until soon Shirataka's corpse resembled a golden statue more than an actual physical body.

Raniel, meanwhile, stared at her intensely, seemingly having forgotten everyone and everything else. The crowd became silent as well, allowing Hal to hear the occasional flapping of the wings of the pegasuses overhead, as well as the bubbling of the river flowing through the city.

Then Raniel stood up and, looking around at the crowd, said, "Shirataka's spirit has been … annihilated."

Gasps of shock and fear swept through the crowd. Multiple angels exchanged uneasy looks with each other while the snooty female angel who had lectured Hal immediately turned and ran as if her life depended on it.

"Annihilated?" Hal whispered to Boca. "What does that mean?"

Boca's frown became even longer. "It means that Shirataka's body wasn't simply killed. Whoever killed her body killed her soul as well, effectively wiping it from existence."

Keershan gasped. "Is that even possible?"

"Apparently so," Boca said. She glanced around furtively. "Perhaps now was not the best time for us to visit. It may still be possible to—"

"Mortals!" Raniel's voice boomed suddenly.

The angelic guardsman was pointing directly at Hal, Keershan, and Boca. The crowd of angels around them all stepped away, their colorful eyes—ranging from red to blue to green and everything in between—warily gazing at them like they were wild animals they could not predict the behavior of.

"Yes?" Boca said, standing up straighter. So did Hal and Keershan, likely thanks to Raniel's authoritative voice.

"You are hereby under arrest for being suspects in the murder of Shirataka, Goddess of Light," Raniel said. "Do not resist."

"You're arresting us?" Hal said. "But we just got here. You don't have any evidence too—"

Boca stepped hard on Hal's boot, snarling, "Shut. Up. It's bad enough that *I* am here. We do not want to test the Divine Guard's patience. They are already biased against mortals. Let us not give them even more reason to hate us."

Hal was tempted to protest their innocence but decided to restrain himself and listen to Boca. She seemed to be the expert in divine matters here, not him, although Hal still didn't like it.

Half a dozen other guardsmen landed around Hal and the others. Hal expected to be cuffed, but instead, Raniel waved his hand and a cage made of brilliant light shone into existence around them. The bright bars dimmed somewhat, making it easier for Hal to see outside, although he still wasn't happy about what he saw.

"What are you going to do with us now?" asked Keershan to Raniel. "Throw us in prison?"

Raniel shook his head. "No. I am going to take you straight to the gods themselves so they can decide your ultimate fate."

With that, Raniel hopped back on Yano and flew through the air, the cage containing Hal, Keershan, and Boca trailing behind them as if tethered to Yano by an invisible rope. The other members of the Divine Guard flew on all other sides, effectively cutting off all potential avenues of escape for them.

Not that Hal intended to escape, however. He just clutched the warm bars, staring at the massive temple in the center of the city where they seemed to be going.

And hoped that Boca had a plan, because he certainly did not.

They reached the huge temple in short order, heading toward a massive golden dome that dominated the rest of the structure. They flew straight toward it, making Hal wonder if they were going to crash directly into it, and if so, how painful the crash was going to be.

But when Raniel and Yano reached the dome, they passed straight through it like it didn't exist. And a moment later, Hal, Keershan, and Boca also passed through it without issue, although Hal did get the feeling they had been scanned by something far more powerful and intelligent than them.

And infinitely less merciful.

Raniel and Yano landed in the center of the huge auditorium they had ended up in, letting Hal look up and see their surroundings.

Hundreds, if not thousands, of thrones rose in varying sizes all around them, and each one was occupied by a different god or goddess. No matter where Hal looked, he saw beings that were clearly divine entities, although he barely recognized most of them.

Some of the gods looked almost human, such as a middle-aged man with a portly stomach who was smiling. Others more closely resembled the angels, with big, white wings, colorful eyes, and an air of otherworldliness about them.

But others looked like animals or other creatures. There was a god who closely resembled a humanoid bear in armor, while another looked like a fish given arms and legs.

And still others were so odd that Hal found it difficult to believe they were gods at all. One was simply a glowing purple orb that hovered above a throne that appeared to have been carved out of volcanic rock. Although the orb had no eyes that Hal could see, he felt like it was watching them more closely than any of the other gods.

"So *these* are the gods," Keershan said, staring in awe at the assembled deities. "There are even more than I thought. Although I don't see Salard."

Hal looked at Keershan. "Salard?"

"The god of dragons," Keershan replied. "All dragons —at least Malarsan dragons—worship him. He is said to reside in the abode as well, but again, I don't see him, either."

Hal pursed his lips. "I understand being excited about seeing your god, Keershan, but I think we have bigger problems to worry about right now. Such as going to jail for being framed for the murder of a goddess, for example."

Keershan's smile faded. "Oh. You're right."

Then Raniel said, in a loud voice, "Gods of the abode! I apologize for my interruption of your convocation, but I have important news to share regarding the recent murder of Shirataka, the goddess of light."

None of the gods looked even remotely surprised to hear that Shirataka had been murdered, which surprised Hal, who whispered, "Shirataka was just murdered, but they already seem to know about it?"

"The gods can feel when one of their own has died," Boca whispered back. "They do not, of course, know *who* did it, but they can certainly feel it. Although I find it very interesting that we timed our visit with their recent convocation. I didn't expect so many gods to be present here today."

"So where's this Gotcham Nubor you said could help

us?" Hal replied, scanning the thousands of gods around them. "I don't see him."

Boca opened her mouth, likely to respond, but then Raniel thrust a hand at them and said, "I have reason to believe that these mortals—the only mortal visitors to the abode in many years—are connected to her murder, for her body was discovered in the streets around the same time they arrived. In fact, I would like to further accuse them of the *murder* of Shirataka."

The gods gasped and muttered among each other. It was difficult for Hal to tell, but he thought that the gods seemed at least a little skeptical of Raniel's assertions.

His theory was partly vindicated when one of the gods —who resembled an incredibly old man in black robes and carrying a small hammer—called out, "What evidence do you have for this assertion, Raniel? I have seen nothing to indicate that these mortals played a role in Shirataka's unfortunate demise, even if the timing of their arrival here is rather suspicious."

Raniel pointed directly at Boca. "Because *this* one, whose previous visit to the abode was an unmitigated disaster, was among them. For it was Shirataka who threw this woman out of the abode for her crimes ages ago. She has every motive to want to take her life. And given her affinity with the darkest magics of the mortal world, she also has the most access to magic that could allow a mortal to murder a goddess."

Hal whipped his head toward Boca. "Is that true? Not the murdering part, I mean. Your history with Shirataka."

Boca twisted her lips. "Shirataka and I did not get along very well during my first visit to the abode. But I also did not kill her, nor would I even attempt such a thing. I may be a witch, but even I know that the consequences for murdering a goddess are too high a price to pay. Only a fool would do such a thing."

"There *is* a rather reliable overlap between fools and mortals, however," another goddess, this one resembling a strange long-necked creature with yellow fur and brown spots that Hal had never seen before, mused.

Raniel nodded. "Yes. Mortals are not known for their foresight or ability to think longer than a hundred years. As well, her companion, Halar Norath, and his dragon Steed, Keershan, have also killed gods before, namely our fallen brother, the Nameless One."

At the mention of the Nameless One, the temperature in the room seemed to drop like a rock. But then Hal realized it was simply the icy feelings that all of the gods felt toward the Nameless One, which told him that they were at least not upset about that.

Although they are clearly afraid we could do it again if we did it once, Keershan said in his head, to which Hal did not disagree.

The only deity who did not seem upset was the mysterious orb, although given its lack of resemblance to any living being Hal had ever seen, he assumed that it simply lacked the physical characteristics necessary to display its emotions like the other gods could.

Raniel lowered his hand. "Although I am but a humble member of the Divine Guard, I suggest that the gods find these mortals guilty of murder and condemn their souls to the Pit, where all of the damned go."

Raniel's argument, which Hal did not find very convincing—probably because he knew that none of them had even touched Shirataka, much less killed her—

seemed to sway the gods. They muttered among themselves, their words in a strange language that was too low and foreign for Hal to hear or understand, but he got the gist of it.

The gods were planning to accept Raniel's recommendations and condemn them to the 'Pit,' whatever that meant.

But then Boca stepped forward, mere inches from the bars of their cage, and held up a hand. "Before you gods hastily announce your verdict, I, Boca Secha, hereby call a testimony in defense of myself and my companions."

Hal pursed his lips. He sincerely doubted that the gods, who already seemed highly prejudiced against them for the crime of being in the wrong place at the wrong time, would listen to Boca's testimony. He appreciated her efforts to save them, however, even if he didn't think it would work.

But apparently, Boca knew what she was doing, because as soon as she said that, a strange energy seemed to settle over the whole room. Gods exchanged looks with each other, ranging from surprise to anger to confusion and everything in between, yet none of them objected to Boca's demands.

Instead, the black-robed judge said, "Speak, Boca Secha, your testimony. It is your right, as prescribed by the Ancient Laws, to speak in defense of yourself and your fellow mortals when accused of this most egregious sin."

Boca nodded. "I am well-acquainted with the Ancient Laws, Judge Noak." She cast her gaze over the gods. "In our defense, I will point out that we arrived in the abode *after* Shirataka's murder. Had we not run into her body in the streets of the city, we would not have even known about her murder. Furthermore, none of us have ever murdered a god aside from the Nameless One, who I am sure none of you mourn."

The gods shifted in their seats, a few still muttering with each other, a handful glaring at Boca as if trying to make her die through bad looks alone.

Boca continued. "Furthermore, Raniel has offered *no* proof or even convincing evidence of our role in this crime. He has only attacked our character and acted as if our presence here alone proves we have done anything wrong. Were that so, then the entire abode ought to be standing trial right now, including all of you, for the apparent crime of merely existing in the same general vicinity as the murder of Shirataka."

That earned Boca more death glares from some of the gods, but others wore thoughtful expressions. Raniel, of course, looked furious, clutching the hilt of his sword, though fortunately he did not try to interrupt Boca.

Boca put her hands on her hips. "Having said that, I acknowledge that the murder of a god or goddess *is* a very serious crime. My companions and I did not travel here to murder a deity. We sought only to get your help in defeating a great evil none of us can stop."

The long-necked goddess snorted. "The Nameless One is already dead and we didn't try to stop him. What makes you think we gods would be interested in helping you deal with a much lesser evil?"

"I am aware of that, Your Divinity," Boca said. "From previous experience, I know how the gods work. You only aid mortals in exchange for something else. Often, it is worship, obedience, sacrifices … or the occasional carnal pleasures of sharing a bed with an attractive mortal. But I know of something of much more value to all of the gods present that we can offer you in exchange for your help."

"And what, pray tell, might that be, Boca?" Judge Noak said, a slightly skeptical expression in his eyes.

Hal, too, was curious about what Boca thought the gods might want. He certainly couldn't think of anything they had that the gods might want even more than justice for the murder of one of their own.

Boca held up a hand. "In exchange for your help, we will personally investigate the murder of Shirataka and bring her *true* killer to justice."

Chapter Five

In Malarsan, far to the south of the Abode of the Gods ...

Surrels found himself wondering, not for the first time in the last week, how his life had gotten to the point where it was.

Of course, Surrels knew the answers: He had joined the Black Soldiers at a young age, served under two different monarchs before rebelling against both (though at different times and for different reasons), befriended a few dragons, and then was framed for the murder of one of said monarchs who had also been one of his closest friends and had to escape from prison, with help from his long-estranged son who had taken an interest in helping him despite resenting him for not being in his life.

Although technically, if Tenka's coronation happens as scheduled, then I will have rebelled against three *different monarchs,* Surrels thought as he walked through the tall grain fields far outside of the capital. *Perhaps I really* do *have a problem with authority. Either that or Anija is rubbing off on me.*

"Father," Kendo's sharp voice came from the shadows. "Are you paying attention?"

Snapping out of his thoughts, Surrels looked at Kendo. Though the moon was out, much of Kendo's face was covered in shadow, other than his judgmental eyes. "Hmm? Sorry. I was lost in thought."

Kendo shook his head. "Now's not the time to think. We have to keep moving if we are going to stop Tenka's men from killing the child before we get there. Or do you *want* Tenka's smug face on the throne?"

Surrels pursed his lips but nodded. He peeked above the heads of grain, catching a glimpse of a small farmhouse on a hill not far from them. A light was on in one of the upper windows, indicating that someone was still up. "I see our destination."

"Do you see any Malarsan soldiers?" Kendo said.

Surrels shook his head. "Hard to tell for certain in this darkness, but it doesn't look like anyone else is there other than the family living there." Surrels pulled Kendo down into the grain and gazed at him. "Are you *sure* this is the place Tonya sent the child?"

Kendo nodded. "Yes. And if not, then I guess we'll find out. Now let's keep moving."

With that, Kendo resumed moving through the grain, his movements surprisingly quiet. It made Surrels wonder, not for the first time, where his adult son had learned such tricks.

I certainly didn't teach him that, Surrels thought, following his son as quietly as he could. *What sort of crimes did he do during my time away from him?*

That was a recurring thought that Surrels had had over the past month and a half or so, ever since he reconnected with Kendo. Kendo had displayed a variety of illicit tricks and skills that he had probably picked up during his criminal career. And while normally Surrels was quite judgmental about his son's criminal past, right now he was thankful for it, because it was probably the only thing that had saved him from the near-execution he barely avoided.

After escaping from Capital City Prison a week ago, Surrels had made his way out to his daughter's house, where he rendezvoused with Kendo, Fralia, and his daughter Lila and her family. There, Surrels learned that Tonya did indeed have a young child at some point who Lila barely remembered, but after a time Tonya had sent the young child off to stay with some distant family of theirs. Kendo hadn't even known the child existed at all, having been born after the child was sent away.

No one knew why Tonya had sent the child away. Lila had speculated that Tonya simply did not want anyone asking her questions about the child and thought that it would be safer in another part of the country.

Whatever Tonya's reasons for doing what she did were, it meant that locating said extended family was a challenge. Fortunately, Lila kept good family records and had been able to pinpoint a location for the family, located out in the farming lands of Malarsan.

Not far from where Hal grew up, now that I think about it, Surrels thought. *I wonder how Hal is doing these days.*

So Surrels and Kendo had headed out shortly after that,

keeping away from major roads and highways to avoid being captured. Surrels was all too aware that his escape from prison made him into Malarsan's most wanted criminal, hence why he wore a cloak and tried to travel only at night.

Fralia had wanted to come, but Surrels told her that she was better suited to stay at the capital and keep an eye on Tenka, who was scheduled to be coronated within the next couple of weeks. Besides, Surrels did not want Tenka to suspect that Fralia might have played a role in Surrels's escape from prison, so it made sense for her to stay put where she was.

As for Tenka, the very thought of the arrogant, manipulative young noble was enough to make Surrels's blood boil. More than anything, he wanted to smack the smirk right off the lips of Tenka, because he had learned that *Tenka* had been the one to order him to murder his wife, not Old Snow, as he previously thought.

Tenka's been playing me for a fool even longer than I can remember, Surrels thought. He sighed. *Which I suppose isn't saying much, seeing as I still barely remember anything before and during my Black Soldier days.*

That was another thing that bothered Surrels. Now that he was on the run, he almost certainly wasn't going to be getting his memories restored anytime soon. His only hope was to expose Tenka for the fraud that he was and clear his name, although neither task was going to be remotely easy, even if Surrels and Kendo successfully located Old Snow's secret second child and proved that he was the true heir to the throne and not Tenka.

So I just need to take things a step at a time, Surrels told himself. *Find the child and get the child to the capital. Even if the child isn't ready for ruling yet, his mere appearance ought to at least throw a wrench into Tenka's carefully laid*—

The sound of glass breaking, followed by a child's scream of terror, broke through the night, causing both Surrels and Kendo to stop.

"What was that?" Kendo said. "Sounds like it came from the house."

Surrels grimaced. "And like someone has already beaten us here. Let's go."

Surrels ran through the heads of grain, no longer caring about stealth. Kendo ran right beside him, and the two ran until they emerged out of the grain field into the clearing around the house.

The gate in front of the house had been ripped off its hinges, lying off to the side of the path. Down the path, Surrels saw that the front door of the modest farmhouse had been kicked in by something, barely hanging onto its hinges. From within the dark house, the sounds of screaming and slashing could be heard, along with what sounded a little too much like the growls of some kind of beast.

"The hell is going on in there?" Kendo said.

Surrels drew his sword. "Nothing good. And if we don't do anything, it will just get even worse."

Just as Surrels said those words, there was another *bang* and then a young boy, no older than five or six, burst out of the front door. The boy ran so fast that he stumbled down the front steps, lying on the ground, clearly dazed by the short fall.

"Kid?" Kendo said in alarm. "What happened?"

The boy, sitting up, looked toward Surrels and Kendo with big, teary eyes. "A m-monster killed my parents."

"A monster——?" Kendo said. "Kid, what are you talking about?"

Surrels suddenly knew exactly what the kid was talking about, remembering something that Tenka had told him not too long ago about his *other* servants. "The kid's talking about——"

A deep growl from within the house interrupted Surrels, prompting everyone to turn their attention to the house.

Then a creature straight out of Surrels's worst nightmares stepped out. The hulking beast looked like a hairless bear crossed with a wolf with dagger-like teeth extending several inches past its mouth. Dead red eyes peered out of a skull covered with papery yet sweaty skin that glistened under the moonlight overhead.

Then the creature looked down at the kid, growled, and leaped toward him.

Chapter Six

BUT SURRELS WAS MOVING EVEN BEFORE THE DEMON DID.

Reaching the child first, Surrels swung his sword at the beast's face. His sword slashed through its nose, sending black blood flying everywhere as the demonic being roared in pain, clutching at its wounded face and staggering backward.

Grabbing the child's arm, Surrels said, "Get up! It won't stay injured forever. Let's go!"

The child did not fight. If anything, the child seemed eager to join them, running away from Surrels toward Kendo, who held his arms open wide to catch the boy. The boy ran into Kendo's arms, who picked up the child and ran into the grain fields around the house to safety.

Surrels would have gone to join them if he didn't hear a deeply inhuman growl behind him. Looking over his shoulder, Surrels saw that the demon—its facial wound having healed up already—was lunging toward him through the air.

Rolling to the side, Surrels barely avoided the demon,

which crashed onto the ground ungracefully before hopping to its feet. Rather than go after Surrels, however, the demon turned its gaze toward the grain fields, sniffing the air, likely trying to track the boy by scent.

Alarmed, Surrels rushed toward the demon, slashing at its hide with his blade. He plunged his sword into its back, causing the demon to let out an earsplitting shriek of pain as more black blood poured out of its wound.

Yanking the sword out of its back, Surrels immediately turned and ran. He headed into the farmhouse, slamming the remains of the door shut behind him, though he knew it wouldn't hold the demon back for very long. That was proved true almost immediately when he heard the demon slam into the broken door, roaring and snarling, the sound of wood being ripped apart by claws filling Surrels's ears.

But Surrels didn't look back. He just took the stairs two steps at a time, heading for the second story. Surrels had no idea where he was going. His only concern, as he panted and sweated, was to perhaps find a small enough room where the demon might have trouble maneuvering and fighting.

Really wish I had a dragon with me right now, Surrels thought as he bounded up the steps. *Or even one of those relics. Should have accepted Hal's offer when I had the chance.*

Surrels reached the top of the stairs just as he heard the demon running up behind him. Looking over his shoulder, Surrels saw the demon surging up the stairs after him, red eyes glowing ominously in the darkness.

But Surrels grabbed a nearby side table and shoved it down the stairs. The table crashed into the demon's face, sending it stumbling down the stairs again, vanishing into the blackness of the night until it hit the lower floor with a loud *crash*.

Panting hard, Surrels ran down the hall, heading for the room at the end of the hall where a single light shone from underneath. He wrenched the door open and slammed it shut, leaning against the door, breathing hard, sweat rushing down his forehead, his armpits slick with wetness.

A glance around the room showed Surrels that he was in what must have been the boy's room. A small bed sat in one corner, along with a dresser on the other side, and a mirror on the wall. Clothes and toys were scattered across the floor, while the light came from a single lit candle that seemed way too bright to Surrels at this time of night. The smell of melting candle filled his nostrils.

The one thing that Surrels did not see, however, was an exit. There was an open closet door and a window, but other than that, the room did not seem to let out into any other rooms.

That demon will be back any second now, Surrels thought, glancing around the room. *Need to buy myself more time.*

Surrels ran over to the dresser, which he pushed in front of the door, along with the bed. He knew his makeshift fortifications would not buy him more than five or six extra minutes, if that, but it was all he could do for now.

Panting, Surrels leaned against the wall, only to hear a far-too-familiar male voice say, "Hello, Surrels."

Startled, Surrels looked around for the source of the voice, but he didn't see anyone else in the room other than himself. "Who said that? Where are you?"

"The mirror has your answers, Surrels," said the male voice.

Surrels looked at the mirror on the other side of the room and started again.

Tenka stood in the mirror, arms crossed in front of his chest, a smirk on his lips.

Even worse, however, were his eyes, which glowed a dull red color, similar to the eyes of the demon.

Anger shot up inside Surrels at the sight of the young noble, causing him to briefly forget the demon. "Tenka. This is your doing."

"Naturally," Tenka said, "although I did not expect to see you here. After becoming the kingdom's most wanted criminal, I assumed that you would do the smart thing and lay low for a while or even flee the country, but I see you've decided to interfere with my ambitions instead."

Surrels tightened the grip on his sword's leather handle. "I'm here to protect a young child from monsters, Tenka. Monsters like *you*."

Tenka chuckled. "Monster? I am the rightful heir to the throne of Malarsan. No one in the court knows about the boy and, if all goes according to plan, no one ever will. At least, no one *living*, anyway."

Surrels bit his lower lip. "How are you even talking to me right now? You're clearly not here in person."

Tenka tapped the mirror. "I am using demonic magic that allows me to communicate with you via mirrors. Not quite as convenient as Communication Necklaces, but it suffices for my purposes. I saw through the eyes of the demon I sent to kill my long-lost cousin that you and your criminal son are trying to save the boy, so I decided that now was a good time to talk."

"Talk?" Surrels demanded. "About what? I am done talking with you. I have nothing good or kind to say to you, other than I hope your lies are exposed to the entire kingdom and you end up in the gutter right where you belong."

Tenka tsked. "Such anger, although I suppose you have always been a very *angry* man. That is why you have been so easy to manipulate. Anger makes people stupid. Calmness, on the other hand, is what separates the intelligent from the intellectually crippled."

Surrels scowled. "I am perfectly calm right now. Calm enough to not take your crap any longer."

Tenka shook his head. "Lie all you want; perhaps that makes you feel better about yourself. But what you must realize is that you are fighting not merely a losing battle, but a losing war. You have lost your wife, your friends, your reputation, your position in the government, your home, and your servants while I am on the cusp of gaining control of the entire kingdom of Malarsan, becoming the kingdom's most powerful and popular monarch in over a hundred years."

Tenka leaned forward, frowning. "A wise person would have understood this and stayed in prison, awaiting his trial, accepting his fate, rather than risk getting put down like a dog."

Surrels stomped up to the mirror, standing inches from its surface. "I'm not accepting anything, Tenka. Maybe I am fighting a hopeless cause, but better to fight for such a cause than to meekly accept my fate like some kind of obedient small child."

Surrels leaned even closer in until the tip of his nose almost brushed against the mirror, his eyes locked onto Tenka's. "And I *will* avenge my wife and Old Snow and save the kingdom from you."

Tenka raised an eyebrow. "That's nice. Although, you do realize our entire conversation is nothing but a distraction, right?"

Surrels frowned. "A distraction? A distraction from what—"

The demon suddenly burst through the open window, howling and roaring, sending glass and chunks of wood flying everywhere. The candle on the table fell over from the impact of the demon's crash, setting fire to the table, the flames quickly spreading throughout the room.

Surrels had just enough time to whirl around before the demon lunged at him again. Leaping to the side, Surrels dodged the demon, which crashed into the mirror, causing Tenka's smirking form to disappear.

Stepping to the side, Surrels slashed at the demon, but it ducked its head and body slammed him.

The impact of the body slam sent Surrels staggering, though he managed to raise his sword in time to block its next slash. However, the demon clutched his sword with its claws and ripped it out of his hand, throwing the sword through the open window to the ground below.

Alarmed and unarmed, Surrels backed away from the demon even as the flames spread through the room, covering more and more of the boy's room, raising the temperature considerably. Surrels backed up until he almost tripped over the threshold of the closet, but he kept backing up until he hit the back of the closet wall.

The demon appeared in the entryway to the closet, red eyes alight with evil intent, licking the blood on its lips.

"I finally have you where I want you," the demon said in a voice that sounded eerily like Tenka's.

Surrels gulped. "Tenka—?"

The demon grinned. "Did I forget to mention that I can also speak through my demonic servants? I hate doing it because of how ugly these monstrosities are, but it can be very … convenient sometimes. Especially when I want to frighten you."

Surrels wiped the sweat off his forehead. He looked around the closet for anything, anything at all, he could use as a weapon to defend himself, but he saw nothing.

And with no way out, Surrels was well and truly trapped.

Chapter Seven

THE DEMON GROWLED DEEPLY, EYES GLOWING DARKLY IN the shadows. "Not to mention this will give me a front seat view of your impending demise. Pray to the gods if you wish. It won't do you any good."

Surrels licked his lips. Breathing was becoming more difficult now, partly thanks to the smoke from the growing fire, partly thanks to the overwhelming stench of blood and death wafting off of the demon in waves. The smell alone would have probably been enough to kill Surrels, although he doubted the demon would be happy with that.

The demon took another step into the closet, still grinning, still licking its lips. "Why don't you beg for mercy, weakling? I might be gracious enough to give you another half second of life. Although even *I* can feel the hunger this demon has for you and even taste the sweet blood on its lips."

Surrels gritted his teeth. "Finally, Tenka, you have a body that matches the rotten soul within your white-washed tomb."

The demon growled even more deeply than before. "For that comment alone, I am going to make your death as slow and agonizingly *painful* as possible."

The demon sprang toward Surrels, at which point several things happened at once.

Kendo suddenly appeared behind the demon, clutching something in his hand, yelling, "Father! Get out!"

Surrels, not trusting his thinking process at this point, dove underneath the demon. He just barely slipped underneath its massive, hairless body, skidding along the creaky wooden floor until he got out of the closet and rolled onto his back.

That allowed Surrels to see the demon crash into the back of the closet hard enough to crack the wood paneling. But the demon just whirled around in the compressed space, hissing and snarling like the monster it was.

"You again," Tenka hissed at Kendo. "Do you want to die with your murderous father, too?"

Kendo grimaced. "No. But I'm pretty sure *you* do."

Kendo suddenly hurled several small objects into the closet before slamming the door shut. Clutching Surrels's arm, Kendo snapped, "Let's go! We don't have much time."

Surrels scrambled to his feet, following Kendo, not to the door to the room, but to the huge hole in the wall that had once been the window for the room. Surrels and Kendo leaped out of the second-floor window at the same time, landing hard on the ground outside at a roll, the two rolling until they reached the edge of the grain fields.

Breathing hard, Surrels, lying flat on his back, looked at his son in bewilderment. "What did you—"

Boom.

The entire second floor of the farmhouse exploded,

massive flames covering the whole thing. The lower floor groaned under the impact before abruptly giving away, causing the entire house to collapse in on itself in a display of fire and debris that would live in Surrels's nightmares forever.

Among the crashing house and exploding fire, however, Surrels thought he heard Tenka's screams of anger, crossed with the painful shrieking of the demon, but that sound went away as quickly as it came.

In seconds, silence had once again descended on the grain fields, other than the crackling of the fire slowly devouring the remains of the once proud farmhouse.

"Wow," Kendo said, rising to his feet and dusting off his pants, "that was even more explosive than I thought it would be."

Surrels, feeling every bone in his body aching from the jump, also rose to his feet unsteadily. "What did you *do?*"

Kendo suddenly held out a small, round ridged object in his hand. "Tipjokian hand bombs. Designed from the Tipjokian exploding fruit, these hand bombs are supposed to pack quite a punch. And technically, you are only supposed to use one at a time, but since we were dealing with an honest-to-god demon, I decided it didn't hurt to go a little overboard."

Surrels's eyes widened. "You mean you've been walking around with literal hand bombs in your pockets this entire time and yet you never told me? And where did you even *get* those things, anyway? Aren't they illegal in Malarsan?"

Kendo shrugged. "I know some people who know some people in Tipjok who are happy to sell their weapons for the right price outside of the law. Besides, I've never been one to care much for legality, although given how you are now a criminal on the run like me, I'm surprised you still give a damn about laws."

"Because I am *not* a criminal like you," Surrels argued. "I was unjustly framed for murder."

Kendo wagged a finger at Surrels. "But you also escaped from prison, which is definitely a no-no in the Malarsan legal system. So technically, Dad, you *are* a criminal like me, if for different reasons."

Surrels scowled. He was more than willing to continue to debate the point with Kendo, only to hear a rustling in the grain heads before the young boy poked his head out, his eyes wide with fear.

"I heard a loud noise," said the young boy, "what hap —"

The young boy's eyes widened even more when he saw the burning remains of his house, his jaw dropping. "Mommy—?"

Surrels bit his lower lip. He had almost forgotten about Old Snow's son, realizing that this was his home. No wonder the boy looked so shocked to see it in flames.

Kendo turned toward the boy and held out a hand. "We need to get going. The demon is dead, but the person who sent the demon after you will probably send more. We need to get to safety."

Surrels was shocked by Kendo's surprisingly gentle attitude toward the young boy. He hadn't realized that Kendo was good with kids.

The boy hesitated, but then took Kendo's hand and the two of them entered the heads of grain again.

Surrels followed, only briefly looking over his shoulder at the burning house. He half-expected to see the demon rise out of the remnants of the house again, but he didn't

see anything except fire and burning wood that would probably burn through the whole night.

Although they had no way of knowing whether the demon
had come by itself or had traveled with others, Surrels and
Kendo agreed it would be wise to take the boy as far away
from the farmhouse as they could. They headed generally
south, going in a more or less random direction in an effort
to throw off any potential pursuers.

They walked for several hours before reaching another
farmhouse, this one genuinely abandoned, where they
settled down for the night.

The boy was quiet during the walk, which surprised
Surrels, because he thought the boy would have all sorts of
questions about them and why they had come to save him
and who wanted him dead. But the boy didn't utter a single
word until they got to the farmhouse and asked him his
name.

"My name?" the boy repeated. "Stebo. Stebo Megat."

Surrels, sitting across from the boy in the abandoned
barn, bit his lower lip. "Megat, you say?"

The boy nodded. He was sitting on the hay-strewn floor
of the barn as well, clutching his toy bear. "Yes. It's my last
name. What's yours?"

"Just call me Surrels," Surrels said. He gestured at
Kendo. "And this is my son, Kendo."

Kendo, standing beside Surrels, nodded at Stebo before
looking down at Surrels. "Father, keep an eye on Stebo. I'm
going to glow Fralia and let her know that our mission was
successful."

Surrels nodded as Kendo stepped out of the barn, clutching his Communication Necklace. He soon heard both Kendo and Fralia's voices as the two spoke through their magical necklaces, although their slightly muffled voices made it hard to tell what they were saying.

"Mission?" Stebo said, bringing Surrels's attention back to him. "Did someone send you to save me?"

Surrels pursed his lips. "Your dad did."

Stebo frowned. "My dad? But he's dead. So is mommy. They were both killed by that monster."

Surrels grimaced. "I'm sorry, Stebo, but those two … they weren't your *real* parents. They may have raised you, but you come from another couple."

Stebo blinked. "I do?"

Surrels nodded. "Yes. And it was your real father who sent us to protect you from the evil people who want to hurt you. That's why we are here."

Stebo rubbed his eyes. Tears were starting to form. "But … I don't understand. Mommy and daddy were not my real parents?"

Surrels tilted his head to the side. "You mean no one ever told you that you were adopted?"

Stebo sniffled. "No. And I don't even know if you are telling the truth or not. I want my parents."

Surrels bit his lower lip. He had not known that young Stebo didn't know who his real parents were. He wished he had done a bit more research in that regard, but it was too late now. Stebo was clearly getting upset, and Surrels couldn't blame him. The kid's entire life had been turned on its head in less than a night.

Who knows how long it will take for him to process everything that has happened? Surrels thought. *This would be a lot even for a full-grown adult. And he's not even ten years old yet.*

Surrels reached out and patted Stebo on the shoulder. "I know you've been through a lot tonight, kid, but you can trust me. I was a good friend of your real father before he died. But even if you are having trouble believing, you saw that demon. You know there are people out there who want to hurt you. Kendo and I will protect you."

Stebo gazed up at Surrels, his eyes wide and brown. Somewhere in the back of Surrels's mind, a mental image of a boy similar in age to Stebo rose up. It was vague and Surrels could barely make out the details, but he thought it was Kendo.

A memory? Surrels thought in alarm, his own eyes widening at the implications. *How—?*

"Did I do something wrong?" Stebo asked suddenly.

Snapping out of his thoughts, Surrels looked at the young boy in confusion. "What?"

"You look worried," Stebo said. He wrapped his arms around his body. "I'm sorry."

Surrels shook his head. "You didn't do anything wrong. I was just remembering something important, something I thought I had forgotten a long time ago."

Stebo pursed his lips before yawning. He leaned against the pile of hay that he sat before, his eyes barely open. "Sleepy …"

Surrels smiled. "Go ahead and rest. Kendo and I will keep watch."

Stebo nodded, yawned one more time, and then closed his eyes. He must have fallen asleep quickly, because not even a second after he closed his eyes, he started snoring loudly. Surrels was jealous that the boy could fall asleep so quickly, mostly because as an adult, he couldn't.

But I am glad that he can *sleep,* Surrels thought, rubbing his eyes. *And that he is safe.*

Kendo suddenly poked his head through the barn doors and said, "Dad, can you step outside with me? I have some news from Fralia."

Surrels, frowning, rose from the floor of the barn and stepped outside with Kendo. He hated leaving Stebo alone even for a second, however, so he made sure to stand in such a position that he could still keep an eye on the young boy's resting form while still facing Kendo.

"What is it?" Surrels asked.

Kendo put his hands into his pockets. "Firstly, Anija Ti, your friend and fellow council member, has finally returned to Malarsan. Says Wilme is getting her up to speed on recent developments in the kingdom, including Old Snow's death and Tenka's ascension to the throne. Anija herself is also going to give us the most recent update on Halar Norath and Keershan, plus what is going on in the Glaci Empire and Kryo Kardia's next moves."

Surrels looked at Kendo in surprise. Anija had disappeared about a month and a half ago under mysterious circumstances that Surrels still did not entirely understand himself. Last he had heard from Fralia, Anija had been in the Northern Circle, the capital of the Glaci Empire, though how and why she went there, Surrels still didn't know himself.

"That's great news," Surrels said with a smile. "It will be nice to have another friend in high places for us. And, of course, I am happy to hear that Anija is alive and well."

Kendo pursed his lips. "The bad news is that a date for Tenka's coronation has finally been set. It's next week."

Surrels's eyebrows shot into his hair. "Next week—? But I thought it wouldn't be for another month. Don't they still need to finish the investigation of Old Snow's death?"

Kendo shook his head. "Apparently not. According to Fralia, Tenka convinced the other nobles that leaving the throne empty for so long, especially in light of Hal and Anija's recent disappearances, is not good for the kingdom, so they are speeding up the typical coronation process. As well, since 'everyone' knows you murdered Old Snow, there is little political will to do a full-fledged investigation into the matter."

Surrels scowled. "I imagine Tenka is stonewalling it. After all, any honest investigation into the facts would only serve to vindicate me and make Tenka look bad."

Kendo shrugged. "Either way, this means all three of us need to get back to the capital as soon as possible if we are going to stop the coronation. Fralia also did research into the matter and found out that if we can prove that Stebo is Old Snow's son, then Tenka will not be allowed to take the throne."

"We knew that already," Surrels said. He folded his arms in front of his chest and glanced at the sleeping boy. "The question is, *how* do we prove that Stebo is Old Snow's son?"

"Fralia is still looking into that," Kendo said, "but either way, the most important thing is keeping Stebo alive and safe until we get back to the capital."

Surrels cocked his head to the side. "I agree, but now that I think about it, *how* are we going to get back into the capital, exactly? I imagine security will be beefed up considerably with the coronation just around the corner, plus you and I are both wanted men at this point. If either of us are seen in public—"

Kendo clasped Surrels's shoulder. "Don't worry about that, Dad. I've asked some favors of a few friends of mine who have experience getting things into and out of places they aren't supposed to be."

Surrels narrowed his eyes. "And who, pray tell, are these 'friends' of yours?"

Kendo smiled. He gestured at the dragon tattoo on his face. "You see this tattoo? I'm not just wearing it because it looks cool. It signifies my membership in a very select group of people who are not on good terms with the law."

Surrels frowned. "And who are they, if I may ask?"

Kendo's smile became even bigger. "The Dead Dragon Syndicate. And they are the only people who can get us into the capital without Tenka or his goons being the wiser."

Chapter Eight

ON ONE HAND, ANIJA TI WAS HAPPY TO BE BACK IN
Malarsan. Although she had only been absent from the
country for a little over a month, it had been perhaps the
most difficult month of her life, not including the first
month after she had been abandoned by her parents as a
young child. She had been possessed by the evil spirit of her
former boss, slaughtered an entire room of professional
assassins and thieves, and then traveled to a far-flung
foreign country to kill the single most powerful mortal individual on the planet (and failed).

Somehow, though, Anija survived all of that.

On the other hand, Anija's return to Malarsan couldn't
have been worse.

Mostly because she learned that a *lot* had happened
since her departure.

"So let me get this straight," Anija said slowly, sitting at
the desk in what had been Hal's office in the town of
Mysteria, staring at the elderly woman sitting across from

her. "Old Snow was assassinated by Surrels, but only because Old Snow's nephew, Tenka, tricked him into doing it. Not only that, but Old Snow apparently had a secret second child he didn't tell anyone about until the night of his murder, a child who has a better claim to the throne than Tenka, so now Surrels and his long-lost son are trying to save the child before Tenka kills him to remove a threat to his claim. Oh, and Tenka apparently also was the one who ordered Surrels to murder his wife, too, a long time ago. Did I get all of that right?"

The old woman sitting across from Anija, Wilme, another member of the council and the woman left in charge of the Dragon Rider School in Hal's absence, nodded once. "More or less, yes."

Anija shook her head, leaning back in the creaky wooden chair. "And I thought that *I* had been on some pretty wild adventures recently. Nothing ever stays quiet, huh?"

Wilme nodded again. "It would be boring if it did."

Anija chuckled. "Honestly, despite how much I like action, I wouldn't mind a little boring now and then."

We must remain ever vigilant, Anija, said a deeper female voice in her head. *Surrels told Fralia and Kendo that Tenka is apparently affiliated with the demons now. And you know what that means.*

Anija grimaced. The voice in her head belonged to Rialo, her dragon Steed. It had been mostly thanks to Rialo that Anija had managed to free herself from Shadow Mask's control and get back to Malarsan in a timely fashion. "Yes. But do we know that for sure?"

Yes, said Rialo. *Fralia performed a memory spell to observe*

Surrels's memories, and she saw what he saw in prison. Knowing how dangerous the demons are, this makes it even more urgent that we stop Tenka from becoming king.

I don't disagree, Anija replied. *This situation just keeps getting worse and worse.*

Rialo growled. *Very. Although I am happy you are back.*

Anija smiled. She was happy she was back, too. She wished Rialo could be there with them, but Rialo was too big to enter the building with them, so the dragon was forced to sit outside the window of the office and communicate primarily through telepathy via their bond.

"Rialo says that Tenka has demons working for him, too," Anija said to Wilme. "If this is true, then we need to act *now* to stop him."

Wilme pursed her lips. "That would be very unwise, Anija."

Anija scowled, leaning forward in her chair. "Why? We've overthrown corrupt demon-possessed monarchs before. I don't see how Tenka is any different."

Wilme held up her hand. "For one, we have no proof that Tenka is responsible for Old Snow's murder. So far, all of the evidence points to Surrels, so in the eyes of the court and the public, Surrels is the criminal here, not Tenka. Additionally, Malarsan *does* need a king, and Tenka is the only living relative of both Old Snow and Marial who is eligible to sit on the throne. Until Surrels and Kendo return with Old Snow's true heir, we have no choice but to wait."

"The coronation is next week, though," Anija said. "That's barely enough time to find a hidden child in a country the size of Malarsan."

Wilme brushed her gray hair out of her face. "I understand, but Surrels and Kendo are on it. We have to let them do their roles. In the meantime, we must do ours."

Anija sat back and folded her arms in front of her chest. "Fine. What *are* our roles, exactly? What are we going to do?"

"Wait until Surrels and Kendo return with the child, mostly," said Wilme. "There isn't much any of us can do until then. But more importantly, we are happy to hear that Hal and Keershan are still alive. Where did you say they went again?"

Anija furrowed her brows. "They went with one of the Snow Witches to some place called the Endless Cliffs. Supposedly, the Endless Cliffs lead to the Abode of the Gods. The plan is to appeal to the gods for help against Kryo Kardia, but I'm not sure how high the odds of them getting help actually is."

The Abode of the Gods? Rialo repeated in excitement. *When Keershan gets back, I will have to ask him if he saw Salard.*

Anija frowned. *Who?*

Salard is the god of dragons, Rialo explained. *According to legend, he is the biggest dragon in the world. But not only is he huge, he is also extremely powerful, said to be the father of all dragons, and full of wisdom and courage. I aspire to be just like him, as any good dragon does.*

Before Anija could respond to that, Wilme leaned forward slightly and said, "Did you say the Abode of the Gods, Anija? I didn't realize that place existed."

"Neither did I, but the Snow Witches seemed convinced that it does," Anija said. "And in any case, we're going to need all the help we can get. Kryo Kardia is even more powerful than any of us thought, and not just because he is the emperor of the Glaci Empire, either."

"Yes," said Wilme, "your report about his real powers was very disturbing. Legions of undead creatures, himself being an unnatural abomination animated through dark magic ... and somehow he accomplished all of that without the aid of demons."

Anija chuckled. "Trust me, Wilme, Kryo Kardia makes the demons look like fluffy kittens."

Do we know if he is planning to invade Malarsan or not? Rialo asked. *I still am not clear on that.*

Neither am I, Anija replied, *but I think it's safe to assume that he is.*

When Anija had escaped the Northern Circle, thanks to the other two Snow Witches, Ericha and Kiko, she had heard only that Kryo Kardia's Undead Legion had successfully annihilated the rebel forces. She did not know what the empire's next move might be, exactly, but she didn't think Kryo Kardia would forgive them for everything they did or tried to do to him.

Especially me, Anija thought. *I tried to kill him* twice.

Aloud, Anija said to Wilme, "We'll have to beef up the kingdom's northern defenses, just in case the Glacians decide to invade. Particularly, we will need Dragon Riders to counter Kryo Kardia's own."

Wilme sighed. "I knew we had our suspicions about Kryo Kardia stealing our relics, but I wish they had been false. Especially now that Kryo Kardia himself is apparently a Dragon Rider."

"Yeah, but we just have to do the best we can with what we have," Anija said, "although this is another reason why Hal and Keershan's mission to the gods is so important. We're going to need every bit of help we can get if we are going to stop—"

Anija, said Rialo suddenly, *you and Wilme need to get out here immediately.*

Fear rising in her stomach, Anija said, *Why? Is the Glaci Empire attacking already?*

No, said Rialo. *Tenka is here. And he is asking to meet you.*

Chapter Nine

As it turned out, Rialo was correct. When Anija and Wilme stepped out of the Dragon Rider Order headquarters, Anija saw a handsome, young dark-haired man in royal robes standing on the street in front of the building. He was surrounded by half a dozen tough-looking bodyguards, clad in thick armor and carrying swords, spears, and shields.

Nor was Tenka unnoticed by the inhabitants of Mysteria. Dragons and humans alike had formed a loose gathering on the street, ogling the soon-to-be king of Malarsan, though Anija noticed some of them left when she and Wilme showed up.

Probably don't want to get into trouble, Anija thought, *which is understandable, because depending on what Tenka is doing here, there might be a* lot *of trouble.*

Anija felt relieved to see Rialo standing on the other side of the steps. The huge black dragon stared down at Tenka and his bodyguards with her green eyes, not quite threatening them, but looking intimidating nonetheless.

Anija could feel every ounce of distrust Rialo felt toward
Tenka, feelings she certainly reciprocated, knowing Tenka's
role in Malarsan's current troubles.

Tenka's bodyguards looked rather intimidated by Rialo,
but Tenka, surprisingly enough, did not. He simply met the
black dragon's gaze with a strong gaze of his own, as if he
was used to being stared down by massive dragons
every day.

He probably thinks he can take her in a fight thanks to his demons,
Anija thought.

"Are you Tenka?" Anija said as she and Wilme stopped
halfway down the steps, staring at the young man.

Tenka tore his gaze away from Rialo to look at Anija.
"Oh? Why yes, yes I am. You must be Anija Ti. I was just
admiring your pet dragon's black scales."

"The name is Rialo, human," Rialo growled. "I am not
a pet."

"She's right," Anija told Tenka. "Steeds are life partners, not just simple pets."

Tenka held up his hands. "Apologies. I did not mean to
cause any offense. I simply don't have much direct experience with dragons, so I don't know much about their
culture or language. I will do my best to treat her with more
respect going forward."

Although Tenka looked and sounded polite enough,
Anija wasn't fooled. Even if she hadn't known Tenka's true
colors, Anija had spent enough time in the world of criminals to tell the difference between real politeness and fake
politeness.

And right now, Tenka couldn't have looked faker if he
tried.

"It is a surprise to see you here, Noble Hojara," said

Wilme, taking a tone that Anija felt was more diplomatic than Tenka deserved. "We had no idea you were coming to visit."

Tenka bowed respectfully. "If I am going to be Malarsan's next king, then I need to become familiar with every part of the kingdom. That includes the Tops, home to both the Dragon Riders and the Relic Crafters."

Anija tensed. "You know about the Relic Crafters? How … interesting. Most people don't realize they used to live here."

Tenka smiled. "I'm something of a bookworm, as my parents and teachers would attest. I love delving deeply into history and myth, including consulting some very obscure sources. I didn't realize a place as remote as this had such a complex and fascinating history. A lesson in not judging a location by its appearance, wouldn't you say?"

Anija pursed her lips. "I … suppose. What are you doing here, anyway? Especially on such short notice."

Tenka folded his arms behind his back, the cool wind blowing through his hair. "Aside, as I said, from wanting to learn more about this grand kingdom that I will soon be presiding over, I also wanted to personally welcome you back to the kingdom of Malarsan. I understand you have been missing for quite some time, although I have yet to learn where you spent the last month and a half."

Anija licked her lips. She had not been back in Malarsan long enough to have come up with a good cover story for what had happened to her. She didn't want to explain to Tenka about her quest to kill Kryo Kardia, but she knew he was smart enough to see through any obvious lies on her part.

Wilme, however, stepped forward and said, "Anija was

kidnapped by the Dark Tigers, who took her out of the country. She only recently managed to escape on her own and make it back here in one piece."

Tenka raised an eyebrow. "Really? I heard that the Dark Tiger Guild was destroyed by someone recently. I had assumed it was Anija."

Anija shook her head. As grateful as she was for Wilme's lying for her, she knew she needed to take it from here. "No. That happened after they took me out of Malarsan. I spent a long time in prison, so I am just getting up to speed on everything that has happened myself."

Tenka nodded. "I see. Then I suppose that means that the rumors about you traveling to the Northern Circle were false, then."

Anija stood still and calm, although deep down, she was a storm of emotions. "Totally. I've never even been that far north."

"I've heard it's a beautiful place," Tenka said after a pause. He looked at Wilme. "What of Commander Norath and his Steed, Keershan? I assume they are still missing after their diplomatic mission to the Glaci Empire?"

"Yes," said Wilme without hesitation. "Emperor Kryo Kardia says that the White Foxes, a terrorist group in the Northern Circle, are holding them ransom. Says that the empire is doing everything in their power to save them, though no luck yet."

Tenka sighed. "Disappointing. I was hoping to have the first Dragon Rider and his Steed present for my coronation next week. At least I can still invite the *second* Dragon Rider and her Steed, who also happens to be the Chief of the Clawfoot Clan."

Anija stared at Tenka. "The coronation is next week? But didn't Old Snow die last week?"

Tenka rubbed his chin. "My uncle did get murdered by a former friend of his a week ago, true. But right now, as we rebuild from the Dragon War and deal with possible encroachment from the Glaci Empire, we need strong leadership more than ever. What is a kingdom without a king, after all?"

"Or a king without a kingdom," Wilme muttered.

Tenka chuckled. "My late uncle would have known about that, given how long he spent in exile up here. Which is another reason for my visit. I wanted to see the place where the previous king of Malarsan spent the last decade of his life."

Anija put her hands on her hips. "So you are inviting Rialo and me to your coronation?"

Tenka nodded. He pulled out an envelope from his robes and handed it to Anija. "Yes. Normally, coronation invitations are sent by messenger, but since you just got back, I wanted to invite you myself." He winked. "And you never know what the future may hold. I will need a queen at some point, after all."

Anija, taking the envelope, glared at Tenka. "What does that mean?"

Tenka smiled mysteriously. "Nothing, other than having now met you, I am convinced that the future holds all sorts of interesting possibilities for the two of us. We will be working very closely to rebuild the kingdom, after all. You never know what might happen."

Anija met Tenka's eyes without hesitation, although she wanted to clock him. "You're right. Although I'm pretty happy where I am."

So am I, Rialo said mentally.

"How long are you going to stay up here, Noble Hojara?" Wilme asked, before Anija or Tenka could speak. "We have plenty of lodging for you and your bodyguards and servants."

Tenka waved a hand at her. "Only for the day. Then we will head back to the capital to prepare for the coronation, which will be the biggest celebration of the year."

"Perhaps I can give you a personal tour of Mysteria, Your Majesty," said Wilme. "After all, despite how small this town is, we have much to see."

Tenka nodded. "I would like that, Wilme. Especially the Forgotten Temple, said to be the birthplace of the Dragon Riders, and home of the Relic Crafters."

Anija gulped. She looked at Wilme, trying to mentally communicate to her why that would be a bad idea without Tenka catching on.

Wilme, fortunately, seemed to be on the same wavelength as her, because she said, "The Forgotten Temple can wait until later, Noble Hojara. We can start with the main Dragon Rider School, where you can see exactly how we train new Dragon Riders and their Steeds."

A look of slight disappointment crossed Tenka's features before being replaced with a soft smile. "Very well, then. You are the expert here. I will let you show us whatever you deem fit in whatever order you think is best."

Wilme nodded. She walked down the steps, gesturing for Tenka and his bodyguards and servants to follow. They did, following Wilme away from the headquarters to the huge structure on the other side of the town where the Dragon Rider students did most of their learning.

As for Anija, she and Rialo went the opposite direction, to the Forgotten Temple.

Creep, Anija thought as she walked. *If I ever get married, it certainly won't be to* him.

Wise decision, sister, said Rialo. *He probably only wants you for your position in the order. He is not the sort of male I would mate with, either.*

Anija chuckled. *Glad we have the same taste—or distaste—in men.*

Anyway, why are we going to the Forgotten Temple, Anija? Rialo asked as they walked. *We do not have any business there today.*

Anija sighed. *Normally, yes. But if Tenka knows about the Tops's connection to the Relic Crafters, then we need to warn our* own *Relic Crafter about this. Because I doubt Tenka has any good intentions for him.*

Chapter Ten

If Anija hadn't known that a Relic Crafter was now inhabiting the secret basement level of the Forgotten Temple, which had once been a Relic Crafter workshop, then she would not have realized the place was still in use at all.

Prior to Lom the Relic Crafter moving in, the hidden workshop had been clearly abandoned with dust covering tools and equipment, the smell of stale air indicating that the place had not been used in years, since whenever its previous owners had used it. That had probably been thousands or at least hundreds of years ago.

But Anija supposed there was one key difference she noticed as she entered the workshop.

It was now *even messier* than it had been before.

Piles of tools, equipment, and half-finished inventions or objects stood high on the worktables, some even spilling onto the floor, leaving just a couple of narrow pathways for a person to walk through. Anija nearly tripped over a wrench when she entered the room, staggering forward slightly before catching herself.

Anija, are you okay? Rialo asked. *I sensed you almost fell.*

Anija scowled. *I'm fine, sister, but thanks for asking. Just a wrench Lom left lying around, as usual.*

All right, Rialo said. *I wish I could join you, but I am too big to go down there with you. I will let you know if I see Tenka or anyone else approaching the temple, at least.*

Thanks, Anija said.

Anija's attention shifted when she heard a series of loud banging noises followed by surprisingly strong curses coming from one corner of the workshop. Carefully picking her way through the mess, Anija followed the sounds of cursing and hammer-banging until she found what she was looking for.

An almost skeletally thin man, clad in heavily-patched clothing with a thick work apron over it and wearing comically huge leather crafter's gloves on his hands, was slamming a hammer against some kind of metal object that Anija could not divine the purpose of. Every time he banged it, the man would pause, lean in close to observe it, curse loudly, and then resume banging it, seemingly oblivious to anything else in the room other than the thing he was working on.

Clearing her throat loudly, Anija said, "Lom? Lom, can you hear me? Lom?"

But Lom apparently did not hear her, because he just kept banging on the metal object. He did pause briefly to tinker with a loose screw, but only for a split second before resuming his hammer banging.

Annoyed, Anija walked up and grabbed his shoulder,

shouting, "Lom! Would you stop banging that hammer for one gods-damn second—"

Lom let out a squeak like a mouse and whirled around, waving his hammer madly at Anija. But Anija caught his wrist and twisted it, forcing Lom to drop the hammer at his feet, its thick head banging against the stone floor.

"Huh? What?" Lom said, his eyebrow-less eyes wide. Then he looked at Anija and confusion appeared across his face. "Anija? What are you doing here?"

Anija nodded at the metal object on Lom's worktable. "I was going to ask you what *you* were doing, other than making a terrible racket."

"Oh!" Lom said, nodding. He gestured with his free hand toward the worktable. "I was just in the middle of designing some neat metal boots I thought might be helpful for traversing the Tops's rugged terrain."

Anija raised an eyebrow. "And how does hammering a piece of metal do that?"

Lom grimaced. "I was testing the metal to see how it would, um, handle repeated stress. Thus far, the metal seems to be holding up, although it's just a prototype."

Anija glanced at the metal, noting that despite the fact that Lom had clearly been hammering it for who-knew-how-long, there wasn't a single dent or scratch in it. "What kind of metal is it made out of?"

"Malarsan blacksteel," Lom explained, "from the southern part of the region. Difficult metal to get a hold of, but it's great for making nigh-unbreakable armor and equipment. And not just for combat, either."

Anija frowned. "Sounds like something we might need if the Glaci Empire decides to invade. Could make useful armor."

Lom gave her a horrified look. "Are they here already? If so, tell them I'm dead. You can even tell them you murdered me because I annoyed you too much. I won't be offended."

Anija sighed in frustration. "They aren't here *yet*. I just came down to check on you and make sure you were okay."

Lom relaxed slightly, although his nervous expression and body language reminded Anija of a frightened cotton-tail rabbit nonetheless. "Oh, good. Hopefully, Hal and Keershan stop Kryo Kardia before they get here."

"Hopefully," Anija agreed.

Lom bit his lower lip. "Um, can you let go of my wrist now, please? It hurts."

Anija, having forgotten she had grabbed his wrist, immediately let go, allowing Lom to pull his hand back to his chest, rubbing his wrist like it was his baby. "Sorry. I guess all the banging and mess distracted me."

Lom nodded. "No problem. I understand that humans like you aren't used to the organization of a Relic Crafter. Our minds tend to work differently from normal humans. Where you might see chaos, I see unconventional order."

Anija, thinking of the wrench she nearly tripped over on her way in, eyed him skeptically but did not say anything.

After Hal and Keershan went with Boca to the Abode of the Gods, Anija had decided to head back to Malarsan herself. Her main goal had been to return to the kingdom with news about Kryo Kardia's true nature and power, but she had not traveled alone. Lom the Relic Crafter had tagged along with her.

The reason for that was simple. Because Kryo Kardia knew that a Relic Crafter existed within the borders of the

Glaci Empire, the Snow Witches had worried that Lom was no longer safe in the Northern Circle. And because the Snow Witches had actively come out against Kryo Kardia, it meant Lom could not stay with them in their compound anymore, either.

So, after Lom repaired Hal's relic, it had fallen on Anija to safely transport Lom to Malarsan.

Which Anija really did not mind. She knew how power-hungry Kryo Kardia was. It was a big enough problem that Kryo Kardia had stolen a lot of their relics to make his own Dragon Riders. She didn't even want to think about how bad things would get if Kryo Kardia had a full-time Relic Crafter under his employ, not merely to repair the relics he already owned, but to create brand new ones, thus allowing Kryo Kardia to expand his Dragon Rider forces almost infinitely.

But there was one small problem with Lom: He was a complete coward. Anija was practically convinced at this point that Lom had been a particularly cowardly rabbit in his previous life, which explained why he was so jumpy and fearful. The trip from the Northern Circle to Malarsan had been particularly difficult, due to the inherent danger of the journey forcing Anija to have to constantly calm down Lom and reassure him that everything was going to be okay at multiple points along the journey.

Granted, Lom had improved a lot once they actually arrived in Malarsan and Anija had moved him into the once abandoned crafters' workshop underneath the Forgotten Temple. Even though they had only been in Malarsan for a couple of days, Lom had already accumulated an impressive collection of tools and materials to make things.

That prompted Anija to ask, "Exactly where *did* you get all of this stuff from, anyway?"

Lom folded his arms behind his back. "I've mostly been scavenging what I can find around the town, though it's difficult because I'm not supposed to be seen in public. Also, my travel-space necklace has been useful in that regard."

Anija did a double take. "Your travel what?"

Lom closed his mouth. "Nothing. It's a Relic Crafter secret. Part of the Ancient Laws and blood oath we swore."

Anija gazed at Lom hard again. She remembered Lom explaining to her once that all Relic Crafters had sworn a blood oath that prevented them from divulging their secrets to non-Crafters. She had mostly assumed it was secrets related to crafting techniques and ideas, but it sounded like Lom was hiding a lot more than that from them.

Regardless, Anija did not come here to interrogate Lom about the secrets of his brethren. She asked, "How are you liking this workshop, by the way? Hal told me about your old one in the north, which was apparently a lot bigger than this one."

Lom shrugged. "It's fine for my purposes. As you said, definitely smaller, but not too small. Although I find it interesting just how *old* it is."

Anija frowned. "Aren't all of you Relic Crafters thousands of years old or something like that?"

Lom nodded. "Yes, but this place is even older than my workshop. There's a certain energy about the place that I can't put my finger on but which I can feel. I'm surprised you can't."

"I don't feel anything other than claustrophobic," Anija said.

Lom shook his head. "I suppose you aren't a Crafter, so naturally you can't feel it. But I can. A lot of things were made here, mostly good things, but … also some bad things."

"Bad things—? As in—?"

Lom shuddered. "I shouldn't say. It's considered bad luck among the Relic Crafters to talk about our failures. Better to focus on the successes. Although truth be told, I probably have a lot more failures than the average Relic Crafter, so I'm very sensitive to this sort of thing."

Anija narrowed her eyes but nodded. "Well, I'm just glad you seem to be adjusting. I'd recommend not going out for the rest of the day, though."

Lom gave her a curious look. "Why?"

"Because there is a certain individual in town who you definitely do not want anything to do with," Anija said. "A very dangerous man. Not quite Kryo Kardia level of dangerous, but someone you don't want to associate with anyway."

Lom gulped. "Well, I wasn't planning to go out today, anyway. I have so much work to do that I couldn't spare the time even if I wanted. Thanks for the warning, though."

Anija smiled. That was good to hear. Although Anija was not worried about Lom exploring Mysteria—he wasn't a very adventurous type—she still worried about what Tenka might do if he discovered Lom dwelling there. Given Tenka's association with the demons, Anija did not want Lom anywhere near Tenka if she could help it.

With another nod, Anija said, "Good to hear. Guess I'll see you later."

With that, Anija turned and made her way back to the exit. With Lom taken care of, Anija planned to return to the surface and join Wilme's tour of Mysteria, mostly to keep an eye on Tenka.

You definitely don't want a guy like that running around town unobserved, Anija thought, *which I'm sure is why Wilme invited him on the tour in the first place. Smart woman.*

Anija was about to put her hand on the door when it opened on its own …

Revealing a curious-looking Tenka on the other side.

Chapter Eleven

THE SILENCE WHICH HAD BEFALLEN THE GODS WAS deafening. All chatter ceased as all eyes fixed on Hal, Keershan, and Boca in the center of the chamber.

Well, the eyes of the gods were really just on Boca. The ancient witch, however, showed no fear or worry in the face of so many powerful deities. She stood tall and proud, seemingly daring them to speak first.

"Is she joking?" Keershan whispered to Hal. "Because I can't tell if she's joking or not."

Hal pursed his lips, but before he could reply, the long-necked goddess from before said, "What an … *interesting* proposition, Boca. Although I can't tell if this is a mortal joke or you are being serious."

"I am being *quite* serious, Jio," Boca said. She gestured at herself, Hal, and Keershan. "To prove our innocence, the three of us will conduct a full investigation of Shirataka's murder. If we bring the real murderer to justice, then you will hear our plea and give us the aid we need to defeat Kryo Kardia."

"And if you do not?" Judge Noak said, raising a skeptical eyebrow.

Boca folded her arms in front of her chest. "Then we will take the place of the real murderer and allow you to execute us."

Hal bit his lower lip. He saw what Boca was doing. The Snow Witch was clearly trying to save their lives by forcing the gods to grant them time to find the murderer.

And it wasn't even a bad plan, necessarily. Hal just did not see how or why the gods would agree to it.

The gods themselves apparently thought the same thing, because another god, this one with the head of a hawk, said, "But Raniel has already made a convincing claim for your guilt in Shirataka's murder, a claim which I believe has persuaded most of us already."

Raniel smirked at that, which made Hal hate him even more than he already did.

"Raniel proved nothing other than how easily one can use circumstantial evidence to make anyone look guilty," Boca said. "There was an entire crowd of people staring at Shirataka's corpse, not to mention the hundreds of thousands who call the abode their home. How likely is it that we, three mortals who literally just arrived, could have killed a god from a distance?"

"You obviously had help on the inside," Raniel snapped. He gazed toward the gods. "The Divine Guard shall do a full investigation into the matter until we find whoever the accomplices of these murderous mortals are."

"*Alleged* murderous mortals," Boca replied. "You still have not offered proof of your accusation. Besides, your assurance that you will weed out potential accomplices means that you already implicitly agree with the premise behind my argument, which is that our absence from the abode means we couldn't have killed Shirataka, certainly not on our own, anyway. If we did it at all, that is."

Raniel glared at Boca again, but Boca simply met his gaze without flinching.

Hal noticed that Boca's words seemed to be reaching the gods. Earlier, most of the gods had looked more than willing to condemn Hal and the others to death per Raniel's suggestion, but now many of them looked uncertain. A few were whispering furiously among themselves, though they were too far away for Hal to hear.

I think Boca's plan is working, Keershan said mentally. *The gods seem to be arguing with each other.*

Yes, Hal agreed. *I think it's time I jumped in, however, because I still don't think they are going to grant Boca's request without more convincing.*

Stepping up beside Boca, Hal raised a hand and said, "Gods of the world! My name is Halar Norath, and I agree with Boca. We will happily investigate Shirataka's murder for you in exchange for our lives and aid for our battle against Kryo Kardia in the mortal world."

"And just why should anyone care what you think, mortal?" said the long-necked goddess, gazing upon Hal with skeptical eyes.

Hal took a deep breath. "Because I am not just any mortal. I am the same Halar Norath who, along with my Steed Keershan, killed the Nameless One, preventing him from rising from the dead again. I know that this was used against me earlier, but I also know that none of you gods were very fond of the Nameless One in the first place."

"Meaning—?" Judge Noak said.

Hal gazed around at the gods. "Meaning that I am also

on your side. I do not hate the gods or wish to overthrow, oppose, or harm any of you in any way. My parents raised me from a young age to have respect and reverence for the gods, so knowing that someone out there has murdered a goddess in cold blood offends me as much as it does any of you. That is why you can rest assured that we will do everything in our power to get true justice for Shirataka, if you would but let us try."

Hal stopped speaking, waiting for the gods' reactions. While he couldn't predict exactly how each god or goddess might respond to his short speech, Hal had reason to believe that at least some of the gods were on his side already.

A year ago, during Hal and Keershan's final battle with the Nameless One, the Nameless One had implied that Hal and Keershan had been chosen by the gods in some capacity to oppose and defeat him. While Hal had killed the Nameless One before he could get more information or clarification on what the demonic god had meant, Hal nonetheless suspected that it meant some of the gods were already carefully tracking Hal and Keershan.

Meaning that at least some *of these gods must know we are innocent of this crime,* Hal thought, gazing around at the assembled deities, *even if I don't know which ones.*

Sure hope you are right about that, Keershan said. *Because I'm not feeling good about our odds here, despite your speech.*

Neither was Hal, if he was to be honest. The gods still looked uncertain, with the furious whispers simply gaining strength as time went on. It looked to Hal like perhaps the gods were evenly divided on the issue, although Hal did not know what that meant. If there was a tie, was there someone who could step in and break it if needed?

Judge Noak banged his gavel against the table in front of him, however, bringing the constant whispers and arguments of the gods among themselves to a sudden halt.

"We have heard arguments from both sides of the issue regarding Shirataka's murder," Judge Noak said, "and now, it is clear that we are no longer of one mind as to the guilt of the mortals. Therefore, I submit that we call a recess on this session to reconvene at a later date to make our final —"

"No."

That single word seemed to make the entire chamber freeze. All of the eyes of the gods turned toward one of the thrones before Hal and the others, so Hal followed their gazes until he was looking at the same entity they were.

It was the swirling sphere of purple from before, the one that Hal thought was watching them more carefully than the others. It took Hal a moment to realize that the sphere had actually spoken.

"Excuse me, Demo," Judge Noak said slowly, "but did you just speak?"

The sphere, apparently named Demo, swirled, which Hal took to be its way of nodding. "Yes."

"I don't understand," Keershan said, scratching his nose with one of his claws. "Why is everyone surprised to hear this sphere talking?"

Boca looked at Keershan as if he had just said something very ignorant. Even she wore an expression of pure shock on her face. "Because Demo *never* talks. He is not called the Silent God for no reason. The last time anyone heard him speak was … well, I doubt even the gods themselves can remember."

"What domain does he rule over?" Hal asked. "Because out of all of the gods, I can't say I have ever heard of him."

"He's the God of Mystery," Boca said. "He presides over everything that is unknown, especially to mortals and even to the gods. Out of all of the gods, he is the most mysterious. Some say he's the eldest god, while others say he isn't even a god at all, but belonged to some group of beings who predate even the gods. No one even knows if he has any worshipers or not."

"Wow," Hal said. "I take it that no one knows who or what he really is, then."

Boca nodded. "You would be correct. Still, the gods do accept him as one of their own. While he is not the leader of the gods, his insight is valued greatly by his fellow deities due to his great wisdom and understanding. Whenever he talks, others listen."

"Fascinating," Keershan said, gazing at Demo with more respect and curiosity now. "So if he's speaking up—"

"Then that means our situation is about to get *very* interesting," Boca said with a small smile that Hal was not sure he liked.

"Honorable Demo," said the long-necked goddess from before. "You said 'no' to reconvening at a later date. Why do you oppose Judge Noak's decision?"

The light inside Demo shined briefly. "Because the mortals are correct that we do not have nearly enough evidence to convict anyone of Shirataka's murder, mortal or otherwise."

"Are you implying that one of our own might have killed Shirataka?" the hawk-headed god demanded. "Because that is even more outrageous than the mortals' suggestion that one of our angels might have done it."

"I say nothing definitively one way or another," Demo replied, "other than I believe we should give the mortals a chance to prove their innocence and find the murderer."

The gods immediately exploded into shouts and bickering. Half of the gods were pointing fingers at and yelling at Demo while the others loudly came to his defense. Unfortunately, the gods had devolved into using what Hal assumed was their native language, meaning he didn't understand a word of what anyone was saying.

But he read the tones and body languages of each god and knew that Demo's words had been like an explosion going off in their midst.

A thundering, slamming sound cracked the air, overwhelming even the loudest of the gods, followed by Judge Noak's authoritative voice bellowing, "Order, I say! Order in the court!"

Surprisingly, the gods once again simmered down, although none of them looked the least bit happy about being silenced. Demo was the only deity who did not look upset, although that probably had more to do with Demo's lack of a face or body to communicate his thoughts and feelings than anything.

"I know we are all on edge because of this most horrendous crime that happened in our midst, but we mustn't be like the mortals and let our passions cloud our judgment and divide us," Judge Noak said, gesturing at the gods. "Even if you disagree with Demo, we all realize he is one of the wisest and most intelligent among us. If he believes that the mortals should be given a chance to prove their innocence, then I say we let them."

Hal noticed a hint of doubt in Judge Noak's voice. No doubt Judge Noak still considered Hal and the others guilty, but it was equally clear Judge Noak had great respect for Demo and didn't want the gods to divide over this issue.

"With all due respect, Judge Noak, Demo is not all-knowing," said the long-necked goddess. "If we let the mortals simply wander about the abode unsupervised, running their silly little 'investigation,' giving them all the time they need to fabricate evidence or frame others for their crime, then—"

"We will do none of that, Jio," said Demo, interrupting her without so much as an apology. "I was not done speaking earlier before everyone decided to share their opinions on my incomplete thoughts. I do not believe we should let the mortals move freely about the abode unsupervised. They need accountability, and I suggest that Raniel be their escort."

"Me?" Raniel said in surprise, putting a hand on his chest. "You would entrust me with that duty, Lord Demo?"

"Yes," said Demo. "You are one of our most loyal and faithful servants. In addition, you already have a clear dislike of the mortals, so we do not have to worry about them corrupting you should they turn out to be the guilty party. This will, in turn, give you a chance to find more evidence incriminating them, if indeed these mortals are behind Shirataka's untimely demise."

Raniel shifted from foot to foot, clearly unsure whether to be happy about Demo's suggestion or not.

Hal certainly wasn't. Raniel was already convinced of their guilt. He would probably stonewall their investigation, which would make it far more difficult, perhaps even impossible, for them to prove their innocence.

"We accept Demo's offer," Boca said without hesitation. "We will happily work with Raniel and the rest of the

Divine Guard to track down Shirataka's murderer, if that will please the gods."

Hal whipped his head toward Boca in shock. "What? But Raniel might—"

"Shut up," Boca whispered. "The gods would never let us travel around the abode unsupervised regardless. If we do not accept this stipulation, then all three of us will die *very* horrible deaths very soon."

Hal gritted his teeth, but he could not argue with Boca's logic. Boca seemed to understand the gods and their ways of thinking much better than he or Keershan did. He supposed she was probably right, though that did nothing to make him feel any friendlier or kinder toward Raniel.

"We see that the mortals have already agreed to Demo's stipulations," Judge Noak said, "but first, we, the gods, must vote on whether to accept Demo's idea or not. A simple majority is all we need one way or another. All in favor of giving the mortals a chance to prove their innocence under the watchful eye of the Divine Guard, including Raniel?"

At least half of the gods' hands shot up into the air, although with so many gods, Hal couldn't be sure if this was the more than half they needed or not.

Judge Noak nodded. "And against?"

The other half of the room raised their hands, although to Hal's eyes, the number of hands that went up looked smaller than the number that went up in favor of Demo's plan. A handful of gods kept their hands down the entire time, however, which made Hal wonder why they were abstaining from voting.

Not that it mattered particularly, however, because Judge Noak said, "Then the decision is settled. Mortals, the gods have voted, sixty/forty, to allow you to investigate

Shirataka's murder and to bring the real murderer to justice alongside Raniel and any other members of the Divine Guard who may be able to help you."

Hal breathed a sigh of relief, but Boca said, "Thank you, Your Honor, but is there a deadline by which we must report our findings?"

Judge Noak nodded. "Yes. Tomorrow morning. And if you do not present us with enough evidence to clear your names or incriminate someone else by then … well, we will revisit the issue and your roles in it."

Chapter Twelve

"ONE DAY *IS NOT* ENOUGH TIME TO INVESTIGATE THE murder of a goddess and bring the real murderer to justice," Keershan said about half an hour later, sitting on the ground, frowning, his head resting on his paws.

Hal, sitting at the small outdoor table outside of the cafe near the Temple of the Gods, nodded. "I agree. But knowing that we don't have all the time in the world to investigate Shirataka's murder, I wonder why we are sitting here at this cafe rather than pounding the streets of the abode looking for evidence to clear our names and find Shirataka's real murderer. Boca?"

Boca, sipping her tea, said, "Because we should eat first. I am sure the two of you are very hungry after climbing the Endless Cliffs and dealing with the gods in one day. We will conduct the investigation far more efficiently with full, rather than empty, stomachs."

Hal's stomach growled in agreement with Boca, causing Hal to put his hands on his belly. "I don't know. I'm still not sure this is the best use of our time."

"It doesn't matter how much time the gods might give you," Raniel said suddenly, his shadow falling over Hal. "Either way, you won't be able to find the 'real' murderer because *you* are the real murderers."

Hal looked over his shoulder to see Raniel standing not far behind him, the angel's arms crossed in front of his chest. "I forgot you were there."

"You had better not," Raniel warned Hal, "because I am keeping an eye on you at all times. That is the holy duty that the gods gave me, and it is a holy duty I fully intend to uphold, regardless of what mortal tricks you might try to use on me."

"No one is trying to trick you, Raniel," Boca said in a slightly bored tone. "Although it would not be very difficult to do, given how dull you are."

Raniel glared at Boca, his hand going to his sword. "Insult me one more time and—"

"And what?" Boca prodded. "You'll kill me? Before the gods have even passed judgment on me? You know very well how the gods feel when judgment is carried out in their name before they even get a chance to pass it themselves."

Raniel closed his mouth, and just in time, too, because an angelic waitress stopped by their table and placed a tray with three large lamb sandwiches on it in front of them. "Here you go."

"Thank you," Boca said to the waitress, who simply nodded and walked back into the cafe, likely to go fulfill another customer's order. She picked up her sandwich and sniffed it. "Ah. I forgot how delicious the sandwiches they make here smell."

Hal had to admit that Boca had a point. The sandwich set in front of him smelled of fresh bread, tomato, and cooked mutton. His stomach growled even more, causing Hal to pick up the surprisingly light sandwich and bite into it.

It felt as if Hal's taste buds exploded from the taste. The bread was light and fluffy yet with a satisfying crunch, while the lamb, tomato, lettuce, and special sauce used in it were a perfectly flavorful combination of ingredients. A few more bites and Hal felt back to full strength already.

"Wow," Hal said when he was halfway through his sandwich, looking at it in amazement. "This food is utterly amazing. I feel refreshed already, but I still want more."

Keershan snapped his lamb sandwich up in one bite, chewed it up a few times, and then sighed. "You're right. This was the greatest lamb sandwich I've ever eaten, maybe the greatest lamb I have ever had, period. Truly the food of the gods."

"*All* food made in the abode is of superior quality to anything you might find in the mortal world," Raniel said with a hint of smugness. He gestured at the cafe. "And this is what we consider street food here. The food served at the gods' banquets are of such high quality that you cannot even begin to imagine it."

Hal shook his head. No wonder everyone in the abode seemed happy all the time. He would be, too, if he had daily access to such delicious food as this sandwich.

Keershan sighed. "I would love to attend a banquet of the gods. Sounds amazing."

"We will probably not stay here long enough to attend any banquets, of the gods or otherwise," Boca said, sipping her coffee. "Either we will prove our innocence and leave the abode with the help we need to stop Kryo Kardia … or we fail and perish."

Raniel brushed back a thin strand of golden-yellow hair from in front of his face, grinning. "My money is on the latter. I know you are guilty. And it is only a matter of time until the gods themselves realize that, too."

Keershan cocked his head to the side and gazed toward the gates, which stood in the distance. "Suppose, for the sake of argument, that we fail to prove our innocence by tomorrow. What is to stop us from fleeing the abode before the gods can condemn us to death?"

Raniel chuckled. "The gates are protected and operated by the Divine Guard. Without our approval, no one can get in or out of the city. Should any of you try to flee, you will find yourselves suffering the full force of the Divine Guard."

Hal grimaced. It had occurred to him, like Keershan, that fleeing was always a possibility, but if Raniel was telling the truth, then running was not actually an option. "Then I guess we have no choice but to do this investigation, then."

"Exactly," Boca said. "I, myself, could have told you that, but I thought it might be more convincing coming from Raniel. Although I am sure that that lockdown order also applies to everyone else living in the abode, right, Raniel?"

Raniel scowled. "How did you know?"

Boca gestured toward the Temple of the Gods. "Because, although we may be the main suspects in the murder case of Shirataka, no one has yet proved anything one way or the other. There is always the possibility—a very *high* possibility, in my humble estimation—that the real murderer either lives here or frequently visits."

Raniel stepped toward Boca, his eyes practically bugging out of his skull. "But that would include not only the angels, but the gods themselves! Are you implying that one of the other gods is behind Shirataka's untimely demise?"

Boca shrugged. "I'm merely saying that whoever is in charge of the gates—which clearly isn't you—must think that that is at least a possibility. After all, who is more likely to be able to kill a god: A mortal or another god?"

Raniel glared at Hal. "Given how one of you has killed a god already, my money is on the mortal."

Hal glared right back at Raniel. "I killed the Nameless One because he was evil and posed a threat not just to Malarsan, but to the whole world. I have never even met Shirataka, nor do I know anything about her. You know very well I have no reason to want her dead."

Raniel cocked his head to the side. "Do I? I don't know you. You could be lying. Perhaps you and your fellow mortals have a vendetta against the gods, or against Shirataka specifically."

"Enough, Raniel," Boca said with a wave of her hand. "There is nothing to be gained from senseless bickering among ourselves, other than mild amusement. With how limited our time here is, we must make our moves quickly if we are to meet the deadline that Judge Noak gave us."

Keershan nodded. "I agree, Boca, but where do we even start? I've never investigated a murder before, especially not the murder of a goddess."

Boca nodded. "I understand. Firstly, we will need to talk with the gods who knew her best."

"We won't investigate the scene of the crime?" Hal said.

Boca shook her head. "There isn't much to see, especially since we do not have Shirataka's body anymore, thanks to Raniel."

"Actually, we *do* still have her body," Raniel said. "I simply teleported it to a safe place until justice could be served."

Hal scratched the back of his head. "Hold on. Boca, you told me that the gods' physical bodies are just vessels to allow them to act in the mortal realm, right? Wouldn't that mean that Shirataka's spirit is back in the actual spiritual realm?"

Keershan scratched his nose. "I see where you're going. If Shirataka's spirit is still alive, then why don't we just contact her that way and find out what she knows?"

Boca sighed. "It's not that simple. Yes, if Shirataka had voluntarily given up her physical body, we could have contacted her. But because she was murdered in cold blood, her spirit has probably not made it back to the spiritual realm yet, if it has at all."

Hal furrowed his brow. "Why wouldn't it make it back to the spiritual realm? Where else could it go?"

Raniel scowled even more. "Don't tell me that you are going to accuse one of the other gods of having kidnapped her spirit as well, Boca."

Boca sipped her coffee again. "All I am saying is that Shirataka's spirit being kidnapped explains why the other gods have not been able to reach her since her death. Thus, we aren't trying to solve a mere murder, but also a kidnapping."

Keershan grimaced. "Man, this case just gets worse and worse the more I hear about it. And our odds of actually solving it, clearing our names, and going home seem to drop with every new fact we learn."

"Hope is not yet lost, Keershan," Boca said. She looked at Raniel. "Raniel, could you please give us a full report on

Shirataka's corpse? Including any wounds, poison samples, and so on?"

Hal looked at Raniel in surprise. "You can do that?"

Raniel nodded, although only begrudgingly. "Yes. I can order another one of the guard to analyze the body and write up a report. It should not take long, although I am curious as to why you do not wish to view it yourself."

"Because we are going to pay a very important god a visit," Boca said, "one who might be able to shed some light on who would want to murder Shirataka."

"And which god would that be?" asked Hal.

Boca glanced at Keershan. "The god who Keershan asked about earlier but who, curiously enough, was not at the temple today."

Keershan stood up, his eyes wide. "Wait a minute. You don't mean *him*, do you?"

Boca smiled. "I do. Salard, the god of the dragons, and the only god who Shirataka considered a good friend."

Chapter Thirteen

"I CAN'T BELIEVE I AM FINALLY GOING TO GET TO MEET Salard in person," Keershan said less than an hour later, walking beside Hal up one of the abode's many hilly streets. "This is an opportunity that every dragon and hatchling dreams of from a young age."

Hal nodded. "I'm glad you are excited, Keershan, even if I don't really understand it myself."

Keershan whipped his head toward Hal in surprise. "You don't? Well, I suppose that makes sense, since you are human and humans don't actually worship Salard. But we dragons do because, without Salard, dragons wouldn't even *exist*."

Hal raised an eyebrow in surprise. "Really? Did Salard create the dragons?"

"In a way, yes," Keershan said with a quick nod. "Legend has it that at the dawn of creation, Salard laid the first dragon eggs, from which the First Dragons were born. After growing up, these twelve dragons scattered across the world, where they founded each of the major twelve dragon clans, and through the clans, each tribe, including my own."

"Wow," Hal said. "How come I didn't know that, even though we've been bonded for over a year?"

Keershan shrugged. "Honestly, with everything else we had going on, there just wasn't time to talk about our mythology in great detail. Fun fact: Clawfoot was the name of one of the First Dragons, who was the founder of the Clawfoot Clan."

Hal furrowed his brow. "So does that make all dragons part-god or—?"

Keershan shook his head as they passed an angel riding a cart drawn by a pegasus. "No. Though the First Dragons were all demigods, our divinity gradually bled out of the bloodline as we bred with other mortal creatures until soon we dragons were just regular mortals like humans. Although it does explain why we live for so much longer than other species, which we attribute to lingering divinity."

"Other mortal creatures?" Hal repeated. "Do you mean that dragons are not fully, er, dragon?"

Keershan shrugged. "The First Dragons are said to have been very different from modern dragons, including having fur, for example. Certain traits were lost over the years as their descendants bred with other creatures in the mortal realm, including wyrms, which are basically smaller dragons without wings."

Hal cocked his head to the side. "I've never heard of wyrms."

"Because they basically don't exist," Keershan explained. "Not anymore, anyway. Technically speaking, the current dragon race is an entirely new species that has traits from both the First Dragons and the wyrms. It's very interesting once you start delving deep into the history of the dragons, including the forging of the legendary divine weapon Scalebreaker from one of Salard's scales at the dawn of creation and—"

"I'm sure Lord Salard will be very impressed to hear you recite your peoples' entire history from the Day of Creation until this very moment to him, dragon," Raniel said, walking just behind them, his left hand resting on the hilt of his blade. "Assuming he even grants an audience with accused murderers at all, that is, which is highly doubtful."

Boca, walking on Hal's other side, rolled her eyes. "Why don't you let Salard decide if he will talk to us himself, Raniel? I'm sure he doesn't need a lowly angel like you making that decision for him."

Raniel sputtered. "Lowly—? Strong words coming from the mortal who directly challenged the gods' judgment. Or have you forgotten what you did during your last visit here? I hear that elderly mortals like yourself have weak memories."

"I remember quite well what happened during my last visit, Raniel," Boca said, "which has absolutely no bearing whatsoever on our current investigation into Shirataka's unjust murder."

Keershan looked from Boca to Raniel and back again, curiosity creeping onto his features. "What exactly *did* happen on your last visit here? Everyone is acting really cagey about it for some reason."

Boca waved a hand dismissively at Keershan. "As I said, it's irrelevant. Raniel is simply upset that the gods did not immediately execute us on the spot based on his trumped-up charges. I would not take heed of anything he says."

"Because I speak the truth?" Raniel said. He chuckled. "Perhaps I shouldn't be surprised. After all, witches are hardly known for their adherence to the truth. Or facts. What is a witch, after all, other than a female mortal who seeks to warp reality to fit her delusions?"

Boca did not respond, but Hal could tell that Raniel was getting under her skin based on how tightly her hands balled into fists. As frustrating as it was not to know what Boca did the last time she was in the abode, Hal had to admit that she had a point about it not being important to their investigation right now.

Keershan gazed ahead. "So where *is* Salard, anyway?"

"He has a cave up in the peaks where he stays during his visits to the abode," Raniel said. He pointed at a yawning cave mouth up ahead. "Specifically, that one."

"You mean he just sits inside that cave all day without a door or even guards to protect him?" Hal said skeptically. "That doesn't seem safe."

Raniel snorted. "Lord Salard doesn't *need* protection. If anything, I would say it is any would-be assailants who need protection from *him*. I once was called to deal with a potential assassination on Lord Salard's life some years ago. But by the time I got there, there was no sign of the assassin other than a bloody stump that might have been his right leg. Or his left. It was hard to tell."

Hal grimaced while Keershan said, "That is so cool! Man, I wish I could be like Salard. Then I might not have gotten bullied so much by my siblings when I was a hatchling."

"You will get to meet him soon enough," Boca said. "His cave isn't far off now."

Boca was correct. A few minutes later, they reached the

entrance to Salard's cave, which was even bigger than Hal thought. It was nearly as big as the Temple of the Gods back in the main area of the city, the opening so wide that Hal thought you could march the entirety of the Dragon Rider Order through it side by side and still leave everyone plenty of personal space.

Warm air wafted out of the open cave mouth, along with the familiar smell of dried dragon dung and blood. Hal supposed that Salard was apparently as messy as his children, to which Keershan did not respond or disagree, although that may have been because Keershan was in so much awe that he wasn't even listening to Hal's thoughts at the moment.

"This is it?" Hal said, staring up at the cave mouth. "I don't see Salard."

"That is because he is likely at the *back* of the cave," Raniel said. "If I had to guess, he is probably napping, because this is usually the time of day when he rests."

"Is that why he was not present at the meeting?" Hal said, glancing at Raniel incredulously. "Because he was asleep?"

"Do not question the gods' choices, mortal," Raniel said, shooting Hal another scowl. "The gods' ways are far above our own. We cannot question them, much less understand them."

"Perhaps," Boca said, "but we can certainly ask them if they know anything about the murder of one of their own, especially if the victim was a good friend."

"So you said Shirataka and Salard are good friends," Hal said, "but you didn't explain how they know each other."

Boca folded her arms in front of her chest. "In short,

Shirataka and Salard are both worshiped by the Tipjokian people and have been for centuries. In particular, Shirataka is considered a mother goddess figure among the Tipjokians, while Salard is considered more of a fatherly deity. They are near equal gods in the eyes of the Tipjokians, however, which is what brings them together."

Hal furrowed his brows again. "Even if the Tipjokians worship both of them equally, I don't understand how or why that would make them friends."

Raniel huffed. "Because you, being a mortal, fail to understand the relationship between gods and mortals. When mortals worship a god or gods, they have some degree of influence over that god, including that god's relationships with other deities."

Keershan perked his head up just then. "We do? Does that mean we can make the gods do whatever we want?"

Raniel glared knives at Keershan. "Of course not! The gods will do as they see fit. At best, mortal worship allows you to influence the gods in a very minor way. The more a particular form of worship is focused toward the gods, the stronger that influence will be over said deity."

Boca nodded. "And because the Tipjokians have designed their entire religion around Shirataka and Salard, this has created a link between the two deities that did not exist before. As a result, Shirataka and Salard are now good friends with each other and have been for a very long time."

Hal supposed Raniel and Boca probably knew more about the gods and their relationships with each other than he or Keershan did, although he still found the concept of mortals influencing gods difficult to grasp. He had always been told by his parents that they worshiped the gods because the gods were greater than them, but Hal wondered if there was more to it than that, more that perhaps even his parents did not know.

In any case, Hal said, "Very well. If Salard was indeed good friends with Shirataka, then let's go talk to him."

Hal took a step toward the open cave mouth, only for one of Boca's skeletally-thin hands to wrap around his upper arm as she said, "Don't. Not unless you want to die."

Hal looked back at Boca in alarm, seeing her very serious expression. "Die? But it's wide-open and I don't see anyone around."

"Only because, like most mortals, you are blind to the dangers everywhere," Raniel said. "As well, Salard does not accept random visitors. You must first request an audience with him before you can enter his private cave."

Hal folded his arms in front of his chest. "Okay. How do we request an audience with him, then?"

"You talk to me," said a feminine yet deep voice from within the cave.

A massive crystalline dragon stepped out of the cave, though only partially. Even so, she was probably the biggest dragon Hal had ever seen in his life, dwarfing even Rialo. Perched atop her long neck was an impatient-looking face, gazing down on Hal and the others as if expecting them to start justifying their existence right there and then. Tufts of fur lined her head, which Hal had never seen on a dragon before.

Hal's eyebrows shot into his hair. "Whoa. You're—"

"Vilona!" Keershan said, almost squealing. "I can't believe it. You're real, too."

The female dragon gazed at Keershan in confusion. "Why wouldn't I be real?"

Keershan licked his lips nervously. "Er, I mean, that the legends that my people have about you are true, of course."

"Keershan," Hal said to Keershan, "who *is* Vilona?"

"Lord Salard's right-claw servant," Keershan said quickly. "Legend has it that Vilona was the only child of Salard not to leave the nest. She instead stayed to serve him and be his mediator with the outside world. The old stories claim that she is second only in power to Salard himself, making her more powerful than any other dragon living today."

Vilona smirked. "Thank you for the compliments, youngling, but flattery by itself won't get you an audience with Salard."

"You know that's what we are looking for?" Hal said, craning his neck to look at Vilona.

Vilona nodded. "Yes. I heard every word of your conversation from within the cave. I take it you are the mortals who the other gods charged with investigating Shirataka's murder."

Vilona said that with a clearly skeptical tone, telling Hal that she probably wasn't convinced of the success of their mission. Either that or she just didn't like mortals, which seemed to be the common bias among the people who lived here. Gods and angels did not seem to like mortals very much.

Regardless, Hal stepped forward and said, "Yes. We would like to speak with Lord Salard, who was a good friend of Shirataka. We think he may have some insight into who may have murdered her."

Vilona raised an eyebrow, an odd look on a dragon, though Hal recalled what Keershan said earlier about the original dragons having fur. "Do you? Lord Salard is currently resting. Due to his vast age, he prefers sleeping more than anything else and rarely awakens for anything that is not an immediate emergency."

"The murder of a goddess doesn't count as an immediate emergency in his eyes?" Hal said incredulously. "I mean no disrespect to Lord Salard, Vilona, but—"

"If you mean no disrespect, then why do you have to say it?" said Vilona, cutting Hal off rudely. She glared at the mortals. "Lord Salard does not need to be interrupted by you mortals. I suggest taking your investigation elsewhere, because Lord Salard doesn't know anything about Shirataka's murder, at least no more than—"

Vilona suddenly stopped speaking herself. She looked over her shoulder, eyes narrowed, as if listening very closely to only a voice she could hear. It made Hal wonder what she was listening to.

Then Vilona whipped her head back toward Hal and the others, with less hostility in her eyes. "Lord Salard has awakened and has accepted your request to have an audience with him. Please follow me."

With that, Vilona turned and vanished back into the shadows. Boca immediately went in after her, as did an excited-looking Keershan, and then Hal, who heard Raniel follow behind him.

I can't believe we're going to meet Salard himself! Keershan said mentally to Hal. *Isn't this exciting?*

Thinking about how abruptly Vilona changed her tone, as well as the serious expression on her face when she told them Salard's orders, Hal shrugged. *Hopefully, it will be informative and get us one step closer to clearing our names, at least.*

Chapter Fourteen

As it turned out, Salard's cave wasn't nearly as dark on the inside as it had looked from the outside. In fact, the second Hal stepped through the threshold, he found himself in a well-lit, warm, enormous cavern with a ceiling so high he could barely see it.

Looking over his shoulder, Hal saw Raniel, the last of their party, step through the wall of shadow denoting the entrance. Raniel actually stumbled slightly, as if disoriented by the dark wall, before standing up to his usual tall height and walking forward past Hal. "What are you looking at?"

"The wall," Hal said, looking at Raniel. "I thought the cave was very dark."

Raniel shook his head. "The wall is an illusion, meant to give Lord Salard privacy. It also acts as a security measure, capable of keeping out all but the darkest of magic. Had any of us tried to enter it without his permission, the results would have been … painful, to put it in terms a mortal such as you can understand."

Hal wasn't sure if Raniel was telling the truth or simply playing up how dangerous the dark wall was for his own amusement, though given how serious Raniel usually was, Hal opted for the latter.

"Hey, Hal, Raniel!" Keershan said. "What are you two doing? We're going to see Lord Salard."

Snapped out of his thoughts, Hal and Raniel walked quickly to rejoin Keershan and Boca, who walked right behind Vilona. The divine dragon seemed even bigger than before, her silver scales partially covered with white fur that looked almost like snow. She was also a good deal taller and ganglier than any dragon Hal had seen, making him wonder if that was another physical trait that Keershan's people had lost when they mated with the wyrms.

As big as the cavern was, however, Hal was struck by how empty and even ordinary it seemed. It reminded him of many of the dragon caves in Dragon Valley, where the dragons made their nests. Evidently, Salard's children had not changed their dwelling habits much since splitting off from their father however many eons ago they had been born.

But despite that, it still smelled very much like dragons, meaning dragon dung, blood, and various other bodily smells that the average dragon had. Being a Dragon Rider, Hal had grown used to those smells, but he could tell that both Boca and Raniel—especially Raniel—had not, based on their facial expressions. Yet neither of them complained, perhaps because they knew Vilona and Salard would not appreciate complaints from them about Salard's scent.

Soon, they reached the opening of another cave, this one so huge and wide that Hal couldn't even see the ceiling.

A gaping hole nearly as big around as the castle back in the capitol dominated the center of the room while a simple stone peninsula jutted out into the open air above it.

"Here we are," said Vilona, coming to a stop. She gestured with her claw. "Lord Salard's room."

Hal looked around, frowning. "And where is Lord Salard—?"

A deep rumbling sound echoed from the hole in front of them, and then a huge dragon head rose. 'Huge' was an understatement. Its head alone was nearly as big as one of the Glacian war balloons, connected to a body that Hal could not see, although he guessed that it had to be absolutely enormous to support such a massive head.

The dragon head resembled Vilona's to a degree, but was flatter and gold and red instead of silver. Two huge golden eyes stared out of the massive skull, hints of smoke rising from its nostrils. The mere presence of the head was enough to make Hal and the others back off abruptly.

Vilona, on the other hand, bowed respectfully toward the dragon. "Lord Salard, Father, the mortals charged by the gods to investigate Shirataka's murder have arrived for an audience with you."

"Thank you, daughter Vilona," Salard said, his voice surprisingly soft despite his enormous form. His eyes shifted from Vilona to Hal and the others, making Hal feel supremely uncomfortable. "What brings you here?"

Hal cleared his throat. "Um, we came to find out if you know anything about Shirataka's murder."

Salard's eyes widened. "Am I a suspect in this investigation?"

When Salard said that, the anger in his voice was palpable. It was nearly enough to make Hal wet himself. He had never seen a dragon anywhere close to this big before, and even though he intellectually *knew* that Salard wouldn't kill them, every instinct in his body told him to run.

"No, Lord Salard, you are not a suspect," Keershan said quickly, stepping forward. "We would never suspect you of having murdered your friend. That would be ridiculous."

Salard growled. "That is good to hear. Because if my fellow gods had suspected me of murdering Shirataka, then that would have made me even less likely to want anything to do with your pointless investigation."

"Pointless?" Keershan repeated. "Why do you think this investigation is pointless, sir?"

Salard shook his head. "Because whoever killed Shirataka covered his tracks very well. No one would ever carelessly kill a god or goddess. It would have to be well-planned by necessity, with every possibility accounted for. The killer would have had to know how serious this crime is. Therefore, I doubt you mortals will catch them."

Hal raised an eyebrow. "I see you've given this a lot of thought, Lord Salard."

Salard glared at Hal again, making Hal's heart rate spike. "Why wouldn't I? As you yourself stated, Shirataka and I were not merely good friends, but best of friends. When she died, I felt her loss as clearly as I would have felt my own death."

Hal heard real pain in Salard's voice when the god said that, making Hal believe him. Hal knew dragons well enough by now to be able to read their emotions with a good degree of accuracy, and right now Salard was wearing all of his emotions on his sleeve.

"Even if the killer accounted for every possibility, the

killer couldn't have accounted for us," Boca said, raising a hand. "No one knew we were coming to the abode, after all. It's possible there may be evidence you or the other gods have overlooked."

Salard grunted. "Be that as it may, I sincerely doubt your investigation will succeed. One day is simply not enough time for any mortal to catch a god-killer. That my fellow gods gave you such a strict deadline tells me that they already believe you are guilty and are only doing this as a way to waste your time."

Keershan gasped. "I said the same thing earlier! We truly must be related."

Salard shifted his gaze back to Keershan, frowning. "State your parentage, young one."

Keershan stood up a little straighter. "I am Keershan Clawfoot, Lord Salard, of the Clawfoot Clan. Son of Chief Bronda of the Clawfoot Clan, though the youngest."

Salard's eyes widened, this time in shock. He looked to Hal and said, "Identify yourself, human."

Hal, also standing up straighter like Keershan, said, "Halar Norath, Commander of the Dragon Rider Order of Malarsan and Rider of Keershan, who is my Steed."

Salard looked almost like someone had slapped him. "Dragon Rider … that is a name I haven't heard in centuries. Are you wearing the Final Relic?"

Hal nodded, not sure where Salard was going with this. "Yes. It is the source of my bond with—"

"I know how relics work, Rider," Salard said without hesitation. He peered closely at Hal's helmet. "Yes, that is most certainly the Final Relic, although it appears to have been repaired recently."

"It was, actually," Hal said. "Have you seen it before?"

Salard looked at Hal with an amused expression. "Seen it before? Why, young Rider, I was there when the Final Relic was first forged eons ago … and I also helped defeat the Nameless One the very first time."

Chapter Fifteen

SURRELS DID NOT KNOW WHAT HE LIKED LESS ABOUT THEIR current situation: That Kendo knew the Dead Dragon Syndicate or that Kendo was still a member in good standing with the Dead Dragon Syndicate.

"Are you sure this is our best option, Kendo?" Surrels said as they walked the crowded streets of the port city of Faifa. "Because I am almost certain there are other options. Such as asking Fralia's mages to teleport us into the capital directly, for example."

Kendo, wearing a hood over his head, shook his head. "Knowing Tenka, he probably has the entire capital protected with demonic magic, not counting the normal mages who work for him already. Besides, we are trying to avoid implicating the rest of the council in the conspiracy, remember? As far as Tenka knows, we are the only two actively involved in saving Stebo and opposing his ascension to the throne."

Surrels bit his lower lip and looked to his side, where Stebo was walking. "Still, I'm not sure about—"

Surrels stopped speaking when he noticed that Stebo—who had been walking quietly by his side since their arrival in Faifa—was missing.

Looking around in alarm, Surrels spotted Stebo standing in front of a merchant's booth, manned by a merchant with a face ugly enough to make him look like a member of the Dead Dragon Syndicate as well. The merchant held out some type of fried fish on a stick to Stebo, which Stebo reached for with his little arms with an excited look on his face.

Rushing over to Stebo, Surrels grabbed the boy's shoulder and said, "Stebo! What are you doing over here? I nearly had a heart attack when I looked and didn't see you."

Stebo frowned at Surrels. "I was hungry and smelled this fish on a stick. Isn't it amazing? I've never even heard of such a thing before."

"Aye, sir, I wasn't doing nothing bad to your grandson," said the merchant in a gravelly voice, his breath smelling of fish. "The boy reminds me of my own grandson, so I thought I'd give him one of my fresh fish on a stick."

Grandson? Surrels wondered if he actually looked that old.

Probably all the stress of killing one of my best friends and being on the run from someone I thought *was a friend,* Surrels thought. *I live a very stress-free life.*

Aloud, Surrels said, "Sorry, sir, but we don't have any money for your, er, fish on a stick, so—"

"Please, this one is on me," the merchant insisted. He pulled out a couple more and held them out to Surrels. "Here. Take three. One for your grandson, one for your son over there, and one for yourself. No charge."

Surrels raised an eyebrow. "No charge?"

The merchant nodded, a friendly smile on his face. "Sure. I know what it's like to be a grandfather with a wandering grandson. Even grandparents need a treat every now and then, too."

Surrels frowned even more, but since Stebo seemed happy, he decided not to push it. He just thanked the merchant for the food and led Stebo back to Kendo, who had stopped in the street to watch their interaction with the merchant with amusement.

"I see you got us free food," Kendo said, taking the third fish stick meant for him and biting into it. He sighed in relief. "I forgot how good seafood around here is."

Surrels scowled, though he had to admit the fresh fish did smell good. "We didn't come here for the seafood. And we are also supposed to be not drawing attention to ourselves by interacting with too many people."

Stebo looked up at Surrels. "But I was *hungry*. I haven't eaten since breakfast."

Surrels shook his head. He had forgotten how much children, especially boys, needed to eat. It reminded him of when Kendo was a little boy and how he would seemingly always be hungry no matter how much Tonya fed him—

Another memory? Surrels thought in alarm. *Spurred on by Stebo. Again.*

Surrels was starting to notice a pattern. Ever since saving Stebo from Tenka's demon, Surrels found himself regaining memories he hadn't even realized he had. Most of them centered around Lila and Kendo, his daughter and son, when they were not much older than Stebo, though a few were from later in life.

Such a revelation might not seem like much to most

people, but it meant a lot to Surrels. After all, he was really only in this situation in the first place because of his quest to regain his long-lost memories from before his time as a Black Soldier. The promise of restoring his memories had been what made Surrels so easily manipulated by Tenka.

And deep down inside, it was still something Surrels wanted more than anything, even knowing what he did about his past now.

And Stebo is helping me somehow, Surrels thought. *Maybe he just bears a striking resemblance to Kendo when he was his age. Or maybe my memories are coming back on their own. Guess we'll wait and see.*

Taking a bite out of his own fried fish stick—and noticing how deliciously crunchy it was—Surrels said to Kendo, "Regardless, I still think approaching the Dead Dragon Syndicate for help seems extreme."

"Extreme times call for extreme measures, Father," Kendo said as they resumed walking. He gestured at his facial tattoos. "Besides, once the Dead Dragons see my tattoos, they'll accept me as one of their own and will be more than willing to help us. After all, their leader, Mama Dragon, owes me one."

Surrels pursed his lips and looked around the city of Faifa as they walked.

Faifa was a large port city on the southern shore of Malarsan, second in population only to the capital. It was also a huge economic driver of the kingdom, because the vast majority of ships carrying cargo from other nations, including nations as far south as the Islands of Hopar, delivered their cargo here. Surrels himself had visited the city more than once under several different circumstances, including as a Black Soldier.

Unlike the capital, however, Faifa was infamous for its high crime rate and connection to organized crime. It was said that more crimes were committed in Faifa in one day than in an entire month at the capital, which didn't surprise Surrels. Due to its strategic economic and political location, both legal and illegal goods passed through the city in huge numbers and it was home to a number of smuggling and criminal groups.

Such as the Dead Dragon Syndicate, for example.

The Dead Dragon Syndicate was the biggest and most notorious smuggling ring in Malarsan. Primarily based out of Faifa, the Dead Dragons were the biggest distributors of illegal goods to the kingdom, including human—and non-human—slaves. While they rarely engaged in outright murder like the Dark Tigers used to, the Dead Dragons were a ruthless criminal organization that even the enforcers feared to confront. Some even said that the Dead Dragons really owned Faifa and that its mayor, Mayor Yola, had been paid off by them, but whether those accusations were true, Surrels did not know.

He *did* know, however, that the Black Soldiers and the Dead Dragons had clashed on more than one occasion in the past. Surrels even recalled once being ordered by Queen Marial to kill a high-ranking Dead Dragon smuggler who had tried to sell stolen relics.

His death had been *very* messy.

But Kendo insisted that the Dead Dragons were their best hope for infiltrating the capital in time to prevent the coronation of Tenka. His reasoning that the Dead Dragons knew ways to sneak into the city without tripping any alarms, so they could probably get them into the capital no problem.

Surrels supposed that was probably true, but that didn't mean he liked having to recruit the help of known criminals to prevent Tenka's rise.

Then again, as my son always reminds me, we *are technically criminals now,* Surrels thought as they walked through the crowded streets of Faifa.

Kendo suddenly led them down a nondescript alleyway that Surrels would have completely overlooked himself. The narrow alleyway, strewn with trash and smelling of sea brine and fish, took them away from the bustling main streets of Faifa into the complex, almost maze-like alleyways of the city.

At least, to Surrels, who was not used to the layout of the city, Faifa's alleyways seemed like a maze to him. But Kendo showed no hesitation in leading them through the twisting, turning alleys, acting as if he was going to start his shift at the docks for the day and not meet with the leader of a dangerous criminal gang.

And the deeper they delved into the back alleys of Faifa, the more aware Surrels became of their surroundings. The alleys were narrow and long, with little room to hide or take cover in the case of a fight. Not to mention Surrels thought he caught glimpses of gaunt, ghostly faces in the windows of the buildings around them, though they would disappear just as soon as he looked at them directly.

Even Stebo seemed to feel the danger they were in. The young boy, the now bare fish stick in his hand, clutched the stick like a weapon while clinging closely to Surrels. His fearful brown eyes glanced about the place, making Surrels feel more protective than ever over Stebo.

Kendo, however, looked perfectly at ease in the alleys of Faifa and didn't slow down or hesitate until they reached a building set on the docks of Faifa, although it was a secluded part that clearly hadn't seen business in ages. Old wooden shipping barges clung to the docks with frayed ropes, their sails limply blowing in the wind. Empty crates and barrels stood along the docks, stayed by the water and what looked like blood in Surrels's professional opinion.

There were no living creatures from what Surrels could see, other than a black bird sitting atop the mast of one of the abandoned ships. The black bird squawked as soon as it saw them, however, and flew into the air, heading toward an open window at the top of the rundown building they were approaching. The squawking of the bird made Stebo clutch Surrels even more tightly, for which Surrels did not blame the kid.

This was a dangerous situation.

Unfortunately, it would only get more dangerous from here.

Kendo, of course, didn't seem even remotely put off by the creepy environment or the squawking black bird. Instead, he marched straight up to the door, which Surrels expected him to knock on.

Instead, Kendo kicked the door open and, storming inside the building, shouted, "I want to see the Mama!"

Even before Kendo finished speaking, an uproar inside the building erupted. Surrels heard a variety of harsh voices and dozens of running footsteps, followed by what sounded like fighting. He heard fists being thrown, people being kicked, and glass and wood breaking. It sounded like an all-out brawl was going on inside the building and Kendo was right in the middle of it.

Stebo, clutching Surrels's leg so tightly now that Surrels

could not feel the blood flow anymore, said, "Is Kendo okay?"

Drawing his sword, Surrels said, "Stay here while I go in and back him up."

Before Surrels could leave, however, the sounds of fighting abruptly stopped. Silence reigned for several seconds, the only sounds being the waves beating against the docks underneath them, along with the occasional foghorn somewhere in the distance.

Surrels stepped forward. "Kendo—?"

A man stepped out of the building just then, a man who was almost certainly not Kendo. He was short and stout, more fat than anything, with a wild gray beard and thick gray hair poking out from underneath a tricorn hat. One of his eyes was covered with a black fraying patch while the other seemed to be bulging out of his skull, particularly when he raised his hat with a hook hand as if to see Surrels and Stebo more clearly.

"Are you Kendo's friend?" said the man, his voice harsh and crackly, with a trilling 'r' that made it clear he was not from Malarsan.

Surrels gulped, but just raised his sword. "Maybe I am. What do you want?"

The man jerked a thumb over his shoulder. "The Mama wants to see you. Both of you."

Stebo shrank slightly while Surrels said, "I'm sorry, but until you can reassure us that Kendo is safe, we want nothing to do with your so-called 'Mama.'"

A blade suddenly appeared at Surrels's neck, making his eyes dart to the side to see a young woman—more like a girl, really—standing at his side, holding a knife at his throat. Her eyes were dark and difficult to read, though given how she held the knife against his throat, Surrels easily guessed at her intentions.

The patch-eye man smiled, revealing that he was missing more than a few teeth in his mouth. "When the Mama invites someone into her home, you *can't* refuse. Put away that sword and no one gets hurt."

Surrels scowled, but without knowing if Kendo was even still alive, he sheathed his sword. He noticed Stebo tried to 'sheathe' his stick, but without a proper sheath, the young boy simply slipped the greasy stick into a belt loop.

Then the two of them walked toward the building, the mysterious young woman walking behind them, the grinning old man before them.

And Surrels, once again, found himself wondering how much worse his life was going to get before it got better.

Chapter Sixteen

STEPPING INTO WHAT SURRELS PRESUMED WAS THE headquarters for the Dead Dragon Syndicate, Surrels's nostrils were immediately assaulted by the stench of sweat, fish, and brine that seemed to permeate the entire building. Granted, those stenches were everywhere in Faifa to some degree, but they were even worse inside the dank headquarters. There was little light outside of a torch that the old man lit, which illuminated just enough of the building's interior for Surrels to feel disgusted by his environment.

Although Surrels did not get a chance to be properly disgusted by the stenches. The old man and the young woman herded Surrels and Stebo down a long, creaky narrow hallway, paint peeling off the walls, broken picture frames hanging on rusty nails. Oddly, Surrels saw no sign of the brawl that he had heard happening inside the building. No bodies, no blood, not even any broken furniture or windows to indicate that a brawl had just occurred.

Either the brawl wasn't nearly as bad as it sounded or the Dead

Dragons are really good at cleaning up after themselves, Surrels thought. *Although I still don't see Kendo, either.*

That was when Surrels suddenly heard noises up ahead. It sounded like … music, surprisingly.

Specifically, Surrels heard slightly muffled trumpets, pianos, violins, and a variety of other instruments being played. The music was mixed in with bawdy singing and laughter, punctuated by wooden mugs being slammed together and the clinking of silverware against glass plates.

"Excuse me again," Surrels said to the old man in front of them, "but where are you taking us, exactly?"

The old man grinned, showing every missing tooth in his mouth. "You'll see."

Not a helpful answer, although Surrels supposed he couldn't expect a helpful answer from people who were not trying to be helpful.

Finally, they reached a door at the end of a hallway, light spilling out from underneath it. Before Surrels even had a chance to stop, the old man pulled the door open and shoved both of them through it. Gasping in surprise, Surrels immediately regained his balance and drew his sword again, pointing his blade in every direction, certain that the Dead Dragons were going to descend on them at any moment to kill them like they killed Kendo.

Instead, however, Surrels saw the exact last thing he expected to see in a place as grim and dark as this.

A riotous party, complete with a band and food.

Over on the left side of the room, a band composed of several men dressed in rags played the variety of instruments Surrels had heard from within the hall, along with a few he hadn't recognized. A large scantily-clad woman with her skin covered in tattoos stood on the stage, doing some

… *interesting* dances for the laughing and watching pirates, who kept throwing coins at her while making a variety of requests that she performed for their entertainment.

On the right side of the room, even more pirates sat around tables or lounged around on sofas, devouring chunks of meat, downing massive mugs of beer, and in a few cases even fighting or wrestling with each other. Some were even having a drinking contest. And based on how many lay unconscious on the floor with beer spilled all over them, it was obvious that the contest had been going on for a while.

And in the center of the huge room was an open pit of water, apparently indicating that the building had been built directly over the sea. Without any railings, it seemed like it would be easy for someone to accidentally fall in there, though Surrels didn't think it was that dangerous until he saw the fin of what looked like a shark pierce the surface.

Surrels's eyes, however, were drawn to the platform situated above the water. Reached only by two sets of rickety-looking stairs on either side of the platform, the figures sitting on the platform were a sight to behold.

A large woman—bigger and fatter than the stripper on stage—lay on top of a variety of soft pillows on a half-sofa, half-chair. She was alternating between tearing off huge chunks of meat from the chicken legs offered to her by a servant, guzzling so much beer it made Surrels sick just to watch her, and joking with the man sitting on the smaller and much less extravagant chair before her. The black bird from earlier, which Surrels now realized was a black seagull, perched on the back of her chair, its beady dark eyes glaring directly at him.

As for the man sitting across from the woman, Surrels realized that he was a smiling, laughing, and joking Kendo.

Stebo's eyes widened. "Wow. This is the biggest party I've ever been to."

Surrels would have said something similar, but Kendo looked down and waved at them. "You two! Come up and join us. The party is just getting started."

Surrels raised an eyebrow. "Party—?"

A fist came out of nowhere and slammed into the side of Surrels's face. The unexpected blow nearly knocked Surrels off his feet, but he leaned on Stebo for support as a slurred voice nearby said, "Take that, you sword-swinging loser!"

Rubbing his face, Surrels looked to see a drunk pirate, this one as stout as the old man but easily more muscle than fat, standing with his fists raised. Behind the drunk pirate, a couple of his friends sitting at a nearby table roared in laughter and one of them shouted, "Do it again, Veg! But better this time. You missed his nose."

Veg hiccupped and glared at his friends. "You try to aim for such an itty-bitty little nose while drunk off your rockers if you think it's so easy!"

Surrels narrowed his eyes. "Did you punch me on a dare from your friends?"

Veg looked back at Surrels, hiccupping again and wiping spittle out of the corner of his mouth. His eyes darted to Surrels's sword. "Naw, mate. Saw you brandishing that sword of yours. Around here, that means you're looking for a fight."

Surrels immediately sheathed his sword and held up his hands defensively. "No trouble. I'm just here to see the Mama. Not looking for a fight."

"See the Mama?" Veg eyed Surrels more carefully. "You don't look like the sort of man *she* likes. Not enough meat."

Surrels raised an eyebrow. "What is that supposed to—"

"Veg!" Kendo called out suddenly from the platform overhead. "Leave those two alone! They're with me."

Like flipping a switch, Veg's entire demeanor changed in an instant. He looked at Surrels apologetically and said with a series of increasingly worse hiccups, "You're with Kendo? My apologies! I didn't mean to get in your way. Have a nice day, sir."

With that, Veg spun around on his heel and walked straight into the wall to the left of the door into the room, causing him to fall down on his back and his friends to roar in laughter again, with one of them shouting, "Do it again! But harder this time!"

Surrels, deciding that the drunk pirate lifestyle was almost certainly not for him, held Stebo tightly to his side as they made their way up the stairs to the platform.

Reaching the top of the platform, Surrels said to Kendo, "Kendo, what is going *on* here? We thought the Dead Dragons had killed you."

The large woman sitting before them laughed so hard that she sounded like she was choking on her chicken. "Kendo? Killed by *these* drunks? As if anyone could kill this scrappy little punk. Even Toothy couldn't lay a finger on *him*."

As the woman said that, she dropped her chicken bone into the water below, where it was immediately snapped up by the shark before the large fish disappeared underneath the murky water.

"You flatter too much, Mama," Kendo said. He

gestured at Surrels and Stebo. "Mama, allow me to introduce you to Surrels, my father, and Stebo, my son."

Surrels resisted the urge to raise an eyebrow. Stebo? Kendo's son? Had Kendo overheard what the fish merchant said earlier and decided it was a good cover? Surrels supposed he couldn't argue with it, as he didn't trust the Dead Dragons with the knowledge of Stebo's true identity.

The huge woman looked at Stebo in annoyance. "Your son? Kendo, what did the Mama teach you about avoiding *that* particular problem?"

Kendo shrugged. "I didn't know he was mine until his mother, this pretty redhead I slept with a while back, dropped him off at my front door about a week ago and told me he was mine."

The woman laughed. "Good one! Well, I suppose it can't be helped. But next time, make sure you get what *you* want and not what *she* wants. Got it?"

Kendo nodded. "Of course, Mama, of course."

Surrels narrowed his eyes. "Mama—?"

Kendo started. "Oh! I forgot my manners. Father, son, meet Mama Dragon, leader and founder of the Dead Dragon Syndicate. And, in a way, the mother I never had."

Mama Dragon blushed, although her face was so red with alcohol that she might have just been very drunk. "Who's the flatterer now, Kendo? I'm a mama to *all* of my men." Then she said, in a whisper, "But don't tell anyone that you are my favorite. Otherwise, they might get jealous."

Kendo laughed. "Of course, Mama! Some of the things you taught me have stuck, even if certain *other* things—" he gestured at Stebo when he said that. "—did not."

"Things sticking is exactly what got you into this mess in the first place, Kendo," Mama Dragon scolded him, though it was with a wink and a smile. "I hope she was a hot one, at least."

Kendo chuckled. "Very. Anyway, Father, Stebo, why don't you both take a seat?"

"Yes, join us!" Mama Dragon said. She gestured at the pile of food on the table. "Eat until your stomach can't take it anymore, vomit it up, and then eat again!"

Surrels grimaced as he and Stebo took seats beside Kendo. "Thank you for the, er, generous offer, Mama, but we ate on the way here, so—"

"So?" Mama Dragon demanded. She waved a turkey leg at Stebo. "The boy is all skin and bones! And he could probably use a good beer, too."

"He's not even ten," Surrels said.

Mama Dragon stared at Surrels in genuine confusion. "What of it? Me father gave me my first drink when I was six. Or, if you want to get real technical, me mother drank when I was in her womb. And look how well I turned out."

Surrels bit his lower lip and, deciding to change the subject, said to Kendo, "What happened back there, Kendo? Stebo and I heard a brawl. We thought you were dead."

Mama Dragon burped. "And what a brawl it was! Really, though, none of those drunk assholes below could have stood a chance against 'im. Kendo's always been a wily one, more brains than brawn."

Kendo shrugged. "What Mama Dragon means is that a brawl is the proper way for a prodigal son such as myself to be welcomed back into the Syndicate. I fully expected it, so I went in knowing what was going to happen. A few cracked skulls and kicked groins later, Mama Dragon was more than happy to welcome me back into the gang."

Stebo, who was chowing down on a piece of steak, looked at Kendo in amazement. "So you were never in danger of getting killed at all?"

"Oh, no, I could have easily been killed if I didn't keep my guard up," Kendo said. He gestured at the party below. "Fortunately, we chose to show up when Mama is throwing one of her big parties, so half of them are drunk and the other half are so full of food they can barely walk, much less fight."

Mama Dragon nodded, wiping her mouth with the back of her hand. "Aye! And if you hadn't been able to handle a bunch of drunk pirates, I wouldn't have welcomed you back into the fold. Indeed, I would have made you shark food for Toothy. He hasn't gotten to eat a full-grown man in at least a week."

Surrels assumed 'Toothy' was the name of the shark circling the water below them. Though the platform felt sturdy enough, Surrels did not like the implication of Mama Dragon's statement regarding the shark's diet.

"So," Surrels said, looking at Kendo again, "how long have you been a member of the Dead Dragons?"

"Since I turned thirteen," Kendo replied, "so not long after you left the family."

"Youngest member of the syndicate we've ever had," Mama Dragon said proudly. She burped. "That's why he's the son I never had."

"Thirteen?" Surrels repeated in disbelief. "That seems … really young."

Kendo shrugged. "I left home early because I couldn't stand being around Mother or Lila. Traveled across the kingdom for a bit until I ended up in Faifa, where I tried to pickpocket Mama Dragon herself."

Mama Dragon chuckled. "Good times! If you hadn't been such a cute boy, I would have beheaded you myself and fed you to Toothy's dad!"

Surrels blinked. "Toothy's dad?"

Mama Dragon gestured carelessly at the shark below. "This isn't the first Toothy. In fact, they're not even related. But I call 'em Toothy anyway because they have teeth."

Surrels nodded, though more out of politeness than anything. "I see. And Kendo, how did you end up in prison—?"

Kendo sighed. "A business deal gone wrong. I was taking a shipment of illegal goods up to the capital to deliver to a client, only for said client to rat us out at the last second. And then I spent the next several years rotting away inside the Capital City Prison until you freed me."

Mama Dragon looked at Surrels with respect. "So it was you who busted Kendo out of prison? What a good—" she hiccupped and burped several times, "—father you are. Not like mine, who beat me silly every day until I couldn't stand it and shoved him off a ship in the middle of the worst storm Faifa has seen in two hundred years!"

Surrels bit his lower lip and glanced at Kendo. Though Kendo did not disagree with Mama Dragon's assessment of him as a 'good' father openly, Surrels knew that he and Kendo still had a long way to go before they could fully mend their relationship.

And with Lila as well, Surrels thought, rubbing his hands together anxiously. *I will still have a lot of work to do even after we stop Tenka. If we stop Tenka, at any rate.*

Mama Dragon suddenly slammed her empty beer mug

on the table between them, prompting a young woman—
the same one who had nearly slit Surrels's throat earlier—to
step forward with a huge jug of beer in her hands and pour
it into the cup.

As soon as the young woman finished refilling her cup,
Mama Dragon brought it up to her lips again, downed half
of it in one gulp, burped, and said to the girl, "Thank you,
girlie."

The young woman bowed respectfully. "You're
welcome, Mama."

Wiping the excess alcohol off of her lips, Mama
Dragon turned her eyes toward Surrels, Kendo, and Stebo
again. "All right, Kendo, you rascally devil, I know you
didn't just come here to catch up on old times. You want
something, don't you?"

Surrels pursed his lips while Kendo said, "As astute as
ever, Mama. While I would love to rejoin the syndicate as
an active member, the truth is that I do need a favor from
you and your men."

"A favor, eh?" said Mama Dragon. She waved at him.
"Go ahead. Make your request. As my favorite 'son,' I'll
happily give you anything you want."

Surrels raised an eyebrow. He knew that Kendo had
said the Mama owed him a favor, but he hadn't realized just
how much the Mama liked Kendo. Perhaps getting into the
capital would be even easier than he thought.

Kendo sipped from his beer mug. "A simple request,
really: We would like the aid of the Dead Dragons in infiltrating the capital, preferably in time for Tenka's
coronation."

The jovial smile on Mama Dragon's face faltered ever-
so-slightly at Kendo's request. "Why would you need our

help to infiltrate the capital? Surely you can do it on your own."

Kendo sighed. "We could, Mama, but the thing is, my father, son, and I are wanted criminals. There will be guards at every entrance, checking everyone going into and out of the city, not to mention the variety of mages who will be using magic to keep the peace during Tenka's coronation. But I know that the syndicate has many ways into the city that allow us to easily circumvent even the tightest security, so—"

Mama Dragon ripped meat off of a chicken leg, speaking in between bites. "So you want *us* to help."

"Exactly, Mama," Kendo said. "And it is urgent that we do so."

Mama Dragon cocked her head to the side. "Why? Do you want to see that spoiled royal brat get a shiny piece of metal placed on his head?"

Kendo pursed his lips. "Unfortunately, Mama, I cannot tell you our reasons for doing so. They are, er, very private."

Mama Dragon seemed to consider Kendo's point. "Hmm … they wouldn't have anything to do with your 'son,' now would they?"

Surrels heard a shriek and looked to his left, where Stebo had been …

Only to see that Stebo was missing entirely.

Another shriek brought Surrels's attention back to Mama Dragon, where he saw a disturbing sight:

Stebo floated beside Mama Dragon's head, held up by a fist made of water that rose from the ocean below, gripping him tightly. Stebo wriggled intensely to escape but it was clear he couldn't break free of the watery fist on his own.

"Stebo!" Surrels said, rising to his feet, reaching for his sword.

Mama Dragon wagged a finger. "Ah, ah, ah. Draw that sword and the brat becomes shark food."

Surrels glanced at Toothy below, whose fin was now very visible as it swam in its enclosure. "But I don't understand. How—?"

Mama Dragon chuckled. "I'm not just the Mama of the Dead Dragon Syndicate. I am also a powerful water mage … and unless you tell me who you really are and why you *really* want to go to the capital, the boy will make excellent shark food for Toothy."

Chapter Seventeen

THE MUSIC IN THE ROOM DIED AS ABRUPTLY AS THEIR chances of making it into the capital with the help of the Dead Dragons.

Surrels felt every eye in the room turn to look at them. He heard the chuckles and sneers of the Dead Dragons below as they took bets on how long Surrels and Kendo would last against Mama Dragon. Somehow, the stench of sweat, alcohol, and grease radiating off of Mama Dragon, along with the briny scent of seawater below, seemed to become stronger, and Surrels could feel the sweat running down the side of his face.

"Mama, what are you doing?" Kendo said in a pacifying voice. "Stebo here is my son."

Mama Dragon hocked and spat a loogie onto the table. "Bullshit, Kendo. I taught you everything I know about lying. And I can tell you are lying harder than the whore who lied to you about this child being yours."

Surrels widened his eyes. He had thought Mama

Dragon was a dumb drunk, but she was apparently far more aware and intelligent than she appeared.

Kendo, still smiling in the way a diplomat might smile when speaking with the representative of another country they were at war with, said, "So you did, Mama, so you did. You caught me."

Mama Dragon leaned forward just then, one eye bigger than the other. "And do you know what I do to my children who lie to me, Kendo? You remember Bart, don't you?"

"Bart?" Surrels said. "Who was that?"

Mama Dragon looked at Surrels with a ghoulish grin. "My *original* favorite son, before Kendo. Handsome, smart, strong … but very, *very* greedy. And Mama don't like it when her greedy children steal from her and lie to her face about it. No, Mama don't like it one bit."

Surrels gulped. He got the implication of what happened to Bart, which he suspected had something to do with the shark below.

"Kendo," Surrels said, leaning toward Kendo, "why didn't you mention that Mama Dragon is a water mage?"

Kendo gave Surrels an annoyed look. "Because I didn't know that until now, either, Father."

Mama Dragon grinned. "My magic is not something I show off all the time, mostly because it's not necessary. But I may have picked up a magic trick here and there along the way during my long and illustrious criminal career."

Surrels could tell she was deliberately downplaying her abilities. While not a mage himself, Surrels had had enough conversations with Fralia and other mages over the last year to know that the level control Mama Dragon asserted over the water right now was advanced magic. He didn't doubt she had some formal magical training, if not a mentor who taught her everything she knew.

Though I can't imagine a magical school that would ever allow a woman like her to enroll, Surrels thought.

Kendo raised his hands. "Fine! I lied. The truth is, Stebo is *not* my son, although I am very impressed that you figured that out so quickly."

Mama Dragon snorted. "When your father first entered the room and I saw how protective he was of the boy, I figured the boy was more important than a *mere* grandson. In fact, I'd even say he's probably the whole reason you want to infiltrate the capital in the first place. Someone somewhere wants him either dead or kept out of the city, and you need my help to get the boy past them without being killed."

Surrels's mouth dropped open. "You figured out all of that just by looking at us?"

"Of course," said Mama Dragon with a sneer. "I'm the Mama of the Dead Dragons. I've trafficked so many human slaves over the years that I can instantly smell when someone else is doing the same thing. The only thing I haven't quite figured out is *why* the boy is so important. Skin and bones are all I see, although I'm sure Toothy will find him a delectable snack nonetheless."

The watery fist floated away from Mama Dragon slightly toward the open water below, making Stebo instantly start crying.

Surrels instantly shot to his feet and said, "Wait! Don't kill him. Please. I beg of you."

Mama Dragon gave Surrels an amused look. "You *beg* of me? Smart man. Most men look at me and say they would never beg a woman for anything. Of course, those men don't last too long. I see we have a smart one here."

Surrels gulped. He didn't say anything to that, mostly because he was worried about what Mama Dragon might do if he said the wrong thing at the wrong time. He was just grateful she wasn't going to kill Stebo.

Stebo floating beside her again, Mama Dragon said, "I won't kill the boy if you promise to tell me who this kid *really* is and why it is so important for you to get him into the capital without anyone knowing. Who exactly is this brat related to that makes him so important?"

Surrels bit his lower lip. Telling Mama Dragon that Stebo was the long-lost son of Old Snow would be a terrible mistake, Surrels knew. Given how the Dead Dragons were masters of blackmail and human trafficking, Surrels did not even want to think about what Mama Dragon might do if she knew who Stebo actually was.

And unfortunately, Kendo and I don't have either the time or a way to figure out a convincing lie, either, Surrels thought. *Wish we had that telepathy that the Dragon Riders have with their Steeds. Would be very useful right now.*

Mama Dragon drummed her fat fingers against the arm of her chair. "Time is ticking, Kendo, Surrels. And I am getting a bit tired of having to concentrate so in order to maintain this construct. Magic always requires a lot of concentration, and I am so drunk that I might just drop the poor boy into Toothy's tank any second now. That would be rather unfortunate, wouldn't you say?"

Surrels rested a hand on the hilt of his sword. He saw no way out for them except to attack Mama Dragon and hope they could kill her before she dropped Stebo into the water. That would inevitably mean having to fight the entire Dead Dragon Syndicate just to escape, but given how drunk most of them were, Surrels hoped that their odds were better than they seemed.

That is, until Kendo rose, pointed at Stebo, and said, "That boy is the long-lost second son of Old Snow and the actual rightful heir to the throne of Malarsan."

Stunned silence dominated the room at Kendo's words. A glance around their surroundings showed Surrels that every single pirate in the room looked as if Kendo had personally slapped each one of them in the face.

The most stunned of all, however, was clearly Mama Dragon. She looked from Stebo to Kendo and back again, disbelief etched into her chunky features. "This boy is King Rikas's *son*? Impossible. You be lying to the Mama again."

Kendo shook his head. "No. This time, I am really telling the truth."

Surrels didn't know what to say. Did Kendo *want* to give the Dead Dragons information they could use against them? Already, he could see the gears turning in Mama Dragon's mind as her brain processed this information and how she could use it to her personal advantage.

"Kendo," Surrels whispered, "what the hell?"

Kendo stomped his foot on Surrels's boot. "Shut up. I know what I am doing."

Surrels doubted that. He doubted that so much, in fact, that he started drawing his sword, knowing that violence was their only real option at this point.

Finally, Mama Dragon smiled. "Ahhhh … *now* I see. I have always heard rumors of a long-lost son of King Rikas, said to have been born in an illicit love affair between the king and one of his servants. Never in my wildest dreams, however, did I think those rumors were true or that I would get to see them proved in front of my very eyes. What interesting times we live in indeed."

The water hand moved Stebo closer to Mama Dragon, who examined his face. "Yes … I can even see a bit of that stubborn old fool of a king in those frightened little eyes. What a catch. What. A. Catch."

Then Mama Dragon looked back toward Surrels and Kendo. "And now I understand why you want to enter the capital before Tenka's coronation. You want to throw a wrench into the process, plunge the country into disarray, and probably profit off of it in a way I haven't quite figured out yet."

Surrels blinked. "That actually isn't—"

Kendo stomped on Surrels's foot again, making Surrels cringe as Kendo said, "That's exactly it, Mama. But we know that Tenka knows about the boy's existence and has probably given orders to the city guard not to let any boy who looks like Stebo into the city. Hence why we can't do it ourselves."

"That young noble is a clever one, no doubt," Mama Dragon agreed. She looked at Stebo again, stroking her chin interestedly. "Yes, this is very interesting. Children of royalty make excellent hostages. Their parents are so desperate to have their little ones back that they will often pay any price we ask. And the son of Rikas … my, there's no limit to how much money this little one might make me. I could ask for the entire treasury of the kingdom, and I might just get it."

Surrels scowled. He knew this would happen. As soon as Mama Dragon realized that Stebo was Rikas's child, she would probably just take Stebo outright and hold him as her hostage. He could already guess that Mama Dragon planned to kill him and Kendo now that she had Stebo and knew exactly who he was.

That was why Surrels was shocked when the water fist floated back toward him and Kendo. The hand dropped Stebo back onto his chair, but Stebo jumped up and immediately hid behind Surrels and Kendo, shivering uncontrollably, his eyes wide with fear underneath his sopping wet hair.

"And that is why you can have him back," Mama Dragon concluded. She picked a piece of chicken out from between her teeth and flicked it over the edge of the platform, grinning all the time. "And we will be more than happy, of course, to help you infiltrate the capital in time for the coronation."

Surrels's jaw dropped again. "Wait … what? You're going to *help* us?"

Mama Dragon glared at Surrels. "What are you so upset about? Didn't you want the boy back? And here I thought you were a *smart* one."

Surrels shook his head. "No, I'm happy that you gave us back Stebo, but I thought for sure you were going to hold him hostage to get money from the government, like you said."

Mama Dragon rolled her eyes. "How am I going to make money off *this* one? Both of his parents are dead, and his closest living relative probably doesn't care if he lives or not. I can't make money off a brat like this, so I have no reason to keep him around. I hate kids, anyway. So disgusting and annoying."

Mama Dragon punctuated that last sentence by guzzling down another beer, burping, and dropping the wooden mug onto the floor, wiping her mouth clean with the back of her hand again.

Surrels was not sure if Mama Dragon was lying to them or not. He looked to Kendo for confirmation, only to see that Kendo appeared as puzzled as he did.

"So you're going to help us infiltrate the capital out of the goodness of your own heart?" Kendo said.

Mama Dragon laughed. "Ha! I *have* no heart, Kendo. You should know that better than anyone. Sold it a long time ago when I founded the most powerful crime syndicate in the entire kingdom of Malarsan. No, I am going to help you because I see opportunities in the political chaos the mere presence of the young boy will inflict on the entire kingdom."

"Political chaos?" Surrels repeated in confusion.

Mama Dragon rubbed her hands together. "Aye! Consider what will happen when, on the day of Tenka's coronation, someone else with an even greater claim to the Throne than he does shows up and claims to be the son of King Rikas himself! Never in the history of the kingdom has such a thing happened. Right, Catol?"

Catol, apparently the name of the girl who refilled Mama Dragon's beer mug, nodded. "Yes. At least, not in living memory, anyway."

Mama Dragon sighed. "It will be so delicious. The court will likely become divided between the Tenka loyalists and the Rikas loyalists. Given the pressure on the country at the moment, it might even lead to outright civil war, much like in Tipjok. And that's not even getting into what the Glaci Empire might do. That old glacier Kryo Kardia might like to seem like a distant observer, but even I can tell he's as power and money hungry as the rest of us. The refugees, the complete breakdown of law and order, the number of officials we could bribe … why, I am getting excited just *thinking* about it."

Surrels thought Mama Dragon was getting more than *excited* thinking about it. She was practically salivating at the thought of the chaos that would spread across the kingdom in the wake of a divided court and no clear heir to the throne of Malarsan.

In fact, it now got Surrels worried about the political ramifications of their actions. Up until now, Surrels had assumed that the nobles of the court would naturally side with Stebo once the boy showed up, and Tenka's ambitions would be thwarted, if not crushed outright.

But what if that *didn't* happen? What if some of the court sided with Tenka, some sided with Stebo, and others were caught in the middle? Not to mention how the public would react upon learning about the existence of the second son of Old Snow and Marial who had been missing up until now.

Despite that, I think the kingdom will be better off than it would be under a demon-influenced Tenka, Surrels thought, *although I am not sure that Mama Dragon knows that particular fact about Tenka yet.*

Kendo, as usual, was all smiles. "That is wonderful to hear, Mama! I knew we could count on you to come through for us."

Mama Dragon blushed. "Please, Kendo, your flattery is entirely unnecessary, although much appreciated. After all, when has the Mama ever *not* come through for her children?"

Then Mama Dragon raised two huge frothing mugs of beer into the air and shouted, loud enough for everyone in the room to hear, "Dead Dragons! Let us eat and drink, because by this time next week, the entire kingdom of Malarsan will become our playground, and we will become richer than any of us can possibly imagine! The best days are yet to come!"

Riotous laughter, cheering, and clinking of wooden and glass mugs filled the air, along with the band on the stage resuming their music, only this time at a faster, more exciting tempo. The barely clothed woman on the stage even started singing an incredibly gleeful (if also very bawdy) pirate song, prompting nearly everyone else in the room to start singing along.

Not Mama Dragon, however. She rested the mugs on the table and looked Surrels and Kendo straight in the eyes, leaning forward with her eyes bulging out of her face greedily.

"Now, let's get down to business, shall we?" said Mama Dragon, licking her lips. "And figure out exactly how we are going to plunge the entire kingdom of Malarsan into profitable chaos."

Chapter Eighteen

It took Anija several seconds to realize that Tenka was standing in the doorway before her. The young noble also looked a bit surprised, his long hair slightly windswept, probably thanks to the constant winds of the Tops.

Tenka smiled in a way he had clearly used to charm women more naive than Anija before. "I didn't expect to run into you down here, Anija. What a pleasant coincidence."

Resisting the urge to slam the door in his arrogant face, Anija said, "Rialo is up there. You should have seen her."

Tenka shrugged. "I did, but I didn't know that meant you were here. It appears that Dragon Riders and their Steeds are always together. Another thing for me to learn about your kind."

Anija scowled but did not respond. She sent a mental message to Rialo, asking, *What the hell, Rialo? Why did you let Tenka come down here?*

Tenka is down there with you? said Rialo in genuine surprise. *But I just saw him and his entourage with Wilme standing outside the temple. She told him that it was unsafe for him to enter, so they continued their tour of Mysteria. Are you sure he's down there?*

Anija opened her bond a bit larger, letting Rialo see through her eyes just long enough to confirm Tenka's identity. Rialo cursed.

You're right, Rialo said. *I don't know how he slipped past me or Wilme.*

Demon magic, probably, Anija thought. *This just confirms he knows Lom is here and is looking for him. I need to keep him from finding Lom.*

Rialo growled in frustration. *Do you want me to go tell Wilme? She probably isn't too far away from the temple yet.*

No, because I don't want Tenka to suspect that anything is up, Anija replied. *He's into me, so I'll just distract him long enough for Lom to hide.*

"Anija?" Tenka said with a frown. "Are you all right?"

Snapping out of her thoughts, Anija looked at Tenka in alarm. "Hmm? Oh, sorry. I was just surprised to see you down here. Most people, even the people who live in Mysteria year-round, don't know this place exists."

"Rialo told me about it," Tenka said. "Said it was the abandoned workshop of the Crafters. And I, being the history enthusiast I am, could not resist the temptation to see the place where the legendary relics of the Relic Crafters were forged myself."

Liar, Rialo snarled. *It's still not too late for me to tell Wilme.*

Anija shook her head slightly, partially in response to Rialo's offer, but also doubling as a way to deny Tenka's request. "Sorry about that, but this place is off-limits to visitors. As you might imagine, underground chambers that have been abandoned for thousands of years are not structurally-sound. It would be a very unfortunate thing if part of the roof caved in right on top of you, for example. Hard to be king when you are buried alive."

Although quite poetic, Anija thought but did not say aloud.

Tenka laughed. "Thank you for the concern, Anija, but since you clearly have not been buried alive yet, it's a risk I am willing to take."

Anija bit her lower lip. "Okay, but still, I don't have authorization from Hal or Wilme, so I can't let you in. Bye."

Anija tried to close the door in Tenka's face, only for Tenka to catch the door with one hand. It was like slamming the door into a wall, Tenka's strength belying his rather slender form.

If Anija didn't believe Tenka was working with the demons before, she certainly did now. Especially since she had used her own dragon-powered strength to close the door.

Tenka kept smiling. "If this gets you in trouble with Commander Norath and Wilme, then you can just blame me. I don't mind getting blamed for a beautiful woman's problems. Not in the slightest."

Now Anija wanted to slam the door in Tenka's face even more, albeit for reasons which had nothing to do with protecting Lom this time.

Still, Anija knew Tenka was just going to keep pushing and wouldn't leave, so she opened the door and, stepping aside, said, "All right. You can come in. But don't touch anything, all right? This is historical stuff. Very valuable. Irreplaceable, even."

Tenka nodded as he stepped inside. "Of course. I know better than to touch history. I wouldn't want to ruin it, after all."

Anija bit her lower lip. She looked toward Lom's work-table, expecting to see the Crafter still banging on the metal boots he was making …

Only to see that Lom was completely missing. Not only that, but the worktable itself was covered in pieces of junk, looking as if it had also stood abandoned for years.

Where did he go? Anija thought in alarm. *There's nowhere Lom could have hidden. And why would he? Does he somehow know that Tenka is after him?*

Anija, unfortunately, had neither the time nor the energy to find the answers to those questions, because Tenka was already giving himself a tour of the workshop. His eyes scanned the piles of tools, abandoned inventions, and various other bits and bobs with utter fascination. Yet he, too, seemed to be searching for something, something that was undoubtedly Lom.

Tenka made his way carefully through the tall stacks of junk strewn everywhere, eyes darting about quickly. "Amazing. The history books have few facts on the Relic Crafters, such as what they were like, where they lived, even how they crafted the relics. I feel as if I stepped back in time five thousand years to before the Fall, if not longer."

Anija pursed her lips. "I suppose it's interesting, but there's honestly not much to see down here."

Tenka stopped and pointed at one of the walls. "If there's nothing much to see down here, then what is that?"

At first, Anija thought Tenka had spotted Lom, which would definitely get her in trouble.

But then Anija followed Tenka's finger and saw he was pointing at a slightly faded painting on the wall of the workshop.

Specifically, Tenka was pointing at a painting on the

wall that showed a Dragon Rider pair who bore a striking resemblance to Hal and Keershan. Anija recognized the painting. Hal had told her that the Relic Crafters had painted it ages ago, a sort of visual prophecy of when Hal and Keershan would find the Final Relic and use it to become the first Dragon Rider pair since the Fall.

Despite that, though, Anija never quite bought that interpretation herself. After all, how could the Relic Crafters have known about Hal and Keershan? They weren't future-seers. True, they did commune with the gods on a fairly regular basis if the legends were to be believed, but Anija still thought it was probably a coincidence more than anything.

Regardless, Anija was no expert on Relic Crafters, prophecies, or ancient paintings, so she never argued with them about it, despite her own reservations about its interpretation.

"That?" Anija said. She cleared her throat. "A painting by the Relic Crafters of old. Supposedly, it shows Hal and Keershan gaining the Final Relic and using it to become the first Dragon Rider pair in five thousand years. Think of it as a visual prophecy of sorts."

Tenka nodded in fascination. "Some of the oldest books I read mentioned that the Relic Crafters often had visions of the future and would draw them so that others could see them. Never did I think they were true, however, or that I would lay eyes on one. I feel deeply honored."

Despite Tenka's glowing praise for the painting, however, Anija caught more than a whiff of anger in Tenka's voice. His hands balled into tight fists, his eyes hard, as if the very nature of the image offended him on a primal level that he could not quite articulate.

It's probably the demons inside him angry about the prophecy of the rebirth of the Dragon Rider Order, Rialo spoke up. *No doubt they're channeling it through Tenka, even if Tenka is unaware of it himself.*

I don't know about that, Anija replied. *He seems awfully offended by it just on his lonesome.*

"Well, you still can't touch it," Anija said aloud. "And since that's all there is to see down here, you might as well go back up to your entourage and finish your tour of the town."

Tenka, however, looked over at Lom's worktable. Walking over to it, he said, "Interesting."

Anija raised an eyebrow. "What's interesting?"

Tenka stopped in front of the worktable and laid his hands on its surface, his back to Anija. "This worktable looks like it was used recently. It's less dusty than the rest of the workshop, plus I see filings and pieces from what is obviously the work of someone making something here."

Anija's heart raced. "That would be me. I was messing around with some of the stuff here, although I am not supposed to—"

Anija was interrupted by the sound of pieces of metal shifting in a pile right next to the worktable. The sound was subtle enough that Anija hoped Tenka would not notice.

Unfortunately, he did.

Tenka whipped his head toward the pile of pieces, raising an eyebrow. "Is someone in there?"

Anija folded her arms behind her back. "No. Of course not. We're the only two people down here. Why would you ever think someone is hiding there?"

Tenka's eyes narrowed. "If someone is spying on us, then that poses a threat. Perhaps a Glacian spy, sent by

Kryo Kardia to scout out Mysteria in preparation for the invasion of the kingdom."

Tenka slowly walked toward the pile, prompting Anija to step forward and say, "H-Hey, Tenka, why don't you let me look instead? If it's a spy—"

Anija never got to finish her sentence before Tenka drew a sword from his cloak and slammed it into the pile of junk in one swift motion.

For a split second, Anija expected to hear Lom's cry of pain as Tenka's sword stabbed through his heart.

But all that happened was that the pile of junk collapsed, revealing nothing except more, well, junk.

Tenka was still for a moment, holding his sword out into nothingness, before pulling it back, sheathing it, and turning back to Anija with a smile on his face. "Guess it was nothing. Probably just a mouse foraging for food or something."

Anija nodded once, although seeing Tenka's reflexes confirmed to her that he was *definitely* demon-possessed. "Yeah. Probably."

Tenka shrugged. "Anyway, while this was a fascinating visit, I am afraid I have to rejoin my entourage. We plan to fully tour the entire town before heading back south. I am thinking of visiting Faifa next. It's usually nice this time of year."

Anija nodded. Faifa was all the way on the southern coast of Malarsan, as far away from the Tops as one could get while still remaining within Malarsan's borders. She had to resist the urge to tell him to get on a boat and go even farther, however. "Yes. I'm sure it is."

With that, Tenka walked past Anija. She watched him

go up the stairs, not daring to close the door until she saw him disappear around the corner of the stairs.

With a sigh of relief, Anija closed the door and leaned against it. She touched her forehead and realized she was sweating a lot more than she thought.

Tenka is heading back up to the temple, Rialo, Anija said. *Watch out.*

I will, said Rialo, *but did he see Lom?*

Anija shook her head. *No. Which is weird, because even* I *don't see Lom. I have no idea where he is. I don't even know if he's—*

Without warning, Lom burst out from the pile of junk next to the one that Tenka had stabbed, breathing hard and startling Anija, who nearly launched a fireball at him on instinct.

"Lom!" Anija said, half-annoyed, half-relieved. "What were you doing?"

Lom looked around in alarm, his eyes wide with fear. "The bad man. Is he gone? For real?"

Anija blinked. "Yes. He's gone. For real."

Lom sighed. He pulled himself out of the junk pile, wiping dust and dirt off his clothes. "It has been ages since I sensed that much evil in one person. Even Kryo Kardia doesn't exude that kind of sheer malevolence. I thought for sure he was going to kill you, Anija."

"Kill *me*?" Anija said. "You do realize he was looking for *you*, right?"

Lom looked at Anija in surprise. "You mean you didn't sense the sheer blood lust he felt toward you? To me, it felt as if it took every bit of willpower he had not to murder you on the spot."

An ominous feeling went up Anija's spine. "No, I didn't sense that at all. How did you sense it?"

Lom shuddered. "Relic Crafters have a unique ability to sense the good and evil in others. Most of the time, we don't actively use the ability, but I didn't have to activate it in order to feel *his* evil. It was like he was screaming about how much he liked eating babies at the top of his lungs in a crowded market and no one paid him any attention."

Anija gulped. She had thought she could read people pretty well, but she hadn't picked up on Tenka's murderous rage toward her at all.

It made her feel very unsafe.

Shaking her head, Anija said, "Good thing he didn't find you, then. I don't even want to think about what he would have done to you."

Lom shuddered. "Tell me about it. I haven't felt that much evil since … since the Fall, at least, when the Nameless One died."

Anija pursed her lips. Although Lom physically resembled a human man in his late thirties or early forties, the truth was that he was infinitely older than that. He was actually at least five thousand years old, if not older, because the Relic Crafters had fled after the Fall five thousand years ago.

It made Anija wonder what immortality was like. Never dying seemed like a good thing to her, even though Lom did not seem to be particularly enjoying it.

Then again, Lom is kind of a coward, so maybe that's why, Anija thought.

Supposedly, Dragon Riders like herself could live forever. Or at least for a very long time. Due to the scarce knowledge about the old Dragon Riders, the exact powers and abilities of the Dragon Riders were still largely unknown, even to modern Dragon Riders like Anija and Hal.

Does that mean that Rialo and I will live for as long as Lom? Anija thought. *That's crazy to think about.*

Aloud, however, Anija said to Lom, "That's because we are pretty sure that man is demon-possessed. Or at least is working with them."

Lom's eyes widened in alarm. "Demon-possessed? Good Lord, I thought you guys said that Hal and Keershan killed the Nameless One again."

"They did, but there are apparently still a few demons lurking in the shadows," Anija said. She smiled. "But don't worry. We're working on a plan to stop him before he can hurt anyone else."

Lom sighed. "Good to hear. I remember those awful things. I still sometimes have nightmares about them."

Anija nodded before hearing Rialo's voice in her head say, *Coast is clear. I just saw Tenka leave the temple. He's heading toward the school.*

Thanks.

Aloud, Anija said, "All right, Lom. I guess I'll leave you to your work, then … Lom?"

Lom was apparently not paying attention to anything she said. He was looking at the image of Hal and Keershan on the wall, his mouth open slightly. "Is that a painting of Hal and Keershan?"

Anija frowned. "Didn't you hear me explaining to Tenka what it is?"

Lom shrugged. "Sorry. When I get stressed out about being killed by evil people, I rarely pay attention as well as I should."

Anija sighed, but said, "Yes. It's a visual prophecy of

Hal and Keershan using the Final Relic. It was painted by one of your fellow Crafters, though we don't know who."

Lom looked at Anija in surprise. "One of my fellow Crafters painted this? Fascinating. Very fascinating."

Without warning, Lom shoved aside several piles of junk and parts, metal and wood clattering against the stone floor. He got right up against the painting, his eyes darting across it as he ran his hands across every inch his arms could reach.

"What are you doing?" Anija said, raising a questioning eyebrow. "Other than making a big mess?"

"Looking for something …" Lom made a sound of triumph. "Ah! Here it is."

Lom pressed on a loose stone in the wall, and it sank into the wall. A second later, the wall itself rumbled, making the room shake and causing Anija to wonder if she hadn't been lying about the structural soundness and safety of the workshop.

But the workshop did not cave in on both of them. Instead, the wall slid to the side very slowly, stone scraping against stone as the ancient mechanisms inside the walls came to life for the first time in who-knew-how-many years.

"Ah-ha!" Lom said, smiling triumphantly as the wall slid aside. "I *knew* there was something hidden behind here. Let's see what—"

Without warning, a corpse fell out of the opening beyond the wall and into Lom's arms.

Chapter Nineteen

UNSURPRISINGLY, LOM SCREAMED LIKE A GIRL AND DROPPED the corpse onto the floor. He rushed over to the other side of the room, hiding behind the dormant furnace for safety, making sobbing sounds as if he had just been assaulted by a monster.

Anija, although surprised by the corpse's appearance, nonetheless stepped forward, carefully looking at the corpse.

Anija did not know what she was looking at. At first, she thought it was a human being, because of its vaguely humanoid shape: A head, two arms, and two legs.

Then she noticed the extra two arms growing out of its sides, directly underneath the first set, and she realized this thing, whatever it was, definitely *wasn't* human.

The corpse was roughly the height of Lom, but even thinner than him. Wrapped in strange burial clothing, the corpse lay on its front, making it impossible to tell what its face looked like. She did notice what seemed to be a bright purple jewel hanging from the necklace around its neck, though her instincts told her not to touch it.

"The hell—?" Anija said, staring at the corpse. "I didn't know there was a dead body hidden in the walls of this place."

Lom peeked out from behind the furnace, though just barely. "Is it dead?"

Anija gave Lom a sardonic look. "What do *you* think, O wise Crafter?"

Taking a deep breath, Lom stepped out from behind the furnace. He carefully walked over to Anija, eyes fixed on the corpse. He looked very disturbed, although Anija couldn't blame him. She felt very similarly, even if she expressed it in a less cowardly way.

Lom nudged the corpse with the toe of his boot and nodded. "Definitely dead. And not *un*dead."

That may have seemed like an odd concern to have, but given how they had just escaped from Kryo Kardia's army of undead creatures, Anija didn't judge him for wanting to make sure.

"Yes," Anija said. She stroked her chin. "But *what* is it? It's obviously not human, since humans don't have four arms."

Lom looked at Anija in surprise. "You don't?"

Anija held up her arms. "See? Only two."

Lom blinked. "Oh. Sorry. I assumed you were hiding them."

"Hiding them?" Anija said. "Hiding what?"

Still frowning, Lom unhitched the odd patches on the inner sides of his shirt, patches that Anija originally thought were just normal patches meant to keep his clothing from falling apart.

At least, Anija thought that until two extra arms popped out of the newly revealed holes, arms identical in size and length to Lom's normal arms, albeit skinnier, like they hadn't been used in a while.

"What the hell?" Anija said again, taking a step backward in surprise. "Since when do *you* have four arms?"

Flexing the muscles on both sets of arms, Lom cocked his head to the side. "I have always had four arms. Anyone who knows anything about the Relic Crafters knows about our distinctive four arms. How else do you think we are so productive and inventive?"

Anija opened and closed her mouth several times. She wasn't quite sure why seeing a four-armed man shocked her so much, since she had seen—and experienced—far stranger things over the past couple of years.

But it did anyway, prompting her to say, "Well, *I* didn't know about your four arms. And I'm pretty sure no one else does, either."

Lom slapped his face with his right arm. That was, the one connected to his shoulder, not to his waist. "Right, sorry. I keep forgetting that outsiders like you don't know anything about us other than hearsay and legend. So yes, we *do* have four arms, but best practice dictates keeping them secret from outsiders except in extreme circumstances, such as now."

"Oh," Anija said. She glanced at the paintings of the Relic Crafters on the walls. "But these paintings of your people show them with only two arms each."

Lom snorted. "I noticed that, too. Probably, the Crafter who owned this workshop got lazy and didn't want to draw the extra arms. Crafters can be lazy as well, though not as lazy as outsiders, of course."

Rialo, are you seeing this? Anija said mentally. *Lom has four arms.*

And? Rialo said. *You humans have two. To a four-legged dragon like me, Lom's body design makes far more sense than your two-armed human one.*

Anija rolled her eyes, but then looked at the corpse at her feet and said, "So this isn't a human being. This is the corpse of a—"

"Relic Crafter, yes," Lom agreed somberly. He gazed at the four-armed corpse. "Probably the original owner of this workshop. We Crafters have a tendency to bury ourselves in our workshops when we die. Partly to be with our creations in the afterlife, partly to make sure no one breaks into our workshops and steals our secrets after we depart."

Anija looked at Lom in alarm. "But this guy is dead."

"Maybe so, but his spirit is probably still hanging around somewhere," Lom said. He scratched his head with his upper left arm. "Only I don't feel it at all. He must have perished a long time ago. Or his spirit, assuming it hasn't moved on, is probably so tiny it might as well not exist."

Anija's head spun at this revelation. "How did you know it was behind the painting in the first place?"

Lom shrugged, which looked very strange with four arms. "I didn't. When you mentioned the painting, I recalled how common it is for my people to hide our best inventions behind walls. Often, we hide them behind paintings, because no one would think of messing with a beautiful piece of art on the off-chance that something may or may not be hidden behind it."

Anija furrowed her brow. "Guess that makes sense. But when you say your 'best inventions,' what do you mean, exactly?"

"Not sure," Lom admitted. "It varies from Crafter to Crafter. For some, it might be a finely-crafted hammer designed to be perfect at nailing in nails. For others … it might be a doomsday weapon that we would probably be better off *not* finding."

Anija frowned. "That seems like a pretty big range."

"The range of the Crafters is as big as the range of creativity itself," Lom replied. He gestured at the opening in the wall. "Anyway, there's only one way to find out what is on the other side of this wall. And that is by going through it."

Cocking her head to the side, Anija said, "That's awfully brave of you, Lom. After all, we have no idea what your dead cousin was hiding in there."

Lom waved off her concerns. "I doubt it's anything that I can't handle. As a Relic Crafter, I am pretty familiar with how other Crafters make things, so let's go in and see what we can find."

Thus, the unusually adventurous and confident Lom walked past the Crafter's corpse and disappeared into the shadows. Almost as soon as he did, a high-pitched scream came from within the dark opening.

"Lom!" Anija said in alarm.

Drawing her daggers, Anija launched herself into the darkness. As soon as she passed the threshold, her dragon-enhanced night vision kicked in, allowing her to see what Lom did.

They stood on a platform overlooking a massive tomb full of dragon skeletons.

Chapter Twenty

ANIJA HAD NEVER SEEN ANYTHING LIKE THE ROOM LAID OUT before them. A gigantic ceiling supported by massive stone pillars stretched out across the chamber for as far as the eye could see. Underneath the ceiling, dozens, if not hundreds, of dragon and human skeletons were scattered.

'Scattered' wasn't the best word. They were clearly organized, the dragons resting on top of huge stone slabs while the humans lay inside glass cases beside them, arms crossed in front of their chests. The air was dry, dusty, and dull, though Anija's enhanced senses caught a faint whiff of death, too.

A sobbing sound in front of her made Anija look down at her feet. Lom was on his hands and knees, his huge eyes gazing out over the gigantic tomb, his body trembling uncontrollably.

"What is it, Lom?" Anija said. She looked around the chamber again. "What *is* this place?"

Lom gulped. "A place of death. A tomb. A graveyard."

"Graveyard?" Anija said. "Of what?"

Lom looked up at Anija shakily. "Can't you see? It's a Dragon Rider Graveyard. These are the remains of the Dragon Riders—and their Steeds—who came before you. They're all dead."

Anija didn't understand why Lom looked so deathly afraid. As far as she could tell, the skeletons were just that: Skeletons that could not move, breathe, think, or even feel.

Probably just being a coward like always, Anija thought.

Stepping closer to the edge of the platform, Anija said, "So this is where all of the Dragon Riders of old were buried? Weird. Given how long ago they all died, I'm shocked that there's anything left."

"T-They were probably preserved by magic," Lom said. "O-Or maybe the lack of exposure to the outside world meant that their corpses decayed more slowly than they otherwise would. Either way, we need to get out of here. Now."

Anija looked at Lom in annoyance. "Why? Are you afraid of a bunch of dead people who probably don't even know you exist?"

Lom rubbed his hands together anxiously. "It's not that. It's that I have a *very* bad feeling about all of this. Disturbing places of the dead is never a wise move. And disturbing places of the dead sealed off by a Crafter? That's like asking for bad luck."

Anija rolled her eyes again. "By the gods, Lom, you really need to stop thinking about how scary everything is. Look, we've been standing here for five minutes and nothing bad has happened to either of us."

"Yet," Lom said.

Anija continued, ignoring Lom. "And even if this place was sealed off for a reason, it's still good we found it. Think about all of the history of the Dragon Riders we might find down here. There's still so much we don't know about ourselves or our powers. This could be a good way for us to reconnect with our ancestors and become better Dragon Riders."

"Or a good way to die horribly," Lom said. "That is also possible, you know."

Sighing, Anija said, "Okay. Lom, you can stay here if you want. I'm going in deeper to see what I can find."

"Are you sure that is wise?" Lom said. "Going by yourself, I mean."

Anija smirked. "Are you offering to accompany me, Lom? Very chivalrous of you."

Lom shook his head so rapidly that it looked like it was in danger of flying off his shoulders. "No, no, no! I was just saying that maybe you should go back to the surface first and see if you can find someone to come with you."

"Rialo is always with me, even if not physically," Anija said.

True, sister, said Rialo. *And like you, I also think this is worth exploring so we can learn more about our Dragon Rider ancestors. I think this is an important discovery for the Dragon Riders, so it's worth exploring.*

Anija tapped the side of her head. "Rialo agrees. And since two outvote one, I think it's clear that I get to do what I want."

Lom frowned. "I've never been a fan of democracy, honestly."

Doing her best not to roll her eyes yet again, Anija jumped off of the platform and landed on the stone pathway between the skeletons. Rising to her feet, Anija looked back up at the platform, seeing Lom's bald head peering over the edge at her, his eyes big and wide.

Waving a hand, Anija said, "Don't worry about me, Lom! I will be back before you know it."

"Okay," Lom said with a gulp, "I'll go get the others if you—"

Lom must have slipped for some reason, because he suddenly let out a yelp and fell toward Anija. Anija caught Lom in her arms and looked at him. "I guess you're joining me after all, it seems. How chivalrous of you."

Lom sighed, but did not argue as Anija let him down.

With Lom by her side, Anija made her way down the path, gazing at the skeletons on either side.

Despite not being a 'history enthusiast' like Tenka or even Keershan, Anija nonetheless found herself fascinated by the deceased Dragon Riders and Steeds she saw around her. More than that, however, was how surprised she was to see so many. She had not realized how many Dragon Riders had existed in the past. There were at least several hundred down here alone with more appearing the deeper in they walked.

Even more interestingly, however, were the plaques inscribed at the base of each stone slab. Most of them were covered in thick dust, though it was swept away easily enough by Anija's hand, letting her see a strange form of writing she could not read.

Squinting her eyes at the plaque on one of the slabs, Anija said, "What does this say?"

"It says, 'Here lies Frade De and his valiant Steed, Pokano,'" Lom said suddenly. He leaned in closer and grimaced. "One of the many casualties during the war against the Nameless One, apparently. Seems like he was an important figure."

Anija whistled. "You can read that?"

Lom rubbed the back of his head sheepishly. "More or less. The language is Ancient Malarsan, the language spoken during the pre-Fall years. I remember speaking it all the time back in the day. Been a long time since I've seen it written down, though I can still translate it pretty easily."

"You make it sound like you didn't know this 'Frade De' person," Anija said, "even though he lived around the same time as you?"

Lom gestured at the vast tomb. "Look at all of the skeletons down here. Do you think it would even be possible for someone like me to know each and every one of them individually?"

Anija shook her head. "I suppose not. Especially since you don't seem like much of a social butterfly yourself."

Lom shuddered. "It's not even that. It's just that there are so many of them everywhere. A person can only know so many people, after all."

"True enough," Anija said, "especially since this isn't even connected to your workshop, but to the workshop of … whoever we found buried inside the wall like that."

Lom grabbed his mouth with all four of his hands. "And we disturbed the corpse of one of my former Crafters. Yeah, we definitely should never have come down here."

Anija sighed in frustration. "It will be fine, Lom. Just keep an eye out for anything interesting. And if it really bothers you that much, we can always go back."

Lom looked at Anija hopefully. "Really?"

Anija smiled. "Yes. After, of course, we thoroughly explore the place."

Lom sighed heavily, but then his head whipped in one direction and he squinted his eyes. "Wait … is that who I think …"

Without any other explanation, Lom hurried down the path between the skeletons, forcing Anija to practically run to keep up with him. "Where are you going, Lom? Did you see something?"

But Lom did not answer. He just kept running until he stopped in front of a particularly large stone slab and gazed up at it. "I thought so."

Anija, stopping beside Lom, looked at the stone slab as well.

At first glance, the stone slab didn't look much different from the stone slabs that were in the rest of the tomb. She did note that it was larger than the others, however, which most likely had to do with the size of the dead dragon lying upon it.

The skeleton of this dragon was huge, almost twice as big as the surrounding skeletons. It was crouched on the slab, its sightless eyes gazing down at Anija and Lom. A huge necklace was draped over its neck, a dusty ruby gem set inside it.

In a glass case beside the dragon, the skeleton of what Anija assumed was a man stood upright. Clad in purple-and-black armor, the deceased Dragon Rider must have cut an imposing look when he was alive. Anija was especially impressed by the broadsword his skeletal form clutched with one hand, because it was nearly as long as the Rider was tall. His skeleton face was slightly narrow, giving Anija the impression that he must have looked a bit like a dragon himself when he was alive.

Lom was studying both skeletons very intently, his head darting from the Steed to the Rider again in utter fascination. "Yes, yes, that's *him*, no doubt. I'd recognize that broadsword anywhere, though I guess his hair didn't survive the burial process …"

Tapping her foot impatiently, Anija said, "Who is this man again? Someone you knew?"

Lom, apparently snapped out of whatever spell he had fallen under, looked over his shoulder at Anija sheepishly. "Sorry! I forgot you were standing there. Yes, this is definitely someone I know. Or knew, since he obviously died a long time ago, given the fact that he's, well, down here with all of the other skeletons."

"Thank you for that observation, Captain Obvious," Anija said sarcastically. "I still don't know who he is."

"Oh?" Lom said. He smacked his forehead. "Right. You can't read Ancient Malarsan. His name is Domon Azertan, and his Steed is Mathoh."

Anija furrowed her brow. "You say those names like I should know who they are."

Lom turned to face Anija fully, excitement on his face. "You should, because Domon Azertan is the last of the original Dragon Riders, the one who wore the Final Relic before Hal … and the Dragon Rider who dealt the finishing blow to the Nameless One over five thousand years ago."

Chapter Twenty-One

Touching the Final Relic on his head, Hal said to Salard, "You mean you actually were present when the Final Relic was made five thousand years ago?"

Salard nodded, the movement causing sparks and smoke to shoot out of his nostrils and hit the ground before them. "Yes. I witnessed the best of the Relic Crafters putting their all into making the most powerful relic that has ever been created. Indeed, making such a powerful relic wouldn't have even been possible without my help."

"What do you mean, Lord Salard?" Keershan said anxiously. "Did you grant the Relic Crafters the knowledge they needed to craft it?"

Salard shook his head. "More important than that. I gave them a physical part of my own body to make it."

Hal blinked. "I don't understand."

"I do," Boca said. She gazed at Salard. "It has to do with how relics are created. Relics are created from the bones and scales of dragons."

"The witch is partially correct," Salard said with a nod.

"A relic can only be created by using the scales of dragons and the bones of humans. By doing so, they have a bit of humanity and dragonkind in them, which is what allows them to form bonds between humans and dragons and make it possible for the Dragon Riders to exist at all."

Hal tried to wrap his mind around that concept. "So the metal of the Final Relic was made from one of your scales?"

"Precisely," Salard said with another nod. "I donated the scale myself, knowing that it would give the Final Relic the divine energy it needed to become the only weapon capable of killing the Nameless One."

Keershan gasped. "Just like the legendary sword, Scalebreaker! Do you have it?"

Salard shrugged. "We do, but it has been ages since I last used it. Vilona? Do you know where Scalebreaker is?"

Vilona scratched the ground with her claw. "Where it always is: In the armory, of course."

Hal, still trying to understand the origin of the Final Relic, rubbed the cold metallic surface of the Final Relic again. "If you provided the scale, who provided the human bones? Doesn't it seem a little morbid that bones from dead human beings are required to make relics?"

Salard frowned. "Since when did you humans consider that morbid? The last time I visited the human world, the bones of the deceased were used by their living relatives in many different ways."

"That is because, Father, the last time you visited the human world was over five thousand years ago," said Vilona dryly. "Mortal cultures and mores tend to change over time."

Salard scowled. "They do? Humans are very inconsistent. Regardless, the bones came from a fallen Dragon Rider who was also a king of Malarsan at the time. He had fallen in battle against the demons and specifically requested that his bones be used to make the relic that would defeat the Nameless One. I believe it was his son, Domon Azertan, who wore the Final Relic."

"In other words, the Relic Crafters who designed and built the Final Relic together were simply following Father's wishes," said Vilona simply. "Nothing more, nothing less."

Hal pursed his lips. He supposed that he couldn't see anything wrong with that, even if he couldn't quite understand it himself. It was mostly because he would never have considered having his own bones used that way. He would prefer them to stay in the ground.

As Vilona said, human cultures do change a lot, Keershan said, *so I doubt anyone back home is waiting to use your bones to make new relics. Not even Lom. But honestly, I don't see what you're so upset about. All of this is amazing.*

Is it? Hal replied. *Because this discussion is making me feel a little queasy, to be honest.*

But we're learning so much about how relics are made, Keershan said excitedly. *We're even learning a bit about the original Dragon Riders. We're learning history. Isn't that amazing?*

Academically, yes, Hal said. *Emotionally, no.*

"Yes," Salard said. He grinned, showing his massive teeth, each tooth as tall as a full-grown man. "By giving the Crafters the materials that they needed, I indirectly helped the Dragon Riders kill the Nameless One. I am quite proud of that accomplishment, in case you couldn't tell."

"So the Final Relic has divine energy flowing through it?" Hal said, stroking his chin. "That explains why it is so much more powerful than the other relics."

"Indeed," Salard said. "Only a god can kill a god."

"Speaking of gods killing gods," Boca said, "why don't we return to our original reason for talking to you: The murder of Shirataka."

Salard's smile turned into a harsh scowl. "As I said before, I know nothing about that awful, awful crime. Your investigation was clearly designed by the other gods to fail from the start. If I were you, I would leave the abode entirely and hope you can hide in the mortal world before my brothers and sisters find you."

"That's why I am here, Lord Salard," Raniel said smugly, patting Hal on the shoulder, "to make sure that these murder suspects do not take advantage of the gods' generosity to escape justice."

Hal glared at Raniel while Boca said, "With all due respect, Lord Salard, it is not your place to question the judgment of your fellow gods. Your job is to cooperate with us to the best of your ability. I promise you we will not bother you anymore once you answer some of our questions."

Salard grunted, a noise which sounded a bit like a muted cannonball to Hal. "Then ask your questions."

Boca stood up straighter. "First, when was the last time you saw Shirataka alive?"

"Yesterday," Salard said without hesitation. "She came to visit me in my cave, having just recently arrived in the abode to participate in a meeting of the gods."

Hal raised an eyebrow. "A meeting of the gods—?"

"The gods meet together once a year in the abode to share news, discuss recent events happening in both the mortal and divine realms, and keep up with each other," Raniel explained. "You mortals just so happened to arrive on the day of this year's meeting, which is why the gods are present in the abode. Not that the murder of one of their own wouldn't prompt every god and goddess in the universe to drop what they were doing and head straight here, however."

"Certainly," Boca said. "What did Shirataka visit you about, Lord Salard?"

"She mostly wanted to talk," Salard said. He tilted his head to the side. "She seemed … disturbed. I believe it had something to do with the mortal known as Kryo Kardia."

Hal tensed. "Kryo Kardia? You mean the emperor of the Glaci Empire?"

"Yes, I believe so," Salard said. "She seemed disturbed by his use of dark magic to blur the difference between the living and the dead. I told her that such experimentations were normal for mortals to play with but, like all mortals who rise above their station, Kryo Kardia would probably extend his reach a little too far and pay a very harsh price for it."

Hal wasn't so sure about that. Based on the skeptical expressions of both Keershan and Boca, he could tell they weren't, either.

"Still, Shirataka wasn't comforted by my words," Salard said, "so I suggested she speak to Demo, as he understands the secrets of dark magic and similar areas better than I do. He might have a better understanding of what Kryo Kardia is trying to do."

"Demo?" Hal said. "You mean the God of Mystery?"

"There is only one," Salard replied. "And in any case, Shirataka left me, probably to do just that."

"Did she?" Boca asked.

Salard shrugged. "I don't know. Most likely, but I also

know that Shirataka and Demo have never gotten along. Probably because of their differing natures. Shirataka was open and hated keeping secrets, whereas Demo is all about mystery and obscurity."

Hal was starting to think they had a suspect. "Do you think that Demo, then, might know something about Shirataka's death?"

Salard gave Hal a very indignant look. "I would never accuse one of my fellow gods of deicide if that is what you are implying. For if the gods were to fight and kill each other as you mortals do, the consequences for the world would be so grave that even I couldn't begin to imagine them. That is why, when we gods do wish to oppose each other, we work through mortals such as you. Much safer."

"Such as in the case of the Nameless One, for instance?" Boca said.

Salard rumbled. "Yes, though that was a very special case, because the Nameless One had crossed a line a long time ago and needed to be dealt with, for the good of the gods, the mortals, and the world as a whole. Although I will have you know that we still did not fight the Nameless One ourselves then."

"I see," Boca said. She bowed respectfully. "Thank you for your time, Lord Salard. You have answered all of the questions we wanted to ask."

Hal gave Boca a questioning look. "Are you sure? Because I can think of several more questions we might want to ask him, such as—"

"Hal," Boca said, interrupting him, "we cannot waste Lord Salard's time with more irrelevant questions. I feel like we have gotten the information we needed from him, unless there is anything else he wishes to share with us."

"There isn't," Salard said. "I have told you all I know. Now leave my cave." He leaned in closer, making his face and eyes look bigger than ever as he glared at them. "Or else."

Boca bowed respectfully again. "Yes, sir. Again, thank you for your time and your help."

With that, Boca turned and walked away from Lord Salard toward the cave exit. Surprised, Hal and Keershan hurried after her, with Raniel bringing up the rear. The shaking of the ground told Hal that Vilona was also following, probably to make sure that they made it out of the cave safely and did not stick around longer than they should.

Hal tried to get Boca to talk, but she wouldn't answer any of his questions, simply walking as quickly as her long legs would let her.

So Hal fell into silence, though he did look over his shoulder one last time to catch a glimpse of Salard between Vilona's legs.

And saw that the god's head had disappeared.

Yet Hal still felt as if Salard was looking at them, even though he was no longer visible.

Chapter Twenty-Two

"WHAT A PRODUCTIVE MEETING THAT WAS," BOCA FINALLY said ten minutes later, when they emerged from Salard's cave and stood on the side of the winding road they had taken to get up here. The cave's perch offered them an excellent view of the rest of the abode, letting Hal see other angels and pegasuses in the skies overhead, as well as catch glimpses of divine and semi-divine beings walking in the streets below.

But Hal's attention was fixed primarily on Boca and what she just said. "Productive? Salard didn't seem like he wanted to cooperate with us. I felt like we were talking to a stone wall half the time."

"But he gave us some very important information about the Final Relic," Keershan objected. "I know that's perhaps not exactly relevant to the investigation, but——"

"Actually, Keershan, it is," Boca said, interrupting Keershan as if he wasn't talking. "Everything he told us, even the bits about the Final Relic, was entirely relevant to our investigation and has helped me focus the investigation in the right direction."

Raniel, standing a few feet from Hal and the others like he didn't want to be seen associating with them, gave Boca a puzzled look. "And how, pray tell, does trivia about a trivial item such as the Final Relic help you identify who killed Shirataka, witch?"

Boca folded her arms in front of her chest. "Firstly, we learned that Shirataka was worried about Kryo Kardia. This tells me that at least some of the gods are paying attention to what is going on in the mortal world. More importantly, she was worried enough about Kryo Kardia to want to do something about him."

"But she didn't," Hal said. "She was killed before she could talk to anyone other than Salard."

"And Demo," Boca said. "At this point, I am almost certainly convinced that Shirataka spoke to Demo at some point yesterday or possibly this morning before she got murdered. In fact, I would even go as far as to say that Shirataka likely would have brought up Kryo Kardia at the gods' annual convocation, if she had been able to attend."

"Why do you think that?" Keershan said.

Boca gestured at the city. "Because I think that whoever killed Shirataka did so in order to keep Kryo Kardia off the gods' radar. If the gods do not know about, or take seriously, the threat that Kryo Kardia poses to the world, then they will not oppose him."

Hal's eyes widened as the implications of Boca's statement sank in. "Are you saying that Kryo Kardia killed Shirataka?"

"Or someone working for him did," Boca said. "I

sincerely doubt Kryo Kardia is in the abode. He's far more likely to have someone on the inside who did it for him."

"If you are again accusing the gods of having killed one of their own—" Raniel began.

Boca snorted. "Of course not. Salard already gave us another suspect: A mortal or semidivine being carrying a weapon with divine energy in it. By using such a weapon, even a mortal could kill a god. Right, Hal?"

Hal, thinking back to when he and Keershan killed the Nameless One using the power of the Final Relic, nodded once. "Yes, that's right, Boca. I see where you are going with this."

"We both do," Keershan said. "You're thinking that the murderer is either a mortal or semidivine being living within the abode, secretly working for Kryo Kardia to make sure that the gods do not learn about his crimes and punish him or intervene in some way, right?"

"On the dot," Boca said. "You two are smarter than you look. You, on the other hand, are not."

Boca addressed Raniel with her last sentence, earning a death glare from the angel. Hal noticed Raniel's hand tremble on the handle of his sword, but he still refrained from drawing it.

Must be pretty disciplined, Hal thought, *which I can respect, even if he is a bit of an idiot like Boca said.*

"So … where do we go from here?" Keershan said, looking around at everyone in confusion. "What are we supposed to do with this information?"

Boca held up a finger. "First, we need that report on Shirataka's body. Raniel, I believe you said you would handle that."

"I said I would send someone to do it for us," Raniel

replied, "which I already have. I am still awaiting their report back."

"Why do we need that autopsy report?" Hal said. "How will that help our investigation?"

Boca wagged a finger at Hal. "I am hoping to find evidence of the weapon used to kill her. We still do not know what murder weapon was used to kill Shirataka. If we can narrow it down to one kind of weapon, then that will give us an idea about how Shirataka may have perished and what divine weapons to look for."

Hal nodded. "Got it. Raniel, when will that report be ready?"

Raniel folded his arms in front of his chest. "Probably not for another half hour, hour or so."

"That's fine," Boca said. "In the meantime, there's another god we should pay a visit to."

"Demo," Keershan said. "Right?"

"Correct," Boca said, "although I am surprised you managed to guess that right off the bat, Keershan."

Keershan shrugged. "Given how Demo is one of the two people who last saw Shirataka before her death, he just seemed like the most logical person to talk to next."

Hal looked at Raniel. "You're the expert on gods here, Raniel. Where does Demo stay in the abode while he is visiting?"

Raniel scowled. "No one knows."

Hal glared at Raniel. "That's not a funny joke."

"It's not a joke," Raniel insisted. "I'm serious. Demo is such a mysterious deity that no one even knows where he stays during his visits to the city. The most likely place would be the temple itself, as it has hundreds of extra rooms for visiting gods and is where most of the other gods who do not live in the abode stay, but even that is not certain."

"As much as I'd love to talk to Demo, Raniel is correct that he's very difficult to get a hold of due to his reclusive nature," Boca said. "But there is one god who should be easier to find: Gotcham Nubor."

"Gotcham Nubor?" Keershan repeated. "I believe you mentioned him before. Wasn't he the god who you thought could help us with Kryo Kardia in the first place?"

Raniel's eyes widened. "Gotcham Nubor? There is no way in hell that Gotcham Nubor would *ever* speak with you, woman. Not after what you did during your last visit."

Boca rolled her eyes. "Please, Raniel. That was thousands of years ago. Even Gotcham doesn't hold a grudge *that* long."

Hal stepped between Boca and Raniel before an argument could break out between them. "Hold your horses! Boca, you still haven't told us who Gotcham Nubor is, how he could help us, or what you did during your last visit to the abode. If we are finally going to meet this Gotcham Nubor guy, I think we deserve to know that much."

Keershan nodded. "I agree with Hal. If we're going to be your partners in this investigation, then we need to know *everything*, lady."

Boca sighed in annoyance, rubbing the back of her neck. "All right. I suppose you two deserve to know the truth, especially if we are going to meet Gotcham Nubor in person. Once we see him, you will find out the truth anyway. Might as well hear it from me first so you aren't entirely blindsided. What would you like to know first?"

Hal put his hands on his hips. "First off, who *is* Gotcham Nubor? I've never heard of him."

"He's a god," Boca said, "but not just any god. He is the king of the gods, the strongest, oldest, and mightiest god of all. Every other god is subject to him, including the Nameless One."

Keershan gave Boca a look of deep respect. "Wow. Do you mean you are on speaking terms with the king of the gods? That's impressive."

Raniel snarled. "She *was* on speaking terms with him, dragon. Not anymore. Not after what she did."

Hal pursed his lips. "Then I guess that's the second thing I want to know: What did you do to Gotcham Nubor that made everyone in the abode seemingly hate you?"

Boca brushed a strand of gray hair out of her blue eyes. "I was his lover. And then I broke his heart cleanly in two."

Chapter Twenty-Three

"You were Gotcham Nubor's *lover*?" Keershan said a few minutes later as they walked down the road to the abode, away from Salard's cave above. "As in—?"

"Physically making love, yes," Boca said in a slightly bored voice. "Do you want the details?"

Keershan shook his head wildly. "Of course not! I just … wow. When you said you knew him, I didn't know that you meant you *knew* him, as well."

Boca shrugged. "It was a long, long time ago. We haven't spoken since my last visit here."

Hal, still trying to process this revelation himself, said, "I don't understand. How can gods and humans, well—?"

"Gods can make physical bodies for themselves that are … physically compatible with human bodies," Raniel said, walking just behind them, a look of absolute disgust on his face. "Every now and then, a particularly beautiful or hand-some mortal will catch a deity's eye, and they will go after them. It's disgraceful, if you ask me."

"No one did," Boca said idly.

Keershan looked at Boca again, disbelief etched over his dragon features. "I take it Gotcham Nubor approached you first?"

Boca laughed. "Nope. I seduced him."

Hal gasped. "You seduced the king of the gods?"

Boca gave Hal a dismissive look. "I didn't always look like a crooked old woman, Norath. At one point, I, too, was young and beautiful and very experienced in the ways of making love. Frankly, I found him only slightly more difficult to seduce than the average mortal man, and only because it took him five minutes to make a body suitable for the physical part."

Hal felt sick just thinking about Boca and Gotcham Nubor together, so he did not. "But … why? Why would you even *do* such a thing?"

"And then you went and broke his heart?" Keershan added. "That doesn't seem very nice."

Boca shook her head. "I was being overly dramatic when I described how our relationship ended. The truth is, I simply got what I wanted from Gotcham Nubor and didn't see any reason to stick around longer than needed. That got Gotcham *very* angry with me and is what got me kicked out of the abode the first time."

"It must not have been too bad, whatever you did," Hal said, "otherwise you probably wouldn't have been allowed to come back into the city, right?"

"Wrong," Raniel said. He glared at Boca. "You should not have been allowed in here, woman. I don't know how you even got into the city in the first place, but—"

"Gotcham still has a soft spot for me," Boca interrupted him. "Even though I broke his heart completely, I don't think Gotcham ever got over me completely. If I had to guess, he probably still hopes I'll come back to him. That's why I was able to enter the abode, despite my less than cordial exit the first time."

Hal narrowed his eyes. "Are you planning to come back to him?"

Boca smiled. "Depends on whether or not that will get us what we want."

"You are planning to deceive the king of the gods himself?" Raniel demanded. He flew over them and landed in their path, forcing them to stop. He drew his sword and pointed its tip just underneath Boca's chin. "For that alone, I ought to stab you right here and now."

Hal, surprised by Raniel's sudden violent action, drew his sword and smacked Raniel's blade away from Boca's neck. "Hey! That's no way to treat an innocent woman who has done nothing wrong yet."

Raniel shot Hal a death glare, his golden eyes glowing in a way Hal did not like. "Innocent woman? This woman is the exact opposite of innocent, Halar Norath. She is guilty of seducing and harming the king of the gods, is planning to deceive said king, and is probably also guilty of Shirataka's murder, just like you!"

Raniel swung his sword at Hal, but Hal blocked the blow. Holding Raniel's sword back, Hal grunted, "The hell are you doing? I thought you were supposed to keep an eye on us, not fight us."

Raniel leaned closer to Hal's face, an angry scowl on his deceptively youthful features. "The gods may not have given me the right to kill you yet, but they didn't say anything about sparing. I am sure the gods will understand once I explain to them that I had to put a mouthy, uppity mortal in his place."

Hal hated to admit it, but Raniel was stronger than he looked, maybe even stronger than him. It took all his strength just to hold the angel back, even with Keershan giving him extra strength via their bond. He wasn't at all sure he would win in a fight against Raniel, especially right now.

"Boys, stop your bickering," Boca said. "Do you want to cause a scene?"

Raniel glared at Boca without letting up on the pressure he was putting on Hal. "Silence, woman. Don't butt into this unless you also want to fight me."

Boca rested her chin in her hand, an amused look on her face. "I'm not much of a fighter myself, so I am afraid I will have to decline that offer. But I do think it would be quite amusing to see a human beat up an angel right in the middle of the abode. I wonder what your fellow angels would think about that."

Raniel snarled. "No human would beat me in a fight. Especially not *this* weakling."

"Weakling—?" Hal repeated.

"If that's the case, then I am sure you will duel Hal *properly*, yes?" Boca said, putting her hands on her hips. "Rather than randomly assaulting him like some silly thug?"

Raniel narrowed his eyes. "I am no thug. I am a member of the Divine Guard. That is a respectable position and title for an angel to have."

"Then act like the respectable angel you are and either challenge Hal to a duel or let him go," Boca said. "The choice is yours, although given how limited our time is, I suggest the latter."

Raniel looked back toward Hal. Hal thought the angel looked like he was going to challenge him to a duel, but to his surprise, Raniel pulled his sword away from Hal, stepped back, and sheathed it in one smooth motion.

"I don't need to waste my time and energy dueling a mortal," Raniel grunted, rolling his shoulders. "This isn't even a very good place for a duel, anyway."

Hal, surprised by Raniel's decision, nonetheless sheathed his sword, too. He did it primarily because he noticed some of the other angels passing them had given him a very dirty look while he was holding his sword. That implied to Hal that there was apparently some unspoken social taboo here about walking around with one's weapons drawn, and the last thing Hal wanted was to draw the negative attention of another angry angel.

Raniel looked at the others. "What are you mortals waiting for? If you want to see Gotcham Nubor, we have no time to waste."

Raniel turned and resumed walking down the path, stomping his foot every step of the way. After a moment, Hal, Keershan, and Boca followed, though they kept their distance this time.

"Geez, what is his problem?" Keershan said. "I know that Shirataka's death has everyone on edge, but he almost snapped back there."

"In case you hadn't noticed, divine entities tend to be very prideful," Boca said. She patted Hal on the shoulder. "Especially when it comes to dealing with mortals. Raniel didn't want to duel you because he didn't want to risk losing to a mortal in public."

Hal frowned, feeling the soreness in his arms from

where Raniel had pressed against him. "Not sure that was a realistic risk."

"More so than you might think," Boca said. "I once heard a legend that a Dragon Rider was said to have bested an angel in combat right in the town square of the abode. Ever since then, angels have been wary about fighting your kind, despite being stronger than you."

Hal looked at Raniel, who walked with his back toward them, clearly grumbling under his breath. "So Raniel really didn't want to embarrass himself in front of his fellow angels, then."

"Yes," Boca said. "It's all very silly if you ask me, but using the gods' egos against them is the most effective way to manipulate them. Most of my seduction of Gotcham consisted of me complimenting his intelligence and good looks, although it helped that I was his type."

Hal pursed his lips. The more Boca talked, the less and less respect Hal felt for the gods and for divine beings in general. They seemed no better than mortals, at least from what he'd seen of them so far.

Better not say that aloud, though, Hal thought. *Otherwise I probably will get in trouble.*

"Anyway, I assume Gotcham Nubor is in the temple?" Keershan said, glancing at the huge building built into the mountain.

Boca nodded. "Of course. The temple also doubles as his royal palace. If Gotcham is anywhere, it has to be there."

Hal supposed Boca was the expert here, and so he followed Boca down the path toward the temple.

At the same time, however, Hal found himself wondering if the story of the Dragon Rider defeating an angel was true or not, and, if so, who was that Dragon Rider and why had he or she dueled with the angel in the first place.

But Hal figured that would be a story for another time. For now, they had an audience with the king of the gods himself.

Chapter Twenty-Four

THROUGHOUT SURRELS'S LIFE, HE HAD DONE A LOT OF things and seen even more. He had been a soldier in the Malarsan Army, fighting on the front lines against the dragons during the Dragon War. He had then served as a member of the Black Soldier Corps, undergoing clandestine missions for the king and queen of Malarsan, doing a variety of licit and illicit actions for the safety of the country.

Then Surrels had been drafted into a rebellion against the queen of Malarsan against his will, only to discover that Queen Marial had been just as bad as the rebels had said she was, and voluntarily joined the rebellion to oust her from the throne. The rebellion had been successful.

That successful rebellion then catapulted Surrels to the position of General of the Malarsan Army, where he then found himself manipulated by an evil prince into murdering one of his best friends, nearly alienating the rest of his friends and making the kingdom itself hate him as a result.

But none of them came close in weirdness to his current role.

Pretending to be a corpse being taken to the capital for its final burial.

Lying inside the coffin, feeling every bump in the road that jostled the carriage his coffin was being transported in, Surrels was wondering if allying with the Dead Dragons had indeed been a wise decision.

One week ago, Surrels, Kendo, and Stebo had sat down with Mama Dragon, the leader of the Dead Dragons, to work out a plan to break into the capital without Tenka or his men knowing. Mama Dragon had promised to give them access to the full resources of the Dead Dragon Syndicate. She had even promised that they would get all three of them into the city without Tenka or his loyalists being aware.

That seemed like a big promise to Surrels, but he had agreed to their demands anyway, because they really had no other choice at this point. Security around the city had supposedly been heightened in preparation for the coronation of Tenka to the throne, meaning they certainly couldn't get in on their own.

And that doesn't take into account the demonic servants who work for Tenka, either, Surrels thought.

Of course, Tenka's association with the demons was still not public knowledge, so Surrels doubted that there would be any posted at any of the city gates looking for them. Most likely, it would just be human guards using human methods to make sure no one was sneaking into the city who wasn't supposed to be.

Hence the coffin. It was apparently a common practice for the Dead Dragons to use coffins to transport illegal goods, because once a coffin was sealed with a corpse inside, the laws of the land forbid even the government from opening it and looking inside. Mama Dragon had insisted that they had used this method several times to successfully transport their illicit products into and out of the capital without raising suspicions from the guards.

Did it work?

Surrels couldn't tell. The coffin he lay in was practically soundproof. While he could feel the bumps of the road, as well as stops and starts of the cart upon which his coffin was being transported, Surrels couldn't see anything. Any noises he could hear were dampened so much that he could barely make out who was saying what to who or if anyone was talking at all.

Even worse, Surrels couldn't tell where Kendo and Stebo were. They had been put inside separate coffins, mostly because the coffins that the Dead Dragons used were not big enough for multiple people. Not that Surrels was complaining. Given how he barely fit inside the casket himself, Surrels couldn't even imagine how cramped it would have been if his son and Stebo had been stuffed inside with him.

I hope they are all right, Surrels thought. *Especially Stebo.*

The poor young boy seemed to be holding up from what Surrels had seen of him, but Surrels could tell that Stebo was still struggling to make sense of everything that had happened to him since his foster parents had been killed by Tenka's demon. Surrels had tried to be of some comfort to the boy, but since Surrels didn't consider himself a very comforting person, he often wasn't sure what to say to Stebo.

He reminds me a bit of how I was when I was his age, Surrels thought. *And how Kendo was, too.*

Over the past week since allying with the Dead Dragons, Surrels had been slowly regaining more and more memories of his time with his family. Most of them had to do with either Kendo or Lila when they were about Stebo's age, but every now and then Surrels would remember things involving Tonya, his wife, or other situations that had nothing to do with his children.

Why Stebo's mere presence brought back so many memories, Surrels still didn't know. Anna, his memory mage, probably would have been able to tell him, but since Anna believed him to be the assassin of Old Snow like everyone else in the kingdom other than his close friends and allies, Surrels couldn't just ask her about it.

Regardless, Surrels was finally starting to think that perhaps his quest to regain his memories wasn't going to be entirely fruitless after all. Stebo might have even been just what he needed in order to remember who he was.

What Surrels would do with those memories, he wasn't sure. And frankly, at this point, it didn't even matter. Until they stopped Tenka from ascending to the throne, Surrels would worry about that later.

Without warning, the carriage stopped, the abrupt stop jostling Surrels. For a moment, Surrels feared that perhaps their cart had been stopped at the city gates by the guards, that perhaps the guards would realize there was something off, and that their entire plan would fall apart as a result.

That was when Surrels heard someone striking the coffin on the outside with a hard metal object. *Thunk, thunk, thunk …* it was a steady rhythm, almost in tune with Surrels's heartbeat.

Damn it, Surrels thought. He reached for his sword, before remembering that he had given it to one of the Dead Dragons because there was no need for him to carry his sword in the coffin.

This wasn't good. Without his sword or any other weapon he could use, Surrels's odds of escaping from the city guards were not particularly encouraging. He just prepared himself to jump out and run as fast as he could away from the city. He didn't know if he'd be able to outrun the guards, but it wasn't like he had any decent backup plans.

Finally, without warning, the lid of the coffin burst open, and before Surrels could jump out, Stebo's young face peered inside, a concerned look on his face.

"Surrels?" Stebo said. "Are you okay?"

Blinking into the light, Surrels sat up, rubbing his eyes. "Stebo? What—? Where are we?"

"We made it into the city without alerting the guards," Kendo's voice said to his right. "It went as smoothly as butter. Right, Argon?"

"Right you are, young man," said the familiar boisterous voice of Argon, also to his right. "Those dumb guards really bought the poor widow act from Catol here."

A distinctly feminine *humph* was the only sound in response to Argon's statement.

His eyes finally adjusting to the light, Surrels looked around at his new surroundings.

They were inside a big, dusty, mostly empty warehouse. Aside from a few stacked crates here and there, the warehouse looked like it hadn't been used in years. The windows near the ceiling were cracked or busted out, a heavy heat making Surrels sweat even more than he had while inside the coffin.

Rubbing the sweat off his forehead, Surrels looked to his right to see Kendo standing nearby, arms folded in front of his chest. To his left was Argon, the patch-eyed Dead Dragon from before, and Catol, the young woman who had threatened to slit his throat back in Faifa, who looked quite bored with the proceedings. A small wooden table stood behind them, though it was currently bare.

"Where are we?" Surrels said. "I don't recognize this place."

"Officially, it's a condemned warehouse in the shipping district of the capital, set to be demolished any day now," Argon said. He cracked a grin. "Unofficially, it's one of our many less-than-legal warehouses where the syndicate stores and distributes our goods. This particular warehouse has quite a lot of illegal weapons, though you might find a crate or two of the really good drugs hidden here and there."

Surrels rubbed his eyes again and frowned. "Never in my life did I imagine I would be spending time inside a Dead Dragon warehouse. And I hope to never be here again."

"That's an odd way of thanking us for risking our lives to get you and the boy in here," said Catol coldly. She glanced at Stebo. "I honestly don't know what the Mama sees in you."

Stebo shrank slightly while Kendo said, "Lay off him, Catol. If I remember correctly, you weren't much younger than him when the Mama took you in."

Catol rolled her eyes. "Whatever. As long as I don't have to babysit him, I'll do what the Mama wants."

Surrels decided that he did not care for Catol. Then

again, he also did not care for the Dead Dragons in general, other than Kendo, who was his son. He noticed two other coffins on the floor nearby, including a child-sized one he assumed was the one that Stebo had been transported in.

Jumping out of the coffin, Surrels said, "So the guards didn't even suspect us?"

"Not a word," Argon said. He clasped a hand on Catol's shoulder. "Of course, they could never say no to a poor, pretty widow coming to the capital to lay to rest her dad, husband, *and* young son, who all died in a boating accident in Faifa not even a week ago. They are to be buried in their family tomb in the Capital Graveyard, where they will presumably be given proper burial rites by a priest to ensure that they join the gods in the afterlife."

Surrels frowned. "Was that really the story you gave the guards?"

Catol sniffled. "Yes. I'm really good at crying on command. Especially when those big, mean guards start asking invasive questions about my background. I was very stressed."

"It was quite impressive, and this isn't even the first time I've seen her use it," Argon added. "She is a true actress."

Catol glared at Argon. "I'm still not going to sleep with you, you dirty old man."

Argon sighed. "A man can try, can't he?"

Surrels shook his head. "How far is this warehouse from the coronation?"

Argon pulled out a map of the capital and ran his finger down it. "Let's see … we're about six blocks northwest of Castle Lamor, where the coronation is scheduled to take place this afternoon."

Kendo glanced out the windows at the sun. "Looks like

we've got a couple of hours before the ceremony starts, so we should have plenty of time to get there in time to ruin Tenka's day."

Surrels pursed his lips. "I hope so, but how are we going to travel the streets without being seen? In case you all forgot, I am currently the most wanted 'criminal' in Malarsan. There are wanted posters of me up all over the city. Not to mention that the guards are going to be looking for me specifically, and probably Kendo and Stebo as well."

Argon suddenly threw Surrels a dark cloak. "Just wear this cloak. It will hide your features and make people over-look you."

Surrels held up the smooth cloak, feeling the cotton under his fingers. "Is this a magical cloak or something?"

Argon shook his head. "Nope. Just a regular old cloak. No magic needed."

Kendo stepped forward. "My father's questions bring up an excellent point, however, which is that we need to go over the plan before we leave the warehouse."

Catol pouted. "We already went over the plan in Faifa. Do we really need to go over it again?"

"Do you *remember* the plan?" Kendo asked.

Catol pouted even more, prompting Kendo to say, "Exactly. Anyway, it helps to review the plan so we can all have it fresh in our minds when we leave this place."

Kendo grabbed Argon's map of the city and spread it out on the small wooden table from before. Everyone gathered around the wooden table, including Stebo, who was just tall enough to be able to see the map like everyone else.

Kendo pointed at the center of the city, where Castle Lamor was. "This is Castle Lamor, where the coronation is scheduled to happen today."

Surrels cocked his head to the side. "Isn't the coronation actually happening *here*, though, since it is a public event?"

Surrels pointed at the square in front of Castle Lamor, prompting Kendo to say, "Yes. That is indeed the actual location of the public ceremonies. As you can see, there are three alleyways connecting to the square in front of the castle, aside from the main roads and streets, of course."

Surrels nodded. Having lived in the capital himself for many years, Surrels was intimately familiar with its layout. "Yes. Are those the same alleyways we are going to use to sneak into the coronation without being seen?"

Kendo nodded. "Of course. They are the easiest, most direct routes into the square, not counting the main streets, which we can't take for obvious reasons."

Stebo held up a hand. "I forgot. Why do we need to know where all of these alleys are?"

Kendo gestured at everyone around the table. "That is because we are not going to enter the coronation as a group. To decrease our odds of getting caught, we are going to split up and approach from three different directions at once."

Kendo pointed at himself and Catol. "Catol and I will enter from the western alleyway, while Argon and Stebo will enter from the eastern alley. Father, that means you will enter from the northern alley by yourself."

Surrels whipped his head toward Kendo again in surprise. "Why is Stebo going with Argon? I thought he was supposed to travel with me."

"Change o' plans, Surrels," Argon said. He scratched his beard. "Because your face is known to Tenka and mine isn't, we figured that Tenka will be looking out for you specifically, thinking you might have the boy. He probably won't suspect Stebo of being with me, since I don't have any particular connection to the boy outside of this mission."

Surrels furrowed his brow. "Who is this 'we' who figured this?"

"Mama Dragon, of course," Kendo said. "She and I had a few private discussions after you and Stebo went to bed after the party last week."

"And you didn't think to share these decisions with me because—?" Surrels said.

Kendo smiled. "Because Mama Dragon hates having her eggs in one basket. But don't worry. We'll only pull out the secret plans if the main plan fails, which it shouldn't."

"Aye," Argon said. "I fully expect our plan to go off without a hitch. And don't worry. I'll keep the boy safe."

As irrational as it was for him to feel this way, Surrels didn't like leaving Stebo with Argon. He knew that Argon would keep Stebo safe until the coronation, but Surrels felt very protective of the young boy and disliked the idea of letting Stebo out of his sight for even a moment.

On the other hand, Mama Dragon's logic made a lot of sense to Surrels. The fact was that he was indeed the most wanted member of their group. The city guards were likely on high alert for him, and if someone saw him and Stebo walking together, then that would be game over for all of them.

Still, Surrels was now sure that allying with the Dead Dragons was not a wise decision. It was obvious that Mama Dragon didn't see Surrels as an equal worthy of consideration in important discussions and decisions.

But we have no choice, Surrels reminded himself. *And besides, the alternative is much worse.*

"Okay," Surrels said, though not without more than a hint of reluctance in his voice. "I'll go by myself, then."

"What do we do when we get to the coronation?" said Catol.

"Simple," Kendo said. He gestured at Stebo. "This is where Stebo comes in. Argon and Stebo will step out into the square, where we will publicly reveal Stebo's heritage. This will undoubtedly cause a huge uproar in the crowd and probably force the ceremonies to be canceled while the nobles attempt to figure out who has a better claim to the throne."

Surrels frowned even more. "That's all well and good, but we still haven't established how we are going to prove Stebo's parentage. What is to stop Tenka from simply accusing us of lying? It would be our word against his, and right now, neither the nobles nor the public is especially likely to take our word seriously."

"That is where I come in," Fralia's voice said from within the shadows of the warehouse.

Fralia stepped out into the light from the sun's rays spreading through the warehouse's windows. She wore simple blue mage's robes and carried a thick, dusty-looking tome under her right arm.

"Fralia?" Surrels said in surprise. "When did you get here?"

Fralia coughed, perhaps because of how dusty the warehouse was. "Just a few minutes ago, though I over-heard your discussion about proving Stebo's heritage."

Surrels looked around at the others. "Am I the only one who didn't know that Fralia would be meeting up with us here?"

"Yes," Kendo said with a nod. "It was another thing

Mama Dragon and I discussed. Honestly, Father, you went to bed way too early. The really interesting discussions happened *after* you and Stebo went to bed."

Surrels pursed his lips but said nothing to that. He just looked at Fralia and said, "You know of a way to prove Stebo's heritage?"

Fralia nodded. She lifted up a book. "Yes. This is an old magical book called *Blood Magic*. Normally, it's housed in the Forbidden Section of the Capital City Magical Library, but as current archmage of the academy, I can get it whenever I want."

"*Blood Magic* sounds like an evil title," Surrels said, looking at the old book warily. "I assume you had a good reason for picking it up?"

Fralia shuddered and looked at the book again. "Yes. There is a reason it's kept in the Forbidden Section and available only to the archmage. It goes deep into black magic, including how to speak with demons. I've read a lot of things in here that will probably haunt my dreams for as long as I live."

Surrels gulped. "Demons, you say? Given how we know Tenka is working with the demons right now, does it have any useful information about how to fight them?"

Fralia shook her head. "Unfortunately, no. It only covers talking to them. But that's not important right now. What is important is that there is a spell in this book which can prove a person's heritage beyond a shadow of a doubt."

Fralia walked up to the table, placed the book on it, and opened it up to a page somewhere in the middle. Pointing at a page, Fralia said, "This is the spell."

Surrels leaned toward the page, as did everyone else, squinting his eyes to read the rather tiny text while sniffing the old parchment the text was written upon. "*Communing with the Spirit of the Departed via Blood*? Sounds like a mouthful."

"What does it mean, miss mage?" Stebo said, looking at Fralia.

Fralia smiled kindly at Stebo. "It means that we will be able to talk to your real parents using your blood. We will be able to make their spirits appear in front of everyone, thereby confirming your heritage and making it impossible for anyone to dispute."

"Seriously?" Surrels said. "That's amazing, if true. Would we really be able to talk to Old Snow again?"

Fralia glanced at the book. "As I said, we should be able to do so, but I haven't tested it yet, so I can't say for sure."

"But you said it would require my blood," Stebo said, rubbing his hands together anxiously. "I don't want to get hurt."

Fralia rubbed Stebo's head affectionately. "Don't worry. It doesn't require much blood to work. Just a simple prick of your index finger ought to be enough for our purposes."

Stebo still looked uncertain, but he said, "Okay. I guess I can do that."

Kendo slapped his hands together, catching everyone's attention. "All right, everyone! Now that everyone knows the plan, as well as Fralia's role in it, it's time to put the plan into action. The goal is to get Stebo to the public square just in time for the coronation ceremony, at which point Fralia will use her new spell to make Old Snow's spirit appear and confirm Stebo's parentage. Any questions?"

Surrels looked around at the others, but no one spoke up. Even Stebo wore an expression of determination on his young face, as if he also understood the gravity of the situation.

Kendo smiled. "Great. Then let's cause some profitable chao—I mean, let's save the kingdom and all that."

Argon bowed toward everyone. "May the gods protect us all."

Catol rolled her eyes. "Whatever. Let's just get this over with."

Surrels nodded. Like Catol, he also hoped that the situation would be done sometime within the next hour.

Although knowing my luck, things are going to get very sticky very soon, Surrels thought. *I just hope we can handle it.*

Chapter Twenty-Five

AN HOUR LATER, THE PARTY SPLIT UP. KENDO AND CATOL went to the eastern alley, per the plan, while a hooded Argon and Stebo went to the western alley. As for Fralia, she had to return to the pre-coronation party that all high-ranking officials in the kingdom had to attend. Due to being the archmage of the academy, Fralia had been invited to the festivities and couldn't be late, not unless she wanted to arouse the suspicion of Tenka, at any rate. They didn't want Tenka to suspect that Fralia was part of their plan to prevent his coronation, at least not until it was too late for him to do anything about it.

And finally, Surrels made his way through the back streets and alleyways of the capital to the northern alley. In his mind, he visualized everyone as little dots moving along the map, at first going in seemingly opposite directions, only to converge on a single point—the public square—eventually.

But Surrels did find it challenging to move unseen through the streets of the capital, even when he stuck religiously to the back streets and mostly empty alleys where few people lived. The streets of the capital were packed with people from all over the kingdom, many of them also heading to the coronation, expecting to see the coronation of the first new king of Malarsan in many years. Merchants hawked wares in the streets while street performers put on shows for the visitors to the capital, earning themselves a decent amount of money from what Surrels saw.

The excitement in the air was almost tangible. No doubt everyone was expecting to see a grand coronation ceremony as the handsome young Tenka Hojara was crowned king of Malarsan today.

But Surrels felt less excited and more nervous, for reasons that were obvious. He kept looking over his shoulder, paying careful attention to his surroundings to make sure that no one was following him. It was probably irrational to worry that much about the demons, given how the Dead Dragons had successfully gotten him, Kendo, and Stebo past human security without issue, but he worried nonetheless.

Demons are tricky bastards, Surrels thought, pausing in the shadows of an alleyway to allow a large family to walk the street before him on their way to the coronation before he quickly crossed the street himself into an alley on the opposite side. *They always strike you when you least expect it.*

But Surrels did not run into any demons, guards, or any other obstacles on his way to the coronation. The most tense moment was when he accidentally stumbled over a homeless old man lying on one of the back streets, but the old man didn't even wake up. And if he had, Surrels doubted he would have been sober enough to recognize

Surrels, given the number of empty alcohol bottles spread around the homeless man like flowers in a field.

Soon, Surrels reached the northern alley, just as planned. Hiding behind a couple of trash cans, Surrels peered out at the public square beyond, trying to get a good look at how everything was set up.

The square in front of Castle Lamor was normally quite empty at this time of day. Aside from the castle guards protecting the main gate, the square was not an especially popular spot, mostly because merchants were not allowed to set up shop there and street performing was definitely not allowed there. Only occasionally would people gather, usually for a royal edict from the current monarch, and even then only sometimes.

However, Surrels assumed they must have decided to loosen the restrictions considerably, because Surrels saw several merchants in booths lining the perimeter of the square. As well, a large stage had been constructed in the center of the square, although it was currently empty. Still, Surrels identified the stage as the location where the coronation itself would soon take place.

Hundreds of people gathered in front of the stage, chatting and talking loudly with each other. Surrels spotted walking merchants holding boxes and selling what looked like snacks and drinks to the spectators, which didn't surprise Surrels, as the coronation hadn't started yet and many of these people were probably very hungry.

Heck, I'm hungry at the moment, Surrels thought, rubbing his stomach and sniffing the scent of fried food in the air. *I could go for a chicken breast on a stick right about now.*

Then Surrels shook his head. *Focus. Don't let your appetite distract you from your very important mission.*

Due to the massive crowds of people, Surrels couldn't see Kendo, Catol, Argon, or especially Stebo. But he knew they were all probably close by, waiting for the right opportunity to do their part of the plan.

Unless they got caught on their way here, Surrels thought. *By demons.*

Surrels shook his head again. Thinking such thoughts was not going to be very helpful right now. Surrels needed to focus on what was happening before him, not worry about things he had no control over.

Even so, Surrels couldn't stop worrying about Stebo in particular, who was the most vulnerable out of all of them. Argon may have promised to keep Stebo safe, but such promises meant little when they were going up against the most powerful man in Malarsan, who also had demons at his beck and call.

But Surrels's worrying was interrupted by the blaring of what sounded like dozens of trumpets at once. The blasting of the trumpets completely overwhelmed the noises made by the crowds, causing the spectators to turn their attention to Castle Lamor's main gate.

The main gate had apparently already opened at some point. A troop of trumpeters marched out, their trumpets blasting the Malarsan national anthem at full volume. Behind them came a veritable army of drummers, followed by a smaller army of tuba players, and then a few violinists. Yet somehow their music, despite coming from vastly different instruments, flowed together in a surprisingly harmonious way, making Surrels feel very patriotic.

But Surrels didn't let himself get caught up in the music. He stood very still, watching and waiting for Tenka to make his appearance.

It seemed, however, that Surrels would have to wait a while longer, because after the parade came the entire court of the Malarsan royal family. Dozens of well-dressed members of the nobility streamed through the gate in neat, orderly rows. A few of the elderly nobles had to ride on horses or carriages, but otherwise, it was a very dignified group. The nobles made their way onto the stage, each one taking a seat on the empty chairs that stood on the stage.

Among them was Fralia, who walked with the other master mages and academy faculty. She had seemingly ditched her blue robes for white mage robes that looked rather pretty on her. Though Fralia was smiling and waving like the other nobles and high-ranking officials, Surrels noticed her eyes scan the crowd, probably looking for him and the others.

Can't show ourselves yet, though, Surrels thought, kneeling lower behind the trash cans in the dark alley to avoid being seen. *Just a few more minutes and then we can strike.*

Next was the military leadership, who Surrels recognized easily enough from his time in the Malarsan Army. It burned him to see the men and women who he had worked with for years showing up in their nice clothes to the coronation of an evil man who had ruined his life and tried to kill him, but Surrels had to remind himself that they probably did not know about Tenka's true nature or that Surrels was innocent.

If everything goes according to plan, however, then everyone *will know what Tenka truly is soon enough,* Surrels thought, clasping the hilt of his sword hidden underneath his cloak.

Finally, once all of the nobles were seated, a portly man in white-and-black robes who Surrels recognized as a priest of the gods stepped to the front of the stage. Raising his hands into the air, the priest said, in a voice that seemed to be magnified by magic, "Citizens of the kingdom of Malarsan! It is with great pleasure and even greater honor that I will begin the coronation ceremonies for the new king of Malarsan. His Majesty, Noble Tenka Hojara, the nephew of King Rikas and Queen Marial, shall shortly join us on stage. But first, let me lead us in prayer to the gods for their blessing on Noble Hojara before he appears."

The priest lowered his head and clasped his hands together, as did the nobles, the military leadership, the master mages, and everyone else in the crowds watching the scene. The priest started praying out loud, but Surrels—who had never been a particularly religious or spiritual man—paid little attention. He was just waiting for Tenka to appear so they could begin the next phase of the plan.

A shadow suddenly flashed by out of the corner of his eyes, making Surrels start and whirl around, thinking it was a demon.

But it turned out to be a simple pigeon, which flapped by overhead, disappearing over the top of a nearby building.

Breathing a sigh of relief, Surrels turned around just in time to hear the last words of the priest's prayer.

"… And O great gods, we ask for endless blessings for our incoming king and this nation," the priest finished. "In the names of every god in the abode, we pray, amen."

That last word echoed across the crowd as everyone finished their prayers.

Surrels tensed. *This is it. Tenka should be showing up any second now.*

As if on cue, the trumpeters resumed blasting their trumpets in the air. A white coach, drawn by equally white horses, emerged from within the walls of Castle Lamor and rolled across the bridge to the main gate. The white cart came to a stop at the foot of the stage, where the driver hopped from his seat and rushed over to the passenger door. Pulling open the door, the driver bowed deeply as a man in white stepped out.

It was Tenka. Although Tenka had traded in his normal dark cloak for snow-white robes lined with gold, Surrels would recognize that smirk anywhere. The young noble waved at the crowds as he ascended to the platform, prompting cheers and shrieks of joy from the civilians, especially from the young women in attendance.

"He's so handsome," Surrels overheard a young woman near his alley say to another young woman who was probably her friend.

"Yeah," said the other young woman with a nod. She sighed. "Imagine being *his* queen."

Surrels shuddered. If those women could only know how terrible Tenka actually was, then they probably wouldn't find him very attractive anymore.

Once Tenka reached the stage itself, he walked over to stand beside the priest, who was much shorter than him.

"Hello, citizens of the kingdom of Malarsan!" Tenka called out, his voice also seemingly magically magnified to well beyond its usual output. "I am beyond honored to see such a large crowd for this momentous, even historical, event. As your new king of Malarsan, I promise to lead the country with the full wisdom and knowledge of all the monarchs who lived before me, including my beloved aunt and uncle, who passed away far too soon."

Surrels scowled. Tenka may or may not have been upset about Marial's demise, but he was definitely not at all sad about Old Snow's death. Surrels felt sick just listening to the arrogant young man pretend to care about Old Snow.

Even worse, the crowd seemed to be gobbling up his lies. The two young women before him made sympathetic sounds, with one of the women saying to the other, "Hasn't he had such a hard life? I don't know what I'd do if I lost both my aunt and uncle one after the other like he did."

The other woman sighed. "I wish I could comfort him."

Surrels pursed his lips. He had to restrain himself to keep him from shouting at the ignorant women. Settling himself, Surrels tried to focus more on the priest and Tenka rather than the crowd.

"Yes, their deaths were truly tragic," the priest agreed, "but let us not dwell on such sad thoughts. Today is a day of celebration and joy, for we shall now have a proper king on the throne. Today will be the start of a new era for the kingdom of Malarsan."

"I couldn't agree more, Priest Om," Tenka said. "Before we begin the proceedings, however, do you mind if I give a few words to the crowd? I wrote up a short speech before coming here that I wish to share with the people of this great kingdom."

Priest Om appeared slightly taken aback by Tenka's request, but nodded. "Of course, sir, of course. I am sure that everyone is dying to hear what you intend to do as king of Malarsan."

I know I am, Surrels thought as the crowd spontaneously erupted into cheers, as well as chants demanding that Tenka speak.

Waving his hands at the crowd to quiet them down, Tenka said, "Do not worry. This speech won't take long. I'll be done in five minutes, maybe less. Then we can move on to the actual coronation itself."

Stepping forward, Tenka looked across the crowd with a kind expression. Surrels, however, pulled his hood slightly farther over his face and hid even more behind the trash cans. He sincerely doubted that Tenka could see him from up there, but he didn't want to risk Tenka seeing him before he had to reveal himself.

Evidently, it worked, because Tenka then shifted his attention to the crowd as a whole, saying, "Ever since I was a young boy, I have dreamed of sitting on the throne of Malarsan as king. But I always assumed I would gain that role once I was old and gray myself, as 'old and gray' seemed like requirements to becoming a monarch to me when I was a young child in my uncle's court."

The crowd chuckled at Tenka's comments, although Surrels didn't find them funny in the slightest, if only because he knew exactly how Tenka had managed to get such power at such a young age.

Still speaking, Tenka continued. "But then tragedy struck. First, my aunt, Queen Marial, turned out to be a slave to the demons. She perished at the hands of the vicious demons a little over a year ago today in a series of tragic events that are too long to go into here. Suffice to say, however, that the queen's demise struck a terrible blow to the kingdom, leaving us without a leader.

"That is, until my equally beloved uncle, King Rikas, took the throne again and restored order and peace to the kingdom, even signing a peace treaty with the Clawfoot Tribe of Dragon Valley to end the decade-long Dragon War. But then tragedy struck again and he was murdered in cold blood by a man who he thought was his friend over a week ago today. Once again, the kingdom of Malarsan was left without a leader."

Surrels wanted to run up onto the stage and punch Tenka out. Even though he had been aware that Tenka was spreading these lies about him, that did not make them any easier to listen to, much less accept.

But again, the time wasn't right. If Surrels ran out there right now, he would just draw a target on his back. He had to wait on Argon and Stebo to appear, and then for Fralia to do her magic. Literally, in this case.

So Surrels continued listening to Tenka's speech.

Tenka sighed and gazed down at his feet. "Truthfully, I had expected to ascend to the throne in much happier times. But fate never gives us a choice when greatness is thrust upon us. And right now, fate has thrust greatness upon me in a time that may be the most difficult time that the kingdom has faced since the First Dragon War. I think you all know what I am talking about."

Surrels didn't, but he also didn't say that aloud. He gazed at the confused looks among the crowds, who were also anxiously hanging onto every word Tenka spoke.

Tenka raised his head again, steel in his gaze. "The Glaci Empire. Although the Glaci Empire has provided us with great support since the demise of Queen Marial, that support comes attached to many strings. Such as risking becoming entirely dependent on the empire for aid, for example. And I have every reason to believe that Emperor Kryo Kardia seeks to annex Malarsan into the Glaci Empire, taking away our sovereignty and reducing our proud kingdom to a mere vassal state.

"But once I am king, I will make sure that doesn't happen. For the first time in his life, Kryo Kardia will be told no, you may not have that, this is not yours, go away. And if he doesn't like that, then he will finally know what it feels like for the rest of us mortals when we do not get what we want."

More cheering from the crowd, which Surrels could not exactly disagree with himself. He was no fan of Kryo Kardia or the Glaci Empire himself, but frankly, he suspected that Tenka would not be a much better or less oppressive ruler than Kryo Kardia.

Tenka's hands balled into fists. "Yet the greatest threats to a nation are rarely external. The greatest dangers almost always come from within. By that, I mean I have uncovered a conspiracy within the court and the council to not merely oppose my own coronation, but to help the Glaci Empire annex Malarsan and take away our independence."

Shocked whispers spread throughout the crowd like wildfire. Even Surrels found himself interested, leaning forward to hear exactly what Tenka was going to say. He guessed Tenka was going to mention the now-defunct Silver Sun Society, a group of nobles, businessmen, mages, and various other influential individuals in the kingdom who had helped Tenka rise to power but who he now no longer needed.

Tenka told me that he was going to out them as conspirators and have them all executed to solidify his power over the kingdom, Surrels thought. *If he hasn't done that already, I imagine that is what he is going to do now. I would feel sorry for those bastards, but since they actively supported Tenka, I can't say I do.*

"As you all know, it was General Surrels Megat who assassinated Old Snow and broke out of Capital City Prison, all in the same night," Tenka said. "But what you may not know is that Surrels had accomplices. He was no lone wolf. He had the full support of the council, including the support of Archmage Fralia Jeniq, Councilwoman Wilme Irad, and Dragon Rider Anija Ti and her Steed, Rialo."

The crowd exploded into a huge uproar, yelling and screaming and demanding answers. The uproar was so great that Surrels genuinely feared that a riot would happen, and a riot would ruin their plans as much as it would ruin Tenka's coronation.

But Tenka, again displaying an unusual level of control over the crowd, waved his hands again, shouting, "I know, I know! This is a terrible revelation with many shocking implications for the kingdom, but it is indeed true."

"True?" Fralia spoke up suddenly, her voice also louder than normal. "Noble Hojara, what are you talking about? You do realize I am sitting right here, don't you? Do you think I am just going to sit here while you blatantly accuse me of sedition with no evidence?"

Tenka turned to face Fralia, an angry expression on his face. "Do not feign ignorance, Fralia. It is well-known that you and Surrels were close friends and allies. How else could Surrels have escaped from prison, if not for your magical aid? And were you not present at the very same dinner where King Rikas was assassinated? Did your magic not fail to detect Surrels's own magical weapon?"

Fralia gulped. "I … I …"

"And where did Surrels even get his hands on such a weapon in the first place, anyway?" Tenka continued. "He was not a mage. He had no access to any sort of magic. Not on his own, anyway. But he *was* good friends with the arch-mage herself, who has unlimited access to the magical resources of not just the academy, but the kingdom itself. It wouldn't be difficult for you to have obtained a magical weapon for your friend Surrels without anyone being the wiser. Who would question the archmage's need for a magical weapon, after all?"

Surrels could not believe what he was hearing. He certainly hadn't expected Tenka to turn on Fralia in public like this. Was Tenka already aware of their plan to interrupt the coronation and prevent his rise to the throne? That seemed possible, given how Tenka knew they had Stebo.

But how could he know when and where we'd try to do it? Surrels thought in alarm. *Does he have a mole on the inside? Perhaps a demon following us without our knowledge? Or is he just really good at guessing this sort of thing?*

Surrels, unfortunately, had no time to consider the different possibilities, because two of Tenka's bodyguards rose up and grabbed Fralia. Raising her to her feet, the guards walked Fralia over to Tenka against her protests.

"Let me go!" Fralia said, struggling against the guards. "This is illegal! You haven't even formally arrested me according to the law."

"Plotting to overthrow the Malarsan royal family is also illegal, traitor," Tenka said coldly. He pulled out a knife and held it against Fralia's throat. "But I'm sure you knew the consequences of failure, of course."

"Your Majesty?" Priest Om said, staring at the knife in alarm. "What are you going to do to Archmage Jeniq?"

"Kill her, naturally," Tenka said, glancing at Priest Om. "Do you disagree that traitors and assassins deserve the death penalty?"

Priest Om gulped. "N-No, of course not, sir, but usually there is a trial first."

Tenka shook his head. "We don't have time for a trial."

He gazed across the square at everyone. "Because today, an attempt will be made on my life, and it will be made by Archmage Jeniq herself."

The crowd gasped in shock, including the young women near Surrels.

As for Surrels, he reached for his sword. Although this wasn't how the plan was supposed to go at all, Surrels did not care. He couldn't let Tenka kill Fralia. She was his friend, and he could not live with himself if Tenka got to kill yet another one of his friends because he couldn't stop him.

But it will be damn near impossible to get through the crowd in time to save Fralia, Surrels thought, looking with despair at the huge crowd between the northern alley and the square. *I should have gotten closer to the stage earlier. Perhaps then, I would have been able to save her in time.*

As it was, Surrels could only watch as Tenka raised his knife and slashed it across Fralia's throat.

Chapter Twenty-Six

OR RATHER, WATCHED AS TENKA *TRIED* TO DO THAT.

What actually happened took even Surrels by surprise.

A fireball flew out of the sky toward Tenka, hurtling at such speeds that it would have been impossible for a normal human to dodge or deflect.

But Tenka immediately whirled around and slashed at the fireball with his knife. Shadowy energy bands expanded from the blade and devoured the fireball, energy bands that Surrels recognized as being demonic in origin.

More shocked gasps came from the crowd as the people became torn between watching the stage and looking at the sky. Surrels also turned his gaze to the sky overhead, wondering who might have interrupted the coronation.

A massive black dragon soared down from the clouds suddenly, followed by at least a dozen other dragons.

No, Surrels thought, a smile curling across his lips. *Not dragons. Dragon Riders.*

The black dragon was Rialo, and seated upon Rialo's

back was Anija. The Dragon Riders and their Steeds circled the square overhead before Anija jumped off of Rialo's back and landed on the stage near Tenka and Fralia.

The guards immediately let go of Fralia, reaching for their swords, but Anija jumped forward and knocked them both off the stage with simple kicks. Tenka and Priest Om, on the other hand, immediately backed away from Anija and Fralia, the two wearing shocked expressions on their faces as they stared at Anija and the Dragon Riders.

Surrels was surprised to see Anija and the Dragon Riders, as well. He had heard that the Dragon Riders would not be attending the coronation because the capital's streets and buildings were not designed for dragons.

This is definitely not part of the plan, Surrels thought, *but I can't say it* hurts *the plan, either.*

The dragons overhead landed on the rooftops of nearby buildings, digging their claws into the roof tiles and brick for support. The crowd of people gazed around at the dragons, seemingly unsure about whether they should flee or not.

"The Dragon Riders?" Tenka said, glaring at Anija. "What is the meaning of this? I thought you said you were not going to attend the coronation."

Anija shrugged. "Changed our minds at the last minute. Fun fact: Dragons *love* parties. Although they love crashing them even more."

Tenka scowled, but shouted to the crowd, "See? I told you that the Dragon Riders were in on the coup. This is proof that they planned King Rikas's assassination. And now, they want to kill me and take control of the kingdom themselves!"

Anija gave Tenka a look of sheer disbelief. "Please don't

tell me you actually believe your own crap. Otherwise, I'm going to have to rethink how smart you actually are."

Tenka glared at Anija again, his hands balled into fists. "You will never get away with this. I can mobilize the total might of the Malarsan Army against all of you right away."

Anija raised an eyebrow. "Sorry, Tenka, but we're not trying to kill you. We're just trying to keep an innocent woman from being murdered on trumped-up charges. Although I must say, you are really good at projecting your own faults onto others."

"What is that supposed to mean?" Tenka demanded.

Anija met Tenka's gaze without hesitation. "It means that *you* murdered Old Snow, that is, King Rikas, in order to ascend to the throne yourself. That means, in effect, you are the very traitor you are accusing poor Fralia, Surrels, and the rest of us of being."

More shocked gasps broke out among the crowd, and Surrels heard one of the young women say to her friend, "Tenka killed his uncle? I can't believe that."

"She must be lying," the other woman insisted. "No way a man as handsome as Tenka could ever do such a horrible thing."

Surrels pursed his lips. He still wasn't sure if now was the right time to show himself or not. He was as taken aback by the arrival of the Dragon Riders as anyone else, so he decided not to intervene. Instead, Surrels made his way through the crowd slowly, trying to get as close to the stage as possible so he could be in place for his part of the plan.

Tenka put his hands on his chest. "*I* was the one who assassinated King Rikas? What a ridiculous, baseless claim."

"It gets even more ridiculous than that," Anija said. She pointed at Tenka. "You are also a collaborator with the very same demons that killed your beloved aunt."

The crowd gasped yet again, making Surrels wonder how much more gasps the people had in them. Not that he minded. The fact that the crowd was so fixed on the drama on the stage made it easier for him to move around unseen among them, getting closer and closer to the stage.

But however much Surrels might have enjoyed taking advantage of the crowd's distraction, he also had no idea what Anija's game here was. Sure, everything she said was true, but until she could prove it, Surrels didn't see how this wouldn't backfire on her eventually.

Maybe she's hoping we will get Stebo out here soon, Surrels thought. He scanned the crowds for Stebo and Argon as he walked. *But I still don't see him myself.*

Pushing his anxiety down, Surrels looked up at the stage to see what Tenka's reaction was going to be.

As to be expected, Tenka looked deeply offended by Anija's very truthful words. "Demons? I seriously have no idea what you are ranting about. After seeing what the demons did to Queen Marial, I want nothing to do with them, just as any decent person would."

"Problem is, you're not a 'decent person' by any stretch of the imagination," Anija said. "You're a despicable, lying son of a bitch who will never be king."

Tenka's eyes seemed to briefly glow red when Anija said that.

Then he laughed.

"Is that all you have?" Tenka said in between bouts of laughter. He gazed toward the crowd. "Are you listening to her, my fellow citizens? Rider Anija has just accused me of orchestrating King Rikas's assassination, as well as heavily implying that I may have had something to do with Queen Marial's murder, too. All without a single shred of proof. Who is convinced of these allegations, other than the ones who are making them?"

No one in the crowd spoke up in Anija's defense. Not that Surrels could blame them. Even though Anija spoke the truth, no one else knew that. The average person, indeed, had no reason to suspect Tenka of doing any of what Anija had just accused him of.

As if to add insult to injury, Anija added, "Oh, and Tenka doesn't have a legitimate claim to the throne, either. Old—I mean, King Rikas and Queen Marial had another son they hid for years, a direct descendant who Tenka has actively tried to kill multiple times over the past week or so. This entire coronation is illegitimate and must be stopped. Now."

The anger which flashed across Tenka's face when Anija said that was unmistakable even by the average person. More than a handful of people in the crowd exchanged confused and disbelieving looks when Anija said that, though still no one spoke up.

"A hidden heir?" Tenka repeated. He laughed again. "I hope no one here is actually tempted to *believe* such fairy tales. Clearly, someone has been listening to too many campfire tales told by bards with more imagination than sense if they believe that nonsense."

Surrels got as close to the stage as he dared and stopped. He looked up at the stage again, at both Anija and Tenka. He also briefly glanced around for Argon and Stebo but saw neither of them. Nor did he see Kendo and Catol, either, making him wonder where everyone was.

They'd better show up soon, Surrels thought. *The guards won't let Anija keep talking forever.*

Indeed, Surrels could already see the guards who had accompanied both the nobles and the master mages starting to assemble. At the moment, Anija could probably escape if she needed to, but her window of successfully escaping was shortening, and Surrels figured it was only a matter of time before the guards cut off most of her potential escape routes.

She might still be able to get away on Rialo, though, Surrels thought, glancing at the dragon flying in the sky overhead. *I hope.*

"Nonsense?" Anija said. "I noticed you haven't disproved any of my accusations, Tenka, probably because you can't."

"That isn't how accusations work, Anija," Tenka said smoothly. "I am innocent until proven guilty. It is up to *you* to prove that I have done any of those things of which you have just accused me. And seeing as you have not offered even one shred of proof for your wild claims, I think it's safe to say that you—"

"—are telling the truth!" Argon's voice suddenly broke out across the crowds.

Hope filling his heart, Surrels looked in the direction from which Argon's voice came, from the west, and saw two hooded figures making their way through the crowd toward the stage. Based on their sizes, Surrels could tell that they were Argon and Stebo.

They made it here safely after all, Surrels thought in relief. *Wonderful. Looks like Tenka is about to go down.*

Tenka had also looked toward Argon, his eyes skeptical. "And just who are you, old man?"

Argon, still pushing his way through the crowd, shouted back, "My identity doesn't matter! But do you know whose identity *does* matter?"

Stopping several feet from Surrels, Argon bent over and picked up Stebo, raising him for everyone to see. "This boy's identity! He is the most important person in the entire city, nay, the entire *kingdom* at this point. For the fate of the kingdom itself rests on the identity of this boy!"

Tenka's eyes narrowed, and recognition clearly flashed across them, though he quickly put on a stoic face. "And who, may I ask, is that boy?"

Argon smiled. "This *boy* is a young farm boy named Stebo, but *you* probably better know him as the missing son of King Rikas and Queen Marial, as well as the true heir to the throne of Malarsan."

The crowd's attention turned from the scene on the stage to Argon and Stebo among them. Surrels, knowing it was still not yet time for him to show himself, shrank back slightly into the crowd, but he felt truly victorious.

Stebo was here. All they needed to do now was have Fralia perform her blood spell on Stebo, and then Tenka's whole plan would come crashing down around him.

"So that boy is the fake hidden son of my late aunt and uncle?" Tenka said, skeptically eyeing Stebo. He gazed at Anija. "I appreciate the effort at realism, Anija, but your lies have simply gone too far."

"I could say the same about yours, liar," Anija said. She gestured toward Argon and Stebo. "Go ahead, kid. Take off your hood so everyone can see your face."

Stebo reached up to remove his hood. The hood fell down onto his shoulders, and Surrels felt his heart sink straight into his stomach.

The boy who Argon held in his hands did not look anything at all like Stebo.

Chapter Twenty-Seven

One week ago, in the Tomb of the Riders ...

Anija looked over at the human skeleton in the case before her. "This is Domon Azertan? And the dragon is Mathoh, his Steed?"

Lom nodded eagerly, rubbing all four of his hands together. "Yes! And I knew them before they died. Hal and Keershan remind me of them a lot, actually."

Anija looked at Domon's skeleton again. "Domon is definitely bigger than Hal. And Mathoh is much bigger than Keershan, for that matter."

Lom shook his head. "I don't mean Hal and Keershan *physically* remind me of them. I mean in terms of their helpful personalities and kindness. No wonder the Crafter who owned this workshop foresaw Hal and Keershan using the Final Relic like Domon and Mathoh. It makes a lot of sense."

Anija folded her arms in front of her chest. Unlike Hal and Keershan, Anija had not been super interested in the myths and history of the Dragon Riders. Her interest lay only in learning more about how the original Dragon Riders' powers worked, as well as what kind of powers they had. She cared not for history for history's sake, as Keershan did. It helped that her Steed, Rialo, felt the same way.

Even so, Anija could not help but acknowledge the sense of history she felt standing in the tomb. She could only imagine how Domon Azertan and Mathoh must have looked when they were still alive.

"And you say these are the same two who defeated the Nameless One the first time," Anija said, glancing at Lom.

"Of course," Lom said. He scratched his chin. "I always wondered what happened to these two after the Fall. That's about the same time my fellow Crafters and I decided to go into hiding. It was a very chaotic time for all of us."

"Interesting," Anija said. She brushed a strand of red hair out of her face. "I assume the Final Relic is the only thing he left."

"Yes," Lom said with a nod. "At least, as far as I know. A fun fact about the Final Relic is that it was infused with divine energy by Salard, the god of dragons, himself."

"It was?" Anija said. "I suppose that explains how it could kill a god."

Lom smiled. "Yes. But Domon didn't just use it to kill the Nameless One. He often sparred with King Gotcham Nubor, the king of the gods, himself in the days leading up to the final defeat of the Nameless One."

Anija rested her chin in the palm of her hand. "So not

only did he know how to kill a god, but even how to fight them. He must have been an impressive Rider."

"He most certainly was," Lom said. He put a hand on the glass case. "I am glad we managed to find his burial place, although it makes sense that he would be buried here. He was, after all, born in the Tops. So was Mathoh, for that matter."

"They were born in the same place?" Anija said. "What a coincidence."

Lom folded his arms behind his back. "Actually, that was standard fair for Dragon Rider pairs prior to the Fall. Humans and dragons often lived side by side in Dragon Rider settlements. It wasn't uncommon for baby humans and dragons to bond with each other as they grew up with their relic often solidifying a bond that was already there."

Anija looked at Lom in surprise. "But I thought a Rider and Steed can only be bonded by wearing relics."

"It's actually not necessary," Lom insisted. "Relics just make the process easier and quicker, particularly for adults. But bonds can be formed voluntarily or through close association over time. It's your modern-day methods of bonding adult humans and dragons that, historically speaking, is unusual."

Anija tapped her chin in thought. "So if I had a baby and raised it alongside Rialo's kids, then would my kid form a bond with one of them at some point?"

Lom shrugged. "Maybe. Maybe not. It really depends on how much time they spend with each other, as well as if they like each other or not. Like I said, relics were made to speed up the process and make it more efficient. They really aren't necessary."

That was very useful information to know. In fact, Anija

could already see how it might play out for them in the future. As Mysteria developed as a town, she could easily foresee a time when both human and dragon children were born together. These children would undoubtedly grow up side by side, in which case it was possible that some might naturally bond with each other over time.

If so, then the relics stolen by the Glacians might not hamper the growth of the Dragon Riders at all, especially if more humans and dragons kept moving to Mysteria and having children there.

Plus, I somehow doubt this will be the only Dragon Rider settlement we will found, Anija thought. *Hal and Keershan were working on a human-dragon town somewhere out in the rural parts of the kingdom. Who knows how that will work out?*

The implications were staggering, and Anija had only just started to think about it. She decided to put that aside for later, however, when Hal and Keershan returned and she could relay this information to them then. They would probably have a better idea of what to do with it than she did.

"All right," Anija said. She looked up and down the tomb. "I think we've seen enough for now. Let's head back to the surface and see if Tenka and his entourage have—"

A cold wind suddenly blew through just then, making Anija and Lom shiver.

Wrapping all four of his arms around his body in a tight hug, Lom said, "Wh-What was that?"

Anija, reaching for her daggers, said, "Don't know. Rialo?"

I can't tell from up here, Anija, Rialo said. *But whatever it is, it can't be good. Get out of there. Now.*

Before Anija or Lom could move, however, a sickly

green light suddenly flashed at the end of the tomb. Something green and shiny shot toward them with shocking speed, but Anija was quick enough to grab Lom and pull him out of the path of the shiny green thing, which disappeared into the shadows behind them.

"Whoa!" Anija said, looking in the direction that the green bolt had disappeared. "What was that?"

Lom suddenly pointed down the hall. "It probably came from … from that."

Anija followed Lom's finger, only to immediately regret it when she did so.

A massive dragon skeleton surrounded by a green glow was walking toward them. Eyeholes lit with green fire, the dragon let loose a rattling growl that sent shivers up Anija's spine.

"What the *hell* is that thing?" Anija said. "Rialo, are you seeing this?"

I am, Rialo said. A hint of frustration colored her next words. *But I can't go down there and help you with it.*

Lom took a step backward. "I think we should run. It doesn't look nice."

Anija, deciding that Lom had the right idea, whirled around and darted down the hallway back toward the workshop. She grabbed one of Lom's arms as she passed him, almost dragging him along behind her as she ran as fast as her feet could carry her. Faster, actually, because she drew upon Rialo's dragon strength via their bond to make her run well past her normal limits.

Even so, the ghostly dragon was still on their tail. It growled and clicked, its green aura casting the whole Tomb in a sickly green light. The temperature in the tomb grew colder and colder the closer that thing got to them, forcing

Anija to draw upon Rialo's dragonfire to make sure her limbs didn't freeze.

Although it wasn't a physical cold, necessarily. It was more like a mental or spiritual coldness, seeping into her mind and spirit. Her thinking process slowed down considerably, making even the most basic of thoughts require a great deal of effort.

In fact, Anija no longer even knew what she was running *from*. Or why she was running. Somewhere in the back of her mind lay the answer, but for the moment, Anija was tempted to stop and perhaps ask Lom if he knew what was going on, because right now, she didn't see any reason for them to keep—

Ghost dragon! Rialo yelled in her mind suddenly. *Right behind you! Keep running!*

Rialo's voice was like a splash of cold water on her mind, instantly making Anija far more alert than she had been even a few seconds ago. She remembered everything now and forced herself to run to her absolute limits.

Only she wasn't just physically running anymore. Her mind was also running from the ghostly dragon's influence or magic or whatever the hell it was doing to her.

Somehow, she suspected that what the ghostly dragon would do to her mind would be worse than whatever it might do to her body.

But before Anija and Lom could go much farther, there was another flash of green light before them. Thinking it was some sort of attack, Anija came to a stop, reaching for her daggers at her side.

Only for a ghostly voice from within the light to say, "Don't. You can't win down here, woman, and you know it."

The voice's commanding tone made even Anija hesitate. She looked over her shoulder at the ghost dragon to see that it, too, had stopped, though it didn't look nearly as afraid as Anija did. It merely blocked their path deeper into the tomb, glaring at them with its dead green eyes.

"Why did it stop?" Lom whispered.

"Because I told him to," said the voice from within the green light. "That's why."

The green light soon faded, revealing yet another ghostly figure, though this one appeared to be the ghost of a human.

A skeletal, ghostly figure stood before Anija and Lom. Clad in black armor, the ghost clutched a long, thin scythe in one hand while carrying a shield in the other. Rather than a helmet, the figure's head was covered by a hood, from which his glinting green eyes peered out with clear judgment at them. The lingering stench of death wafting from his form filled Anija's nostrils, and she shuddered from the cold.

"Who are you?" Anija said, scowling.

"I am the Tomb Guardian," said the ghost.

Anija raised an eyebrow. "No, I mean what is your actual name? Not your title?"

The Tomb Guardian cocked his head to the side. "I gave up my real name ages ago when I took the oath to protect the bodies of my brothers and sisters in arms. I no longer even remember it."

Anija's eyes widened. "Brothers and sisters … wait a second, are you one of the original Dragon Riders?"

The Tomb Guardian nodded, his bony joints cracking with every movement. "I was. The dragon behind you was my Steed, whose name I also do not remember. I call him the Ghost Dragon, however."

The Ghost Dragon growled deeply. "I do not care what you call me. All I care about is protecting the tomb from intruders like these two."

"We are *not* intruders," Anija argued. "Okay, maybe by the technical definition of that term we are, but we didn't come here to rob graves or do anything like that."

"Yes," Lom said, visibly shaking. He pointed at the exit overhead. "We just want to go back to my workshop."

The Tomb Guardian blinked. "work … shop?"

The Tomb Guardian disappeared in the blink of an eye and reappeared not even a foot from Lom. Anija drew her daggers and slashed them at the Tomb Guardian, but her blades merely passed through his ghostly form without so much as touching him.

The Tomb Guardian didn't even seem to notice her attack. He just leaned in close to Lom's face, his glowing green eyes boring into Lom's own.

"But you do not look like Okana …" the Tomb Guardian said. "You're different."

"I don't know who the hell 'Okana' is," Anija said, "but maybe take a step back, buddy. You're intruding on our space."

The Tomb Guardian glanced at Anija and narrowed his eyes. "And you … you are a Rider, are you not?"

"Uh, yes," Anija said, deciding not to lie to the ghost she couldn't kill. "How did you guess?"

The Tomb Guardian's eyes flicked to her chest. "Your necklace. I recognize it."

Anija glanced down at her necklace, which was the relic she used to bond with Rialo. "You do?"

"Yes," said the Tomb Guardian, a slight hiss to his words. He stood up straight. "It was the relic of Era Ponga and her Steed, the mighty Jin-Ah. I thought it lost in the Fall, but I see that it survived after all."

Anija did her best not to show any fear or weakness in the face of the ghostly Tomb Guardian, even though she was well aware of how powerless she was to hurt him. "I didn't know that. I don't even know who Era Ponga or Jin-Ah are."

The Tomb Guardian frowned. "Then … time has passed." He sniffed the air. "Yes, you smell young." He looked at Lom again. "You must be a Relic Crafter, then, though not one I recognize."

Lom gulped. "Does this mean you aren't going to kill us?"

The Tomb Guardian's eyes glowed ominously. "I will reserve judgment. Ghost Dragon, you are dismissed."

Ghost Dragon growled again, only to dissipate into soft green mist.

But Anija noticed that the mist did not disappear. It simply hung in the air behind them, seemingly of its own accord.

Must be an alternate form for the Ghost Dragon, Rialo said.

You seeing this? Anija replied.

I am, Rialo said. *And I am not sure what to make of it.*

That makes two of us, Anija said.

Aloud, Anija said to the Tomb Guardian, "Thanks for not killing us and all, but we still don't know who you are, exactly."

The Tomb Guardian stared at Anija. "I am the Tomb Guardian. I protect the tomb of the Dragon Riders, along with my Steed, the Ghost Dragon."

Anija resisted the urge to roll her eyes. "We know that already. I mean, how did you get here? How long have you been protecting the tomb? What's your story, in other words?"

The Tomb Guardian appeared to be having trouble comprehending her words. "My … story? I do not have a story. I am the Tomb Guardian. But if you mean how I got here …"

The Tomb Guardian's voice trailed off. It occurred to Anija that the Tomb Guardian may not have spoken to anyone else in a very long time and thus was probably not used to conversing with other people.

Finally, the Tomb Guardian said, "I do not remember much, but I do remember, after the Fall, vowing to protect the bodies of my fallen brothers and sisters from the Nameless One and his foul demons. The demons … they were out for blood after Captain Azertan and faithful Mathoh killed their master." His eyes darkened. "I killed many, *many* demons until they stopped coming. And then I was forgotten, much like the rest of the tomb."

The Tomb Guardian did not sound at all upset about having to kill demons. If anything, there was a hint of bloodthirsty pleasure in his voice, as if he was recounting a time he had fond memories of.

"So you've been down here since at least the Fall," Anija said. "That was … quite some time ago."

"Indeed it was," said the Tomb Guardian, "if your complete lack of respect for your elders is indicative of your age."

Anija bit her lower lip. She'd been scolded by her elders before, but this was the first time she got scolded by a literal dead man. She didn't know how she felt about that.

"You mentioned someone named Okana earlier," Lom said. "Was that the name of a Crafter, perchance?"

The Tomb Guardian nodded. "Yes. She was the one who lived in the workshop above. Is she still with us?"

Lom sighed. "Unfortunately … she is not."

The Tomb Guardian's shoulders slumped slightly. "Oh. I did not know that. I have slept for a long time."

Anija found both of their reactions interesting. The Tomb Guardian appeared to be genuinely sad about the demise of Okana, which made sense given the proximity of the tomb to her workshop.

But Lom acted as if he, too, had known Okana. Granted, they were both Relic Crafters, so perhaps that made sense, but Anija had been under the impression that Lom didn't know who owned the workshop above. Maybe she had been someone he knew after all.

Then the Tomb Guardian turned his gaze back to Anija. "But if you are indeed a new Dragon Rider, then that must mean that the Dragon Riders have returned. Yet how can that be, when the Nameless One's curse divided humanity and dragonkind?"

"The Nameless One is gone," Anija said. "Another Dragon Rider killed him last year. The curse is broken. While we're not quite up to the original number of Dragon Riders like in your day, we've grown a lot and now have lots and lots of Dragon Riders and Steeds in training, with more bonding all the time."

"You do?" said the Tomb Guardian, sounding as if he didn't dare believe what Anija was saying. He sighed very deeply. "That is … wonderful news. I thought I would spend the rest of eternity watching over the bodies of my fellow Riders and their Steeds, yet it seems like Okana was correct in foreseeing the rebirth of our kind."

If Anija didn't know any better, she would almost say that the Tomb Guardian was close to tears. He sounded very relieved, as if a heavy burden had just been lifted off his shoulders.

As if to accentuate that point, the Tomb Guardian gazed up at the ceiling and whispered, "Your sacrifice was not in vain, Captain … we survived …"

"That's nice and all, but Lom and I really need to get going," Anija said, grabbing one of Lom's arms and leading him around the Tomb Guardian. "While I'm sure you have lots of fascinating information on the early years of the Dragon Riders, we have some important things to do, so—"

The Tomb Guardian suddenly appeared in Anija's path again, causing her to look up at him.

And see that he was not happy.

"You said that the demons have been defeated," the Tomb Guardian said. He glanced at the ceiling. "So why do I sense their evil wandering around on the surface now?"

Anija gulped. *He senses Tenka.*

I know, said Rialo. *Still can't help.*

Anija pursed her lips, but before she could say anything, the Tomb Guardian raised his scythe over his head. "If you have lied to me, then you must perish."

Chapter Twenty-Eight

"I DIDN'T LIE ABOUT THE DEMONS!" ANIJA SAID. "I JUST——"

The Tomb Guardian brought his scythe down on Anija and Lom, forcing them to jump back to avoid getting hit. Throwing Lom behind her, Anija raised her daggers, channeling dragonfire along them as she faced the Tomb Guardian.

The Tomb Guardian raised his scythe again. "You dare to use dragonfire against me? That is proof of your Dragon Riderhood, perhaps. But not of much else."

Anija scowled. "I said I didn't lie. Even though the Nameless One is dead, there are still some demons running around. And right now, someone who is a friend of those demons is going to take over the country unless we put a stop to him."

The Tomb Guardian hissed. "Why not kill him here and now if that is the case? I sense other Dragon Riders up on the surface. He is outnumbered. There is no reason not to kill him."

"Because it would be … complicated, politically-speaking," Anija said. "But believe me, we are working on a plan to stop him. You just have to trust us."

"Trust those I have just met and know almost nothing about?" the Tomb Guardian said. Green fire erupted along his scythe. "I wonder if the demons have corrupted you somehow as well. You would not be the first Dragon Rider to fall to their wicked lies."

The Tomb Guardian took a step forward, and then another. Anija did not know why he was walking rather than teleporting, but she supposed it didn't matter.

"He's going to kill us," Lom whispered frantically to Anija. He hid behind her, clutching her back with all four of his hands. "We're going to die."

"We are not going to die," Anija whispered back. "Maybe we can run deeper into the tomb and double back after throwing him off of our trail."

"What about the Ghost Dragon?" Lom said.

Anija whipped her head over her shoulder to see that the Ghost Dragon had reformed behind them. It now completely blocked off their only path of escape, trapping them between it and the Tomb Guardian, who was still advancing on them, each step seemingly slower but far more dangerous than the last.

"We are going to die," Lom said again.

Anija bit her lower lip. Telling Lom to shut up was getting old and wouldn't actually help them in their current situation, as much as she wanted to do it.

At the same time, however, Anija saw no way out for them. She supposed she could try drawing upon Rialo's dragon strength to give her legs the power necessary to make the jump to the exit overhead, but that was assuming that the Tomb Guardian or the Ghost Dragon wouldn't be expecting that and wouldn't try to stop her.

You need to somehow convince them that you are not working with the demons, Rialo said in Anija's mind suddenly.

Good idea, but how do I do that? Anija asked. *I've already told him he's wrong. Not like I can prove a negative.*

Rialo grunted. *I'm just throwing ideas out here. If I were there, I would fight alongside you, but I'm not.*

It's not your fault, Anija said. *It's not even like you would be able to fight them, either. They're spirits. Physical attacks probably can't hurt—*

An idea hit Anija just then. Like many of her last-minute ideas, it was crazy, but it was also their only chance of survival.

Looking over her shoulder at Lom, Anija said, "Lom, stay here. I am going to give the Tomb Guardian proof that we are not the enemy."

Lom looked at her frantically. "And leave me to die?"

"With luck, neither of us is going to die today," Anija said.

Without another word, Anija ran toward the Tomb Guardian. The spirit of the departed Dragon Rider raised his flaming scythe defensively, perhaps thinking that Anija was going to attack him.

She wasn't.

Not physically, anyway, and not even spiritually.

Anija had experience fighting spirits.

And so she knew exactly what to do.

Passing through the handle of the Tomb Guardian's scythe, Anija reached out with a hand toward his face. Right before her hand passed through his head, Anija opened her bond with Rialo wide, hoping against hope to include the Tomb Guardian and the Ghost Dragon in it.

At first, Anija felt nothing other than the confusion and hostility of the Tomb Guardian before her. She also thought she heard Lom's screams of terror somewhere behind her, though he sounded distant and far away despite not being even fifteen feet away from her.

In the next second, however, Anija felt another presence in her mind that wasn't Rialo. It was the Tomb Guardian, whose eyes widened in shock in the real world, perhaps realizing what Anija had just done.

But the Tomb Guardian had no time to react before Anija's hand made contact with his face.

In a flash, Anija opened her mind to the Tomb Guardian. She showed him *everything* from her life, from her earliest childhood memories, through meeting Hal and the others, bonding with Rialo, and even being possessed by Shadow Mask and forced to do his bidding.

She showed everything. She felt vulnerable, exposed, even naked, but she didn't hide anything. She wanted the Tomb Guardian to trust her, to believe her, and she couldn't do that if she hid or held back anything.

But apparently, the bond was a two-way street, because Anija caught glimpses of the Tomb Guardian's previous life. Only glimpses, because unlike Anija, the Tomb Guardian wasn't trying to share everything with her.

She saw enough, however. She saw the Tomb Guardian as a young boy playing with a green hatchling that bore a suspicious resemblance to the Ghost Dragon. She saw the Tomb Guardian as a young man, along with his now grown-up dragon, being given a relic by none other than Domon Azertan himself in what seemed to be a ceremony inducting them into the Dragon Rider Order. She felt his happiness as his wife gave birth to their first child.

And his fear and determination as he and hundreds of other Dragon Riders flew across a sea of pure blackness, which Anija realized wasn't a sea at all. It was hundreds of thousands of demons, their black bodies packed so tightly together in the valley that they looked like an ocean of death from above.

Finally, Anija saw the Tomb Guardian standing at the entrance to the tomb of the Dragon Riders, gazing at the cases and platforms full of deceased Dragon Riders and their Steeds. He clutched a dagger in his right hand, prayed a silent prayer to the gods, and then brought up the knife to his throat and slit it.

It all seemed to take an eternity but it was perhaps a second later that Anija felt the Tomb Guardian forcibly break off their bond.

Landing on her behind, Anija shuddered. Bonding with the Tomb Guardian had reminded her of her bonding with Rialo, only not nearly as pleasant. She felt both like she had been violated and had, in turn, violated the Tomb Guardian.

It was a feeling she would never forget.

"Anija, are you okay?" Lom said suddenly. She looked over her shoulder to see Lom, an alarmed expression on his face, standing behind her. "Can you stand?"

Anija groaned and rose to her feet, dusting off her pants. "I think so. That was just so … so *intense*."

Even as Anija said that, 'intense' felt like a severe understatement to her. Perhaps it was because it was the first time she'd ever tried to bond with a human, but the experience left her feeling drained. Her knees wobbled, and her joints burned, making even the simple act of standing a great challenge.

Rialo, did you see all that, too? Anija asked.

Some of it, Rialo said. *But I don't know what you just did. Or what you thought you were doing.*

Trying to prove our innocence so a ghost warrior wouldn't kill us, Anija replied. *Let's see if it worked.*

The Tomb Guardian stood unnaturally still, even by his standards. Because he normally didn't breathe, Anija couldn't tell if he was still 'alive' or not or whatever you called a ghost's visible existence in the real world.

Then the Tomb Guardian's shoulders relaxed and he gazed at Anija. "I … am sorry. I should not have accused you or your friend of being friends with the demons. I should have been more careful with my words."

Anija, slightly taken aback by the Tomb Guardian's frank apology, said, "Don't worry. I know you sense the evil one up there, but trust me, we are working on taking him down. Just have to do it the smart way."

The Tomb Guardian nodded. "Yes … I understand. The Nameless One also required much planning and thought to defeat. And … sacrifice. Much, much sacrifice."

Although the Tomb Guardian's expression was almost impossible to read, Anija recalled the images she'd seen in the Tomb Guardian's mind. In particular, she remembered the next to final memory, of the Tomb Guardian and his fellow Riders flying into battle against a veritable army of demons.

And she understood what he meant by sacrifice.

"So does that mean you will let us go?" Lom said hopefully.

The Tomb Guardian stepped aside. "I must, now that I

know who you are. And, while I find your quest admirable, I must warn you that the demons are not to be taken lightly. I only wish I could join you in your battle against them."

Anija shrugged. "It's fine. We've dealt with the demons before. I think we can handle them again."

The Tomb Guardian cocked his head to the side. "Yet it seems to me that the bigger issue you face is not the demons, but proving the young boy's royal parentage. Otherwise, all your planning will have gone to naught, will it not?"

Anija started before she remembered that the Tomb Guardian had seen everything in her memories, including the plan to defeat Tenka. "Yeah, I guess you're right. But Fralia, our mage friend, is working on it."

The Tomb Guardian's eyes narrowed. "There is a spell I recall one of my fellow Dragon Riders having used prior to the Nameless One's demise, which we used to speak with the departed spirits of one of our distant ancestors. We sought knowledge about how to destroy the Nameless One, and this spirit gave it to us. Without that knowledge, the Nameless One and his army of vile demons likely would have overwhelmed the whole world with their evil."

Anija and Lom exchanged significant looks before Anija looked back at the Tomb Guardian. "This spell … you wouldn't happen to remember it, would you?"

"Unfortunately, I don't," said the Tomb Guardian. "But I believe it was written down in an ancient book called *Blood Magic*, although it has been many ages since we used that spell, so I know not if the book is still around or not. Your mage friend may wish to look for that book."

"I'll definitely tell her about it," Anija said with a quick nod. "You wouldn't happen to have any other demon-related knowledge, would you?"

"Nothing that would help you," said the Tomb Guardian. He gazed at the ceiling again. "And I can't leave this place. I can only help if Mysteria itself ever comes under attack."

"That may not be unlikely," Anija said. She tapped the side of her head. "You saw the Glaci Empire and Kryo Kardia. If they decided to invade the kingdom, this is where they will probably hit first."

The Tomb Guardian's eyes dimmed slightly. "Yes. This Kryo Kardia … he reminds me far too much of the Nameless One."

"Yeah, but he's not an actual *god*, right?" Anija said. "So he'll probably be easier to defeat than the Nameless One."

The Tomb Guardian gave her a long look. "One does not need to be a god to be dangerous. Indeed, Kryo Kardia strikes me as dangerous precisely *because* he isn't a god, but a power-hungry mortal with too much ambition and the might to make that ambition a reality. I only pray that you and the rest of your Dragon Rider brothers and sisters will have the courage and strength to withstand his power and overcome his ambition."

With that, the Tomb Guardian dissipated into mist. So did the Ghost Dragon behind Anija and Lom, leaving the two of them standing alone in the tomb of the Riders again.

Lom gulped. "Well, that went better than expected."

"Definitely," Anija said. She looked around at the entombed corpses around them. "But I can't really blame the guy for being so tense. After everything he's been through, it's understandable."

Lom nodded. "I'm mostly relieved that I finally know what happened to Okana. I'd been wondering that."

"Who *is* Okana, anyway?" Anija said. "I mean, I know she's another Relic Crafter, but was she a close friend to you or something?"

Lom rubbed his arms. "She was not just a close friend. She was my older sister. My bossy, but kind, older sister."

The sadness in Lom's voice was evident. It made Anija feel sorry for him. However annoying or weak Lom might sometimes be, she could tell he was truly sad over the loss of his sister.

Rubbing his shoulder, Anija said, "At least we've found her body. We can give her a proper funeral if you want."

Lom, however, shrugged her hand off his shoulder and shook his head. "Thanks, but Relic Crafters are supposed to die—and be buried in—our workshops. I'll focus on finding a new place to put her body. You just go and help the others stop Tenka."

Anija pursed her lips. "But—"

Lom whirled to face her, a serious look on his face. "You heard the Tomb Guardian. Between Kryo Kardia and Tenka, we don't have time to mourn. You didn't even know Okana. You need to do your part, and I'll … I'll do my part, the part that only I can do. Okay?"

Anija raised an eyebrow. She had not thought Lom capable of speaking so decisively and assertively before, but this was clearly something that Lom felt strongly about, and for good reason, too.

Rather than argue with him, Anija merely nodded once. "Fair enough. Now let's get out of here. We have a lot to do."

Chapter Twenty-Nine

BACK IN THE PRESENT ...

Anija was worried.

That was unusual. Anija rarely worried about anything. While not exactly a laid-back person, Anija wasn't prone to anxiety and indecision like some people she knew. Anytime she ran into a problem that seemed impossible to handle, Anija would always fight her way out of it or sneak her way out of it.

Thus, it took a lot to worry Anija.

And the reveal of the young boy in the crowd, held up by the Dead Dragon Syndicate member Argon, was enough.

Now, Anija had never seen Stebo, Old Snow's son, in person before. She didn't quite know what he looked like. She had received a description of Stebo from Fralia a while ago, who in turn had received it from Kendo and Surrels.

And to Anija, that boy didn't look anything like Stebo.

For one, the boy's hair was too dark, much darker than the blond hair Stebo was supposed to have. His skin, too, was paler, and he seemed smaller and skinnier than Kendo's description of the boy. It didn't help that the young boy wore a frankly bewildered expression on his face, blinking rapidly as he looked around at the crowds around him, like he was just as surprised as anyone else to be here.

But what really made Anija worried was when Tenka smirked.

"Who, may I ask, is that boy, stranger?" asked Tenka. "Your son?"

Argon gulped. "Why it's … well, it's *supposed* to be Stebo, the long-lost second son of King Rikas and Queen Marial."

That confirmed it to Anija: That boy wasn't Stebo, otherwise Argon wouldn't have used the word 'supposed.'

Anija couldn't say she was actually surprised. During her time in the Dark Tigers, Anija had encountered members of the Dead Dragon Syndicate on more than a few occasions. The two criminal groups' paths crossed frequently, because even though the Dead Dragons cared more about smuggling than assassination, it wasn't uncommon for the Dark Tigers to be hired by others to take out certain members of the Dead Dragons by their enemies.

Hell, Mama Dragon herself had been a frequent target of the Dark Tigers. After losing several of their best assassins to her, however, Shadow Mask had put a moratorium on accepting jobs to kill anyone from the Dead Dragons. Likewise, Mama Dragon had forbade her men from stealing from the Dark Tigers to avoid any unnecessary unpleasantness.

As a result, the two groups had formed a sort of cease-fire between them, doing their best not to interact with each other except only when necessary. As Anija recalled, however, the ceasefire definitely had been violated on more than a few occasions, usually from the Dead Dragons' side.

And while Anija found the Dark Tigers to be a group of murderous thugs who cared about nothing other than money, the Dead Dragons were even worse. Mama Dragon was a genius negotiator and manipulator who taught her men how to best go back on deals with others, use alliances for their own benefit, and stab others in the back when it benefited them the most.

In Anija's personal dealings with the Dead Dragons, she had always had to keep her guard up. Not because they would try to steal her money, necessarily, but rather because they would try to get her to steal something for them, then steal it from her, and try to throw her to the enforcers.

That was why Anija was surprised, and hesitant, when she first heard from Fralia that the Dead Dragons would be helping them in their plan to prevent Tenka's coronation from happening. Unlike the other members of the council, Anija was well-versed in Malarsan's criminal underworld, and so she understood that if the Dead Dragons were helping them, then they were definitely not doing it out of the goodness of their hearts.

Even so, Anija had not voiced her concerns aloud at the time. She had decided to take a wait-and-see approach to the issue, thinking that maybe the Dead Dragons wouldn't bait and switch them or betray them at the last possible moment.

Unfortunately, it looked like Anija should have listened to her instincts, because they were being proven right even as she stood there on the stage under the warm midday sun.

"*Supposed* to be, eh?" Tenka said. "You don't sound entirely sure of that yourself, old man."

"But it is him," Argon said. He looked at the boy again. "I think. Right, Stebo?"

The boy looked down at Argon in confusion. "Who is Stebo?"

Crap. That all but confirmed it.

Anija could guess what happened. The Dead Dragons had probably switched out Stebo with another boy, most likely an orphan they picked off the street at random, without telling Surrels or the others. In all likelihood, the Dead Dragons wanted to hold onto Stebo for blackmail purposes while throwing Anija and the others to the wolves.

Right out of their game plan, Anija thought, her hands curling into fists. *I feel like a fool.*

What do you think we should do, Anija? Rialo asked. *Run?*

Anija shook her head slightly. *No. We need to see what happens. We might still be able to salvage this situation.*

Even as Anija said that, however, she didn't know how they were going to turn things around. Stebo was their trump card, their main—and only—way to challenge Tenka's claim to the Throne.

Without Stebo, their entire plan fell apart.

Tenka gazed over the crowd, a strong breeze blowing through his long, dark hair. "What do you think, my fellow citizens? Do you think that this boy, who doesn't even seem to know his own name, could possibly be the long-lost son of my deceased aunt and uncle?"

The crowd shifted. Lots of people wore uncertain or

skeptical looks on their faces. Not that Anija could blame them.

She, after all, had failed to be as skeptical of the Dead Dragons as she should have been.

And now, they were about to face the consequences for trusting the wrong people.

Tenka shook his head. "I know what happened. The council probably kidnapped a young boy from his family with the aid of the vile Dead Dragon Syndicate with the intent of causing chaos among the court as to who should rightfully sit on the throne. The boy was clearly supposed to pretend to be the long-lost second son of King Rikas and Queen Marial, but I suppose the boy forgot his lines under pressure. Children do make terrible actors, after all. They're too honest."

The crowd laughed at that, while Argon lowered the boy to the ground, a look of shame on his face.

Argon looks ashamed, Rialo noted. *Do you think that maybe they accidentally got the wrong boy?*

I'm not sure about that, Anija said. *The Dead Dragons are not even remotely trustworthy. I wouldn't put a bait and switch past them. Especially when you consider what is at stake here.*

Yet Anija had to admit, something did feel off about this situation. She didn't know why Argon seemed so embarrassed. After all, if the Dead Dragons had indeed been attempting to perform a bait and switch, surely Argon would have been included in it.

Either Argon had been set up as the fall guy for the plan … or perhaps Stebo *had* been with Argon at some point and the real Stebo had been switched out without even Argon knowing.

Anija flicked her eyes toward Tenka. She noticed how

calm and collected the young noble seemed. He looked totally unfazed by the presence of Argon and the wrong boy. Indeed, he almost looked like he'd been expecting it.

Tenka knows something, Anija said to Rialo. *He definitely has something to do with this.*

Do you think Tenka had Stebo switched out for that other boy? Rialo said. *If so, where is Stebo? Do you think he's even still—?*

I don't know, Anija said. *But if Tenka is behind this, then he's even more dangerous than I thought. We might need to abort the mission.*

Tenka snorted and waved a hand. "Guards, please arrest and remove the Dead Dragon from the square. As for the young boy, make sure to get him back to his loving parents, who are no doubt worried sick about his disappearance."

Guards standing on the perimeter of the crowd made their way toward the center, near where Argon and the boy were. Argon looked around in alarm, but it was clear that the pirate had no easy or obvious escape route, if indeed he could escape at all.

That was when a hooded cloaked figure jumped out of the crowd, rushing toward Argon and the boy. Drawing a sword from within his cloak, the figure reached Argon before the guards and brought his sword down …

On the boy's head.

The hooded man's sword split the boy's head open cleanly in two. The boy didn't even scream, but the crowd sure did. Screams of shock and horror erupted from the crowd at the hooded man's sudden attack. A wide circle formed around Argon, the boy, and the hooded man as people tried to keep their distance from the crazy guy with the sword. That made it more difficult for the guards to get to them, slowing their progress considerably.

Even Anija was shocked by the hooded figure's attack. Killing a child? That seemed like a step too far to her. She didn't know who the hooded man was but figured he couldn't have been a good person if he was willing to murder a young boy in broad daylight.

Tenka was evidently thinking the same thing, because he shouted, "You monster! I don't know who you are, but murdering a young child is a grievous evil. Do you want to go to prison with the Dead Dragon?"

The hooded man looked up at Tenka defiantly. "The boy is not dead."

Anija thought the hooded man was delusional until she noticed that the boy, despite having his skull cleaved in two, was still standing.

And did not look even remotely happy about having been attacked.

Without warning, black tendrils erupted from within the young boy's skull. Argon and the hooded man backed away from the flailing tendrils, which immediately slammed into the ground. The tendrils, now more closely resembling spider legs, raised the 'boy' into the air, still glaring at the hooded man and his bloody sword.

That was when Anija felt it. A sinking coldness, like being out in the middle of a snowstorm at midnight, filled the air. It was a sensation she had not felt in a long time, not since the—

"Demons," Anija whispered. In a louder voice, she pointed her dagger at the boy and said, "That boy is a demon!"

The 'boy' flicked his eyes toward Anija. "Took you long

enough to figure out. Although I wonder how *this* one knew."

The demon gestured with a hand toward the hooded man. The hooded man raised his sword, although Anija doubted he would last long against the demon.

"'This one' has had plenty of experience fighting demons like you," the hooded man said in a familiar voice. "But if you want to know who 'this one' really is, then let me show you."

The hooded man ripped the hood off his head, revealing the familiar aged face of Surrels.

The surrounding crowd gasped, both in horror at the sight of the demon, and shock at the sight of Surrels. Even the guards had stopped, watching the scene in utter amazement and bewilderment.

"Surrels?" Tenka growled. "Of course. I should have realized you wouldn't miss my coronation. Or rather, miss the perfect opportunity to ruin it."

"Ruin your fake coronation?" Surrels said. "You are not the rightful heir to the Throne, and you know it, Tenka. Stebo is still alive. You just had one of your demons replace him at the last second to thwart our plans, didn't you?"

Tenka put his hands on his chest. "*My* demons? I have no idea what you are talking about, Surrels. I have never worked with a demon before in my life. I certainly have never seen *this* particular demon before. More pathetic lies, which I am not surprised to hear, given how you and Anija are clearly working together in this conspiracy."

Even as Tenka said that, however, Anija noticed the noble's hands shaking slightly. She realized that Tenka had not expected his demonic ally to be exposed so quickly, which told her that they had finally done something he had not planned for or expected.

The only question is, can we actually prove that he and the demon are in league? Anija thought.

The Steeds on the roofs of the nearby buildings snarled and hissed at the demon, but did not attack just yet.

The demon, by contrast, looked remarkably calm, if a bit annoyed. "Well, this is inconvenient. But I suppose there is no further point in pretending I am anything other than what I am. Right, Tenka?"

All eyes in the crowd turned from the demon to Tenka, whose eyes bulged when the demon used his name.

"H-How do you know my name?" Tenka demanded. "I have n-never seen you before in my life, demon."

The demon chuckled. "Please, Tenka. There is no further point in this charade. Even I know that, and I am a demon."

Shocked gasps and cries rang out throughout the crowd. Whispers and murmurs swept through the people as they processed this shocking revelation. Even Anija was shocked by the frankness of the demon.

Tenka then pointed at the demon, his face red with rage. "You idiot! You are ruining my perfect plan right when it was about to succeed."

The demon sneered. "Your perfect plan? Please. You speak as if you have been in control of us, when truthfully, it was I and my brothers and sisters who have been influencing your actions this entire time. Just as the Nameless One controlled your dear aunt, so, too, have we controlled you."

The shadows around Tenka's feet suddenly expanded, forming a wide circle around him that also encircled Priest

Om. Anija, Fralia, and everyone else on the stage backed away from the shadowy circle, though it stopped expanding after encompassing Tenka and Priest Om.

"What the—?" Priest Om stuttered. He shot a horrified look at the demon. "We had a deal, demon!"

The demon cocked its head to the side. "When has making a deal with a *demon* ever worked out for the humans foolish enough to make it?"

Shadow tendrils ending in sharp-looking claws erupted from the black circle. The claws sank into Tenka's and Priest Om's skin, making them bleed profusely as the shadows pulled them into the circle.

"No!" Tenka cried out, struggling against the tendrils, blood staining his perfect skin. "I can't die! I am destined to be the king of Malarsan! I am destined to be the king of—"

Then Tenka and Priest Om vanished into the circle in the blink of an eye.

Chapter Thirty

THE TEMPLE OF THE GODS WAS JUST AS BIG AS HAL remembered. Up close and outside, however, it looked even bigger. A massive gold dome stood atop an even bigger multi-story structure with countless windows covering its exterior, probably the rooms of the various deities visiting the abode.

Rather than fly into the temple like before, however, Raniel led them to the front gates, which were across a crystal bridge, which in turn spanned a moat so deep that Hal could not see the bottom. The surface was opaque as well, only occasionally broken by a fin or tentacle, though never long enough to give Hal a clear idea about exactly what lurked within the moat.

Given how this moat is clearly designed to protect the gods, I'm not sure I want to see what is in there, Hal thought as he walked along the bridge.

You're braver than me in even looking at the moat in the first place, Keershan replied with a shudder. *I hate water and I especially hate water I can't see through.*

Hal looked at Keershan in surprise as they walked side by side. *You're afraid of water? I never knew that.*

Deep, opaque water, Keershan corrected, *like in a lake or the ocean. As a matter of fact, it's a common fear among dragons. Why else do you think we prefer living in mountains or valleys, where we can see everything clearly below us while we are flying?*

Hal had not thought about that, but it made sense. While dragons had amazing eyesight that let them see even the smallest creatures moving on the ground miles below them, Hal could see how the sea might scare them. It wasn't like they could see under the surface, which meant they had no way of knowing what was or wasn't lurking underwater just out of sight.

Hal continued to muse on this as Raniel led them through the front gates into the lobby of the temple itself.

Although Hal had been here inside the temple once before, that had been a completely different part from the front lobby. And when he stepped through the doorway and looked around, his jaw fell. "Keershan, are you seeing what I'm seeing?"

Keershan, standing beside him, nodded, disbelief on his features. "I am. I'm not believing it, but I sure am seeing it."

Boca gave them a puzzled look. "What is so surprising? I know the Temple of the Gods can be a bit much when you first visit, but—"

"We've been here before," Hal said. "At least, we've been somewhere *similar* to here before. Right, Keershan?"

Raniel, who had been walking before them, paused and turned around to face them in the vast lobby. "Nowhere in the mortal realm is even remotely similar to the Temple of the Gods."

"That's where you're wrong, Raniel," Keershan said

with a shake of his head. "Because the Temple of the Gods —at least, the interior—looks almost exactly like the interior of the Forgotten Temple back home in Malarsan."

Hal agreed with Keershan. The lobby of the divine temple was almost identical to the lobby of the Forgotten Temple, except cleaner, nicer, and fancier. It had the same basic layout, complete with vast open space and a ceiling supported by massive stone columns. The statues set along the path were different, being statues of various gods and goddesses rather than of dragons, but other than that, the lobby looked like how Hal thought the lobby of the Forgotten Temple had probably appeared before it was abandoned after the Fall.

"I've never been to the Forgotten Temple myself," Boca said, gazing at Hal questioningly, "but even I find your claim hard to believe."

"You will have to visit us in Malarsan after this," Keershan insisted. "We will definitely show you the Forgotten Temple, and you'll see for yourself just how similar they are."

Raniel shook his head. "We have no time to be discussing random architectural coincidences. We are here to see Gotcham Nubor, the king of the gods, himself."

"I know," Hal said, "but—"

Raniel, however, had clearly stopped listening at this point. The angel resumed walking ahead of them, forcing Hal, Keershan, and Boca to walk quickly to follow him.

Yet Hal could not get over just how eerily similar the entire lobby was to the Forgotten Temple back in Mysteria. He felt like he'd walked back in time, to an era when the Forgotten Temple had been in better shape than it currently was. He wondered if the Forgotten Temple had looked as beautiful and glorious in its day as the Temple of the Gods did today.

What do you think, Keershan? Hal asked mentally, deciding not to bother either Raniel or Boca with his observations and questions.

I don't know what to think, Hal, Keershan replied, also looking around in awe at the lobby. *It seems like whoever built the Forgotten Temple must have based its design off of the Temple of the Gods.*

How do we know they weren't built by the same people? Hal asked.

Seems way too unlikely to me, Hal, Keershan said. *After all, the Temple of the Gods has probably stood for, what, eons? The Forgotten Temple, by contrast, is probably only about five thousand years old. I doubt there is any real connection between the two.*

Other than the fact that they are carbon copies of each other, sure.

I mean that they were probably not built by the same people, Keershan clarified. *Maybe whoever built the Forgotten Temple visited the abode once and was inspired by the temple here. You never know. Either way, the similarities between them are still mind-blowing, that's for sure.*

Hal, of course, could not disagree. He only wished they could speak with whoever had built the Forgotten Temple, although that was probably impossible, seeing as the Forgotten Temple had been built ages ago. Whoever had designed the building was probably not even alive anymore. The same was likely true of whoever built the Temple of the Gods, unless that person was a god.

With no way to get to the bottom of this particular mystery at the moment, Hal put it off to focus on their current objective.

Meeting with Gotcham Nubor, the king of the gods and Boca's former lover.

Raniel led the three of them through the winding hallways of the Temple of the Gods. The similarities between the Temple of the Gods and the Forgotten Temple back home ended at the lobbies.

Because the Temple of the Gods was *huge*. It seemed like one massive hallway after one massive hallway, a maze of hallways and corridors that Hal was sure he would have gotten very lost in if he were to explore the place on his own. Dozens of angels and other semidivine beings Hal could not identify walked or flew up and down the hallways, seemingly running tasks and errands for whichever god or goddess they worked for.

Very few of the busy angels took note of Hal or his friends, though he did notice a few glance their way. He guessed that the other angels somehow knew that Raniel was watching them so they did not feel a need to keep a careful eye on them, which Hal was fine with. The last thing they needed was to draw more unwanted attention to themselves, especially after the gods already suspected them of being Shirataka's murderers.

"Where exactly does Gotcham Nubor stay in the temple?" Keershan asked after about five minutes of walking. "Does he have his own apartment like the other visiting gods?"

Raniel gave Keershan an offended look. "The entire temple is technically His Majesty's house. He only lets the other gods stay as his guests. Thus, he could conceivably be in any of the rooms, though if I know His Majesty—and I do—then he is probably sparring."

"Sparring?" Hal repeated. "With who?"

Raniel came to an abrupt stop and said, "We are about to find out."

Raniel had come to a stop in front of two massive golden doors that Hal had not noticed, mostly because there were a lot of golden doors in the temple. Raniel pushed them open without another word and stepped inside, gesturing for Hal and the others to follow, which they did.

At first, Hal thought they had returned to the meeting room of the gods from earlier, where they had been charged by the gods with finding the true killer by tomorrow.

But then another look around the room told Hal that they had actually stepped into an arena of sorts. Hundreds of seats rose up around a sandpit arena, the seats made of gold and silver. The sand in the pit below them also seemed to glow golden, though whether that was due to the golden light from the chandelier above or the inherent properties of the sand itself, Hal could not say.

The stands in the arena were empty aside from themselves, though Hal wasn't sure why. After all, he could see that there was a match going on in the arena right now.

A powerfully built young man who didn't look much older than Hal, clad in golden armor, stood in the center of the arena. He clutched a single broadsword in his hands, a dragon-shaped golden helmet sitting squarely atop his head.

The man faced off against six armed and armored angels who reminded Hal of Raniel but scarier. These angels were bigger and taller than Raniel, their arms bulging with massive muscles. Each one of them carried two broadswords identical to the young man's, one in each hand.

"Are those guys holding two broadswords?" Keershan said in surprise. "Each?"

Raniel nodded, scowling. "Showing off as usual, I see."

"Who are they?" Hal said.

Boca smirked. "The strapping young men below are elite divine guardsmen, putting them one rank above Raniel in terms of power *and* authority. They are also the personal bodyguards of Gotcham Nubor."

Hal frowned. "Then who is the guy they are fighting in the arena?"

Raniel scowled at Hal. "That is King Nubor himself, mortal."

Hal's eyes widened. "That's King Nubor? But he looks so … so …"

"Young?" Boca finished for Hal. "Handsome? Yes to both. He is a god, so he can look however he wants."

"The witch is correct," Raniel said. "And luckily for us, it looks like we got here just in time to see his sparring."

Raniel took a seat on one of the benches, as did Boca. Hal, figuring they wouldn't get to talk to King Nubor until he was done sparring with his bodyguards, also sat down. Keershan had to stand in the walkway between the stands, however, because the seats were not designed for dragons like him. Nonetheless, he, too, watched the sparring with interested eyes.

King Nubor still hadn't moved from the center of the arena. His eyes kept darting from elite guardsman to elite guardsman, as if daring one of them to make the first move.

Surprisingly—or perhaps not, given who they were

dealing with—none of the elite guardsmen looked at all eager to be the first to try their luck against King Nubor.

That was, until one of them suddenly jumped toward King Nubor, swinging both of his swords at the god king's head. The bladed weapons came so fast that Hal doubted Nubor even saw it coming.

But Nubor ducked at the last second, causing both of the guardsman's swords to miss him completely. Whirling around, Nubor slashed the hands of the guardsman, making him drop his swords, before kicking him in the stomach and sending him flying into one of the arena walls. The guardsman smashed into the arena wall and slumped, clearly out for the count.

"Nice move," Keershan said.

"Yeah, but there are still five more left," Hal pointed out.

Boca rubbed her hands together eagerly. "That simply means there are more people for Nubor to pummel into submission."

Apparently, despite having just witnessed the resounding defeat of one of their own, the rest of the elite guardsmen attacked. They attacked as one, swinging their broadswords in wild yet clearly orchestrated patterns. It was obvious to Hal that the elite guardsmen worked well as one unit, relying on whatever teamwork or strategy they had worked out ahead of time to deal with Nubor.

Unfortunately for them, Nubor was still a god, and they were not.

Nubor spun around so fast he looked like a tornado, blocking or deflecting their striking weapons. His deflecting tornado spin managed to disarm a few of them while knocking down the one who had gotten a little too close to him flat onto his back, his head clearly spinning from the impact of Nubor's blow.

Coming back to a stop, Nubor launched toward the remaining four elite guardsmen like a hungry dragon. The guardsmen were suddenly on the defense, trying to block all of Nubor's constant attacks.

Even knowing that Nubor was a god, Hal could not help but be extremely impressed by Nubor's speed and agility. Somehow, Nubor was keeping four enemies on the defense all by himself, and didn't even seem to be getting tired. If anything, Nubor seemed to be enjoying himself, because Hal was almost certain he heard laughter amid the clanking of steel on steel and metal tearing through flesh.

In seconds, the remaining four guardsmen lay in various states of defeat around Nubor. Aside from a crown of sweat building on his forehead, Nubor looked more like he had just taken a refreshing shower rather than having just finished fighting six elite angels.

"Good game, good game," said Nubor to his guardsmen. He pulled out a towel from nowhere and wiped the sweat off his face. "You actually made me sweat this time. Impressive. Take five minutes to rest up and then we'll be back at it immediately."

Though the guardsmen did not groan or express displeasure with Nubor's orders, Hal sensed that they were not looking forward to another session of getting beaten up by Nubor.

Nonetheless, the guardsmen rose to their feet and began collecting their weapons or dusting themselves off. Nubor watched them for a moment before turning his gaze to the stands.

Nubor instantly froze when his eyes fell on Hal and the

others. He now resembled a hound dog who had just noticed unwanted intruders in his territory.

"Uh-oh," Keershan said with a gulp. "He sees us."

"But he's not going to hurt us, right?" Hal said, trying to sound—and feel—optimistic. "None of us have even met him before."

Boca smiled. "Speak for yourself."

Just as Hal remembered Boca's past with Nubor, the king of the gods appeared in front of them. It was like he had teleported from the arena to the stands. At least, Hal assumed Nubor had teleported, because he definitely hadn't seen the divine king move.

"Boca," said Nubor, his tone flat yet angry at the same time. He looked her up and down. "You aged terribly."

Boca smiled. "I'm still mortal, Nubor. That means I can't remain young and pretty forever, unlike you and the rest of the gods."

Nubor snorted. "And what brings you back here? Surely you don't think I am going to take you back after what you did to me."

Hal looked at Nubor in puzzlement. "You seem less surprised to see Boca here than one would expect."

Nubor glared at Hal. "I have known she was here since your arrival in the city. I was there at the meeting for Shirataka's murder. That's why I haven't killed you three yet, even though mortals are not allowed to watch the training of the gods."

"We aren't?" Keershan said.

Nubor growled. "Normally, no. But because the other gods have voted to give you the chance to prove your innocence, I can't lay a finger on any of you. At least, not until tomorrow, when you hit your deadline and the divine protection wears off."

Hal did not know if he should be impressed that there was a power that even the king of the gods had to obey or nervous that said power would only last for another twelve hours or so at most.

Boca stood up. She was just slightly taller than Nubor, although he was far more muscular. "Then you must know why we are here. We think you may know something about Shirataka's murder. And want your blessing for dealing with Kryo Kardia."

Nubor met Boca's gaze unflinchingly. "And just why would I do either? I didn't witness her murder. And if you are about to accuse me of having murdered her myself—"

"No one is, Your Majesty," Hal interrupted. "We just want your help in finding the murderer."

Nubor pursed his lips. "I see. If that is the case, then perhaps I could tell you what I know, but on one condition."

Boca folded her arms behind her back. "What do you want? I'm sure we can get it for you."

Nubor nodded. "Very well, then. My request is simple: To gain my blessing to defeat Kryo Kardia, I want to duel the Dragon Rider, Halar Norath, for exactly one minute in the arena. I will also answer your questions about Shirataka, of course."

Hal put a hand on his chest. "Wait, you want to duel me? Why?"

Nubor flashed Hal a strange grin. "Because it has been thousands of years since I last dueled a Dragon Rider. Dragon Riders are said to be the mightiest among mortals.

I would like to see if you could last against me for a minute."

Hal frowned. "I am honored that you would want to duel me, Your Majesty, but I don't think it would be very fun for you. A minute doesn't seem like a long time for a fight."

Nubor nodded again. "It is not, but it is how long the last Dragon Rider I fought ages ago lasted."

"Hal, don't fight him," Keershan said. "He's a god. You'll never win."

Nubor waved a hand. "He doesn't have to *beat* me. He just has to survive in a fight with me for one minute. And besides, the fact that I am a god is irrelevant, given how you two are two of the only mortals who have ever killed a god."

Hal pursed his lips. Nubor was clearly referring to the Nameless One. "Is that why you want to duel me? Because we killed the Nameless One?"

"Partially," said Nubor. "That certainly did get my attention. If you can kill a god, you will undoubtedly give me a good fight. Feel free to bring your dragon with you, by the way. It's only fair."

Hal looked at Boca. "Boca, we don't have time for this."

"Actually, Hal, I think we do," Boca said with a wave of her own hand. She looked at Nubor. "Will you agree to answer our questions about Shirataka's demise and give us your blessing for dealing with Kryo Kardia, if Hal and Keershan duel you for one minute?"

"Of course," said Nubor. "And if they don't, then Raniel here will escort you out of the temple and you will have to look elsewhere for clues to Shirataka's murder and the blessing you need to defeat Kryo Kardia. Deal?"

Boca smiled. "Deal."

Nubor turned toward Hal and Keershan, a rather vicious grin on his face. "You heard the witch. Meet me in the arena in five minutes."

With that, Nubor disappeared again, only to reappear in the arena, where he immediately began doing stretches and other things to prepare for the fight.

Hal wasn't sure why, though.

It's not like we'll stand that much of a chance against him, Hal thought.

You're probably right, Keershan said, *but like Nubor himself said, we just need to fight him for one minute. If we are still in fighting shape by the end of the minute, Nubor will basically give us everything we want. Seems like a good deal to me.*

Hal supposed that Keershan had a point.

But watching Nubor's preparations in the sandpit below did not help his confidence one bit. Or the knowledge that the future of their investigation now rested fully on his and Keershan's shoulders.

Still, Hal began making his way down the stairs to the arena sandpit. He would have prayed to the gods for strength and courage, but somehow he doubted the gods would listen to any prayers from him right now.

Chapter Thirty-One

"WHAT'S THE PLAN, HAL?" KEERSHAN SAID AS THEY stepped into the sandy arena pit.

Hal held up one finger. "Survive exactly one minute against the king of the gods."

As Hal said that, he cast his gaze toward the other end of the arena. Gotcham Nubor stood there, along with two elite divine guardsmen, who were apparently massaging his shoulders and oiling up his armor. Nubor flashed Hal an amused grin when he noticed him looking, which did nothing to quell Hal's own nerves.

Keershan looked crestfallen. "Hal, that is a goal, not a plan. Please tell me you have a plan."

Hal rubbed the back of his neck. "We don't know exactly how powerful Gotcham Nubor is or what tricks he has up his sleeve, so I figure we should just try to avoid engaging with him directly for as long as possible. If we can dodge him for a full minute, then that will satisfy his requirements even if we don't actually fight him."

"What about using the Final Relic?" Keershan questioned. "Couldn't we use that to even the odds a bit?"

Hal touched the cold metallic surface of the helmet on his head. "Yes. I was also thinking about using it. That would be our best bet at surviving, since the Final Relic will make us faster and stronger."

Keershan nodded. "Sounds good. I'm still kind of nervous about the fight, though."

Hal patted Keershan on the head. "Don't worry. We don't need to win this fight. We just need to avoid getting knocked out for a full minute. I think we can handle that."

Keershan wagged his tail back and forth. "I suppose."

Hal frowned. Thanks to his bond with Keershan, he could feel Keershan's emotions almost as keenly as he could feel his own. Thus, he felt how worried and anxious Keershan felt as they went into this fight.

Hal, however, was genuinely confident about their chances of success. The Final Relic had been all they needed to defeat the Nameless One, who had also been a god, after all. And while they were not trying to defeat Gotcham Nubor, the power of the Final Relic would undoubtedly give them the edge they needed to survive for the requisite minute in the upcoming duel.

Looking up at the stands, Hal spotted Boca and Raniel sitting in the seats closer to the edge of the arena. Boca waved at them in a friendly way, while Raniel just scowled, arms crossed in front of his chest, clearly seeing this whole thing as a gigantic waste of time.

But Boca and Raniel were not the only spectators. A handful of elite divine guardsmen sat in the stands, along with a growing number of angels and other semi-divine entities. Hal even thought he saw a couple of gods and goddesses in the back rows, apparently interested in watching this fight.

"Looks like we will have an audience for our duel," said Gotcham Nubor suddenly, causing Hal to look at him. The king of the gods was walking toward the middle of the pit, a single golden broadsword in his hand, clad in brilliant ruby-encrusted silver armor, although he did not wear a helmet over his head.

"Yeah, I noticed," Hal said, also walking up to the center of the arena with Keershan by his side. "News apparently travels fast here."

Gotcham Nubor smirked. "I sent a mental notice to everyone in the temple to come and watch me duel a real Dragon Rider. You have quite the reputation around here, so of course the others wanted to watch my gloriousness pound you into the sand."

Hal licked his lips. He didn't feel particularly pressured by the audience, but he could feel Keershan's anxiety growing worse now that he was aware they were being watched.

It's okay, Keershan, Hal said mentally. *Just ignore the people. Remember, we're only fighting one person, not the whole crowd.*

Keershan nodded. Hal felt Keershan calm down under his influence, though the dragon's nerves were quite obvious.

Drawing his sword, Hal said to Gotcham Nubor, "Thanks. We'll make sure to put on a show for everyone who took time out of their day to watch our duel."

Gotcham Nubor rolled his shoulders. "Good to know."

Hal immediately climbed onto Keershan's back. Reaching up to his helmet, Hal said, "You don't mind if we use the Final Relic, do you? Even the odds a little bit."

"Use whatever you want," Gotcham Nubor replied. "As mortals, you will need every bit of help you can get just to survive against me. I'm not worried."

Indeed, Gotcham Nubor didn't look even slightly worried about them. The king of the gods stood tall and proud, silver armor glowing under the crystalline lighting overhead, hands clutching his broadsword tightly. The confidence was particularly evident in his eyes, which glowed a soft golden color, emphasizing his divinity quite well.

Hal, not letting Gotcham Nubor intimidate him, reached into the Final Relic. He tapped into its power just as he had done in the past and suddenly felt raw divine energy flow through his and Keershan's bodies. His own fears and worries were washed away in an instant as the Final Relic's power filled his very self. Even Keershan felt considerably less worried underneath Hal, standing up a little taller, raising his head and giving Gotcham Nubor a challenging look, their armor and scales now glowing as golden as the sun.

Gotcham Nubor nodded approvingly. "Well done. If I didn't know any better, I would say you two aren't mortals. You look far more divine than mortal right now. Such is the power of the gods."

Hal grinned. "You can be afraid if you want."

Gotcham Nubor laughed. "Why would I be afraid of you? After all, the last Dragon Rider I dueled also used the Final Relic … and he only lasted sixty seconds against me."

Hal's eyes widened when Gotcham Nubor said that, but before Hal could rethink his brilliant plan, Gotcham Nubor launched forward, swinging his sword at them.

But Keershan shot into the air, narrowly avoiding

Gotcham Nubor's sword. Even as Keershan flew, however, Gotcham Nubor reached out with his free hand, caught Keershan's tail, and hurled them both across the arena.

Hal and Keershan crashed into the sand, separating from each other upon impact and rolling away in opposite directions. Although the impact didn't exactly hurt thanks to the protection of the Final Relic, it did temporarily stun Hal, who lay on the smooth sand, his heart beating rapidly.

But then Hal heard rushing footsteps coming toward him and rolled out of the way at the last second. Gotcham Nubor's broadsword slammed tip-first into the spot where Hal had been lying, digging deeply into the sand.

Rising to his feet, Hal whirled around and thrust his sword into Gotcham Nubor's unprotected face. But Gotcham Nubor blocked Hal's sword with his own, having pulled it out of the sand with lightning-fast reflexes.

A stream of golden dragonfire slammed into Gotcham Nubor, practically consuming the god. It came from Keershan, who had risen back to his feet, his mouth open as he poured burning dragonfire onto Gotcham Nubor.

Keep it up, Keershan! Hal said mentally, straining against Gotcham Nubor's sword. *We've got him right where we want—*

Gotcham Nubor abruptly spun around, knocking Hal's sword aside. His sword slammed into Hal's chest, once again sending him flying. He slammed into the arena wall and slumped to the ground, breathing hard. This time, he actually felt pain, which made him wonder just how hard Gotcham Nubor had hit him.

Looking up, Hal saw Gotcham Nubor fly through Keershan's dragonfire and slam his fist down on Keershan's head. Keershan cut off his dragonfire and was smashed into the ground as Gotcham Nubor pressed a foot down on his head.

Overhead, the assembled crowd cheered wildly for Gotcham Nubor, chanting his name over and over again. Gotcham Nubor waved at the crowd briefly, clearly basking in their praise.

Coughing, Hal rose to his feet unsteadily, causing Gotcham Nubor to cast a look in his direction.

"Hmm?" said Gotcham Nubor. "You still stand? Impressive. It's been fifteen seconds and yet you are still able to walk. Maybe you are stronger than you look."

Hal's eyes widened. It hadn't felt like fifteen seconds, though he had to admit that his perception of time was very skewed in the abode.

Still, Hal clutched his sword and fired a dragonfire ball at Gotcham Nubor. But Gotcham Nubor casually deflected the fireball before shooting toward Hal faster than a speeding arrow.

Hal just barely brought up his sword in time to block Gotcham Nubor's next blow, and it took all of his agility, experience, and sword training to keep up with the god's next series of attacks. It felt like Gotcham Nubor had twenty swords, rather than one, and he was trying to hit Hal with every last one of them.

Blocking a sword clearly aimed at his head, Hal left himself wide open for a sword aimed at his hands. The sword slashed his right hand, causing him to drop his sword. Gotcham Nubor followed it up with a kick to the chest that knocked Hal flat onto the ground, knocking the breath out of his lungs.

Rolling his shoulders again, Gotcham Nubor said, "Twenty seconds. You can give up now if you want."

Hal scowled, yet he struggled to move. Every bone and nerve in his body felt like it was broken. And it probably would have been broken if not for the power of the Final Relic. Hal didn't even want to know how much pain he would be in right now if not for the Final Relic.

Getting onto his hands and knees, Hal said, "N-No. One minute. We can do this."

Gotcham Nubor shook his head. "Mortal persistence is amusing, but also very sad. Time to end this before I get *too* bored."

Gotcham Nubor pulled his foot back and lashed out with a powerful kick aimed at Hal's face.

But Hal, drawing upon his bond with Keershan, caught Gotcham Nubor's foot with one hand. It felt like holding back a charging bull, but somehow, Hal did it.

A genuinely shocked look appeared on Gotcham Nubor's features just then before Hal shoved Gotcham Nubor back. The king of the gods lost his footing and stumbled. For a moment, Hal thought Gotcham Nubor would fall onto his back.

Instead, Gotcham Nubor somehow pulled off a backflip that no mortal could ever have hoped to. Landing several feet away from Hal, Gotcham Nubor rose to his full height, glaring at Hal, who was now rising to his feet.

"How many seconds has it been, Gotcham?" Hal said. "Thirty? Maybe we'll set a new record for longest mortals fighting against you."

Gotcham Nubor practically growled. "Thirty-one, to be exact. It's clear I underestimated you and your dragon. Let me finish this *now*."

Gotcham Nubor slammed his foot onto the sand underneath them. Without warning, the sand shook and shifted, rapidly turning into quicksand.

Alarmed, Hal fought against the quicksand as hard as he could, but the quicksand seemed to hold him much more tightly than normal quicksand. Hal wondered if this divine quicksand was different from the quicksand in the mortal realm before deciding that it was irrelevant to his current predicament.

Gotcham Nubor stood on what seemed to be the only patch of sand in the arena that hadn't been turned into quicksand. He watched smugly as Hal sank deeper into the quicksand.

"Once you are up to your neck in quicksand in the next two to three seconds, I imagine you will have to forfeit," said Gotcham Nubor. "After all, it is difficult to fight when one has no arms or legs."

Hal scowled, but he couldn't find the words to respond to Gotcham Nubor's taunts. It took all of his strength just to keep his head above the quicksand. He knew that Gotcham Nubor wasn't going to kill him, but his survival instincts didn't know that, forcing him to thrash about to save himself.

But no matter how hard Hal tried, nothing he did worked. He just continued to sink deeper and deeper into the quicksand, his only solace being that he kept his arms raised overhead, although he knew that would not do him any good once his head went under.

A flap of wings overhead caused Hal to look up in time to see Keershan—not bound by the quicksand in the slightest—soaring toward him and Gotcham Nubor. The king of the gods had just enough time to look in Keershan's direction before Keershan slammed into him, knocking the King off his perch and into the quicksand.

Then, displaying a sort of agility Keershan normally never possessed without the influence of the Final Relic, the Steed reached out with his claws and grabbed Hal's outstretched hands. Hal felt the quicksand pulling on him, trying to keep him from escaping, but Keershan's wings, powered by the divine energy of the Final Relic, allowed him to overwhelm the quicksand's grasp.

And with a roar of triumph, Keershan yanked Hal out of the quicksand and into the air, Hal's quicksand-covered legs dangling underneath him as they soared into the air.

"Woohoo!" Keershan cried out as they flew. "Take that, stupid quicksand!"

Hal, clutching Keershan's front claws for dear life, nodded. "Thanks, Keershan! Didn't think I'd survive for a moment there."

"No problem, Hal," Keershan said. "I knew that Gotcham Nubor had forgotten about me, so I used the element of surprise to take him down while he wasn't looking."

Hal smiled and glanced at the sandpit below. "I wonder how much time is left on the clock. Surely the minute should be up any second—"

Without warning, Gotcham Nubor shot into the air from the quicksand, broadsword in hand. He hurtled toward Hal and Keershan like an arrow, eyes blazing with divine energy, an enraged scowl on his lips.

"You … can't … escape *me*, mortal!" Gotcham Nubor cried out, his voice barely audible over the sound of divine energy crackling around him.

Hal gasped. There was no way either he or Keershan

could dodge Gotcham Nubor's next strike, not when Hal was dangling freely like this. He could only watch as Gotcham Nubor's sword swung toward his face—

And then stopped, less than an inch from the very tip of Hal's nose.

"What the—?" Hal said, staring down the tip of the blade at Gotcham Nubor, who was frozen in midair before them. "What happened? Why did you stop?"

Gotcham Nubor gritted his teeth. "One minute … has passed."

Then, without warning, Gotcham Nubor lowered back down onto the sand, which had seemingly returned to normal. Keershan flew down as well, depositing Hal a few feet above the sand before landing himself.

As soon as Hal and Keershan touched down, Hal looked up at the audience around them. Even though he had not been fighting for the amusement of the spectators, he was still curious to see what their responses would be.

Complete and utter silence reigned in the arena. Most of the divine and semidivine entities looked shocked, particularly the gods and goddesses in the back. Hal did not see either Boca or Raniel, however, making him wonder where those two had gone.

Hal felt a powerful, angry divine presence behind him and turned around to find himself face-to-face with Gotcham Nubor. The king of the gods stood less than five feet away from them, glaring down at Hal with absolute hatred on his face.

Hal, deciding to be a good sport about it, held out a hand. "Thanks for the fight, Your Majesty. It was … thrilling. A true challenge."

Gotcham Nubor looked at Hal's hand as if Hal had

offered him a dead rat. "Challenging for you, maybe. But for me ... I didn't even break a sweat."

"Good job, Hal and Keershan," Boca said without warning. She and Raniel stepped into the arena from a nearby entrance, Boca clapping her hands softly. "I knew you could do it."

Raniel pursed his lips. "Dumb luck is all it was. Or perhaps His Majesty was pulling his punches. Either way, I doubt you could do it again."

"Silence, Raniel," Gotcham Nubor said. "The mortal and his dragon survived for exactly one minute. And, while I am no more happy about it than you are, that means I must stay true to my word and tell them what I know about Shirataka."

"And grant us your blessing for stopping Kryo Kardia," Boca added.

Gotcham Nubor sighed. "That, too, I suppose. But not here. Let us go to my throne room to discuss this matter, where there is more privacy."

Hal understood Gotcham Nubor to be referring to the spectators of the duel. While some had left already, many still lingered, gazing at Hal and Keershan with looks that could be described as both respectful and annoyed.

It must be pretty novel for them to see a couple of mortals go toe to toe with Gotcham Nubor himself and survive, Keershan said mentally.

They look as offended as Raniel, Hal noted, *but that's fine. We didn't come here to win their respect. Just solve Shirataka's murder and get the help we need to stop Kryo Kardia for good.*

Chapter Thirty-Two

GOTCHAM NUBOR'S THRONE ROOM, IT TURNED OUT, WAS not very far from the arena pit. His elite divine guardsmen escorted Hal and the others through the halls of the temple to the throne room, while Gotcham Nubor went to shower and prepare himself for the meeting. Hal didn't think Gotcham Nubor looked or smelled sweaty even after their intense duel, but he supposed the king of the gods wanted to look more like he fit the divine king that he was.

By the time they reached the throne room, however, Gotcham Nubor was already sitting on his throne. He looked very different from how he had looked in the arena. His silver armor had been replaced with opulent golden robes lined with a huge variety of gemstones, his fingers lined with rings of every color. A golden crown sat atop his head, under which his watchful gray eyes gazed down at Hal and the others as they assembled before him.

"Where do you wish to start?" said Gotcham Nubor.

Boca held up a finger. "Yesterday, after Shirataka spoke to Salard and went to see Demo."

Hal frowned and gazed around the throne room. "Speaking of Demo, where is he, anyway?"

"Even I do not know that," said Gotcham Nubor, sounding clearly unhappy about his own ignorance. "Demo does what he wants to do, when he wants to do it, how he wants to do it. Even I have no authority over him."

"Plus, we don't actually need to talk to Demo, anyway," Boca said. She pointed at Gotcham Nubor. "Because Shirataka didn't actually go to Demo next, did she? No, she went to *you* next after speaking with Salard."

Gotcham Nubor frowned. "If you are accusing me of having murdered Shirataka *again*—"

"I have made no such accusation, Your Majesty," Boca replied. "In order to solve this murder, we need to retrace Shirataka's steps."

Gotcham Nubor pursed his lips. "You are correct, then. Shirataka did visit me after speaking with Salard. She shared her fears about this Kryo Kardia mortal and the danger he presented to the mortal realm. She even compared him to the Nameless One, a rare thing indeed, for the Nameless One is in a league of his own."

Hal stroked his chin. He had never thought to compare Kryo Kardia to the Nameless One before, although he could certainly see the similarities between the two beings. He still wasn't convinced, however, that Kryo Kardia actually was worse than the Nameless One.

"What did you tell her?" Boca said.

Gotcham Nubor tapped the arms of his throne. "I told her that I did not think that Kryo Kardia was a threat to the gods. And should he ever try to be, we would slap him down, as we have done to every mortal whose power has outpaced their ability to make accurate risk assessments."

Hal frowned. "So you basically told her that her concerns were unfounded, then."

"I told her that she could do what she wanted with him, but that she would not receive help from me or the other gods," Gotcham Nubor replied. "I believe she was mostly concerned because of Kryo Kardia's invasion of the nation of Tipjok, where she is highly revered by the mortals who live there. This probably made her want to look for any way to save them, as Shirataka has always had a soft spot for mortals that the rest of us gods do not have."

Gotcham Nubor spoke of Shirataka's love for mortals in the same way a human might describe another human's over-fondness for certain animals. It made Hal wonder if the gods thought of mortals as little more than animals.

"What did Shirataka do after that?" Boca asked.

Gotcham Nubor folded his arms in front of his chest. "She said she would bring it up at the next convocation of the gods, the very same one that was supposed to happen today, in fact. She said she would seek the support of the other gods, particularly once she revealed certain damning information about Kryo Kardia that she thought would convince the other gods to join her cause."

"Damning information?" Keershan repeated. "What sort of damning information?"

Gotcham Nubor shook his head. "She seemed to think that Kryo Kardia had a spy in the abode, whose job was to keep an eye on the gods and report our movements and decisions to Kryo Kardia. I told her that that was ridiculous, but she said she would find proof and present it at the convocation for all to see."

Hal stroked his chin and glanced at Boca. He could tell that the Snow Witch also found Shirataka's theory about a spy within the abode interesting because it dove-tailed with their own theory as to the identity of Shirataka's killer.

"Where did Shirataka go after that?" Boca inquired.

Gotcham Nubor frowned, as if trying hard to remember. "She said she would go into the city to gather some evidence before the convocation began, but where she went exactly, I do not know. I do know that, shortly after she left this throne room, her body was found in the streets of the abode."

"About how long was it from the time she left your throne room to the time her body was found in the streets?" Boca asked.

Gotcham Nubor rested his chin on his hand. "About an hour and a half, give or take. I am not the God of Time, so I rarely keep track of it very accurately or in any great detail."

"That must have seemed like an instant to you," Hal said, "given how ancient and long-lived you are."

Gotcham Nubor nodded. "It does. It's why we gods have so little respect for you mortals. Especially when you take into account the time differences between the abode and the mortal realm."

"Time differences?" Hal said. "What do you mean?"

Gotcham Nubor gave Hal a puzzled look. "Have you not noticed that time operates at a different pace here than in the mortal realm? While you and your dragon may have only been here for one day, in the mortal realm, a week or more has likely passed already."

Hal felt his heart race at this revelation. "Seriously? A week?"

Gotcham Nubor shrugged. "As I said, I am no God of

Time, but that is usually how the time differences work out."

Hal's mind raced as the implications of Gotcham Nubor's statement sank in. *If we have been gone for a week already …*

A lot can happen in a week, Keershan said mentally. *For all we know, Kryo Kardia may have already invaded the kingdom. We could be too late.*

That occurred to me, too, Hal thought. He glanced at Boca. *I sure hope Boca knows what she's doing, because I fear we don't have nearly as much time as we thought.*

"Ultimately, the time differences are irrelevant to this investigation," Boca said. She then bowed before Gotcham Nubor. "But thank you for your time, Your Majesty. You have given us a lot of useful information about Shirataka and her untimely demise."

Gotcham Nubor glanced at a huge golden clock hanging on the wall nearby. "You have less than twelve hours left to solve this murder, but something tells me you won't."

Standing upright again, Boca said, "On the contrary, Your Majesty, I am convinced that we are this close to proving our innocence *and* revealing the true murderer of Shirataka."

"We are?" Keershan said in surprise. "Because from my point of view, I think we're still kind of stuck."

"Don't worry," Boca said. "We're just waiting on one last piece of evidence that will let us connect the dots *and* solve this murder once and for all."

Raniel put his hands on his hips. "Such arrogance. Do you really think that your last piece of evidence will just walk into the room and hand itself over to you? That's not how actual murder investigations work, you arrogant—"

Without warning, the doors to the throne room burst open and another angel—this one wearing robes and gold-rimmed glasses on his face—stumbled breathlessly into the room, clutching a stack of papers in his arms. "Captain Raniel! I have finally finished putting together the report for—"

The angel stopped speaking as soon as he saw Gotcham Nubor, who was frowning in clear disapproval of the angel's sudden entrance.

The angel immediately knelt, his head bowed, saying, "So sorry for the interruption, Your Majesty Gotcham Nubor. If this is a bad time, I can wait outside the throne room."

Boca gestured for the angel to approach. "No, this is the perfect time, actually. Come over here."

Gotcham Nubor glared at Boca. "You dare order my angels around in my own throne room? While I sit upon my throne?"

Boca met Gotcham Nubor's gaze without flinching. "Perhaps I do. What will you do about it?"

The two stared each other down for what felt like an eternity to Hal before Gotcham Nubor finally looked away. "Angel, you may come forward and present your report to us."

The timid angel, rising to his feet, cautiously but quickly approached the throne. Handing the papers to Raniel, the angel said, in a slightly breathless voice, "Captain Raniel, this is the complete autopsy of Shirataka's corpse. I just finished it less than a minute ago."

"Really?" Raniel said, who sounded both surprised and,

perhaps, a little disappointed at the same time. "That was quicker than I expected."

The angel bowed nervously again. "I know, but the order was to get it done today, so I had to put aside all my other duties to make sure I got it done. Without error, of course."

Boca immediately snatched the papers from Raniel's hand and flipped through them. "Interesting ... interesting ... *very* interesting ..."

Hal, leaning over to read the report Boca held, asked, "What is so interesting, Boca? What does the report say?"

Boca, however, pulled the report closer to her chest, like she didn't want Hal or anyone else to read it. Her eyes shined with a strange light now, a light that Hal had not seen in them before but which he recognized as expressing one simple emotion.

Triumph.

"Thank you for the flawless autopsy report, my friend," Boca said, patting the other angel on the shoulder. She held up the report. "This report confirms my suspicions and proves, beyond a shadow of a doubt, who Shirataka's actual murderer is."

"So it proves that you three did it, then?" Raniel said. "I'm not sure I would be so happy about that if I were you, witch."

Boca shook her head. "You will find out exactly what it says at the next convocation of the gods. Which Gotcham Nubor will be hosting today."

"Today?" Gotcham Nubor said. "You make it sound as if you can tell me what to do."

Boca gave Gotcham Nubor a smug look. "Trust me, I

need to have *all* of the gods together in one room for this revelation. It is the only way we will catch the murderer."

Gotcham Nubor appeared as if he was going to shut down her request and tell them to leave, but then his shoulders slumped and he sighed. "I could never say no to you, Boca, even when I should. Very well. I will call a second convocation of the gods today to discuss the results of your investigation."

"Thank you, Gotcham," Boca said with a wink. "I knew you would see reason eventually."

Hal leaned toward Boca again. "Are you sure that Keershan and I can't see the report yet? We would like to know who the murderer is."

Boca patted Hal on the head like he was a small, ignorant child. "Do not worry, Hal, Keershan. Soon, everyone will know who really murdered Shirataka … and why."

Hal pursed his lips but decided to trust Boca this time. She seemed to know what she was doing and seemed very confident that the autopsy would vindicate them.

Raniel, of course, was glaring at Boca, probably because of how disrespectfully and bluntly she spoke to Gotcham Nubor.

Then Boca turned away from them and said, "Let us head to the meeting chamber of the gods … and finally put this entire mess behind us, once and for all."

Chapter Thirty-Three

SURRELS STARED AT THE SPOT ON THE STAGE WHERE TENKA and Priest Om had once stood. There was nothing left of them, not even one hair on Tenka's head. If he hadn't witnessed their demise himself, Surrels would have thought that neither of them had ever stood on the stage at all.

"Damn," Argon said, standing next to Surrels, holding an ax in his hands, though Surrels wasn't sure where Argon had been hiding that weapon this entire time. He was trembling. "The bedtime stories me old mom used to tell me about the demons are nothing compared to the real things."

Surrels said nothing, mostly because he was more used to fighting demons than Argon was. Even so, Surrels could not deny that this demon felt particularly vicious and cruel.

Killing its own allies like that in broad daylight, where everyone could see it ... Surrels shook his head. *Yet another reminder to never, ever trust a demon.*

The people around them stared in silent horror at the

demon, which was now licking its fingers like it had just enjoyed a good meal.

"Delicious," the demon said between finger licks. "Arrogant humans who think they are in control always taste the best."

"Monster!" one of the guards in the crowd cried. He burst out of the crowd, sword in hand, rushing toward the demon. "For the murder of Noble Hojara, you must be put to—"

The demon's spider-like legs flashed across the guard and, in an instant, the guard lay in bloody pieces on the ground at its feet.

The demon then picked up a chunk of the guard's flesh and popped it into its mouth like it was a snack. "Stupid humans taste even better."

The fearful spell that had fallen over the crowd seemed to break as soon as the demon spoke. Screams of pure terror erupted from the crowd as everyone ran away from the demon, fleeing into the streets and back alleys of the capital. Even many of the guards fled, along with most of the nobles, military leadership, and master mages on the stage. Neither Fralia nor Anija, however, fled, which was nice, because Surrels had a very bad feeling about this particular demon.

"What are you, demon?" Argon demanded. "And what did you do with Stebo?"

The demon cast a careless look at Argon. "You mean the human boy I replaced without you even knowing? He's still alive, if that's what you're asking. Just not here at the moment."

Surrels furrowed his brow. "Argon asked a good question. You don't seem like the other demons we've faced before."

The demon licked his lips. "That's because I am not. The demons you fought served the Nameless One. I, on the other hand, serve myself."

Surrels's eyes widened. "But I thought all demons served the Nameless One."

The demon snorted. "How perfectly appropriate that creatures of the light such as yourself have no idea what is truly going on in the dark. For you see, we demons are creatures of chaos and destruction. We bow to no one except those who bend us to their will, just as the Nameless One did. That is the only reason any of my siblings ever followed him."

"You mean you never did?" Surrels said.

The demon spread his arms. "Of course not. That foolish god got himself kicked out of the heavens, killed once by mortals, and then killed *again*, for a second time, by more mortals. If he hadn't been a fallen god, I would have finished him myself. I do not follow failures like him, even when they make enticing promises of human flesh and souls we can devour."

"Is that what you did to Tenka and Priest Om?" Argon said. "Did you devour their … their souls?"

The demon licked its lips again. "And their bodies. It has been ages since I last tasted human flesh. And now, I have a whole city of humans to devour. Such a feast shall be spoken of in demonic legend for many ages to come, I am sure."

"Sorry, demon," Anija said, still standing on the stage behind the demon. Her daggers burned with dragonfire. "But if you think we're going to sit back and let you have your way with the people of the capital, then you are sorely mistaken."

The demon glanced in Anija's direction. "Ah, the Dragon Riders. If there is one good thing the failed god did, it was ridding the mortal realm of your kind. Unfortunately, it looks like he couldn't even keep you away forever. How disappointing."

"You are severely outnumbered, demon," Fralia said. She gestured at the Dragon Riders perched on the buildings facing the square. "We've got about a dozen Dragon Riders here. And we have a lot of experience slaying demons, in case you weren't aware."

The demon grunted. "I am very aware of my current situation. But just as you Dragon Riders did not come alone, neither did I."

From within the shadows of the Dragon Riders and their Steeds rose dozens of demonic hands and claws, reaching for Rider and Steed alike. The Dragon Riders tried to fly away, but the demonic claws dug into their clothes and scales, while actual demons crawled out and began attacking the trapped Riders and Steeds.

On the stage itself, three demons rose up behind Anija and Fralia. The two women were forced to turn around and fight off the demons, Anija swinging her daggers, Fralia slinging spells left and right as even more demons rose from the shadows to attack them.

The demon smirked. "That should keep them busy for a while." He glanced at Surrels and Argon hungrily. "I sure could go for another snack."

Surrels gulped. "How come there are still so many demons? I thought that when the Nameless One died, you could not enter the mortal realm anymore."

The demon chuckled. "All the Nameless One did was organize us. And any sufficiently powerful demon can lead the others, if we so will it. And I have a will strong enough to raise up a fair army of demons myself."

Then the demon turned to face Surrels and Argon. "But I don't think an army will be necessary to end your pathetic lives."

The demon's spider-like legs lashed out toward Surrels and Argon. Surrels blocked them with his sword, but just barely, only for one to sneak past him and impale Argon. The Dead Dragon cried out in pain as the demon ripped its tendril out of his stomach, causing Argon to collapse onto the street.

"Argon!" Surrels called out. "No!"

Unfortunately, Surrels allowed his concentration to be broken, letting the demon's spidery legs slam into him. The blow knocked Surrels off his feet, and then the demon's legs wrapped around his ankles and started pulling him toward the demon, who watched with hunger and amusement as Surrels drew closer to him.

"You have been a particular thorn in our side for a while now, General Surrels," said the demon as Surrels bumped along the ground toward him. "Although I lack Tenka's personal hatred of you, I still recall how you and your son killed my brother in that farmhouse. And demons are even less forgiving than humans."

With a snap, Surrels found himself dangling upside down before the demon. He tried to hack at the tendril with his sword, only for another tendril to lash out and knock his sword out of his hands. His sword fell onto the street below with a clatter, leaving Surrels entirely defenseless against the demon.

"No need for that weapon of yours, human," said the demon. "I find that metal isn't very appetizing, although the flesh of my enemies is always delicious."

The demon opened its mouth, which opened wider and wider, until Surrels found himself staring into a gaping maw of jagged, bloody teeth that was far too big to fit inside the head of a young boy. The putrid breath of the demon wafted out of its mouth into Surrels's nose, making him gag.

Against Surrels's will, the demon brought him closer and closer to his mouth. Even worse, Surrels knew he couldn't escape. Without his sword, Surrels's options were extremely limited.

That was, until a mighty roar of a dragon above made the demon pause. Its dark eyes flickered up to the sky before he suddenly threw Surrels to the side.

Surrels hit the ground and rolled for several feet, the impact knocking the air from his lungs. Even so, Surrels got up just in time to see a massive ball of dragonfire crash directly down onto the demon, utterly consuming it in dragonfire. The demon didn't even scream as the flames ripped through its body, the bright light of the fire obscuring its body from view.

A moment later, Rialo landed a few feet from Surrels, smoke trailing from her mouth as she glared at the flames that had once been the demon.

Panting hard, Surrels said, "Thanks, Rialo! That dragonfire is very handy sometimes, isn't it?"

"Don't let your guard down," said Rialo roughly, gazing around at the square. "There are still so many demons to kill. Fortunately, I think we should be able to finish them off now that their leader is—"

Thick spikes of shadow erupted underneath Rialo, spearing straight through her body and making her roar in pain. Surrels scrambled away from Rialo as the shadow spikes stabbed her again and again, sending golden dragon blood flying everywhere.

"Rialo!" Anija cried out on the stage, though she was clearly too far away to come to the rescue of her Steed.

As for Surrels, he could only watch in horror as Rialo collapsed onto the ground in a pool of her own blood. The shadow spikes sank back into the ground, her shadow moving away from her until it stopped a good distance from her body.

Then the demon leader rose up from within its shadows, looking no worse the wear for having been burned to a crisp by Rialo's dragonfire earlier.

"Now that was a close one," said the demon leader, brushing ash off its shoulders. "I almost let my hunger get the best of me. Fortunately, I got the best of the dragon."

Surrels shook in his boots. Rialo was, to the best of his knowledge, the strongest dragon in the kingdom. To see her get practically eviscerated like that was enough to make Surrels wonder if the demon leader had had a point in his dismissal of the Nameless One earlier.

There's nothing I can do for Rialo right now, unfortunately, Surrels thought, slowly rising to his feet. *But I might be able to find Stebo. I don't know where the demon put him, but if I can find him, then maybe I can—*

A single shadow tendril launched out and wrapped around Surrels's left wrist, making him feel as if he had just plunged his left wrist into ice water.

The demon leader smirked. "Where are you going, snack? I haven't forgotten about you."

Surrels struggled to break the demon's grip on his wrist, but it was no use. The demon leader's grip was stronger than steel. Even worse, he could practically feel the demon leader sucking the life out of him, making it harder and harder to remain standing, much less fight off its influence.

"That's right," the demon leader purred, its voice audible above the sounds of fighting going on all around them. "Feel the coldness of death seep into your muscles. Let it devour you from the inside. Know that there is no hope, either for you or your friends."

Surrels found that difficult to argue with, mostly because he was so weak and tired and cold. He almost gave into the demon leader's efforts to pull him in, thinking that that might be easier than fighting a losing battle.

The demon opened its mouth again, wide enough to let Surrels see all of its dozens of teeth …

And then a small, round object flew out of nowhere and landed directly inside its maw.

The second the object touched the demon's tongue, it exploded. A fiery blast erupted from the demon's head, causing it to screech in pain as the blast ripped through its form. The tendril attached to Surrels's wrist broke in an instant, causing Surrels to stumble backward away from the burning remains of the demon.

Rubbing his wrist, Surrels gazed uncomprehendingly at the demon's fiery form, saying, "A grenade? Where did that come from?"

"Who else?" said a familiar male voice behind Surrels.

Whipping his head over his shoulder, Surrels's jaw dropped when he saw Kendo and Catol walking out of the alleyway behind him. Kendo carried several grenades in a belt across his chest while Catol carried a bow that she had already nocked with an arrow.

"Kendo? Catol?" Surrels said in surprise. "Where have you two been?"

"Looking for Stebo," Kendo replied. He gestured at Catol. "We think we know where he is."

"You do?" Surrels said in relief. "Where?"

Catol gestured at the demon leader. "The demon leader has put him inside some kind of pocket dimension. We figured this out when we ran into one of his fellow demons in the alleyways and interrogated him. By killing the demon leader, we should be able to free Stebo."

Surrels sighed. "Wonderful news. And it looks like you already killed him, so Stebo should be free soon, right?"

A sound somewhere between the hiss of a snake and the roar of a lion erupted from the fiery remains of the demon leader. Six shadowy tendrils rose out from within the flames and raised out of it a demonic creature truly from nightmares.

It looked like a naked, emaciated human baby, minus any visible genitalia. Tentacles hung from its mouth, its red eyes reflecting the light from the flames underneath it dangerously. Its demonic eyes darted to Surrels, Kendo, and Catol, its purple tongue running across its lip-less mouth.

"That … hurt," the demon leader growled. "Fortunately, my human guise took the brunt of the damage. Otherwise, I might have actually had to retreat."

"That's your real form?" Kendo said. "Definitely an ugly baby."

The demon leader scowled. "Make all the cheap shots you want, humans. I'll happily devour *all* of you just the same."

Chapter Thirty-Four

WHEN THE DEMON LEADER EVISCERATED RIALO, IT TOOK all of Anija's willpower not to utterly collapse alongside her.

Unfortunately, it turned out not to be enough.

Pain unlike anything else Anija had experienced ripped through her body like fire. She gasped and collapsed onto the stage, dropping her weapons and clutching her chest. She felt as if she had been stabbed hundreds of times by extremely sharp knives herself, even though she neither saw nor felt any wounds on her own body.

A flash of light overhead preceded the appearance of a translucent green barrier, which the demons that she and Fralia were fighting immediately started striking with their claws and weapons.

Fralia, panting hard, knelt beside Anija and put a hand on her shoulder. "Anija, what happened? Are you okay?"

Anija gritted her teeth. "Goddamn … it's like *I* got eviscerated, too."

Fralia's eyes widened behind her glasses. "Not good. I'll

do whatever I can to keep the barrier up, though I can't support it forever."

Anija nodded. "Thanks but … but Rialo's pain … I feel every bit of it as if it were my own."

Anija glanced toward Rialo, who lay on the ground below in a pool of her own blood. Rialo wasn't dead, at least not yet, but Anija could also tell that her Steed was not going to be getting back up anytime soon. She reached out through their bond to check on Rialo's health but got no response other than a weak tingle of dread and pain from Rialo.

I'll help you as soon as I can, Rialo, Anija said mentally. *I won't abandon you. I promise.*

"Would casting a healing spell on you help Rialo?" Fralia asked.

Anija shook her head. "Don't think so. Even though I feel Rialo's pain, my body is actually unharmed. You can't heal Rialo by healing me. Dragon Rider bonds don't work like that."

Fralia pursed her lips. She opened her mouth to say something else, but Anija did not get to find out what it was before a particularly bulky demon slammed its rock-like fists into the barrier. The barrier flickered and shuddered but remained standing, only for the bulky demon to strike it again and again, each strike leaving more cracks where it hit.

"How long until the barrier falls?" Anija said.

Fralia put a hand on her forehead. "Based on my current moulash reserves … five, maybe ten, minutes at most."

Anija grimaced. She looked out over the public square

that had now turned into a battlefield between Dragon Riders and demons.

Fortunately, after the initial shock of the surprise demon attack, the Dragon Riders had rallied and recovered enough to fight back. Even better, Anija did not see any dead Riders or Steeds among them. It helped that some of the capital guards, perhaps the braver ones, had chosen to stay and help them fight off the demons.

But for every demon killed, two or three more would take its place. It reminded Anija of the Battle of the Tops, only she didn't know where all of these demons were coming from. She really had thought that the death of the Nameless One would have made the demons disappear forever, but apparently, they had just gone into hiding and had been waiting for the perfect time to strike.

Her eyes were drawn toward Surrels, along with two other people she did not recognize—a young man who bore a startling resemblance to Surrels underneath his facial tattoo and a young woman with a bow—who had to be Kendo and Catol. Surrels was confronting the demon who had identified himself as the lead demon earlier. Its form had changed, however, making it look even less human than before.

The demon leader showed no fear as it faced Surrels and the others. If anything, it looked like it was more angry than fearful, a strange hissing, gurgling sound coming from deep within its throat as it slowly approached them.

There's no way they can kill that thing on their own, Anija thought. *But everyone else is too busy with the demons to save them.*

In addition to that thought, another thought, more like a feeling, filled Anija's mind.

Red-hot revenge.

Pure anger flowed through Anija's soul as she looked at the demon leader. It had been the demon leader, after all, who had nearly killed Rialo. The demon leader was the cause behind the suffering and chaos here.

The demon leader needed to die.

Preferably as painfully as possible.

The anger ripped through Anija's body and soul, burning the pain away. It did not heal—that would have to come from a different source—but it did make the pain feel less overwhelming. The pain became weak enough that Anija could ignore it for now.

Rising to her feet, Anija glared at the demons assaulting the barrier. "Fralia, drop the barrier."

An alarmed look crossed Fralia's face. "Drop the barrier —? But you said—"

"Drop it," Anija said. She raised her knives, which glowed with charged dragonfire. "The barrier isn't protecting us anymore. It is, however, protecting the demons."

Fralia pursed her lips, but nodded. She waved her hands and the barrier fell.

The demons, seeing the barrier fall, roared in triumph and rushed toward Anija and Fralia. They clearly thought that they had the upper hand now that the barrier was no more, that they would be able to attack Anija and Fralia and kill them where they stood.

No one had ever said demons were smart, Anija supposed.

Knives flashing with dragonfire, Anija rushed toward the demons. Every slash of her daggers slashed a throat, gouged out an eye, or carved out a vast swath of flesh and organs from a demon's body. The demons' triumphant roars turned into shrieks of fear and agony as Anija's fiery daggers tore through their vile forms, sending black blood and guts flying in every direction.

Yet Anija barely paid attention to the screams of agony, other than to take primal pleasure in hearing the death throes of her hated enemies as they perished under her relentless attacks, to take in the stench of their blood and guts and practically revel in it. A part of her almost wished the killing would last longer.

But then it would leave her no time to kill the *actual* transgressor.

The demon leader himself.

When the last of the demons on the stage died with a split skull under her knife, Anija whirled around to see the demon leader stalking toward Surrels, the young man, and the young woman. The demon leader didn't even seem to be aware of the massacre on the stage behind him.

His last mistake.

With a roar like a dragon, Anija leaped off the stage toward the demon leader. Dragonfire flashing along her blades, Anija aimed directly for the demon leader's back.

But at the last second, the demon leader looked over his shoulder and vanished into a pool of shadow. Anija's knives slammed into the street, cracking it under the impact of her blow but leaving the daggers themselves unharmed.

"Coward!" Anija screamed into the air, rising to her feet. "Show yourself, you son of a bitch!"

"How rude," came the demon leader's voice seemingly from everywhere at once. "Human women really are the worst."

The demon leader suddenly rose from Surrels's shadow behind him and placed a long, knife-like leg at his throat.

Surrels froze while Kendo and Catol backed away quickly, though the demon leader paid them no heed. His dead red eyes were fixed on Anija, who ripped her daggers out of the street and stood up.

"You are the Rider of the dragon I just eviscerated," said the demon leader. "I see you are quite upset about that."

"That's putting it mildly, demon," Anija growled. "I'm going to do *much* worse to you."

The demon leader shook his head. "Go ahead … if you want your fellow human here to die, of course."

Surrels gulped but did not move or say anything. His eyes were fixed on the sharpened leg at his throat.

Anija stepped forward. "You bastard—!"

The demon leader jerked his leg in a way that made Anija's heart leap but did not actually seem to hurt Surrels. "I know that you care very much about your Steed. I also know you care very much about your friend here. Let's see who Dragon Riders truly love most: Their fellow humans or their precious Steeds. Which one will you choose, I wonder?"

Anija hated the demon leader more than anyone else right now. She wanted to burn his disgusting face straight off his skull.

But the rational part of her restrained her from acting just yet. However much she might have wanted to rip the demon leader apart limb from limb, she knew that the demon leader would probably slit Surrels's throat before she could kill him.

The demon leader was right about one thing: Surrels was her friend and she did care about him.

Yet Anija's desire for revenge made it difficult to think

clearly. She was also aware that killing the demon leader would turn the tide of the battle in the Dragon Riders' favor and might even allow the others to finish off the rest of the demons.

But I can't attack the demon leader without risking Surrels's life, Anija thought, clutching the wooden handles of her knives tightly in frustration. *He's got me.*

Anija looked at Surrels. She expected to see fear in his eyes, which would have been the logical reaction, seeing as Surrels was just an ordinary human at the mercy of a bloodthirsty demon.

Instead, however, Anija saw something else entirely: A steely determination to do what was necessary to end the fight, no matter what.

No words were exchanged between them. All Anija needed was a look into Surrels's gaze to see that he had a plan for dealing with the demon leader.

She just needed to trust him.

Him … and the others.

Raising her knives, Anija said, "I reject your offer, demon."

The demon leader cocked its head to the side. "What do you mean?"

Anija took a deep breath, which steadied her yet did nothing to dilute the intense anger coursing through her veins like lava. "You said I would have to choose between my Steed and my friend, as if Dragon Riders must choose one or the other. But you don't understand that Dragon Riders can choose both."

"So?" said the demon leader. "What difference does that make?"

"All the difference in the world, frankly," Anija said.

"The role of Dragon Riders is not to pick favorites, but to be a bridge between humanity and dragonkind. We don't fight for one or the other. We fight for both. And that is why I reject your offer."

The demon leader scowled, bringing his leg ever so slightly closer to Surrels. "Are you absolutely certain of that choice, Anija? You know what the consequences for your friend will be if you do not stop me."

"I know exactly what you want to do, demon," Anija replied. "But I don't think you will be able to do it."

The demon leader smirked. "Why not?"

"Because you underestimated us," Anija said. "Just like you demons always do. Fralia!"

Without warning, Fralia appeared behind the demon leader, her hands glowing with green moulash. She thrust her hands toward the demon leader, who suddenly began to choke.

"Air—?" the demon leader gasped, clutching at his throat with his hands. "No ... air ...?"

Fralia nodded, still holding her hands up. "That's right, monster. Although you demons are very different from humans and dragons, one thing about you is still true: To exist in this world, your physical body needs to be able to breathe air."

"And Fralia just so happens to specialize in air magic," Anija added, "including creating a vacuum around a person's head."

The demon leader did not respond as he choked to death. But he did let go of Surrels and sink into the shadows at Surrels's feet, perhaps trying to retreat or maybe reappear somewhere else where he had access to air.

But shockingly, Surrels turned around, grabbed one of

the demon leader's legs as he descended into the shadows, and was pulled in right alongside him,

Before the startled eyes of Anija, Fralia, Kendo, and Catol, Surrels vanished into the shadows with the demon leader without a sound.

Chapter Thirty-Five

THE TENSION IN THE AIR OF THE JUDGMENT CHAMBER OF the gods was so thick that Hal could have cut it with a butter knife.

All of the hundreds of thrones of the gods were currently filled, each one having a different god or goddess seated upon it. It seemed as if every god in the world had shown up to this event. Even Demo, that mysterious purple orb that may or may not have been an actual deity, hovered on his throne. Hal also spotted Salard lounging on his throne, though he was much smaller than before, closer in size to a normal dragon than the giant he had been back inside his cavern. His daughter, Vilona, sat silently by his side, her watchful eyes fixed on the mortals in the center of the chamber.

And instead of Judge Noak from the last Convocation, Gotcham Nubor, the king of the gods himself, sat on the judgment seat before them. He was bigger than before, a couple stories tall at least. Combined with Salard's smaller-than-normal size, Hal assumed that the gods could change their forms at will.

"I didn't realize there were so many gods in the world," Keershan whispered to Hal. The young dragon stood next to Hal, his golden eyes scanning the room. "I mean, I've always known there are many gods in the world, but I've never seen so many in one place before. I can't even name them all, and I tried."

Hal rolled his shoulders. "If you can't name all of the gods, then I probably shouldn't try, either. They would probably smite me for disrespect because I forgot about one or two of the minor ones."

"Don't worry," Boca said, standing on Hal's other side. "The gods will not lay even one finger on any of us until we have presented proof of our innocence to them. Then it will be the murderer who will be put to death, and we shall walk free and alive."

Hal looked at Boca. The Snow Witch looked perfectly at ease beside him, brushing aside a strand of long, white hair from her face. Indeed, she seemed to be the only person in the room who was even remotely relaxed. Everyone else, particularly the gods, practically stank of tension and paranoia.

That wasn't surprising. After all, now was the time when Hal and the others would present their proof to the gods. Boca still hadn't shared Shirataka's autopsy results with Hal or Keershan yet, which frustrated Hal because he wanted to know who actually killed Shirataka. Boca had insisted, however, that they wait until the convocation for some reason.

"Don't relax too much, now," Raniel said, the angelic being standing several feet away from them. "After all, you are about to show the gods what I have known all along: That you murdered Shirataka and that you three deserve nothing less than the harshest possible punishment for it."

Boca shrugged. "Thanks for your opinion, Raniel. I am glad we asked you for it."

"We didn't ask for his opinion, though," Keershan said.

Boca smirked. "That's the point, my dragon friend."

Raniel just glared at Boca. "Why am I even down here with you? I should be leading the divine guardsmen who are protecting the temple. At the very least, I should be guarding the doors. I have nothing to present to the gods."

Boca patted Raniel on the shoulder. "Because you were also part of this investigation, Raniel, whether you like it or not. For that matter, you were part of the investigation whether you liked *us* or not. Your word will be quite helpful when it comes to vouching for our innocence to the gods."

Raniel glared even more at Boca, brushing her hand off his shoulder. "You must be truly delusional if you think I would ever testify in defense of murderers such as yourselves."

Boca rolled her eyes. "Just stand there and look pretty until the presentation begins. Your opinion of us might change."

Raniel did indeed remain quiet, but Hal could tell that Raniel had no intention of changing his opinion of them. Nor did Hal expect him to.

He'll probably still think we're murderers even if Boca shows ironclad proof that we are innocent of the crime we've been accused of, Hal thought.

Probably, Keershan agreed. *On the bright side, Raniel's opinion isn't the one that matters. Only the opinions of the gods matter.*

If they think we're innocent, then we're good to go, even if Raniel thinks we're guilty.

Hal gazed around at the gods again. It was difficult to read their expressions and body language. He couldn't tell if most of the gods still thought they were guilty or if perhaps the gods were just tense because of the nature of the meeting. After all, they were about to find out exactly who in the abode had murdered Shirataka, and perhaps even why.

Then a loud bell tolled throughout the temple, the same bell Hal had seen on top of the building when they first entered the abode what felt like a lifetime ago now.

The tolling of the bell instantly silenced the chattering gods and goddesses, though their eyes went from Hal and the others to Gotcham Nubor himself.

Clad in black judge robes, although still wearing his golden crown, Gotcham Nubor raised his hammer into the air. "Brothers and sisters, I call today for the start of this emergency convocation of the gods. I anticipate that this meeting will be short, but highly impactful, for today we will find out the identity of the one who murdered our beloved sister Shirataka earlier today."

Gotcham Nubor gestured at Hal and the others. "Three mortals—Halar Norath, a Dragon Rider, his Steed Keershan, and the Snow Witch known as Boca Secha—were tasked with investigating the murder of Shirataka, with the promise that we would allow them to live if they were able to prove their innocence, having previously been accused of being the murderers themselves. They were carefully watched by Captain Raniel, the loyal Captain of the Divine Guard, to ensure that they did not try to sneak away or evade justice under the pretense of continuing their investigation."

The other deities nodded as Gotcham Nubor spoke, though Hal saw no reason why Gotcham Nubor was repeating information everyone already knew. Perhaps it was part of the judgment process.

"And finally, the mortals approached me less than two hours ago, asking to present the findings of their investigation to the gods in an emergency convocation," Gotcham Nubor continued.

"They have finished their investigation already?" asked a god with a human body but the head of a bull, a puzzled expression on his face.

Gotcham Nubor nodded. "So they have told me. As the murder of one of our own in the streets of the abode is such a serious crime, I made the decision to call this convocation right away. The longer the murderer is allowed to roam free, the more danger we are all in. This is why I have taken on the role of judge as well, for the Ancient Laws say that the king of the gods can act as judge in certain circumstances."

Mutters of agreement flitted through the watching crowd, mostly in agreement with Gotcham Nubor's point about none of them being safe while the real murderer roamed freely. Certainly, several of the deities exchanged fearful looks, perhaps not expecting to hear good news from Hal, Boca, and Keershan.

Gotcham Nubor pointed at Boca. "But that is enough from me. I will now let the mortals speak for themselves and present their findings and conclusions from their investigation to the gods."

Boca stepped forward, arms folded respectfully in front,

and bowed. "Thank you, Your Majesty, for that brief but necessary introduction. Whilst I am sure that all of the gods present know what has been happening in the abode recently, it is good to recap for those who may have been absent for the previous convocation."

"Just get on with it," a goddess with hair that looked like leaves snapped from her throne. "We don't have all day."

"Yes, yes, I will get to the point, don't worry," Boca said. She gazed at Gotcham Nubor. "But first, has the temple and all its known exits been locked down?"

Gotcham Nubor frowned but nodded slightly. "Yes. Per your request, I ordered a complete lockdown of the entire temple as soon as the last of the gods arrived, including a lockdown of this room. No one can get in or out, not even with magic."

"What?" said the leaf-haired goddess, looking at Gotcham Nubor in shock. "Why would you lock us all in here?"

Boca sighed. "Because the real murderer of Shirataka is not out there. They are in here."

"In here?" said the bull-headed god. "As in, inside the temple walls?"

"Not just within the temple," Boca replied. She gestured at the room. "They are inside this very room with us even as we speak."

That got everyone's attention. The gods and goddesses looked around in alarm with more than a few rising halfway from their thrones, as if they were thinking of trying to escape anyway even though everyone was locked inside the room. It was the first time Hal had seen the gods display true fear, which was understandable, although still unnerving given how much power was currently housed in this room. Anything that could scare a god had to be dangerous.

And anyone that can murder *a god must be doubly so,* Hal thought, gazing around the chamber, wondering just who Shirataka's murderer was.

"Do not worry," Boca said, raising her voice to be heard over the ruckus. "The murderer may be among us, but they will not be taking the lives of anyone today. I asked for the room to be locked off precisely to prevent the murderer from escaping justice."

Raniel sneered. "What recklessness! Do you want to put the lives of the gods at risk? If the murderer is still here, then they could conceivably murder another deity."

Raniel's sentiment certainly wasn't uncommon. The gods looked even more nervous than before, muttering anxiously among themselves and looking around the chamber with fear in their eyes.

But most of the eyes of the gods were on Boca in the center of the room, who looked unperturbed despite the revelation she just dropped on them.

Hal was certainly surprised. Boca had not told either him or Keershan that the murderer was in the room with them. Like everyone else, he had assumed that the murderer was outside of the building, perhaps somewhere else in the abode. Now more than ever, Hal was curious to see how Boca intended to prove her statement.

Folding her arms behind her back, Boca said, "Worry not, Raniel. Although the presence of the murderer in this room does put the gods' lives at minor risk, in the end, the murderer is the one who will suffer. They are, after all, entirely on their own. They should be more worried about their own safety than anything at the moment."

"Boca," said Gotcham Nubor in a tense voice. "Please present your evidence and findings to the gods. Now."

Boca waved a hand at Gotcham Nubor. "Of course. Let's start with the autopsy of Shirataka's body, which we received from a helpful angel who is currently not here but who is most certainly not the murderer himself."

Raniel narrowed his eyes. "That seems like a suspiciously specific denial to me, witch."

"Only because I like to be thorough in clearing up potential suspects in a case," Boca said. She pulled the autopsy out from behind her back, unfurled it, and began reading. "Anyway, the autopsy claims that Shirataka was stabbed to death with a sword. Most likely, it was a sword imbued with divine energy."

"Meaning we can safely take the other gods off the list of suspects?" said Gotcham Nubor.

Boca shook her head. "Not quite yet. After all, it is difficult for mortals and even demigods to get their hands on divine weapons. They must either steal them from the gods … or willingly receive them *from* a god."

"Or find them in a long-forgotten temple and use them for their own purposes," Raniel said, shooting a nasty glare at Hal and Keershan. "They have a sword. I'd say they both look rather guilty right now, myself."

Hal could almost physically feel the eyes of the gods glaring at him and Keershan. He tried not to look concerned, but it was difficult with so many powerful entities glaring at him and Keershan like that.

Boca, however, dismissed Raniel's comments with a wave of her hand. "I've already ruled out Hal and Keershan. One, they were with me when Shirataka's body was found, and there is no way either of them could have sneaked off to kill her without me noticing their absence. And two, Hal's sword is, by itself, an ordinary weapon and only becomes divinely powerful when he uses the power of the Final Relic, which Hal has only used once so far in the abode. Plus, neither of them has a good motive for wanting to kill her anyway."

Hal breathed a sigh of relief. Despite knowing that he and Keershan were completely innocent of any crime or wrongdoing, a part of him had been unnecessarily anxious about the result. Hearing Boca so confidently clear their names, however, still brought much relief.

Keershan sighed as well. "Thanks, Boca. Glad you think so highly of us."

"What I think about you has nothing to do with your innocence," Boca said. "The evidence simply doesn't point in that direction. It points elsewhere, to someone already in the abode, someone who has access to divine weapons, and a reason for wanting to use them to kill Shirataka."

"What are you waiting for?" said Gotcham Nubor. "Stop wasting time. Tell us who you think killed Shirataka. And why."

Boca snorted. "'Why' is obvious. Just before her death, Shirataka had voiced concerns over the mortal known as Emperor Kryo Kardia, emperor of the Glaci Empire in the mortal world. She went to many gods to voice her concerns, but at each turn, she found little or no help."

Hal glanced at Gotcham Nubor and Salard when Boca said that. Salard looked sad, gazing at his front claws while Gotcham Nubor bit his lower lip, clearly trying to restrain himself from doing something he would probably regret.

"And then, after meeting with His Majesty, Shirataka left the temple to prepare for the first convocation," Boca continued, "only to be ruthlessly murdered in the streets of the abode by someone who is working with Kryo Kardia but lives here."

"An inhabitant of the abode murdered Shirataka?" Raniel demanded. "Impossible. Everyone who lives here loves the gods, and Shirataka has always been especially popular with the abodians."

Boca looked over her shoulder at Raniel, tapping the side of her head. "But she didn't have *universal* popularity. All it takes is one bitter or angry or self-centered person with sufficient motive, and even a god can be killed."

"Then it must have been one of the angels," Gotcham Nubor concluded. "A member of the Divine Guard, perhaps, having gone rogue, for they all have access to divine weapons."

Boca scratched her chin. "That was my first thought as well. I even thought that Raniel might be the one who did the deed, that his fanaticism and bigotry against us was him projecting his own guilt onto me and my allies. But in the end, I had to reject that thesis."

Raniel scowled. "You thought *I* was the murderer but decided I wasn't? I am not sure if I should be offended or not."

"Feel however you want," Boca said, "but know that I doubt any of your fellow bodyguards or guardsmen are guilty of this crime. But I do think that someone close to the gods *is* responsible, although not a god themselves. Perhaps not directly, anyway."

Hal furrowed his brow. He had to admit, he had also thought that Raniel might be the culprit, mostly due to Raniel's hostile attitude toward them. Yet if Boca was right, then Raniel was innocent.

Doesn't make him any less of a jerk, though, Keershan said mentally.

True, Hal said. *It just means he is slightly less of a jerk than we originally thought.*

"Again, Boca, just tell us who the murderer is," said Gotcham Nubor. "We do not have all the time in the world to listen to you ramble."

Boca shrugged. "Very well. I suppose I'll just get straight to the point. The murderer of Shirataka, the one person who is responsible for killing the goddess of light herself … is right … there."

Boca pointed. Every eye in the room followed her finger, including Hal's and Keershan's.

As for who Boca pointed at … it was Vilona, the daughter of Salard, who wore a surprised expression on her face.

Chapter Thirty-Six

SURRELS WAS NOT NORMALLY THE SORT OF PERSON TO TAKE unnecessary risks like he just did. He liked to play it safe, making sure not to overextend himself or take risks without thinking them through properly.

But this time, Surrels decided that following the demon leader into the shadows was a risk he was willing to take.

His only regret was not communicating that plan to Anija and the others ahead of time.

To be fair, however, Surrels had not expected he would try something so rash, either. He supposed that he was capable of surprising even himself sometimes.

Plunging into the darkness was like plunging into the sea. Ice-cold shadow swept past Surrels as he clung onto one of the demon leader's legs, clutching its thin limb with both hands as tightly as possible. Surrels could neither see nor hear nor feel anything except the icy darkness and the sharp firmness of the demon leader's leg as it bit into the palms of his hands.

Yet Surrels did not let go. He did not panic. He just clung fiercely to the demon leader until a light shone ahead and they emerged from within the darkness into a room he did not recognize. Surrels slammed into the stone floor of the room, letting go of the demon leader's leg and falling flat onto his back. Breathing in and out hard, it took Surrels a moment to catch his breath and make sense of his surroundings.

Note to self: Never follow a demon into the shadows again, Surrels thought, his heart thumping inside his chest, his muscles still quite stiff. *Not unless you want to feel colder than winter in the Tops.*

Surrels's plan had been simple. After learning from Kendo and Catol that Stebo had been kidnapped by the demons and taken somewhere only the demons could reach, Surrels figured that the only way to save Stebo from the demons was to follow them to wherever they retreated whenever they fled into the shadows.

Of course, what seemed like a simple plan to Surrels had turned out to be a lot more difficult to put into practice. It had relied on luck more than anything, as well as gambling that the demons needed to breathe air as much as humans did and would do whatever they could to get relief from a lack of it.

The only question now was, had his plan been successful? Had the demon leader taken him to where Stebo was being kept, and, if so, was Surrels going to be able to take Stebo back to the mortal realm?

Only one way to find out.

The strength in his muscles slowly returning, Surrels rose to his feet and looked around at his surroundings.

As Surrels had noticed earlier, the demon leader had

taken him to a stone chamber, although it was far, far bigger than he had initially realized.

The vast stone chamber had to be as big as the throne room in Castle Lamor, if not bigger. Stalactites and stalagmites hung from the ceiling and jutted from the floor, giving it a very cave-like feel. The only light was the flickering green light from the torches along the walls, which offered very little visibility.

But it did show Surrels the large object in the center of the room. It looked almost like a water well, only much bigger than any well Surrels had ever seen. And he somehow doubted it was full of water or any other liquid a human could drink.

And there was a strong stench of blood and death in the chamber, the same stench that the demons themselves stank of. It was also very cold, although not as cold as the actual shadows themselves were. Even so, it was enough to make Surrels shiver and wish he had brought a proper coat.

Then again, it's not like I was planning to go here in the first place, Surrels thought.

One thing Surrels did not see, however, was Stebo.

"Stebo!" Surrels cried out. "Stebo, are you here? Where are you? Stebo!"

"Surrels …" Stebo's voice sounded weak but close by. "Help me …"

Surrels whipped his head to his left and saw a sight that made his heart clench.

Stebo was chained to the nearby wall by the wrists, his short legs dangling above the ground. He was still clad in the robe and hood he'd worn earlier, although his face was far more cut up and bruised than before. His skin looked especially pale in the illumination from the green torches on the walls.

Surrels rushed over to Stebo, checking the boy's body. "Stebo, are you all right? Are you injured? Did the demons hurt you?"

Stebo, sobbing, said, "N-Not really, but I'm still scared. I just want to go home."

"I just want to go home," repeated the mocking voice of the demon leader behind Surrels. "Human children are so weak."

Surrels whirled around in time to see one of the demon leader's legs coming straight at him. Surrels leaped to the side, avoiding the leg, which embedded itself in the stone wall directly above poor Stebo's head. Stebo cried out in fear as the demon leader yanked its leg out of the wall and turned toward Surrels, who finally got a good look at it.

The demon leader's appearance hadn't changed much since they got here, but somehow, Surrels sensed it was stronger. Its eyes, certainly, glowed a brighter red in the darkness than in the light, gazing hatefully at Surrels from within the demon leader's inhuman face.

"You followed me here," said the demon leader. "I don't know if I should be impressed or offended. You are, perhaps, the first human to have ever entered this place willingly."

Surrels reached for his sword, only to realize it was missing. He must have lost it at some point during the transition from the mortal realm to … to … "Where *is* this place, anyway?"

"Nowhere a mortal could access on their own," said the demon leader. He gestured with one of his short arms. "This is the demon realm, the underworld, as you humans tend to call it. It is where we demons are born and where many, if not most, of us die."

Surrels's eyes darted over to the well-like structure in the center of the room. He recalled something Hal had told him after the death of the Nameless One, about how the demons were born and created. "That's the well, isn't it? From which all demons are born and to which all demons go when they die?"

The demon leader's red eyes glowed. "You seem to know a lot about our kind despite being a human."

"Heard about it from a friend of mine," Surrels said. His eyes flicked to the well. "If I kill you, your soul will go back there, right? That's how the demons work."

The demon leader grinned underneath the tentacles covering his mouth. "In the physical world, yes. Here, however … I can return as soon as I want."

Crap. Surrels had not realized that the demon leader probably had a massive advantage over Surrels here. After all, the demon realm was the home territory of the demon leader. Killing the demon leader here would only inconvenience him for a short time, not stop him entirely.

"I see you have already realized your mistake," said the demon leader. "By allowing me to choose the battlefield, you have unwittingly signed your own death sentence. All to save the worthless life of a small child who isn't even related to you by blood."

Surrels bit his lower lip, his eyes darting to Stebo. The young boy was sobbing again, although much more quietly now, perhaps because he was getting tired. "Stebo's life isn't worthless. He's going to be the next king of Malarsan, whether you like it or not."

The demon leader sneered. "I do not care which

human sits on your human throne. Human politics bore me. All I care about is devouring human souls to my heart's content. That is all any demon desires, truly."

"I-I'm not going to let you do that, either," Surrels said with a gulp. "You aren't going to feed on any human souls today. Not if I have my say."

"As if I care about what *you* say," said the demon leader. "In any case, even if you were to somehow defeat me in combat, you do realize you are stuck here, yes? Only demons can leave and enter the demonic realm. Humans like you, if you are unfortunate enough to end up here, are stuck. Forever."

Surrels had not realized that, either. He hadn't actually thought through how he was going to get Stebo out of here once he defeated the demon leader, or if it was even possible to escape at all.

Perhaps seeing the worry on Surrels's face, the demon leader said, "Yes. Feel that despair. Know that there is nothing you or any of your friends can do for you now. You and the boy will be lost in the shadows forever. Embrace it, for I will ensure you do not live long enough to regret it."

Surrels took a deep breath and gazed at the demon leader. "So what? Even if I can't leave here on my own, I can still fight you."

"To what end?" said the demon leader. "I am far from the only demon here. And not even the most bloodthirsty, either."

Several pairs of red eyes gleamed in the shadows around them suddenly. From within the shadows came growling, snarling demons, ranging from those with goblin-like appearances to hellhounds with fiery manes and burning eyes. Surrels counted at least a dozen demons surrounding him and Stebo, and more still kept emerging from the shadows to join their brothers.

The demon leader spread his arms wide. "There is nowhere for you to run. Nowhere for you to hide. If I do not kill you, one of the others surely will. Your soul will be rend piece by piece until there is nothing left of you other than endless pain and suffering. Does that sound like a fate you wish to endure?"

Surrels's shoulders slumped. As much as he wanted to put on a brave face, like Hal or Anija, the truth was that he couldn't.

He just couldn't.

Surrels fell to his hands and knees, feeling much heavier all of a sudden. He heard the demons growling and moving around him, heard the demon leader's nasty laughter, but he found it harder and harder to care. The very air in the room seemed to be sapping him of energy, slowly but surely killing him.

Surrels had failed. He had failed his son, his daughter, his unborn grandson, his friends, Old Snow, the kingdom of Malarsan … and especially his wife.

But most importantly, most urgently, was that he had failed Stebo. The young boy was now to suffer a fate infinitely worse than death thanks to his failures.

What was I thinking, following the demon leader here? Surrels thought. *I'm not a hero like Hal or Anija. I'm not a powerful mage like Fralia. I'm not even a good organizer like Wilme or know deeply about Malarsan's history like Keershan or a brave leader like Rialo. I'm just a pawn who thought he could redeem himself. There will be no redemption for me. None whatsoever. I might as well let the demons devour us both and get it over with.*

Yes. That seemed like the most logical, the inevitable,

course of action. All Surrels could do was wait and let the demons do what they would with him and Stebo.

Looks like Tenka got the last laugh, after all, Surrels thought bitterly. *Even though the demons may have eaten his soul, Tenka still wins. That bastard.*

The demons were closing in on him and Stebo now. It felt like there wasn't much time before the demons fully devoured his and Stebo's souls.

The demon leader smirked. "Yes. Feel the despair. Let it consume you from the inside out."

That was when a strong, familiar voice bellowed, "The only one feeling despair today will be *you*, demon."

Without warning, a green fireball came out of nowhere, hurtling straight toward the demon leader. The demon leader, however, jumped out of the way at the last possible second, allowing the fireball to strike and destroy several of his fellow demons in the process. The demons who had survived the blast all roared and growled in surprise, turning their heads in the direction from which the green fireball had come. Surrels followed their gaze, too, wondering who had come to save him.

A powerful-looking warrior clad in black armor, his eyes glowing a sickening green from underneath his hood, sat atop a ghost-white dragon. The dragon roared and rushed toward the demons, slamming into them with its body and ripping the demons apart with its powerful claws. Demons shrieked in agony as the dragon bit and snapped at the demons, killing them in one or two blows each, while forcing the rest of them to back off from Surrels and Stebo. Those who avoided the dragon's blows often ended up in the way of the warrior's scythe, which flashed through the air like a predator's claws striking from the shadows.

Surrels gaped at the sight of the slaughter before him. He looked up at the mysterious Dragon Rider and his Steed standing between him and the demons and asked, "Who are you, and where did you come from?"

The Dragon Rider looked over his shoulder at Surrels, showing his skeletal face to Surrels. "Our names are long-forgotten and unimportant. But you may call me the Tomb Guardian and my Steed the Ghost Dragon. And today, we are going to protect you and the boy from these monstrosities."

Chapter Thirty-Seven

ANIJA COULD HARDLY BELIEVE HER EYES.

One moment, Surrels was holding onto the demon leader's leg, perhaps trying to prevent it from escaping.

The next, Surrels was gone, having disappeared into the pool of shadow with the demon leader. Anija reached out with a hand to try to stop him, but she was too far and too late.

"Surrels!" Anija cried out. "Surrels!"

"What happened to Father?" Kendo said, staring at the spot where the shadow pool had once been. "Where did he go?"

Anija rushed over to the spot where Surrels had disappeared and looked around, desperately searching for him but seeing no sign of either him or the demon leader. "I don't know! I don't see them anywhere. I have no idea what happened to him. Or the demon, for that matter."

"Did he die?" said Catol. "Did the demon kill him?"

Anija sighed in frustration again. "I don't know. I didn't know it was even possible for humans to follow demons into their portals like that. This is completely uncharted territory for us. Fralia?"

Fralia pursed her lips, putting her fingers against her mouth. "I … I think *Blood Magic* did mention that it was possible for humans to follow demons into their portals, but I sort of skimmed that passage when I was looking for the spell that would let us talk to Old Snow's spirit, so—"

Kendo whirled around to face Fralia. "Where is the book? Can't you read it and tell us what it says?"

Fralia raised her hands palms-up. "I left the book back in my room in my family's mansion. It would take me a while to go back, get it, read it, understand the spell I'd need to cast to save Surrels, and then actually cast the spell. And that's assuming the spell in question isn't beyond my current magical capabilities or that there even is a way for us to save him at all, which is very far from certain."

"Then what, we're just going to abandon my father?" Kendo said, his hands balling into fists. "Just like that?"

Fralia shot Kendo an offended look. "I'm not saying we should *abandon* Surrels by any means. I'm just pointing out the reality of our situation. Trust me, I don't want to abandon him any more than you do. I just don't see a realistic way for any of us to save him."

Kendo continued to look angry but did not say anything to Fralia. He just glared at the spot where Surrels had disappeared, as if hoping to bring Surrels back through sheer willpower alone.

He must have had a great relationship with Surrels to be this upset about his disappearance, Anija thought. *Wish I'd had a relationship like that with* my *parents.*

Shaking her head, Anija suddenly had an idea and said, "Hey! There are still some demons alive here. If we can capture one of them, maybe we can force it to open a portal to wherever Surrels went and—"

"Captain Anija!" a familiar male voice called out above. "We did it!"

Looking up into the sky, Anija was surprised to see Lieutenant Frik Ragnol, and his Steed, Dinne, flying down toward them. Dinne landed several feet away from Anija, and Ragnol hopped off his back, his green and silver armor clacking as he landed on the cobblestone.

"Ragnol?" Anija said, looking at the Dragon Rider Lieutenant in confusion. "What did you do, exactly?"

Ragnol walked up to Anija with a bit of swagger and jerked a thumb over his shoulder. "We slaughtered all of the demons who had been working for Tenka, Captain."

Anija's jaw fell. "All of them?"

Ragnol nodded proudly. "Yes. Every last one of them. I even personally put the last one to death myself."

"And even better news, we suffered no casualties other than some wounded capital guards," Dinne added with a big dragon grin and a wink. "It was an absolute victory."

Ragnol raised a fist into the air. "Absolute victory, indeed, Dinne. Our victory shall be spoken of in many legends to come! 'Twas truly an epic battle for the ages."

Anija looked around and realize Ragnol and Dinne's report was correct. From what she could see, the public square was entirely devoid of demons now. Meanwhile, the Dragon Riders she had brought with her from the Tops were now congregating around Rialo, trying to tend to her wounds with the medical supplies they had brought with them from Mysteria. Through their bond, Anija could feel Rialo's pain lessening, so she thought that Rialo would be okay for now.

Even so, she asked, *How are you holding up?*

Fine, Rialo said weakly. *Help Surrels. He needs your help more than I do at the moment.*

Anija nodded. *All right. I'll check on you later.*

"Captain?" said Ragnol, apparently noticing her silence. "Are you all right? You look distracted."

Anija waved a hand. "It's nothing, Ragnol. I was just … very surprised to hear that you and the others took care of all of those demons so quickly. Very impressive. Good job and all that."

Dinne frowned. "You don't sound impressed."

"I am, I'm just …" Anija shook her head. "Never mind. Go help Rialo. Fralia and I have other things to deal with at the moment."

Ragnol smiled. "Yes, ma'am! Come, Dinne. Let us go see how we can help Rialo recover from her grievous injuries!"

Ragnol and Dinne rushed over to Rialo's fallen form while Anija ran a hand through her hair. She suddenly felt very useless.

Anija heard running footsteps and saw Catol rush past her. Catol ran over to the fallen Argon, who Anija had almost forgotten about in all of the excitement. Anija then remembered that both Argon and Catol were members of the Dead Dragon Syndicate, which explained why Catol was going to check on him and make sure he was all right.

Anija, however, didn't have it in her to go and check with her. She just turned toward a sullen Fralia and Kendo, her shoulders slumped. "Well, I am officially out of ideas."

Fralia sighed and adjusted her glasses. "I suppose it's never too late to ask the gods for help, but that isn't very certain, either."

Kendo still said nothing. He just continued to stare at the spot where Surrels had disappeared, like he couldn't accept what had just happened.

Anija also couldn't accept it, even if it was true. She knew she should be happy that the rest of the demons were dead, but she couldn't be truly happy until she knew that all of her friends were safe.

If only there was some way I could become a spirit or something and go into the demon realm or wherever they took him, Anija thought, clenching her fists. *Then maybe, I could—*

A thought suddenly occurred to Anija. It was another crazy idea, but it was also their best possible chance at saving Surrels.

Taking a deep breath, Anija closed her eyes and delved deep into her bond with Rialo.

Only this time, Anija wasn't trying to communicate with Rialo. She was trying to communicate with someone else entirely.

It took her a while, but eventually, Anija established a weak link with the person she was trying to talk to.

Tomb Guardian? Anija said mentally, her voice sounding weak even to her. *Are you there? Can you hear me?*

No answer at first, but then the old voice of the Tomb Guardian practically whispered, *You are Anija Ti, aren't you? The Dragon Rider I ran into earlier.*

Yes, Anija said, feeling relieved that her idea had worked. *Sorry to bother you, but we need your help.*

How did you even establish this connection in the first place? the Tomb Guardian demanded. *We are not bonded.*

Anija sighed, but said, *It was a risk. Since I opened my and Rialo's bond to you, I suspected you might still be connected to us somehow. So I tried to reach out to you, and I did. I got lucky.*

Luck has nothing to do with it, the Tomb Guardian replied, his voice more than a little impressed. *You did something even I, a trained and experienced Dragon Rider, never knew was possible.*

Thanks for the compliments, but I need your help, Anija said. *My friend, Surrels, who isn't a Dragon Rider, just got dragged into the demon realm by a demon. Can you save him? Since you're a spirit and all.*

The Tomb Guardian was silent for a long moment, making Anija wonder if their connection had broken already or if maybe she had offended him somehow.

Finally, the Tomb Guardian said, *I will see what I can do. As a spirit, I may be able to enter the demon realm. And since I've seen your memories already, I know what your friend looks like, so it should not be hard for me to find him.*

Thanks, Anija said. *I know Surrels isn't a Dragon Rider, but—*

He is a true friend and warrior, the Tomb Guardian agreed. *One does not need to be a Dragon Rider to be a true hero. I will do what I can for him. Goodbye.*

Then the link broke, and Anija's eyes snapped open as she gasped for breath.

"Anija, are you okay?" asked Fralia, looking at Anija with concern. "What happened?"

Rubbing her forehead, Anija looked at Fralia and Kendo. "I think I just sent someone to save Surrels."

Chapter Thirty-Eight

THE SILENCE THAT NOW REIGNED IN THE CHAMBER WAS beyond deafening. It was downright explosive. Hal's ears hurt just from not hearing anyone say anything.

And he desperately *wanted* someone to speak, if only so the silence would no longer continue.

Because even Hal found it hard to believe that Vilona, the daughter of Salard, the god of dragons, was the murderer of Shirataka.

The expressions of the other gods showed that they were also struggling with that idea. Emotions raging from disbelief to anger to confusion crossed the faces of every deity in attendance. Even the normally unflappable Demo seemed to spin and glow more emotively than before, although that may have just been Hal reading more into him than he was actually showing on his blank physical form.

Finally, Gotcham Nubor, seemingly voicing the thoughts of everyone in the room right now, said, "Vilona … is Shirataka's murderer?"

Boca nodded once. "Yes. Without a doubt, Vilona is not only Shirataka's murderer, but she is even a willing collaborator with Emperor Kryo Kardia himself."

Salard suddenly rose up on all four feet from his throne, his eyes glowing a brilliant golden color. "Arrogant mortal. Do you dare accuse my favorite daughter, who has been loyal to me my entire life, of turning around and murdering my closest friend among the gods? Do you even hear yourself speak when you utter such follies? Will anyone in this room stand to listen to such awful slander?"

Salard's words seemed to break the spell of silence that had befallen the other gods, because the rest of the gods suddenly exploded into shouts, name-calling, and lots of finger-pointing. Most of the shouting and name-calling was hurtled Boca's way, but quite a bit was thrown back to Salard and Vilona. Salard himself, along with a handful of other gods, answered the shouts with shouts of their own.

Hal did note, however, that Vilona herself stayed silent. She just looked down at Boca with her cold silver eyes, both her expression and her body language making it difficult to tell what she was thinking or feeling at the moment.

Keershan, do you believe Boca's accusation? Hal said. *That Vilona is the murderer of Shirataka?*

Keershan shrugged. *I don't know what to believe, Hal. I would like to think that she isn't, seeing as she is one of the First Dragons, but I also don't know what proof Boca has of Vilona's guilt, either.*

True, Hal said. *Boca hasn't actually proved her accusation just yet. Although at this rate, she might not get to if the gods continue to act like this.*

The shouting and screaming of the gods continued to grow louder and louder with more than a handful of gods looking ready to start exchanging blows with one another. Hal was now legitimately worried about getting caught in the middle of a potential battle or conflict among the gods. Given how nearly every god in the world was present here, such a fight would be truly catastrophic on a number of levels.

Finally, however, Gotcham Nubor raised his hammer and slammed it down on the arm of his throne. Indeed, Gotcham Nubor slammed the hammer so hard that it cracked the surface of the arm of his throne, creating an ear-splitting *crack* that echoed above the shouts and screams of the other gods. "Silence!"

Like someone had flipped a switch, the assembled gods and goddesses abruptly went silent. All eyes turned toward Gotcham Nubor, who was now visibly annoyed, his golden eyes glowing dangerously and more brightly than before.

"Boca Secha's accusations against Vilona are, indeed, extraordinary," Gotcham Nubor said, his voice no longer as loud as it once was. "And very serious."

"Serious?" Salard repeated. "They are a terrible lie if you ask me."

Gotcham Nubor held up a finger. "I understand how you feel, Salard, but this behavior is unbecoming of the deities that we all are. Rather than instigate a riot or act like impulsive little children, I suggest that each and every one of us calm down long enough to let Boca present her evidence and explain her reasoning."

Gotcham Nubor used the word 'suggest' the same way a military commander used the word 'order.' Hal should know, because, during his Relic Hunter training days, Hal's trainers had used the exact same tone on him and his fellow Relic Hunter trainees during their training sessions.

Although Hal thought it remarkable how fewer swear words and insults to the others' mothers that Gotcham Nubor used when speaking to the other gods and goddesses.

Fortunately, the rest of the deities seemed to obey Gotcham Nubor's 'suggestion' for now, because they all quieted and settled down. Still, Hal could tell that tensions were running high in the room. It probably would not take much more for someone to cause the arguing and screaming to break out again.

Settling back in his throne himself, Gotcham Nubor gestured toward Boca. "Please continue with the results of your investigation, Boca."

Boca bowed before Gotcham Nubor again. "Thank you, Your Majesty. Like you, I also understand the seriousness of this accusation, but rest assured that I would never make this accusation lightly or without proof or evidence to back it up."

Boca gestured toward Vilona. "First off, Vilona is a resident of the abode. She spends most of her time here, even when Salard does not. Secondly, Vilona is a demigod and has access to the kind of weapon that was used to murder Shirataka. And finally, the autopsy report suggests that Shirataka's corpse has dragonfire marks on it in addition to the stab wounds from the divine sword."

Raniel glared at Keershan. "Keershan is a dragon. Doesn't that implicate him as a suspect, too?"

Boca shook her head. "It does not, Captain, for reasons I have already gone into before. Nor does it implicate Salard, for that matter, because Salard has no reason to murder one of his best friends."

"But why would Vilona have reason to murder Shirataka?" Salard demanded. "She and Shirataka, while not close, were always on good terms with each other. Right, Vilona?"

Vilona nodded, although her expression still remained unreadable. "True, Father. I bear no hate in my heart toward Shirataka or any of the other gods. While I obviously love my own father more than anyone else, I would never even consider taking the life of another deity."

Boca raised an eyebrow. "Not even if you were, perhaps, growing a little jealous of that deity? Or if you were promised a place of prominent power over the mortal world in exchange for ensuring that neither your father nor any of his siblings intervene in the affairs of a certain mortal emperor?"

Vilona narrowed her eyes. "If you think for even a moment that I would have anything to do with Kryo Kardia—"

"Oh, but I do, sweetie," Boca said, interrupting Vilona like she hadn't been talking. "You see, I can tell you're not a very smart dragon. Otherwise, you would have killed us when you had the chance."

Vilona growled, which sounded a bit like thunder in her throat. "Kryo Kardia invaded Tipjok, a nation where both my father and Shirataka were revered by its mortal inhabitants. If anything, I should be the last person you accuse of being Shirataka's murderer."

Boca folded her arms behind her back. "Not necessarily. As I said, I suspect you were jealous of Shirataka. Jealous of her favored position in your father's eyes, jealous of her power and looks, knowing you could never match up to her. She was a goddess, after all, while you were a mere demigod."

Vilona bared her teeth. "Even if I did envy her, I still

would not kill her, much less conspire with a mortal as wicked as Kryo Kardia."

Boca waved a finger at Vilona. "Maybe you didn't envy Shirataka alone. Maybe you also envied your father, Salard, and his position as the god of dragons. You, on the other hand, are destined to remain a relatively powerless demigod for eternity, with no hope of advancement. If Kryo Kardia merely planted the idea in your mind that keeping the gods off his back would, in the long run, benefit *you*, perhaps by giving you your father's position as the god of dragons at some point, then you might be willing to do anything for him. Up to and including the murder of other gods who do want to stop Kryo Kardia."

Vilona rose to her feet next to her father, eyes blazing with cold anger. "You still offer no proof of any of these accusations, you wicked witch. I know nothing about Shirataka's murder or Kryo Kardia or his plans to overthrow the gods or any of the other things you have accused me of. Perhaps Raniel is right. Perhaps you are the real murderers and you are simply accusing me in order to save your own skin."

Boca smiled. "I never said you knew about Kryo Kardia's plans to overthrow the gods. In fact, even *we* didn't know about that ourselves. Care to elaborate?"

All eyes were on Vilona now. The demigod dragon looked taken aback, her silver eyes darting back and forth as she said, "It was just, er, a slip of the tongue. I know nothing about whatever this Kryo Kardia mortal may or may not be trying to do. At the very least, I don't know more than anyone else does."

Boca tapped her finger. "That is an awfully serious 'slip of the tongue' to make, given how no one brought it up until now. Makes me wonder where your mind was during our conversation."

"Isn't everyone thinking about Kryo Kardia to some extent?" Vilona demanded. "He is one of the most powerful mortals in the world at the moment, plus he has invaded several nations whose inhabitants worshiped us. Given how clearly ambitious he is, I think it's fair to assume Kryo Kardia probably would like to overthrow us at some point."

Boca put her hands together. "You don't know that. Yes, Kryo Kardia may be an overly ambitious mortal, but that doesn't automatically mean he is trying to overthrow the gods. You might want to rethink what you just said."

Vilona scowled, but said nothing. That meant either Boca had just made a very good point or Vilona was so offended that she simply couldn't come up with an effective response to Boca's accusations.

Either way, Hal reflected, that did not make Vilona look very good.

Salard looked at Vilona with a hard look now. "As much as it pains me to admit it, Boca may have a point. You are acting a little guilty right now, my daughter. Even so, I still believe in your innocence."

"Even if Vilona is the most likely suspect, what about the sword wounds on Shirataka's body?" Raniel demanded. "Vilona has claws. Not a sword. Plus, how would she have killed Shirataka in public without anyone noticing? She's a full-sized dragon. Hard to sneak around when you are that big."

Boca nodded. "Normally, I would agree with that. But Vilona isn't just a dragon. She is a demigod, meaning she's at least half-god. And just as the gods can change their size and physical forms at will, so, too, I suspect Vilona can do the same thing. She may have taken on a human or humanoid form, dressed herself up in robes to avoid being identified by others, and then stabbed Shirataka to death with a divine weapon."

"All I hear is a lot of conjecture," Salard said. "Until you have hard proof—"

Boca waved a hand. "It would make a lot of sense. Shirataka probably let her guard down around Vilona because she recognized and trusted her. That would explain how Shirataka was killed in the first place, as most gods are good at keeping their wits about themselves and making sure they do not get themselves killed by random strangers. Why would a god let their guard down in public unless it was because they assumed they were with someone they thought they could trust?"

"Again, still no proof of any of your claims," Salard snapped. "If you really want us to believe your ridiculous accusations against my daughter, then you need more than mere conjecture and circumstantial evidence to condemn her."

Boca smiled. "But I do have hard evidence. Let me show you."

Boca clapped her hands, and one of the angels at the doors to the Chamber walked forward. The angel in question carried a long object wrapped in a soft white cloth, which he handed to Boca before walking back to his position by the door.

Boca raised the object for all to see. "This is the proof of Vilona's guilt that you asked for, Salard."

"What is it?" Salard said. "All I see is an object wrapped in a cloth."

Boca wagged a finger at Salard. "But this is no mere object. Allow me to show you exactly what it is."

Boca suddenly unwrapped the object's cloth, allowing the cloth to fall harmlessly to the floor at her feet. Hal and Keershan gasped at what they saw.

The object in question was a golden sword, glowing softly with divine energy and power. And it was covered in the dried gold blood of Shirataka.

"This is the murder weapon used to kill Shirataka," Boca said. "The legendary divine sword known as the Scalebreaker, said to have been forged in the heart of a star at the dawn of creation. With it, even a mortal can kill a god, although a demigod can use it just as well."

All of the gods and goddesses looked nervously at the weapon, and Hal could not blame them. After all, it was one of the few weapons that could not only harm, but even outright kill, the gods. It had even been used recently for that exact purpose, too.

Salard looked as afraid of the weapon as anyone, but at the same time, still unimpressed. "So what if that is the murder weapon? That still does not prove it was used by Vilona. It could have been stolen from the armory in my cave."

Boca lowered the sword. "So you think, but Vilona was not as careful with the weapon as she thought she was. The weapon was found hidden inside a bakery down the street, about a block from the site of the murder. My guess is that Vilona, panicked after killing Shirataka, hid the weapon there intending to return to retrieve it later, only she never did, and it was instead found by the Divine Guard."

Raniel's jaw dropped. "How did I not know about this

until now? I am the Captain of the Divine Guard. I should have known this before anyone else."

Boca shook her head. "Because it was only found in the last couple of hours. I asked Gotcham Nubor to send divine guards to search the area around the site of Shirataka's murder with a fine-tooth comb. I had suspected that the murder weapon might still be hidden somewhere nearby, although even I was shocked at how quickly it was found once the Divine Guard started looking for it."

Hal had to admit he was pretty impressed by Boca's ability to think ahead and do this kind of thing. He had recalled seeing Boca talk to Gotcham Nubor privately after his duel with the king of the gods. When he'd asked her about it afterward, Boca had vaguely said she'd been asking for 'favors,' although Hal didn't interrogate her further due to thinking that her 'favors' were probably personal in nature.

Looks like I should have realized they were connected to this case, Hal thought.

Boca turned the sword over in her hands. "And this sword, in particular, is known to be the property of Salard. Legend has it that the sword's handle was made by melting down some of Salard's scales into the handle, while the blade itself was said to have been forged in the heart of a star. But do you know what other interesting things this weapon can do?"

Boca suddenly pointed the sword toward Vilona. "It won't kill the last person who killed someone with it."

Without warning, Boca threw Scalebreaker toward Vilona. The sword must have been propelled by some kind of magic, because it flew straight and true toward Vilona at an unnaturally fast speed. The other gods sitting around

Vilona ducked to avoid getting hit, but they needn't have worried because Scalebreaker shot past them without slowing down.

Salard raised a claw, perhaps to knock the weapon out of the air, but even he was too slow. Scalebreaker slammed into Vilona's chest …

And bounced off her scales, harmlessly landing at her feet.

Silence once more descended on the Chamber as everyone looked toward Vilona. Hal noticed that the general skepticism among the gods had almost entirely evaporated by now. Even Salard stared with shock at the weapon at Vilona's feet, as if unable to believe what his own eyes were showing him.

As for Vilona, she looked a lot like a cornered animal now, her eyes bulging, her claws digging deeply into her father's throne, shoulders and legs tense.

"Vilona …" Salard sounded heartbroken. "Why?"

Vilona looked at her father, glaring at him. "Because you are *weak*, Father. Because Shirataka would have condemned me to be your good little girl for all of eternity. Because Kryo Kardia offered me the power I deserve. And because he also showed me a vision of a future … a future *without* gods."

Without warning, Vilona snatched Scalebreaker off the ground at her feet and thrust it toward Salard's throat …

Only for Demo to suddenly appear behind Vilona, causing her to freeze mid-swing. She looked over her shoulder at Demo's swirling form, which to Hal, looked as if it was now swirling with anger.

"Demo?" said Vilona. She scowled. "Do you want to die, too?"

Demo's swirling, spherical form glowed a deadly purple. "I was going to ask you the same question."

Without warning, a line appeared in Demo's sphere-like body. Then the top half of Demo's body opened like a hatch and a powerful sucking force suddenly began pulling on Vilona. Vilona dug her claws into the ground even more, but it was clear she couldn't fight the sucking force forever.

With a scream of fear, Vilona flew into Demo's body. Her own body seemed to shrink as she entered his form, becoming smaller and smaller until she disappeared entirely.

Then Demo closed his body with a loud *clunk*, like someone shutting a huge metal hatch, and silence once again descended upon the chamber of the gods.

Chapter Thirty-Nine

SURRELS DID NOT KNOW IF HE SHOULD FEEL LUCKY THAT this mysterious Dragon Rider and his Steed had shown up to save him and Stebo or if he should be terrified by their ghostly appearances.

On the other hand, the demons are far scarier, Surrels thought, scrambling to his feet. *And, unlike this guy, they have already tried to kill me. He certainly can't make the situation any worse, at least.*

A harsh cackling sound interrupted Surrels's thoughts. Through the slightly transparent form of the Tomb Guardian, Surrels saw the demon leader step forward out of the crowd of demons. The demon leader gazed with hatred at the Tomb Guardian and Ghost Dragon, his small hands balled into tight little fists.

"A Dragon Rider," said the demon leader. His red eyes narrowed. "Though not a living one."

The Tomb Guardian nodded, raising his scythe. "That's right, demon. I am not of the current generation of Dragon Riders, but of the one who preceded them. I served under Captain Domon Azertan in the first Dragon Rider Order, the one who originally killed your evil god."

The demon leader nodded. "I thought your armor style looked familiar, but I could not place it. I would ask how you go there, but I don't really need to know the answer to that question to kill you, now do I?"

The Tomb Guardian cocked his head to the side. "Kill me if you want, demon, but know that I am already dead. And death is not the worst thing that can happen to a person. Trust me on that."

The demon leader laughed. "Trust a Dragon Rider? Are you joking? Your kind has hunted and killed my kind for centuries. I would sooner trust an angry rattlesnake than a Rider."

The Tomb Guardian shook his head. "Whether you trust me or not doesn't matter to me. Either way, you will be meeting your end today, monster."

Surrels raised a hand. "That's nice and all and I am sure you are capable of finishing off these demons all by yourself, but how, exactly, do we get back to the mortal realm? Stebo and I aren't ghosts like you, after all. We are stuck."

The Tomb Guardian glanced over his shoulder at Surrels. "I can open a portal for you back to the physical world when you are ready. But I won't be able to hold it open for very long. Especially if I have to fight the demons at the same time that I have to hold the portal open."

Surrels nodded. "That's fine. Just open the portal and Stebo and I will be on our way."

The Tomb Guardian nodded in response. He lifted his free hand, perhaps to open the portal, but before he could do so, the demon leader pointed at the Tomb Guardian and yelled, "Stop the humans from escaping!"

The demonic horde screeched as one and rushed toward Surrels, Stebo, and the Tomb Guardian.

But the Ghost Dragon opened its mouth and spewed even more green dragonfire. The demon horde tried to get out of the way, but they were all bunched together, meaning they got the full brunt of the Ghost Dragon's dragonfire. Demons got incinerated by the flames, forcing the demons at the back of the horde to scatter to avoid joining their brethren. Yet they, too, ended up dying in droves due to the heat of the dragonfire washing over them.

And now that Surrels had a moment to think, he noticed something strange whenever the demons died. Their physical bodies would turn into black smoke that flew back into the well in the middle of the room, disappearing over the rim without a sound.

A second or two later, the Ghost Dragon cut off its fire breath, allowing Surrels to see that not a single demon remained of the larger horde which had just been menacing them.

The only demon left standing was the demon leader, who had apparently not been brave enough to join his siblings in attacking the Ghost Dragon. Despite that, however, the demon leader didn't look at all annoyed or angry, as Surrels thought he might, since he'd just lost his entire fighting force in one go.

Instead, the demon leader appeared almost pleased, his eyes glinting wickedly in the dull light from the green torches along the walls.

"You sacrificed your fellow demons while not daring to lift a finger to help them yourself?" the Tomb Guardian demanded. "Even for a heartless demon such as yourself, that is low."

The demon leader chuckled. "Their sacrifice was far from being in vain, Tomb Guardian. Or have you forgotten already where we are?"

Surrels, suddenly realizing what the demon leader meant, shouted, "The well! The demons are in the—"

Surrels was interrupted by a rumbling sound from within the well, followed by the screams and screeches of newborn demons. Shadowy smoke erupted from within the well, the cloud dividing into dozens of smaller streams that slammed into the floor before them. Each stream resolved into an individual demon, the very same ones they had just killed, in fact.

The Tomb Guardian raised his scythe, a scowl crossing his skeletal features. "Impossible. How did you resurrect all of your fellow demons?"

"The well is the source of all demons," said the demon leader, gesturing at the well. "It is where we are born, where we go when we die, and where we come from again. If this had been in the mortal realm, our deaths would have delayed us from returning for several years. Here, however, we can come back as often as we want no matter how many times we perish."

The demon leader then grinned at the Tomb Guardian. "But something tells me that there is a limit to how many times *you* can return, Dragon Rider. Indeed, you may not even be able to return at all, given your nature."

The Tomb Guardian's scythe burned with green dragonfire, its light reflecting off of his armor. "I will keep killing you demons no matter how many times it takes."

Surrels bit his lower lip. While he appreciated the Tomb

Guardian's bravery and defiance in the face of the demons, he was worried that the Tomb Guardian might not be able to outlast the demons. The fact was that this was the demons' territory, which meant they had the advantage even without the well. That they had direct access to the well meant that this fight would be more of a battle of attrition than anything, meaning that the Tomb Guardian might not actually be able to win against them in any meaningful way.

But that's why we need only to escape, Surrels thought, glancing at Stebo. *So long as Stebo and I can get back to the mortal realm, we should be safe, no matter how many times the demons might resurrect.*

Fortunately, the Tomb Guardian must have been thinking the same thing, because he pointed his scythe at Stebo. Twin jets of dragonfire erupted from the scythe and cut through Stebo's chains, causing the young boy to slump to the floor. Surrels hurried over to Stebo and, holding him in his arms, looked over the boy more closely.

Stebo had his eyes closed, but his small chest still rose and fell with each breath. Yet Stebo felt small and fragile in Surrels's arms, almost like he was holding a piece of delicate glass instead of a human being. He recalled how much the demon realm had drained him of his strength, and he was an adult.

I can't imagine what it must have done to poor Stebo, Surrels thought, clutching Stebo closer to his chest. *I need to get him out of here. Now.*

The Tomb Guardian thrust his free hand to the side. A shining portal suddenly opened a few feet away from Surrels, the bright light making Surrels squint his eyes. He also heard some of the demons growl in pain, no doubt taken aback by the bright light.

"Flee, Surrels!" the Tomb Guardian said, his voice booming across the darkness. "Before the demons attack again!"

Surrels did not ignore the Tomb Guardian's order. Rising to his feet, Stebo clutched tightly in his arms, Surrels rushed toward the portal as quickly as he could. He heard the screams and screeches of the demons behind him as he ran, followed by the roar of the Ghost Dragon and the roar of the Ghost Dragon's dragonfire as it incinerated even more of them.

As tempted as Surrels was to look back, he did not. He just plunged through the portal, Stebo held safely in his arms, and prayed to the gods that the Tomb Guardian would survive his battle with the demons.

Chapter Forty

"Tell me, Anija," Kendo said, hands on his knees, watching her pace back and forth in front of him, "when has pacing ever actually helped in a situation like this?"

Anija came to a halt and glared at Kendo, who sat on the ground a few feet away from her, sweat on his brow. "What else am I supposed to do? I can't go to the demon realm after them. I can't communicate with Surrels or Stebo from here. All I can really do is pace and hope that the Tomb Guardian does what he said he was going to do. Sorry for trying to cope with a stressful situation."

Fralia, who stood next to Kendo, shrugged. "Anija has a point, Kendo. Right now, we're powerless to do anything until either Surrels and Stebo return or, at least, until the Tomb Guardian gives us an update on how they are doing in the demon realm."

Kendo snorted. "What is the use of magic if it can't even save the lives of an old man and a young boy?"

Anija glared at Kendo. "You watch your mouth. Fralia is a better person than you'll ever be. Just because you're too upset to see that doesn't give you the right to talk so disrespectfully toward her."

Fralia sighed. "It's all right, Anija. I think Kendo is just on edge like everyone is. After all, Surrels is his dad. I know what it's like to lose a father."

Anija glanced at Fralia. "Fralia, while I appreciate your ability to look for the best in people, sometimes, it's *really* undeserved."

Kendo rose to his feet, glaring at Anija. "Says the Dragon Rider who can't even *do* magic. Aside from talking to ghosts that may or may not exist, you're even more useless than Fralia."

"Kendo," Fralia said reproachfully. "Don't talk that way to Anija. It's not her fault that Surrels and Stebo ended up in the demon realm. She's just trying to help."

Anija held up a hand toward Fralia, never taking her eyes off Kendo. "Please stay out of this, Fralia. Kendo is really getting on my nerves. If he wants to rumble, then fine. Let me show him just how 'useless' the strength of a dragon actually is."

Kendo raised an eyebrow. "So instead of answering my criticisms, you threaten me with violence. Perhaps you Dragon Riders are not as good as your reputation makes you out to be."

Anija's hands balled into fists, dragonfire sparks shooting off them. "Why, you—"

A portal, shining brighter than the sun, suddenly opened about half a dozen yards from Anija. She turned her gaze toward the portal just as Surrels and Stebo stumbled out of it, the portal winking out of existence behind them as they landed on the street.

An instant later, Kendo was kneeling beside Surrels and

Stebo, checking them both out. "Dad, are you all right? And what about Stebo? How are you both feeling?"

Surrels sat up, still holding a seemingly unconscious Stebo in his arms. He looked slightly dazed. "We're … better than we were, I suppose."

"How did you guys get back here?" Fralia said in amazement as she and Anija walked over to them. "How did you open a portal?"

Surrels shook his head. "We didn't. A spirit calling himself the Tomb Guardian did. He saved us from the demons. Not sure how he is doing against them now, however. Last we saw, he was holding off an entire demon horde by himself, along with help from his Steed."

Anija sighed in relief. It looked like the Tomb Guardian had saved Surrels and Stebo, after all. She made a mental note to thank the Tomb Guardian the next time she saw him, if she did see him again.

Surrels then lifted up Stebo. "But Stebo is not good. He's very ill from the toxic air of the demon realm. We need to get him to a healer ASAP."

Fralia took Stebo in her arms and gave Surrels a concerned look. "You don't look much better yourself."

Surrels rubbed his forehead. "Don't worry about me. I'll be fine. Stebo is far more important."

Anija did not think Surrels would be 'fine.' His skin was paler than snow, and he trembled as if he was freezing, even though the sun was out in full force right now and its hot rays were beating down on them.

Even so, Anija could not disagree with him about Stebo. The young boy, though breathing, didn't even stir when Surrels handed him to Fralia. Evidently, Fralia thought the same thing, because she immediately started calling for any healers nearby to come and help.

As for Kendo, he put a hand on Surrels's shoulder and said, "Dad …"

Surrels looked at Kendo. "Yes, son?"

Kendo shook his head. "Don't do that again."

Surrels smiled weakly. "No promises, but sure."

Without warning, Kendo hugged Surrels and Surrels hugged him back. Anija felt like she was watching a very private family drama coming to an end, which made her feel a bit awkward about getting to see it despite not being part of Surrels's family.

Even so, Anija thought things had ended well enough for all of them. Tenka was dead, the demons were gone, and now Surrels and Stebo were back. True, they had made some sacrifices—both Rialo and Stebo would need time to heal, the status of the Tomb Guardian and Ghost Dragon was unknown, and they'd lost Argon outright, not to mention the potential political implications of Stebo's existence—but all in all, Anija thought things were looking good for them.

Now we just need Hal and Keershan to come back and then things just might go back to normal around here, Anija thought, a small smile appearing on her lips.

A harsh winter wind suddenly blew through the town square, the wind cold enough to make Anija and the other Dragon Riders, along with everyone else, shiver. Looking around, Anija could not see a natural source of the cold wind, especially since it was such a hot day.

Yet it felt very familiar to her, almost as if she had felt it somewhere before recently …

A piece of paper fluttered through the air nearby.

Carried along by the wind, the paper zipped in and around the Dragon Riders and other people in the vicinity of the square. At first, its movements looked random, directed solely by the whims of the wind, going wherever the gods had destined it to go.

But then Anija realized that its movements weren't random. Nor were the whims of the wind quite so whimsical. It had a specific destination that it was going.

And Anija thought she knew what it was.

The paper reached the stage near the front gates of Castle Lamor, falling with a flutter onto the wood. As soon as the paper touched down, it erupted into a brilliant blue flame that made everyone jump.

"Blue fire?" Surrels said, gazing up in confusion at the burning flame. "What does that mean? It can't be the demons, can it?"

Anija knew the answer even before the blue flames roared and twisted. A humanoid shape rapidly took form in the fire, taking on more and more detail as the humanoid figure within the flame took shape.

In seconds, Emperor Kryo Kardia stood within the blue flames atop the stage, his cold purple eyes sweeping across the public square as Dragon Rider, Steed, mage, and guard alike stopped to gawk at the ruler of the Glaci Empire.

Only, of course, Kryo Kardia wasn't actually there. His form shimmered and flickered in the flames, which did not surprise Anija. After all, fire apparition was the Glaci Empire's main form of long-distance communication. She did not know where the paper had come from or how it caught fire on its own, but then again, Anija had also realized that they did not know the full extent of the Glaci

Empire's magical skills and technology. There was no telling what they could or could not do.

Kryo Kardia also looked a lot better than Anija remembered him looking when she saw him last. His skin was smooth and almost young, making her wonder what happened to the curse—the Fracturing, as she recalled Kryo Kardia calling it—that was supposed to have weakened him. Perhaps he was hiding it somehow with magic or good old-fashioned makeup and lighting tricks.

"Citizens of the kingdom of Malarsan," said Kryo Kardia, his voice booming across the public square, sounding much louder than it should have. "Some of you may know who I am already, but for those who have not yet seen me, I am Emperor Kryo Kardia, emperor of the Glaci Empire."

Kendo's eyes widened. "That's Kryo Kardia? Damn. He's huge."

Anija shuddered. "Trust me, he's even bigger—and scarier—in person."

Kryo Kardia continued to speak as if no one else had, saying, "You may be wondering why I have chosen to appear directly before you like this. It is because of recent events which have transpired in the Northern Circle, the capital of the Glaci Empire, that have forced me to deliver a message to you all, one that your leaders will have certainly seen coming, even if you have not."

Anija felt her heart constrict at Kryo Kardia's words. Even before he spoke his next words, Anija knew exactly what he was going to say and just what message he intended to deliver.

Kryo Kardia spread his arms. "Less than two weeks

ago, I was nearly assassinated by Halar Norath, Keershan the dragon, and Anija Ti in my own home. All three are members of the council of Malarsan, the primary governing body of the kingdom of Malarsan to my understanding. And this was no covert assassination. It was performed directly in the sight of my oldest daughter, my most loyal servant, and the citizens of the Northern Circle itself. It was a blatant display of aggression on the part of Malarsan, leaving me with no choice but to respond in kind.

"After much deliberation with my top generals and advisers, I have officially decided to withdraw all aid from the Glaci Empire to the kingdom of Malarsan. It pains me to see that your leaders have shown such ingratitude when we so graciously came to you in your hour of need, but ambition has ruined many a promising political alliance, so I cannot say this is entirely unforeseen."

Then Kryo Kardia looked directly at Anija, or so she thought. He certainly seemed to be looking directly at her, making her tense up.

"Yet that is not all," Kryo Kardia continued. "It is now clear to me that the council of Malarsan has become drunk with power. I fear that your leaders do not have your best interests at heart any longer, which means they will undoubtedly become more and more oppressive as time goes on.

"Therefore, under the guidance of my advisers and in accordance with the justice of the gods themselves, the Glaci Empire, under my direction, has declared a war of liberation on the kingdom of Malarsan. We will be using the full force of the Glaci Empire to liberate the Malarsans from the council and to establish greater justice and peace for the people of your beautiful country. May the grace and hope of the gods be with you all."

With that, the blue flames flickered and died, leaving nothing but a pile of ash where they had once burned.

And the sinking feeling in Anija's stomach that all, perhaps, was not well and that the true hardships for all of them were just about to begin.

Chapter Forty-One

HAL STOOD BEFORE THE HUGE STONE DOOR UNDERNEATH the Temple of the Gods. It was an impressive piece of work, showing the faces of every god in the world carved into its surface. It looked like it had been designed by a master craftsman, who created not just a door, but a work of art in its own right.

But Hal did notice that there was a big hole near the top of the door, where the face of a particular god should have been. It was as if one of the gods' faces had been torn away ages ago, leaving an ugly scar on the door that marred its otherwise perfect appearance.

"Who do you think that was?" Hal said to Keershan, the dragon standing next to him.

Boca, who stood on Hal's other side, gazed down at him. "Isn't it obvious? That was the Nameless One's place on the Door. He's the only fallen god. His face must have once been carved in there like the faces of the other gods. My guess is that they ripped out his face and threw it away when he rebelled."

Hal looked over his shoulder at Raniel, who was leaning against a nearby wall. "What do you think of that theory, Raniel? Is it true or not?"

Raniel huffed. "I do not know. I've never been down here before. I didn't even know this place existed."

Hal raised an eyebrow. Ever since Boca cleared their names before the gods, Raniel had started treating them a lot more politely. He still wasn't exactly respectful, per se, but he now treated them more like guests whose company he did not particularly enjoy but who he couldn't get rid of instead of suspected murderers like before.

Guess that is technically an improvement, Hal thought. *Even if he could be a bit nicer.*

At least he's not threatening to kill us, Keershan commented. *That's an improvement in my eyes.*

"Gotcham Nubor would know," Boca said. She glanced around the room. "Speaking of Gotcham, where is he? I thought he said he was going to meet us down here."

"He will," Raniel said. He gestured at the staircase behind them, which wound up to the right out of sight. "His Majesty is simply dealing with the fallout of your investigation. He will be here shortly."

Hal nodded. He had suspected as much.

Shortly after Demo devoured Vilona, the assembled gods had broken out into yelling and screaming again. Most of that yelling and screaming had been aimed toward Gotcham Nubor, which might have seemed odd, but there was a certain logic to it.

Even though Vilona was dead, the other gods were apparently still afraid that Kryo Kardia might have other spies and assassins in the abode. This was apparently the first time that a semi-divine being such as Vilona had killed a deity in the abode, which, up until this point, had been considered a safe space for all of the gods.

Now, however, that illusion of safety had been shattered to pieces.

Gotcham Nubor had ordered Raniel to escort Hal, Keershan, and Boca to something called the 'Door,' which Hal could only assume was the door standing in front of them. Aside from the masterful carvings of the faces of the gods, however, Hal did not see what was so special or interesting about the door itself.

Maybe it is what is behind the Door that is truly interesting, Hal thought.

In any case, Gotcham Nubor had stayed behind to answer the objections, worries, and fears of the other gods. Given how many of the other gods had been demanding answers from Gotcham Nubor, Hal guessed it would be a while before the king of the gods showed himself.

Then, without warning, Hal heard heavy footsteps coming down the staircase, and Gotcham Nubor himself soon appeared. He looked a good deal more tired, however, than he did back in the Chamber, his shoulders slumping slightly, his brow furrowed. A bead of sweat ran down his forehead, which shocked Hal because Gotcham Nubor hadn't sweat even during their duel.

He must be very stressed, Hal thought to Keershan.

No doubt, Keershan said. *The gods were very scary back there. I certainly wouldn't want to deal with a bunch of angry, fearful gods.*

"There you are," Boca said, raising a questioning eyebrow to the king of the gods. "We've been standing around here for an hour waiting for you."

Raniel gave Boca a death glare. "Just because you are no longer a murder suspect doesn't mean you have the right to speak so disrespectfully to His Majesty."

Gotcham Nubor, however, waved a hand toward Raniel. "It is fine, Raniel. She will be gone soon enough. I was indeed delayed by my brothers and sisters, especially Salard, who I still need to speak with later regarding the betrayal of his daughter."

Hal bit his lower lip. He remembered how heartbroken Salard had looked when Vilona admitted to her crimes and got executed by Demo. He felt bad for Salard, though at the moment he had no way to help him.

All I can do is stop Kryo Kardia, Hal thought. *Or try to, anyway.*

Same, Keershan agreed, *although Vilona's betrayal still blows my mind. Guess I just never thought that one of the twelve dragons of old could be corrupted like she had been.*

Goes to show that being divine doesn't necessarily make you a good person, Hal replied. *I do wonder what she meant about a 'future without gods,' though.*

Keershan shuddered. *Nothing good, I'm sure. Maybe that is what the gods were so scared of. It probably has something to do with whatever Kryo Kardia is doing and planning.*

Hal scratched his chin. *Probably. Hopefully we can stop him before he gets away with it, whatever it is.*

"So what is this place?" Hal said to Gotcham Nubor. He gestured at the Door. "And what is the Door? Why is it so important?"

Gotcham Nubor sighed, rubbing his forehead. "The Door is where the power you need to stop Kryo Kardia lies. If you can survive what is beyond the Door, then you will be deemed worthy of that power."

Hal frowned. "You mean you don't know what is behind the Door?"

Gotcham Nubor shook his head. "The Door was old when the gods came into the world. Demo might know, but as you know, he is not exactly a chatterbox."

Hal looked at the Door again, frowning deeper. "So Keershan and I need to go beyond the Door, complete whatever challenge is beyond it, and then come back?"

"That seems a little convoluted to me," Keershan said. He looked up at Gotcham Nubor. "Couldn't you and the other gods use your powers to destroy Kryo Kardia yourselves? Or at least give us the power directly?"

Gotcham Nubor shook his head. "It isn't that easy, I am afraid. We gods can only kill mortals who directly threaten our existence. Kryo Kardia has not personally tried to kill any of us, so our power is limited. Plus, we believe Kryo Kardia is still within mortal limits, meaning that you mortals should still be able to defeat him so long as you have the right powers and equipment. As for giving you power, you still haven't shown yourselves worthy of the power you will need to stop Kryo Kardia."

"But we solved Shirataka's murder," Keershan said. "Doesn't that make us worthy?"

Gotcham Nubor narrowed his eyes. "As thankful as I am for your role in bringing my sister's murderer to justice, you are not planning to solve more murders with our power. If you wish for our power, then you will need to prove your mettle as warriors and heroes."

Hal sighed, rubbing the back of his neck. "All right. Guess we'll do it. How long does the challenge take to complete?"

Gotcham Nubor shrugged. "I have no idea. It could

take minutes. Or years. All I know is that if you fail, you will not walk out of there again."

Boca put a hand on Hal's shoulder suddenly, making him look up at her grinning face. "Don't worry, Hal. I'll be right here waiting for you two to return. And if you don't, well, consider this my goodbye."

Hal furrowed his brow. "A temporary one, I hope."

"Indeed," Boca said with a mischievous look in her eyes. "And may the gods always be with you. Can I say that, Gotcham?"

Gotcham Nubor rolled his eyes. "If you two are ready to start the challenge, then I can open the Door."

Gotcham Nubor snapped his fingers.

And with very little drama, the Door slowly swung open, revealing a dark opening that even Hal's night vision could not penetrate.

"Once you step through the Door, you will have no choice but to see the challenge through to the end," Gotcham Nubor warned them. "You will not be able to back out of it. Do you still wish to proceed?"

Hal and Keershan exchanged a confident look with each other. Yet even if they hadn't, neither of them had any fear in their heart. They'd already decided that they were willing to do whatever it took to stop Kryo Kardia.

Even if it meant putting their own lives on the line.

"We are," Hal said as he and Keershan nodded.

Gotcham Nubor gestured at the open Door. "Then go! Complete the challenge. Find the power and blessing you desire. And may fate ever guide your steps, Dragon Rider Halar Norath and Steed Keershan."

With that, Hal and Keershan walked toward the Door.

And without looking back, they stepped through the Door.

In the moments before they crossed the threshold, Hal found himself wondering, briefly, how everyone was doing back home. A part of him almost wanted to stop and go back now, but he restrained himself.

Our friends are doing their part, Hal thought, sharing his thoughts with Keershan. *Now it's time for us to do ours.*

Keershan nodded. *Yeah.*

And thus, as soon as they stepped through the Door, the Door slammed shut behind them, although they hardly noticed.

Because once they stepped through the Door, Hal and Keershan found themselves standing in a wide-open field with a small village in the distance that looked an awful lot like …

"Lamb's Hand …" Hal muttered. "My hometown. How—?"

A soft chuckle behind Hal made him start. "Well, I was wondering when *you* would get here."

That voice. Hal had not heard it in a long time, but it was familiar. Was it—?

Hal and Keershan slowly turned around to find themselves face-to-face with the familiar bearded face of Old Snow himself.

Old Snow smiled through his white beard, clutching his staff, standing in the wheat fields like he was always supposed to be there. "Don't look so surprised. The challenge has just begun. And I can only hope, for the sake of both Malarsan and the world, that you two are ready for it."

Don't miss the final book in The Lost Riders series: The Rider Fall.

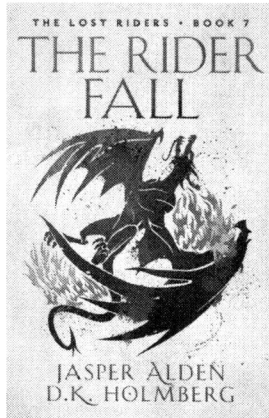

Series by Jasper Alden

The Lost Riders

The Golden Fool

Similar Series by D.K. Holmberg

The Dragonwalkers Series

The Dragonwalker

The Dragon Misfits

The Dragon Thief

Cycle of Dragons

Elemental Warrior Series:

Elemental Academy

The Elemental Warrior

The Cloud Warrior Saga

The Endless War

Made in United States
Troutdale, OR
04/29/2024